A DRAGON LIVES FOREVER . . .

Muscles tensed under Rap's fresh-shaven cheeks. "With respect, your Omnipotence, had we attacked then, the Covin would have released the dragons. We could not risk such a disaster."

The warlock's eyes flamed. "And what makes you think the dwarf will not call out the dragons again?"

Rap drew an audible breath. "We have taken steps—"

"*What?*" Everyone jumped as the warlock's voice cracked through the hall like a whip. He sprang from his chair. His face had flushed to a deep bronze; he was shaking with fury. "What *steps?*"

"To destroy the dragons if they rise again."

"*Idiots!*" The warlock blazed with fury. The sorcerer onlookers cried out and staggered back in unison, and the carnage and the screaming began . . .

By Dave Duncan
Published by Ballantine Books:

The Seventh Sword
THE RELUCTANT SWORDSMAN
THE COMING OF WISDOM
THE DESTINY OF THE SWORD

STRINGS

HERO!

A Man of His Word
MAGIC CASEMENT
FAERY LANDS FORLORN
PERILOUS SEAS
EMPEROR AND CLOWN

THE REAVER ROAD

A Handful of Men
THE CUTTING EDGE
UPLAND OUTLAWS
THE STRICKEN FIELD
THE LIVING GOD

THE
LIVING
GOD

Part Four of
A HANDFUL OF MEN

Dave Duncan

A Del Rey® Book
BALLANTINE BOOKS • NEW YORK

A Del Rey® Book
Published by Ballantine Books

Grateful acknowledgment is made to The Society of Authors, as the literary representative of the Estate of John Masefield, for permission to reprint excerpts from "Tomorrow" by John Masefield.

Library of Congress Catalog Card Number: 93-39290

ISBN 0-345-38878-X

Map by Steve Palmer

Manufactured in the United States of America

First Hardcover Edition: April 1994
First Mass Market Edition: October 1994

10 9 8 7 6 5 4 3 2 1

*To my daughter Jenni,
who most
reasonably points out
that she has never had a
whole book
dedicated to her alone
and who most
certainly deserves one,
this book is belatedly
and lovingly
dedicated*

⫷ CONTENTS ⫸

⫷ PROLOGUE ⫸

The ancient house was hot in the summer night, holding the heat of the day behind windows long sealed. Its many rooms and corridors were stuffy and airless, smelling again of dust as they had before the visitors had come. They had all gone now, the visitors. The people had departed, lords and ladies, maid-servants and manservants. Fireplaces had cooled, doors had been locked again, stillness had returned. For barely half a year the house had been a dwelling and now it was tomb once more, a monument to its own long past.

The old woman wandered the halls and passageways, needing no more light than the beams of summer moonlight angling down from dusty casements. The Voices were upset tonight and her antique bones could not rest.

"What ails, Ghosts?" she called. "Why do you fret?"

No words answered. No wind rattled and wailed tonight, but the little creaks and groans told how the old house was cooling after the long, hot day, and in those tiny sounds she heard the Voices complaining.

"I do not understand!" she cried. "Speak louder."

Pale blue light made angular puddles on the floors. Rafters settled, beams creaked.

Again she called out. "He is gone. He stole away his lady, as you said he would. He took her away, and her child, also. They escaped. The others have departed. Those who came later asking questions have departed, too. There is only me. What ails, Ghosts? You can speak now."

Clicks and creaks and tappings . . .

"Danger? Is that it, then? He is in danger, or his lady? Speak louder. The child? Her child? What is her child to him?"

The old woman stood in darkness beside a patch of moonlight, her head cocked, straining to hear.

"What danger? That one they called *Centurion*? He is the danger? The one I shut in the cellar? I never trusted that one. Yes, you told me to beware of that one. Nasty, violent man. Shut him up in the cellar, we did, and let them escape."

Tap. Creak.

Suddenly she cackled shrilly.

"Child? *Another* child? Well, that's different, isn't it? That's what love brings, isn't it, children?"

Chortling, she turned and wandered back the way she had come, slippers shuffling on the threadbare rugs.

"Nothing you can do about it, Ghosts. Nothing I can do. They're far away now, Ghosts. Have to handle the danger by themselves, won't they?" She chuckled hoarsely. "Another child! Well, what would you expect?" Floorboards creaked as she shuffled to the stairs.

"Going to be a problem, that one, isn't it?" she muttered.

ℂ ONE 𝔻

Still pursuing

1

"Faster, Ylo!" Maya urged. "Make horse go faster!"

She sat on Ylo's lap, jiggling the reins ferociously. As the traces were firmly gripped in Ylo's strong hands, also, the big gray was probably unaware of the divided leadership. It certainly did not care. It plodded doggedly, not even flickering its ears, stoically fulfilling the role the Gods had assigned it. Every second day it would haul some traveler's rig up the hill. The next day it would haul another one down. Nothing about that to puzzle a horse. Not even Ylo's skills would make it go any faster, either, even had he wanted it to.

Huddled in the fur cloak she had not worn in months, Eshiala watched the byplay with heavenly contentment. She, at least, was in no hurry. Days like these could go on forever and she would never tire of them. For the last hour the road had been winding gently upward through a dense mist, so that almost nothing was visible except the well-fitted stones of the road itself, built centuries ago by the legions and still in perfect order. Wiry grass along the verge glistened with dampness and a few ghostly bushes lurked beyond that like predatory wraiths in the fog. Once in a while now she glimpsed ragged remains of the winter's snow. Summer came late to the highlands of the Qoble Range.

"You promised me beautiful scenery when we reached the pass," she teased.

Ylo flashed her a smile. They stopped her heart, those smiles of his, those bright dark eyes, those long lashes. He could say more with a smile than all the poems of all the poets of the Impire. "I said you had never seen anything like the view up here. Well, you still haven't, have you?"

"True!" She laughed.

"And admit it, you are floating in clouds, yes?"

"Yes!" she said. "Very true."

"Well, then!"

"Faster!" Maya demanded.

"Poor old horse!" Ylo said sternly. "He's having to pull all of us up this great, long hill. He's working very hard. He's an old, old horse, that's why his hair's turned all white. You ought to get out and walk, so he doesn't have to work so hard, you great heavy lump!"

That was a mistake. Maya decided she did want to get out and walk, and argued when he would not let her. She was very good at arguing. At times she behaved as if she was the rightful-born impress of Pandemia—which she was, even if Pandemia was no more aware of that than the child herself. How about a birthday party, Ylo suggested, and a cake with two and a half candles . . .

They had seen very little traffic all morning, but now hooves clanked on the stones behind, coming fast. Eshiala turned and peered back through the little window. In a moment a ghostly rider materialized out of the mist, gray on gray, solidifying into color as he approached, scarlet cloak and gold-plumed hat. He swung out to pass the phaeton without slowing down, cantering on ahead, fading as swiftly as he had come, the cloud soon muffling the sound. He had been an Imperial courier, and the fact that he had been only cantering, not galloping, showed how hard the hill was on horses.

She stole a glance at Ylo and thought she detected a hint of a frown. A hint of danger? She said nothing. Something had worried him back at the inn that morning, although he had denied it. She thought he had recognized someone. She would not pry. She would let nothing ruffle her happiness.

It would end soon enough. In a day or two they would be in Gaaze, and what happened then she dared not think.

She was in love, hopelessly in love. Twenty years old, a widow with a child, and she was as heartsick as an adolescent.

However guilty she felt that she should have found such happiness through Shandie's death, the world turned for her with the beating of Ylo's heart. She would lie at night with her head on his chest, listening to that solid, comforting beat.

He was a hero. The army had voted him honors no signifer had received since the previous dynasty. He was a duke by right, although not in law. Shandie had admitted that he had never had a more honest, hardworking aide than Ylo. He was even-tempered, everlasting fun, and good company. He was blindingly handsome, blessed with a perfect complexion very rare for an imp. He was tireless in bed, enormously virile and skilled, able to coax rapture from her body as a musician could pluck music from a lute.

He was a notorious rake, as faithless as a weasel.

She had known. She had let him steal her heart, knowing he would break it. He had not broken it yet. He had done what he set out to do—he had taught her what lovemaking should be, and he had brought her safely to Qoble. In another week or so they would arrive at Gaaze, and then the long journey would be over and Ylo would leave her. That had been the bargain, although never put into words.

No, she was in no hurry.

"Aha!" Ylo said. Shadowy buildings were congealing out of the fog. There was a seasonal post at the top of the pass, where weary horses could be replaced. Tomorrow, doubtless, the old gray would plod its way down again, to one side or the other, pulling some other vehicle.

"You go back to your mother now, Princess." He passed Maya across.

"Do you suppose the food is edible here?" Eshiala asked, adjusting her too-heavy daughter on her lap.

"Probably nothing much. Why don't you buy a snack while I'm changing horses, and we'll eat by the roadside somewhere." He pulled his hat brim down to shield his face.

That was an odd gesture for Ylo, who was well aware of his good looks. It was as if he was frightened of being recognized.

2

Despite her sincere belief, Eshiala was not a widow. Far off to the northeast, in Guwush, her husband bounced around unhappily on the roof of a stagecoach. On one side of him a dealer in raw silk lamented endlessly on the ridiculous prices gnomes expected for their produce these days; on the other a minor Imperial bureaucrat expounded on the impossibility of collecting all the new taxes Hub was demanding to fight the current war. At times they gave up hope of winning any sympathy from Shandie and debated with each other as if he were not there, between them.

The three of them were right at the back, which was the worst place to be, and the motion nauseated him. This was gnome country. The coach was crowded, yet not one passenger was a gnome. If gnomes had any reason to travel, they were required to do so in wagons, by themselves. Raspnex was sitting at the front with another dwarf, a dealer in ironware. All the rest were imps. The driver, of course, was a faun.

Shandie wondered how Inos was doing, crammed inside with the other women. She was probably even less comfortable than he was.

The road wound through darkly forested hills, but at least it was flatter than it had been the day before, without the steep inclines that had required the male passengers to dismount and walk. After a day of dust and wind and summer sunshine, they were heading toward some very unfriendly-looking rain clouds. He felt in dire need of a hot bath and fresh garments, but apparently he was about to receive a cold shower first. The knowledge that he could travel on horseback twice as fast with half the discomfort did nothing to improve his mood. He could recall being very impressed as a child by Inos' horsemanship, and he had no doubt that she could still control a horse superbly, but Raspnex could not. Dwarves fell off horses unless they were tied to the saddle. Besides, the coach fare included the cost of the necessary armed escort.

"Nasty stretch this!" the tax collector bleated, eyeing the sinister woods crowding in on either hand. "Been quite a few ambushes near here."

Shandie uttered a noncommittal grunt that would not have shamed a camel.

"Disgraceful!" the silk merchant agreed. "Don't know why the army doesn't clean out those rebels once and for all."

Shandie could have asked him how. He could have mentioned that he had slaughtered ten thousand gnomes near here less than three years ago. He did not. He had invented a vague cover story about representing a syndicate of Hubban investors looking for opportunities in undeveloped land; it allowed him to be tight-lipped about his plans and background. If he tried to explain that it was precisely because this area was infested by gnomish partisans that he had come here, then his companions would report him to the legionaries of the mounted escort.

The XXVIIth had always been an inferior outfit. Even so, this contingent inspired him with disgust. They were a sloppy bunch. He would dearly enjoy taking them in hand for an hour's drill. Two hours would be even better; then he could skin them completely.

For a moment he toyed with the absurdity of marching over to the leader at the next stop and introducing himself. "Good evening, Optio. I am Emshandar the Fifth, by the grace of the Gods imperor of Pandemia, not to be confused with the imposter presently occupying my throne and claiming to be myself. I am your authentic commander in chief. Now tell me, has this bronze always been green or did you paint it like that for some reason? . . ."

Another hour ought to bring the coach to Yugg, if there was no ambush in the meantime. From what Shandie could recall of Yugg, it had nothing to commend it except that it marked the unofficial border between the rule of law and areas held by rebels—or between Occupied Guwush and Free Guwush, depending on one's point of view. It had a fort with an Imperial garrison. Undoubtedly Oshpoo's forces would have agents in Yugg.

The first problem was going to be making contact with them. They would be very wary of any imp. The second problem would be staying alive afterward.

Without slowing, the coach went rumbling through a hamlet. The huddle of squat cottages glowered at the passing strangers with tiny windows under their heavy thatch. They were obviously gnome dwellings, so small that imps would have to crawl on hands and knees inside them. They seemed deserted, but that would be because the inhabitants preferred to sleep during the day and work at night. For a moment the passengers held their noses, and then the coach was through the little settlement, back in forest again.

Such were the joys of Guwush. Despite the Impire's best efforts, it never managed to do much to improve the place. The parts it did not control were even worse, of course, with most of the population living in burrows, but to see squalor like this on a main Imperial highway was very depressing.

Shandie could not shake off a question Inos had posed that very morning, just before entering the coach. It had been bothering him all day. If gnomes preferred to live like that, she had said sweetly, then why should they not be allowed to do so? Fortunately no one else had heard her, except perhaps Raspnex. In Hub it would be ranked as heresy. In the army the idea would be treason, cause for court-martial if spoken aloud. But by definition the imperor himself could never be guilty of treason, could he? If the imperor decided that the Guwushian war was bleeding his treasury white and the best way to solve the partisan problem was just to go away and let the partisans be the government, then nobody in the world could argue with him. Except the Senate, of course, and most of the clergy and the army hierarchy and all the aristocrats who had acquired title to estates in Guwush and likely other groups that would surface in due course.

Well, fortunately Shandie was not required to make such decisions at the moment. Being an outlaw did have its advantages.

He was still thinking about the matter when he noticed that Raspnex had twisted around and was staring back at him, peering between the much taller impish passengers. His ugly face was screwed up in a curiously agitated expression. There were too many people between them for conversation. In a moment the little man rolled his eyes and turned away again to face the front.

In his shabby dark clothing he looked like a retired mineworker, but he was a potent sorcerer, warden of the north. A dwarf rarely displayed emotion like that. What could he have detected that had so upset him?

3

A one-horse chaise, a stagecoach, and a longship . . .

Farther yet to the northeast, *Blood Wave II* surged over the cold green sea, propelled by the rhythmic swing of her oars, rising and falling in steady beat, with the grace of a gull's wings. Half the crew rowed, most of the rest were asleep under the rowers' feet. Onward to Nordland.

Stroke.

Gath and Vork were crammed in together on one bench, pulling the same oar. Thane Drakkor himself had the helm, and he was keeping a steady eye on those two recruits. He had very bright blue eyes, very deadly eyes, killer's eyes.

Stroke.

Gath had no pore that was not streaming sweat. He was certain he had no skin left on his hands. Every muscle in his body burned.

Stroke.

He wanted to ask Vork how he felt now about being a raider, but he had no breath for speaking. His lungs and throat were raw and there was a sour taste of metal in his mouth. He was starting to feel a stitch in his side.

Stroke.

Oars swung. Thole pins creaked. The coxswain's pipe called the stroke. Water hissed past the thin planks of the narrow hull. Salt-scented sea wind blew blessedly cool on fevered skin.

Stroke.

This was a test, of course. Smart-aleck kids had to learn the rough side of the legend. Two uppity sons of thanes were being shown that they weren't men yet. Even pulling together, they could not keep up with the real sailors, not for long, not for much longer. This was the price of hitching a ride on a thane's longship.

Stroke.

The crew was watching, waiting for the mistake. Gath could feel the grins all around. The stroke was faster than usual. Trouble was, he knew what was going to happen even more surely than the crew did.

Stroke.

Prescience was a blessing and also a terrible curse. It produced invaluable warnings of trouble ahead and wonderful anticipation of pleasures in store. When it showed bad futures and especially inevitable bad futures, then it could drive a man insane.

Stroke.

A trickle of sweat ran down the bare back in front of his eyes. So the others were feeling the pace, too. They could keep it up for hours, though. High behind *Blood Wave* the seabirds floated in the salt air, cool and serene. Lucky birds!

Stroke.

Gath's fingers were knotting, losing their grip on the oar. The blood was making it slippery anyway. Not long now. He and Vork were going to catch a crab. Soon!

Stroke.

Then they were going to be given a taste of the rope's end. Sailor talk for flogging. Toughen up the gazoonies a bit—

evilishly painful. Only consolation was he knew he was going to keep quiet under it. Vork wasn't, not quite.

Stroke.

This is what Vork had thought he wanted, to be a raider like his father before him, and his father, and all their forefathers since the coming of the Gods. Gath didn't want that.

Stroke.

He just wanted to get to Nordland and tell the thanes about the usurper and the overthrow of the wardens and the new protocol Dad had invented before he died. Doing it for Dad's memory—duty.

Stroke.

Doing it for Dad. Here it came now—

Crab!

The oar slammed into the two boys' chests, hurling them backward. Angry yells . . .

4

A one-horse chaise, a stagecoach, a longship, and a leaky old coaster . . .

Still very much alive, Gath's father sailed a distant, warmer ocean. At the far side of the world, *Dreadnought* wallowed over a mirrored sea under a sun of molten brass. The breathless wind was barely able to keep her sails full; gulls preened on the yards rather than bother flying on such a day. A hazy smudge to northward marked the island of Kith.

King Rap of Krasnegar leaned on the rail and thought dark thoughts of failure and defeat. The morning was barely half gone at that longitude, but it had already left a bloody stain on the pages of history: five legions dead, untold thousands of goblins dead.

All of this callous slaughter had apparently been committed just to demonstrate the power of the usurper. Doubtless Zinixo was even now gloating in Hub, master of the world, the self-styled Almighty. Perhaps at that very moment hundreds of free sorcerers were responding to his threats, flocking into the capital to be imprinted with unbreakable loyalty and enrolled in the Covin.

True, Warlock Olybino had proclaimed the new protocol, which was a giant step forward, but he had died doing so. Why should the frees choose to join Rap's mythical resistance when it had failed to save its spokesman? Olybino's sacrifice had revealed the opposition's weakness and lack of organization.

The occult scent of dragon still tainted the ambience. The Covin seemed to be herding the worms home to Dragon Reach from their feast at Bandor. That was a relief, but Rap would not breathe easy until all those monsters were safely penned, back in their nests. Meanwhile he had not a clue as to what he should do next.

His brooding was interrupted by a jingle of human finger bones. Lithe and menacing, Tik Tok stalked across the deck to his side, grinning under the multicolored tattoos that covered his face and most of the rest of him, also. Apparently grinning did not hurt when one wore a bone through the nose, although it seemed as if it should. His teeth had been filed to sharp points. The seashells decorating the thick black bush of his hair were new; apart from them he wore only his customary apron of clattering bones.

"You grieve, my friend? You language unconsolidated?"

"I have a lot to languish about."

Eyes twinkling, the cannibal took hold of Rap's shoulder in an astonishingly powerful grip. He kneaded it appraisingly. "You must not pine! You will shriven up, weather away to skin and bones. We cannot permeate such a waste." His manner implied that he had the perfect recipe in mind already.

"Cheer me up, then."

Tik Tok waved a hand to indicate the shabby old ship. "Twenty-nine sorcerers, eight mages? If we want we can move this old tub to Hub itself in a twiddling."

"Not without giving ourselves away to the Covin, we can't."

The cannibal removed his hand so he could lean back with his elbows on the rail. "But you have other plans ready?"

"Er, not finalized."

Tik Tok pouted dangerously. "Well, we cannot wait around forever! Prognostication is the thief of time."

He was mad because Rap had pulled him away from a fight. Despite his invariant flippancy, he was probably almost as murderous as he looked. Many of the other twenty-four anthropophagi aboard appeared even more bloodcurdling, yet they all accepted Tik Tok as leader. Just because he was a potent sorcerer did not mean he did not want to eat someone.

At that moment another hand descended on Rap's shoulder. In this case the hand was the size of a small pillow. Staggering slightly under the load, he glanced around, annoyed that anyone as enormous as Thrugg should have approached without his noticing.

The troll opened his beard in a friendly smile, revealing enough ivory to furnish a spinet keyboard. Even more than Tik Tok, he could have moonlighted as a nightmare, although his bestial appearance hid a heart as gentle as a daisy. He was without question the most powerful sorcerer aboard, even stronger than his mother the warden. The back of his hand and the visible parts of his face were burned, but most of his great bulk was hidden in loose clothing to keep the sun off. He was still a monster, though.

"He's right, Rap," Thrugg mumbled. "The past is over. What matters is to win the future."

Obviously the whole improbable army was on the verge of mutiny. No one would openly accuse Rap of causing Olybino's death, but his refusal to let the group become involved had been an admission of weakness, and it rankled. He had best rally his troops quickly now, before half of them began eating the other half out of sheer frustration. The entire ill-assorted crew was watching. Near-naked anthropophagi lay sprawled around the deck in twos and threes. Most of the trolls were down in the cabins or the hold, by themselves, staying out of the sun, but they were watching nonetheless. Witch Grunth had appropriated the best hideaway, the chain locker. There she had removed all her clothing for comfort and was combing her shaggy gray hair. Nudity emphasized her grotesque animal bulk, wrinkled and flabby and hideous. She, too, was waiting for Rap's reaction.

Old Doctor Sagorn, the only mundane aboard, held the wheel, playing at being sailor to show how childishly easy that was to one of his intellectual superiority. The effect was rather spoiled by his badly shredded clothing, but he sneered his customary arrogant smile.

"What the gentlemen are implying, your Majesty," he said, "is that the late Warlock Olybino has done your work for you. You no longer need travel the world, whispering news of your counterrevolution. All the free sorcerers are now aware of it. You are the leader? Lead us somewhere."

Leader! What mad whirl of the Gods' dice had ever thrust that honor on Rap? He was about the least powerful sorcerer in Pandemia, so why him? Just because he had invented the new protocol did not mean he was the man to bring it to pass, if anyone ever could. He sensed the dragons again and shivered. He could do nothing until they were safely home in their nests. Nothing violent, that was, nothing to provoke the Covin openly and distract it from worm herding. But yes, there must be other, lesser things to be done, as Tik Tok had suggested.

"I'm greatly relieved that I don't need to visit Sysanasso, anyway," Rap said. "If there are any free faun sorcerers they must have heard Olybino's message as clearly as we did. Does anyone disagree with that?"

Thrugg shook his great head. Tik Tok just wiggled the bone in his nose expectantly. Everyone in the ship was listening— except for a pair of trolls down in the hold who had found more exciting things to do.

"And we continue our journey to Thume?"

Trolls and cannibals all scowled. Witch Grunth snorted disbelievingly in the chain locker. It was one thing to accept in an intellectual way that there must be some vast unknown power at work in Thume. To accept it emotionally was barely possible even inside any occult shielding; out in the open where its aversion spell was effective, Thume seemed like the wildest sort of mirage, irrelevant nonsense.

Perhaps because he was a mundane, Sagorn believed in Thume. He was nodding sardonically. "But it will take us weeks to get there," he said. "Years at this pace. I don't suppose you ladies and gentlemen could magic up a cooling breeze?"

All heads shook. Meddling with the weather would be a recklessly conspicuous use of sorcery, as he well knew. He was just being tiresome.

"Big storm coming," Thrugg mumbled, sniffing the air.

Rap abandoned the idea of Thume. His army would not follow him there. He had better find a better plan, and soon. An idea began to glimmer at the back of his mind. It needed time to germinate, though. Distraction . . .

"Sagorn, you're a historian. In any of the dragon wars, did anyone ever raise *all* the dragons?"

For a moment the old scholar's pale blue eyes went as blank as the sky. Then their usual penetrating gleam returned. "Not that I can recall. But in ancient times there were many more of the worms. What you want me to tell you is whether anyone ever flew as many as Zinixo did today?"

"Er, yes."

"Well? How many was that?" Sagorn demanded triumphantly.

Rap just knew that it had been a lot. He referred the question to the others, whose greater power would have granted them better vision in the ambience.

Tik Tok said three hundred and the anthropophagi backed their chief. Thrugg estimated two hundred and the trolls backed him, although with less fervor. The split was becoming worrisomely obvious. Sagorn had noticed it, and his haggard old face bore a sardonic sneer as he answered Rap's question.

"No. The highest count I can ever recall reading of was fifteen. Of course record keeping, like many other things, tends to become spotty in the aftermath of a dragon wasting. Most areas do not recover for several centuries. But one dragon per legion was regarded as a pushover for the dragon. They're just about indestructible." The gangly old man smirked to himself, admiring his own universal expertise.

"So why did Zinixo raise so many?" Rap demanded.

"Terror?" That thought came from Grunth belowdecks.

"To see if he could control so many?" suggested one of the trolls.

"A little boy playing with Daddy's spear?" said a cannibal.

"Because he is insane," Sagorn snapped. "He is trying to convince himself that he is invincible, and the harder he tries the less he believes himself."

"Don't suppose it matters much." Rap was surprised that no one else had caught up with his idea yet, but he was sure of it now. "What does matter is that here on this ship we have the second-greatest concentration of sorcery in the world, and Dragon Reach is just over there. Thataway. I say that that's our part in the war! We go to Dragon Reach and make certain Zinixo never uses the worms again!"

A flash of satisfaction brightened the ambience and was hastily suppressed.

Tik Tok beamed. "A brilliant perspiration!"

"Clever!" Sagorn murmured. "How do you feel about destroying dragons, Master Thrugg?"

Thrugg was already nodding. "Monsters!" he growled. He would not willingly hurt any person and perhaps no animal, either, but a dragon would be fair game even for him. That was a war that trolls could fight.

"Of course," the old jotunn added, with an admiring glance at Rap, "such an act is a flagrant breach of the Protocol, but the usurper has already nullified the Protocol. Today Zinixo set the precedent, so the warlock of the south can no longer claim the dragons as his prerogative! Oh, very appropriate! You can rid the world of the worms at last!"

Rap had not thought of going that far. He often recalled the breathtaking beauty of the dawn rising he had once witnessed at Wurth Redoubt. That had been one of the most moving experiences of his life, but no beauty could justify the evil those monsters had wrought throughout history. The world would be a better place without the dragons. He nodded sadly.

Lith'rian would be incensed beyond imagining.

"You had better warn him what you plan," Grunth sent. *"He has a soft spot for his dragons."*

She was right, of course. The warlock of the south was the one essential character still missing from the stage. He had not yet been heard from, although he was almost certainly skulking somewhere in Ilrane. Somewhere?—Ilrane was only a subcontinent! He must still control a powerful band of votaries. As an elf he could never support Zinixo, a dwarf. They had been virulent opponents in the past and would always remain so, but elvish thinking was never predictable and Rap could not automatically count on Lith'rian's assistance.

He groaned. "Someone will have to go and explain to him." Everyone smiled encouragingly in his direction.

"I think Witch Grunth is the logical ambassador," he protested. "Wardens should speak to wardens." Lith'rian was fascinating, charming, and infinitely ruthless. Merely thinking about him gave Rap cold shivers.

Sagorn snorted. "I can just see her Omnipotence going ashore in Ilrane unnoticed."

"She would be rather contiguous," Tik Tok agreed thoughtfully. "Unless she was heavily despised."

Now Rap was seriously alarmed. "You're suggesting I go and tell the warlock of the south that we're going to kill off all his rootin' dragons?" he squealed. He glanced around and saw that was exactly what they were suggesting—the ship was full of smiles.

"We'll deal with the dragons," Thrugg rumbled in his cheerful-earthquake register, thumping Rap on the shoulder so enthusiastically that he almost crumpled to the deck. "You deal with the warlock."

"Carried anonymously!" Tik Tok proclaimed.

Rap consoled himself with the thought that nothing was likely to happen for a few days yet. Perhaps he would think up a better idea before then. Meanwhile, he had proposed a definite course of action and won back his army's loyalty, at least for the moment.

"I see I have just been volunteered to be ambassador to Ilrane. Meanwhile, how about lunch?"

"Make up your mind," Tik Tok said. "Which do you want to be?"

5

A phaeton, a stagecoach, a longship, a leaky old coaster—and a rock.

Princess Kadolan, Rap's elder daughter, sat on a boulder on a hilltop. The scenery was heart-achingly familiar, niggling at her homesickness—the slopes all carpeted with low herbs, some bearing tiny flowers as if a shower of many-colored stars had just passed over. Scraggy grass between the rocks fluttered in the cool breeze blowing from the washed-out blue sky, but there were no trees at all here in the tundra. Down in the hollows the ground was bright green with bog moss and sedge.

Just over the northern horizon lay the Winter Ocean, and Krasnegar, the home she had not seen in months and had not truly expected to see again. She shivered with eagerness to get there. Then all those terrible months she had spent with the goblins would fade like a nightmare, wouldn't they? Perhaps her parents would be home before her, and oh, what a welcome they would give her! Even if they weren't there yet, there would be Eva and little Holi, who must have grown a lot and would be talking more now. There would be hundreds of old friends and they would all be eager to hear Kadie's news. She would introduce them all to her new friend and rescuer, Thaïle.

The pixie also sat on the boulder, staring intently at nothing. She had chosen her seat and it was not really large enough for two. There were many other boulders nearby, but Kadie wanted to stay as close to her new protector as possible.

Thaïle was little older than Kadie herself and looked a lot like the pictures of elves Kadie had seen in books. Her ears were pointed, her eyes large and gold, oddly slanted, and she had a wide nose, a little like Dad's. She was very pretty, though, and to be rescued by a pixie sorceress was an *extremely* romantic adventure. No one had seen a pixie in a thousand years.

Kadie was bursting with questions, but she thought it would

be unwise to interrupt a sorceress when she was thinking, or whatever Thaïle was doing. Traveling by magic was a very odd business, not at all what the books had led her to expect. There had been a sort of *whoosh!* and a flying blackness. Then she had expected to be in Krasnegar, but instead the two of them had been here in the tundra, as if they'd fallen a little short, like Gath's arrows when he tried archery. But it wasn't that the magic had run out, or anything. Thaïle had said something about watchers, and needing to plan the last bit.

That had been at least half an hour ago, maybe longer.

The rocks that littered the hills were painted with blotches of pale green and orange and red and white. If she looked at them kind of squinty-sideways she could see pictures in them. Lichens were a plant and very old, Papa had said. He'd shown Kadie a clear image of a face on one rock near the peat diggings and said it had looked just like that when he was a boy, and maybe Inisso had seen that same face, too.

Suddenly Thaïle glanced sideways at Kadie and smiled a sad sort of smile. "I'm sorry! You've been wonderfully patient! I was watching what was going on in Hub."

Hub was more than a thousand leagues away, but Kadie was not going to show surprise. She knew that sorceresses could do things like that.

"No need to apologize! I'm sure you were busy."

The pixie shook her head sadly. "It wasn't very nice. The usurper shouted out to all the sorcerers in the world, telling them to come and join the Covin."

"Oh!" Kadie said, alarmed. "You're not going to, are you?"

Thaïle shuddered and pulled a face. "Never! A few did, but not very many. I don't think very many. There was another sorcerer speaking, too, the warden of the east."

"Warlock Olybino? The imperor said he didn't know where he had gone."

"Well, he's dead now. The Covin just killed him."

Kadie said, "Oh!" again. "Because of what he did to the goblins?"

"That wasn't him. It was the Covin killed the goblins, and the legions, too." Thaïle stood up and smoothed her skirt. It was a very simple garment, in green and beige stripes. Her blouse was plain white, her golden-brown legs were bare above soft half-boots with turned-over tops.

Kadie had never seen garments quite like Thaïle's, and had been admiring them. In spite of their plainness, they looked very good. She thought she might get some like them, once she was home in Krasnegar again. "What people wear in Thume," she would say when asked. After months of scavenging for clothes in deserted ruins, it would be wonderful to put on decent clothes again. Even the familiar old things in her closet would be welcome.

"Warlock Olybino mentioned your father," Thaïle said. "He didn't say where he is now, of course, but I think he must be all right still. The Covin hasn't caught him yet, anyway."

Without any warning, the bleak tundra landscape went strangely soft and misty. "Thank you," Kadie muttered, having trouble swallowing. Mom and Gath were probably all right, because they were with a warlock, and the imperor, but it was wonderful to know that Dad—Papa—was safe, too. They would all have wonderful stories to share when they were reunited, and hers would be as good as any. Rescued by a pixie!

Thaïle turned and stared to the north. She wrung her hands. "But now I don't know what to do!"

"What did you mean, 'watchers'?" Kadie asked.

"I meant there's a spell on Krasnegar. It's a nice place, Kadie, although I wouldn't call it little." She grinned briefly. It was nice to see her happy, if just for a moment. For a sorceress, she seemed extraordinarily sad most of the time.

Krasnegar certainly was little! Still, there were more important things to argue about. "What sort of spell? Are the people hurt?"

"No. No, they can't even know it's there. Most sorcerers wouldn't see it, even." For a moment Thaïle seemed at a loss for words. Probably magic was difficult to explain.

"Are you a specially powerful sorcerer, er, sorceress, then?"

"Very powerful," the pixie said sadly. "That's my problem. I'm probably the greatest sorcerer since Thraine."

Kadie said, "Ooo!" After a moment she said it again, wondering why that could ever be a problem. There were hundreds of legends and old stories about Thraine. Would there be stories and books about Thaïle one day? How she saved Princess Kadolan, for instance?

Perhaps the pixie read her thoughts, for she smiled again. "At least, I'm comparable—very, very strong! But I can't see any way in past the watchers, the spell. That's what it's for, you see. It's been put there like a guard dog, to bark if it detects sorcery." Thaïle looked wonderingly down at Kadie with her big gold eyes. "Your father must be very important to the Covin!"

"I expect he is! He's invented a whole new protocol to replace Emine's Protocol." Kadie was not very clear just what Papa had done, but it did seem to have impressed the imperor.

"Yes, the warlock explained, and the Almighty was annoyed very much that it was mentioned."

"The who?"

"The usurper, Zinixo. He calls himself the Almighty now. He's mad—crazy." Thaïle frowned crossly. "But that means you're important, too! If Zinixo could capture you, then he could hold you for ransom, couldn't he? To make your father give himself up or something?"

Kadie nodded, feeling uncomfortable. She did not want to be kidnapped again, not just yet, anyway. "Suppose so."

"I wouldn't put any evil past him. You see, he must have set the watcher spell on Krasnegar to tell him if your father tries to come home. I can't think what else it's there for. And it's a very strong spell." Thaïle bit her lip. "I only know two people who could make a spell that big and that strong."

"You?"

"Ha! No! If I was that powerful, I could undo it. I meant Zinixo. He's got hundreds of sorcerers to help."

"Who's the other one, then?"

The pixie hesitated. "I'd best not say who."

"A sorcerer stronger than you, and you're as strong as Thraine?"

"Sorceress. Well, not really a sorceress. More than a sorceress!"

"Oo! You mean she's a *demigod*?"

Thaïle started, gold eyes widening. "What do you know of demigods?"

"Papa was a demigod once," Kadie said modestly.

"Once? What do you mean 'once'? Tell me."

"I don't know much. Mama told us some of it, Gath and me, when we'd been captured by the goblins. I've forgotten."

The pixie continued to stare for a while, and then shivered. "You are full of astonishing things, Kadie! Mundanes are not supposed to know such lore at all. I think the Gods sent me to you."

"I certainly thought so!"

Thaïle chuckled, then went suddenly sad again. She ran fingers through her hair. It was wavy hair, pale brown, and she wore it very short. She would look older if she let it grow longer.

"Well, what are we going to do? I don't dare take you to Krasnegar, and it's too far to walk."

Kadie jumped to her feet. "Magic up a couple of horses?"

The pixie shook her head sadly and walked away a couple of paces. "I don't think I can risk that much power so close to the watchers." Her fists were clenched now. "Kadie, I think I ought to go back to Thume and tell the Keeper about all this. She probably knows, but . . . But where am I going to take you? I can't leave you here."

Well, that was certainly a relief! Kadie moved close and adjusted her sword. "I'll come to Thume with you! I'll be safe there, won't I?"

"I don't think so!" Thaïle wrung her hands again. It was a very strange gesture, just as the way she spoke was a little strange, too. "Oh, you'd be safe from the Almighty, at least for a while. But I've already told you too much, and shown you too much. The Keeper wouldn't ever let you leave!"

Kadie thought about that. If she couldn't go home to Krasnegar, then she had nowhere else to go. She decided she would like to stay with Thaïle and visit Thume. Nobody ever did, only her mother had, years ago. She'd been trespassing, though. To be shown around by one of the residents would be quite different. And Thume could never be worse than the goblins.

"I can't think of anywhere that's very safe right now. And why shouldn't the Keeper let me leave? Who's ever going to believe me if I say I've traveled to Thume by magic?"

"Any sorcerer could tell you weren't lying," Thaïle said sharply. "You don't have any friends or family anywhere?"

"In Hub we have some relatives, but I don't know them."

"Hub's out of the question!" Thaïle shrugged. "No, I mustn't take you to Thume. I mustn't!"

Kadie smiled hopefully. "You're the most powerful sorcerer since Thraine, you just said."

"I can't fight the Keeper, Kadie!"

"She's the demigod one? Is she not a good person?"

"No! The Keeper protects Thume. That's her job. And she's *ruthless*!"

"Ruthless? What do you mean, ruthless?"

Thaïle turned her back. Then she said, quite distinctly, "She killed my goodman and my baby."

She stepped over to another large rock and sat down, not looking around.

Kadie gulped. *"That's horrible!"* She would never have thought that Thaïle could have had a baby. She didn't seem nearly old enough.

Then she realized that Thaïle was weeping. *Oh!*

This time the boulder was quite big enough for two. Kadie went and sat down and put an arm around Thaïle. In a moment she had both arms around Thaïle, and Thaïle was sobbing on her shoulder. Kadie began to think about Dad, and Mom, and Krasnegar, and even silly old twin Gath, and soon she was crying, too.

They sat there together on the boulder amid the flowers of the barren lands under the washy blue sky, and wept in unison.

Still pursuing:

> Let us, then, be up and doing,
>   With a heart for any fate;
> Still achieving, still pursuing,
>   Learn to labor and to wait.

—Longfellow, *A Psalm of Life*

❮ TWO ❯

To the appointed place

1

About an hour past the top of the pass, the phaeton emerged at last from the clammy white mist. Angling down the side of an enormous valley, the road had just reached the tree line, where a few stunted pine pioneers seemed to be leading the forest in a general migration upward. Sunlight shone in silver on a lake far below.

"There!" Ylo said proudly. "Scenery!"

"Gorgeous. Are the tops of the hills pretty, too?"

"So I'm told. They've been temporarily removed for cleaning. Let's find a place where we can eat. I'm famished."

There was so little traffic that he could have just stopped on the highway itself, but he seemed reluctant to do that. He drove on for a while, until the trees began to crowd in more thickly. Then he reined in, but he jumped down and led the roan up a gentle slope and around behind a thick clump of conifers, the chaise lurching along behind. Eshiala passed Maya down to him and then accepted his hand to descend, wondering but not commenting. She knew Ylo now, and he would have his reasons. He would also have his reasons for not telling her his reasons.

The sun had begun to peek through the clouds, and the day was warmer. They ate lunch. Maya became engrossed in trying to feed, or possibly catch, a ground squirrel.

Lying back on the cloak Ylo had spread on the grass, Eshiala watched him through half-closed eyes. He was leaning his arms on his knees, staring at nothing. Thinking? Worrying? The sun glinted blue highlights in his black hair and traced out the angles of cheekbone and chin. He was quite the most handsome man she had ever met.

She wished her darling daughter would curl up and go to sleep and leave the two of them alone. This would be a very suitable spot to learn about outdoor loving, even if there weren't any of his precious daffodils about. The wind was warm and gentle, the only sounds the roan's steady munching and an occasional rattle of harness.

Whatever was she going to do when they reached Gaaze and Ylo left her? How could she fend for herself and her daughter? Her share of the gold Lady Eigaze had given them was still intact, because Ylo had insisted on spending his and not hers, and it would suffice to buy a little store, a grocer's store, like her father's. She knew how to serve customers in a store, but she knew nothing about buying stock or keeping books or hiring helpers, and she did not think Imperial law allowed a woman to own anything like that anyway. So she would have to find a man to help her. What man could she trust? What man could ever be as satisfying as . . .

Ylo raised his head. Hooves beat a slow tattoo on the road. Harness jingled, wheels rumbled—a carriage coming up the hill. He relaxed again. The sounds died down until the wind wiped them away. He leaned on an elbow to spot a kiss on the end of Eshiala's nose. "Asleep?"

"Almost. What's my dearest daughter doing?"

"Stalking."

"Stun her with a rock, will you? Gently, of course."

He grinned, eyes close above hers. "Don't be greedy."

"Why not? You taught me to be greedy." She would not have Ylo around to make love to very many more times. They were in Qoble now; at Gaaze he would leave her. That had been the agreement. The dream was almost over. She sighed, and stretched, and then laid an arm around his neck, trying to pull him down. "Time to go, I suppose?"

He resisted, frowning, listening. "In a minute."

More hooves, and this time faster—a horseman, descending. He went by. He stopped, suddenly. The roan looked up and whinnied and was answered.

Ylo sat up, breaking free of her. His hand slid to his sword hilt, but she suspected he was unaware of it.

The hooves returned, slowly. Then the sound ended, as the horse left the roadbed. Eshiala sat up. Ylo floated to his feet, graceful as always.

The rider came into view around the pines, a legionary, mail flashing bright in the sunlight. A swarthy and surprisingly youthful face peered out from his helmet. He reined in a few feet away and saluted.

"Signifer Ylo!"

Ylo hesitated. His fists were clenched tight. Then he laughed. "Hawk! Well, well. Hawk, you old rascal!"

Hawk nodded. His eyes flickered momentarily to Eshiala and then away again. "On vacation . . . sir?"

Ylo was out of uniform. The man's tone was respectful, but it indicated that distinction somehow.

"More or less," Ylo said. "They don't call you Hawk for nothing, do they?"

"A blind bat could see those wheel tracks." The youngster looked pleased by the flattery, though.

"Transferred to first cohort, I see. How's Anlya?"

The legionary's mount began to prance, and he brought it under control with more effort than a skilled horseman would have needed. "She's fine, just fine. Deeded me a big bouncing son couple of months ago." He beamed proudly. "Young bullock, he is."

"Hey, great! Congratulations. Give her my regards."

"Will do." Again Hawk glanced briefly at Eshiala, and then at Maya, who was watching from a safe distance. He regarded Ylo appraisingly.

His horse began to fidget again and he swore at it. "Signifer . . . I think this brute may be going to go a little lame, you know?"

"Want me to take a look?" Ylo asked hesitantly, puzzled.

The legionary shook his head in a blaze of sun on bronze. "It'll slow me, I mean. I may be late arriving. Er, just past the second ford, there's a track goes off to the left. It's a bit rough for wheels, but it takes you around Pinebridge."

Ylo's fists relaxed. "Ah. Thanks, Hawk. Appreciate that information."

"Useful shortcut." The legionary smiled grimly. "Try and stay out of trouble, Signifer." He patted the dispatch pouch at his belt thoughtfully.

"Trouble tells a man who his friends are."

"Well, there's that. The Good be with you. My lady."

The kid nodded, wheeled his horse clumsily, and headed back to the highway. A moment later, hooves clopped on the paving.

Ylo stood stock still, staring after him. Eshiala climbed to her feet, heart thumping.

"Now tell me what all that was about." She waited, aware that she was starting to shake. "Ylo? Tell me!"

He shrugged and turned to smile at her. "It can't be the Covin, obviously. So it's mundanes."

"Who?"

The smile became wooden, a mask hiding his feelings. "Hardgraa, I expect. We made a fool of him, locking him in the cellar. Aunt Eigaze did."

Eshiala moved closer, wanting comfort. "Spell it out, darling, please!"

"It's my own evilish fault!" he said, suddenly furious. "Back at Yewdark I blabbed about looking for a warmer climate. Hardgraa's a lot smarter than he looks. He must've guessed I meant to head back to Qoble. He's still loyal to Shandie's memory. He thinks it's his duty to turn your daughter in at court."

Eshiala shivered. Suddenly the wind seemed much colder. "He's only a centurion!"

Ylo shook his head. "Everyone in the XIIth knows he's Shandie's man. He wouldn't need papers and warrants. He could've reached Gaaze ahead of us, easy. And talked to the legate. The XIIth guards the passes."

"They're going to arrest us?"

His anger was obvious now. "Detain us for questioning. He won't have mentioned who you are, of course. He's probably told them some tale about a high official's wife and the imperor being furious but not wanting a scandal. Hardgraa can spin yarns like that by the league. That would be my guess. And the legate's told them to look out for me."

"They all know you!"

He nodded. "And my reputation."

If he wasn't going to initiate a hug, then she would have to. She stepped close and put her arms around him. He did not respond, just stood there, looking down at her coldly. "Well-earned reputation!"

"The finest lover in Pandemia," she countered.

"Finest seducer of beautiful young women!" he said bitterly.

Surely he was not having an attack of conscience? Not Ylo! "And a hero to the army. Hawk was offering to commit treason for you, darling—wasn't he?"

He blinked in surprise and then laughed uneasily. "I suppose it would be mutiny at least, if you want to put it that way."

Strange and lovely man! Ylo was very conscious of his good looks and sometimes lately he seemed just a little ashamed of the use he put them to, but he never, ever gave himself credit for all his good qualities. Like heroism.

"The legate would put it that way!" She squeezed him tighter. "Hawk's risking his life for you, delaying that dispatch. That's something Hardgraa won't have thought of!"

"Mutiny? Young idiot! You're right." Ylo grinned devilishly. "Know something funny? That son he mentioned? It could be mine. The timing would be right."

Eshiala released him and turned her back. "Pretty, is she, his Anlya?"

"Er ... Well, I thought she was dazzling. Since I've met you I know she was a squint-eyed, flabby, poxy dwarf." Now he tried to put his arms around her and she stepped away.

"So this shortcut could be a trap? Hawk and his friends?"

Ylo gulped audibly and she turned.

He shook his head. "No. Hawk's too impulsive! If he even suspected that, he'd have ridden me down, or run me through right here. He wouldn't set traps, it's not his way. Anlya told me how—well, never mind. If he says we can bypass Pinebridge, then we can bypass Pinebridge. We can skip Gaaze and head east, to Castino or Angot ..."

She laughed sadly. "Oh, Ylo, Ylo, my darling! One of these days some husband's going to come after you with a gang of thugs and—"

"Not any more. I'm trying to tell you—"

"But if you think this shortcut's a good idea, then I suppose we don't have anything much to—"

"Eshiala, will you listen to me a moment?"

"I am listening. Hawk won't be able to give us—"

"No you're not. We ought to separate, really, because it's me the men of the XIIth know, not you, and—"

"No!" she shouted.

"I'm a rake."

"I know that, darling. Just now I'm the one being, er, raked, and I love—"

"I'm landless and penniless and the only skill I've got is seduction. I'm a liar—"

"I know that, too." She doubted that he had ever told her one untrue word. She wanted to hold him, kiss him—anything. She could barely keep her hands off him when they were alone, but they ought to be on their way, not standing here jabbering like a pair of parrots.

"I don't lie to the Gods, though."

"We must— What do you mean?"

"Eshiala, my darling, will ... Will you marry me?"

"Ylo! You don't mean that?"

He shrugged. "Well, I was just hoping. Not just because it'll make Hardgraa's job harder. Not only that. I mean, I'm crazily in love with you, like I've never been with any woman."

"Ylo!"

Wonder in his eyes ... "I just realized now—when Hawk said ... I just thought of them separating us, and knew I couldn't bear the thought of ever losing you, but you would be crazy to trust me, and—"

Her mouth was on his. Then his arms were around her, crushing her to him.

Maya came running over and pounded fists on them, wanting to be included. When she began to scream, Ylo broke off the embrace to scoop her up. His face was as flushed as Eshiala knew her own must be, but the sunlight danced in his eyes.

"That means yes?" he asked, clutching her with one arm and Maya with the other.

"Oh, yes, yes!"

Yes yes yes yes yes yes yes ...

2

The sun was setting in Guwush.

The previous evening, Inos had thought that Highscarp was a horrid little place, ugly and squalid. Now she knew that Yugg was much worse—smaller, uglier, and squalider. The post inn was a hovel of timber and sagging thatch, its stableyard a morass of filth. Yugg looked like it sounded. It smelled even more so.

She thought she would always remember it with love. It was full of birdsong and rainbows for her. *Rap was alive!*

Grumbling passengers were still climbing down from the

stage. The baggage was being unloaded by innumerable gnomes of indiscernible age and sex, grotesque little figures in grimy rags swarming over the carriage like ants. They bore off the booty in streams, four or five to a heavy valise and seven or eight under a trunk, running through the mire, splashing it around gleefully with their bare feet and piping excitedly in high-pitched voices. Whatever their faults, whatever their circumstances, gnomes were usually content.

Inos stood in the mud and stench with Shandie and the warlock, hearing hardly half of what the dwarf was saying. Dragons burning up legions, goblins ripped apart, Olybino dead . . . It was all horrible, yet little of it registered. Olybino had named Rap as the leader of the resistance and the usurper had not denied it, so Rap had certainly not been caught by the Covin and must be assumed to be still at large as far as Zinixo was aware. Rap was alive!

So perhaps one day they would meet again? Back home in distant little Krasnegar, king and queen together once more? That seemed so horribly impossible still, and if it happened she would have to tell him how she had blundered, how she had lost their son and daughter—Gath off adventuring into mortal danger in Nordland and Kadie abducted by goblins. A God had warned him he must lose a child, and Inos had crazily lost two. Even Holi and Eva, back in Krasnegar, might be in danger or even dead for all she knew now. Much as she wanted Rap, could she ever bring herself to look him in the eye again?

Gath might yet survive, but Kadie . . . Oh, *Gods*! She thought back to what Raspnex had said about the goblins' fate. Not dragons, at least. That had been the legions. Anything would be better than dragons.

"Sorcery?" she said, interrupting him. "What did you say happened to the goblins?"

He peered up angrily under his broad-brimmed hat, an aging human nail keg, eyes like gray agates above a beard of iron turnings. Then his glare softened. "Just naked power, ma'am. I couldn't tell much at this distance. I mean, I don't know if it was specifically directed at the greenies or would destroy . . . Sorry, Inos. I just don't know."

"You all right?" Shandie demanded.

Of course she was not all right! "I'm fine," she said. *Oh, Kadie, Kadie!*

Shandie glanced at the inn and pulled a face. "We should go get you a stiff drink." He did not move, though. This open yard was a safer place to talk than anywhere indoors would be. He looked down at the dwarf. "Anything else?"

"Isn't that enough? Slag, what a day!" Raspnex scowled, and even for him it was a vicious grimace. "Who's going to believe in us when we pass up an opportunity like that? We let East get blasted and did nothing! Why didn't Rap sound the charge? Why didn't I?"

The imperor shrugged. "Well, why didn't you?"

"Mostly because the dragons were still in the sky. If the Covin had released its hold on them, they'd have run amok."

The imperor nodded. "Then I expect that's why Rap didn't."

The dwarf nodded and stuffed his big hands in his pockets. He stared down at his boots, seeming oddly childlike for an elderly, tough-as-rocks sorcerer. "So now what?" he growled. "We don't have to spread the news anymore. The word's out, may the Gods cherish his soul."

Shandie flashed a meaningful glance at Inos over the crown of the dwarf's hat. The two warlocks had not been friends. From Raspnex, that had been a rare and precious tribute to a dead hero.

"Amen."

The warlock kicked at a lump of filth. "You don't need to bother with gnomish rebels now. We don't have to stay on in this pigpen, thank the Powers. Leave tomorrow."

Shandie drew a deep breath and almost gagged in consequence. "Well, I'll admit that's a relief. For both reasons. Let's think about it." He turned again to face the inn. "Do you suppose they charge by the bed or by the bug?"

Inos thought, *Kadie!* and squared her shoulders. Kadie might have been dead for months; she could well have died in some much more horrible way than just being blasted by sorcery. She must not dwell on that. Likely she would never know what had happened to her daughter. The Gods would . . . Her hand found something.

She pulled a thin tube from the pocket of her cloak and frowned at it.

"What's that?" Shandie demanded. Very little escaped him.

"I don't know." The paper had a gnomish look to it, tattered and soiled. She unrolled it.

> I have no quarrel with
> Krasnegar and offer safe
> conduct to your friend who

> wishes to meet with me. The
> two of you must come at once to
> the temple, unaccompanied. You
> will be security for his good
> conduct. He knows my hand.

"Someone must have just put it there," she said, passing it to Shandie. She glanced around, but the infestation of gnomes had dispersed. The yard was almost empty. Deft little fingers going by could easily have slipped the paper in her pocket without her noticing. She had been in a daze anyway.

Shandie's face was as wooden as a log pile.

"Is it his writing?" Raspnex demanded. He had not been shown the paper. He was a sorcerer.

"Could be. It's been a long time." The imperor shook his head as if to clear it. "Son of a mule! What matters is that whoever wrote this knows I have seen Oshpoo's hand." He laughed mirthlessly. "Brazen cheek!"

"How do you know his handwriting?" Inos asked. She had never considered the idea that gnomes might read and write, and discovering that blatant prejudice in herself annoyed her considerably. Why shouldn't gnomes read and write?

"After Highscarp he sent me a letter congratulating me on my success." Shandie was being much too casual.

"And?"

"And promising to get even." He smiled wryly, passed the letter back to Inos. "Looks like he may have found his chance."

"You're out of your mind!" Raspnex snapped. "I just told you—you don't have to go talk with mundane leaders anymore. All the sorcerous know about the new protocol now."

"But there are other things I might discuss with that gentleman. I use the word loosely." Shandie was regarding Inos. His dark eyes smoldered with an intensity that she had seen in them only rarely. She thought of that as his imperor look. It was the only thing that would ever make him stand out in a crowd. He was asking if she was willing to put her head in the noose with his.

Right now, more than anything, she would enjoy a hot bath, but that would not likely be obtainable in Yugg's sole hostelry. Besides, the bath would be more appropriate after meeting with gnomes, not before. And if Emshandar V by the grace of the Gods et cetera thought he could outdare Inosolan of

Krasnegar, longtime birds'-nest raiding champion of the North Face, then he was due for a shock.

So what if it was dangerous? Right now danger would be a welcome distraction from brooding. She nodded. The imperor removed his sword and scabbard and handed them to the dwarf.

"Madness!" Raspnex muttered.

"You'll keep an occult eye on us, though?"

"Why bother? Can't do much. Given the choice, which do you want—gnomes or the Covin? Your Oshpoo must have sorcerers of his own, to know who you are."

"There's more to it than that," Shandie said. "Much more! Work it out. Inos, I'm grateful!" He offered his arm as if they were about to enter a ballroom. She smiled and accepted. Together they left the yard and emerged on the main street, which was also the Imperial highway across Guwush. Left led to the stockade of the fort, right to the temple, whose rickety little spire was the only thing in town taller than the cottage chimneys. They turned right.

A bugle called faintly from the fort. She did not ask Shandie what it signified. Chow, perhaps? The sky was growing dark, draining color from the world, and yet few windows showed lights. A dog was barking somewhere. The street did seem deserted, but tiny shadows moved in the corners of the alleys and in the corner of her eye. She was quite certain that the two strangers were being watched as they strode along.

"The Yugg Valley is one of the principal sources of spider silk," Shandie remarked, intent on making casual conversation. He did not even seem to be looking out for danger.

He was behaving very oddly. The previous evening he had warned her against taking an innocent evening stroll in Highscarp, and now he was leading her out without a sword to meet a sworn enemy. His personal courage was unquestioned—the Senate had passed resolutions reprimanding him for it—but she would not have expected him to be quite this foolhardy. He must have some powerful reason for wanting to meet the rebel chief, and she could not imagine what it might be.

Even more curious, perhaps, was the way he had allowed Inos herself to be dragged into an affair where she clearly did not belong. That did not fit with his attitude toward women and their irrelevancy in warfare, danger, and all other serious business.

Yet, come to think of it, Shandie's attitude toward women had not been putting quite such a strain on her tooth enamel recently as it had when she had first met him. She could not recall the last time she had ground or gritted at one of his remarks. Could he possibly have changed his opinions in the past few months? A few houses farther along the road, she came to the conclusion that he definitely must have changed them. She wondered what in the world could have caused such a conversion in anyone as obdurate as Shandie.

They were almost at the temple. He was still talking aimlessly about silk. As they passed a gap between two houses, somebody whistled. There was just enough light to make out a small figure beckoning.

"Whistling!" Shandie said, changing direction. Mud squelched underfoot as soon as they left the paved highway. "Now I am whistled up like a dog?" He sounded amused—slightly.

They entered the alley. A tiny shadow flitted ahead, barely visible even when moving, vanishing whenever it stopped to wait for them.

"All we need now," Inos said, "is for a bunch of horsemen to leave the stockade and ride along the street. That'd do it!"

"Less than that, I expect. A bugle call might be enough, if the man himself is really here in person."

There was barely room for the two of them to walk side by side. The little guide hurried through a muddle of cottages like a maze. There were no organized roads and the footing was treacherous. Yugg was larger than Inos had thought. Suddenly they came to the end of it. Ahead lay brush and trees, and fresh air. Their mysterious guide was still beckoning.

A few steps into the wood, Inos stumbled. Shandie steadied her and stopped.

"We need light!" he called.

Tiny fingers gripped her hand and she jumped. Shandie grunted angrily, and she saw that vague little shapes had materialized beside each of them.

"We shall guide you," said a shrill, thin voice, more like birdsong than human speech.

"Lead on, then."

Shandie went first, Inos followed. In a moment she pulled free of the gnome's grasp and put a hand on her—or his—shoulder. That worked better. She raised an arm to keep branches out of her face. They plodded through the forest, following an invisible path, and eventually a glimmer of light came into view. A small fire smoldered in a hollow. A solitary gnome sat cross-legged at the far side.

The greasy little shoulder twisted away from her and the guides vanished as mysteriously and silently as they had come. Shandie and Inos picked their way down the slope and settled on the ground, facing the gnome.

At first glance he was a pot-bellied, very filthy child. A second look discovered the wrinkles and flabby skin under the caked dirt. The color of his hair and beard were indeterminate. He wore a rag of the same gray as himself; his feet were bare. Like all gnomes, he had very little nose. He stared at the newcomers in silence, black-button eyes shining bright in the firelight.

Inos thought the beating of her heart must be audible for leagues. The woods all around were silent, but she was certain that they were filled with watchers. What had possessed her to come here? This was not her business. Rap would call her an idiot.

"You are older than I expected," Shandie said.

"I am not Leader. I must make sure that it is safe for Leader to come here."

"It is safe as far as I am concerned."

The gnome scratched busily. "You are Imperor? This is Queen, from Krasnegar?"

"Yes. We were invited here."

The tiny old man ignored that. He studied Inos for a moment. "You have gnomes in your land?"

She had half expected that question and had her answer ready. "At the last count there were six, but I expect there are eight now. Pish, Tush, Heug, Phewf, and their children."

"Ah! You know their names?"

"They are the royal rat catchers."

The gnome chuckled hoarsely, obviously pleased.

"They are there by invitation," Inos said.

He nodded. "That sounds like Rap."

Her heart jumped. She thought she knew who this ancient was, then. Shandie made an irritated noise, but she ignored him.

"You have met my husband, sir?"

"Please do not give me titles. Yes, I met Rap once, long ago. He stands out of the light."

"I do not quite follow that . . . Ishist?"

"It is a gnomish saying. Most people cannot see the world for their own shadows."

There was a lump in her throat. "That describes him very well."

The old man picked up a stick and poked at the fire. Sparks rushed upward into the night. "He sees what is and does what he should?"

"Yes, he does." It was Rap exactly.

"And you, Imperor? Why wouldst you speak with Leader?"

"You eavesdropped on her Majesty and myself last night in Highscarp," Shandie said. "When we spoke, at the door of the inn."

Ishist cackled. "I did not. Others did."

There was a pause. Inos wished she could pass a note to Shandie, warning of sorcery. "May I inquire how your wife is, Ishist?"

"She is well. She is visiting with her father at the moment."

Inos flipped a mental coin and decided to press on, aware that she was on dangerous ground. "They are reconciled?"

The old man must know every thought in her head. "Oh, yes. Many years ago."

"That is good news. And Ugish, and the other children?"

"Ugish and two more of my sons died at Highscarp."

Awkward silence.

"I am sorry to hear that, Ishist," Inos said. "Are you still Dragonward?"

Shandie twitched.

"No, I retired," the gnome said. He leered, showing innumerable sharp teeth. "His Omnipotence released me, as is his wont with those who have served him well. My only binding now is not to oppose him. Imp, you did not answer my question."

Shandie cleared his throat harshly. "Yesterday I wanted to speak with, er, General Oshpoo so that I could advise him of the usurper and the Covin and the counterrevolution. Today that is no longer necessary."

"No, it isn't. The letter you received was written before the drama in Hub. So why did you accept the invitation?"

"Because I believe there are other important matters he and I should discuss. I am impressed by his power."

"What power?"

Shandie chuckled. "Your power, perhaps. The usurper Zinixo controls the greatest concentration of sorcery the world has seen in a millennium; perhaps ever. For half a year he has tried to catch me. He came very close, but he failed, thanks to a loyal servant of mine, Signifer Ylo. And yet General Oshpoo located me in a day? Clearly he has no small power at his command."

"He does," the sorcerer said in his squeaky whisper. "And the warden of the east died today."

Meaning, perhaps, that the legions were unprotected now, or that the anti-Covin faction could not defend its own. Shandie did not turn to the lure. "I had never thought . . . No one has ever mentioned gnomish sorcerers in my hearing. But of course sorcerers are solitary people. They must often die alone, and yet to die in peace they need tell their words to somebody. I suppose gnomes are often the only ones around?"

The grubby little man nodded, black eyes shining bright in the firelight. "And gnomes die beside other gnomes. We may have more sorcerers amongst us than any other people."

"Which is what I realized when I saw that letter," Shandie said. He turned to share a smile with Inos. "Rap once told me that words could be looted. I don't think even he had realized that they could be scavenged, also! How many gnomes serve the Covin?" He flashed the question at Ishist.

The sorcerer scratched his caked beard. "None."

"Why none?"

"Because few gnomes ever bother to use their power much, so they rarely get caught. When they do, the dwarf takes their words and puts them to death."

"Then the gnomish sorcerers will aid our cause?"

"You are our enemy, Imperor." The little man raised his voice for the first time. "Why should we seek to restore you to your throne? Why should we restore the wardens? Why should we not just stay neutral and let the day folk fight out their own battles? That has always been our gnomish way." He bared his needle teeth.

"That is what I wish to discuss with General Oshpoo."

The black-button eyes stared hard over the little fire for several very long seconds. Then the tiny shoulders shrugged— Inos could almost imagine grime flaking off.

"I think you are honest," Ishist said. "Leader, it is safe."

Another gnome advanced into the firelight, clutching what seemed to be an old log under his arm. He was indistinguishable from any other gnome, so coated in dirt that his color and age were impossible to make out. Only his beard showed that he was not just a filthy child. He moved nimbly to sit down beside the sorcerer, then looked across at Shandie without expression.

"Speak, then. I am Oshpoo."

"I honor a noble opponent."

"I hate you. I would lay your carcass at my door and dance on it every day until it rotted to mud."

Inos glanced at the imperor to see how he had taken that, but Shandie's face was never readable at the best of times.

"After Highscarp you told me you wanted revenge. I think you got it at Abnilagrad."

"Not enough. Not enough to wash out a generation of killing and oppression." Something about Oshpoo's thin voice made Inos think of snakes. Or perhaps it was the unwinking stare of hatred.

The imperor did not try to argue the point. "We are both outlaws now. You understand that? An imposter rules in my place. Nothing I say tonight has any validity in law."

"Say it anyway so I can refuse."

"I want the help of all free sorcerers in the world to overthrow the Covin and the usurper—including gnomes."

"I am not a sorcerer."

"But you have many supporters who are."

"Why should they help one who has killed so many of our young men and enslaved our land?"

"Because the alternative may be worse."

Inos wondered how many eyes watched from the surrounding darkness. All she could hear was crickets and the fire crackling. She wondered how many bows and spears were out there—how many more sorcerers. She wondered how reliable gnomish safe-conduct was.

"Worse than you?" Oshpoo asked with his mouth full. He had laid the rotted log across his knees and was picking things out of it, eating them with evident enjoyment. "Worse than the Four? Without the warlock of the east meddling, we can use sorcery against your legions. The new order holds promise for gnomes."

"Rubbish," Shandie said calmly. "If Zinixo guesses that you have sorcerers at your beck, then he will blast you without mercy. He has pulled half the legions out of Guwush. Don't think that makes him a gnome supporter. I am sure he is setting a trap for you, although I admit I do not understand it."

Oshpoo sneered, showing even more teeth than the old sorcerer had. "Having no army you now try to defend your realm with words?"

"I think you believe the same, General, or you would have moved by now."

"I am no general. My name is Leader. Your flattery sickens me."

"How many spies do you have at court?" Shandie was keeping his voice flat and steady. His hands lay relaxed on his knees.

"That I will not answer."

"And how many sorcerers here in Guwush?"

"That I will not answer, either."

"Will you ask them to help us against the Almighty when the trumpet sounds?"

Oshpoo shrugged his tiny shoulders. "Why should I? Why should they agree? What can you offer gnomes, Emperor?"

"Surrender."

Inos shot a startled glance at Shandie. Diplomats would not approve of his style—he negotiated with a broadsword. The two gnomes showed no reaction.

"Explain!" Oshpoo broke off a piece of wood and evidently found some treats under it.

Shandie took a moment to gather his words. "This war is costing the Impire far more than Guwush is worth," he said. "More in gold, more in men. I make you this promise: When I am restored to power, I will offer you a treaty withdrawing all the legions from your land and recognizing Guwush as an independent realm."

"On what terms?"

"Merely that all imps may leave safely within, say, three months. That is all I shall ask, uncontested withdrawal."

Oshpoo's beady eyes gleamed in the firelight. "No imperor has ever signed a treaty with gnomes."

"Wrong. There was a treaty in 1342. And I will sign this one."

"The Senate would not ratify it."

"I can handle those old relics," Shandie said grimly. "If they balk, I shall threaten to pull out the legions unilaterally, and they cannot stop me from doing that. The money being wasted here will compensate the losers amply."

Oshpoo took awhile to think, obviously suspicious. "And what exactly do you want of me now?"

"Nothing. Almost nothing. I give you my word without

conditions—if I win, I withdraw the legions, whether your sorcerers have aided me or not. But they may tip the balance when the battle is joined, and I hope that you tell them so. If I win, I shall retire to the borders Abnila recognized. If Zinixo wins, he will rule the world and everyone in it. I am your better bet."

"Bah! Promises!"

The sorcerer said, "Gods, Leader! He means it! He really does!"

This time the silence was even longer, as the rebel balanced future hope against old hatred. He had forgotten his supper. Inos thought she could hear whispers amid the crickets' chirps now, rustlings of excitement like dry leaves out in the dark woods.

"He means it now, perhaps." Oshpoo sneered. "Because the dwarf has a sword between his thighs. But if he wins he won't. Imps forget humility very easily."

"I cannot do more than swear," Shandie said softly. "I told you—anything I sign tonight is worthless."

"And so is anything you swear."

The woods had fallen silent, even the crickets. The offer had been made. Apparently it had been refused.

Inos swallowed and wet her lips. "I witness the imperor's oath," she said, "and will see that my husband is informed of it. If gnomes aid his battle, he will know on what terms they fight. He is a man of his word and he has never left a debt unpaid in his life."

Oshpoo turned his baleful black gaze on her and snarled. "He is king of an arctic trading post. Will he curb the imperor?"

"Yes."

Everyone seemed startled by that monosyllable, even Inos herself. It left an ominous aftertaste of truth, though. If the counterrevolution succeeded, then its leaders would rearrange the world, and not necessarily to the old pattern.

"Ishist said earlier that my husband stands out of the light," she said. "He will not buy with false coin. For what it is worth, Leader, you have my oath on this matter also—that I will do anything I can to make Emshandar keep faith. I do not believe that my efforts will be needed, though."

Ishist nodded.

The gnome leader glared at Shandie. "You would shake hands with a gnome on this?"

Shandie laughed, seeking to break the tension. "I will embrace you on it!"

"Oh, you really must be desperate!" Oshpoo stood up.

Shandie rose to his knees and held out a hand to him. "Forget Highscarp, forget Abnilagrad, forget all of them. Let us put aside the past and agree to make a better world!"

"I will tell my friends what you have promised and let them decide for themselves." Ignoring the offered hand, the rebel leader turned and walked away quickly into the trees, still carrying his log.

Imperor and queen looked to Ishist. The old sorcerer winked. They had won.

3

The sun was setting in Qoble.

Thaïle sat under a willow on a riverbank, chin on knees, watching peaty brown water swirl below her. She wondered how water could be bright and dark at the same time. Opaque brown-black depths hinted at danger and currents and hidden trout, yet shreds of evening sky lay on the surface like pale silk. Cattle placidly grazed the lush pasture at her back and behind them in turn lay farm buildings, hedges, and orchards. A road led off to a town somewhere. This sleepy land was the Impire, populous and prosperous and peaceful, and months would drift by before those contented rural folk learned of the massacre at Bandor. By then the harvest would be garnered and the men would be readying their bows and dogs for the hunting season. Yet behind the summer of their lives lurked the menace of the Almighty and the shadows of war. It was all rather like the river, bright and dark at the same time.

The far bank was lower. There the river chattered over a stony spit, innocent and simple, skirting a marshy area of bulrushes and sedge. The woodland beyond that bore no sign of cattle or farms or people—undisturbed nature. A league away, a rounded hill humped up to form the skyline, but no chimneys or spires or haystacks rose over the trees. Innocent and simple? No, that land was Thume, and nothing was innocent or simple at all.

She felt heartbroken with longing and homesickness, and at the same time repelled by that sinister forest—she, a pixie who loved woods and wild places! She was reacting to the aversion spell, of course, and she could block it out if she wished, but her premonition told her that great danger lurked ahead if she crossed the river. She could see the sorcerous barrier like a faint mist, blurring the trees. Possibly her attention had already alerted the archon. Probably she had never been out of the Keeper's ken since she left.

What was she to do? Danger or not, duty summoned her homeward. Thume was in peril. The College was in peril. *Whom do we serve?* **The Keeper and the College.** Duty and upbringing were calling her back. The ghastly evil of the Covin and the Almighty drove her. As the Keeper had warned, pixies were a legend now. Everybody knew that pixies were extinct; there was nowhere Outside where a pixie would be welcome or could rest. True, Thaïle could make herself look like a dwarf, or a jotunn, or an oak tree, but even her paramount power would be hard-pressed to fashion a glamour invisible to all other sorcerers. Where would be the joy of it? She would live a lie all the rest of her life.

She must go home, across the river.

But what was she to do with the girl, this strange half jotunn, quarter imp, quarter faun? This black-haired, green-eyed young beauty? This queen's daughter, sorcerer's daughter, friend of imperor and warlock? Surely she was significant in some way.

Kadie was lying on the grass at her side, leaning on elbows, sucking a grass stem and contentedly watching the cows. She never strayed out of arm's reach. As long as she was close to Thaïle she seemed happy enough, and secure, but months of nightmare as the goblins' captive had left her fragile as a soap bubble. Even sorcery could not cure a wounded soul.

Kadie, too, needed to go home, to family and friends and safety. She needed a long space of love and comfort and healing, but her home was blocked by the Covin; her family at best was scattered all over Pandemia. At worst they were all dead.

"There it is, Kadie," Thaïle said. "That's Thume."

Kadie rolled over and sat up and regarded the far bank distrustfully. "It doesn't look very inviting."

"That's sorcery."

"What happens if someone from this side goes across?" She frowned uneasily.

"They rarely do, because the spell makes them stay away. Sometimes people try, and then the archons see them and tell the Keeper. The Keeper decides. Usually they just vanish."

"You mean she *kills* them?"

"Sometimes. Or turns them around and sends them back. It's entirely up to the Keeper. Some Keepers have been more ruthless than others. Whole armies have disappeared in Thume."

"But you'll be all right?"

Thaïle nodded sadly, thinking of that book of prophecies she had not been allowed to see. "I'm sure they're expecting me back."

"Then let's go!" Kadie said bravely.

"You don't really want to."

"Yes I do! I know that's just an aversion spell making me want not to. Back home we have a door like that. There's a secret word you have to use if you want to go through it."

Thaïle smiled in wonder. "For a mundane, you have an astonishing knowledge of the occult."

"Papa is a sorcerer. I told you. Even Gath is prescient." She grinned nervously, still studying the far bank.

Thaïle sighed. "And that's another problem! The College would certainly class your family as Gifted. It means that you may have a Faculty for magic, too."

Kadie glanced at her with apprehension. "Me?"

Thaïle nodded. Gifted families were rare and seemed to be becoming rarer, although their women were not limited to two children apiece, as all others were in Thume. The College would only be following its normal practice if it decided to impose a background word on this waif to find out if she had Faculty. There were background words in Krasnegar, too, and one of them had turned her twin brother into a seer.

Even if Kadie had no Faculty of her own, the College might regard her as valuable breeding stock, a brood mare to improve the strain. Thaïle could not bring herself to put that obscenity into words. She must make an effort to warn, though.

"Kadie, nobody from the Outside has been allowed into Thume since the War of the Five Warlocks, a thousand years ago. Even if I take you, the Keeper may send you away. Or she may make you stay forever."

Kadie's fear exploded like red flame in the ambience. "You're not going to leave me here!" she said shrilly. "You promised!"

After all those months of terror, she had seized on Thaïle as her rescuer and protector—and in truth she had no one else to rely on and nowhere else to go. She was almost as much a victim of this terrible war as the legionaries had been.

"Are you quite sure that's what you want?"

Green eyes lit up with relief and excitement. "Why not? I want to see Thume!"

"Let's take a day or two to think about it," Thaïle said. It felt strangely, sadly inevitable. Premonition told her of danger and horror if she went home, but it also hinted at far worse futures if she did not, and in some vague, unlocatable way, it suggested that returning and taking Kadie along might be the best choice of all. Only one thing felt certain—she had a destiny to meet, and a duty.

4

Rap had been wrong; Thrugg had been right.

Rap had thought he would have several days in which to perfect his plans. Thrugg had foreseen the storm. *Dreadnought* was hurtling through Rip Channel like a trout in a water pipe, and leaking at every joint.

The hammocks and sea chests littered around showed that the fo'c's'le had been sleeping quarters for eight men. It was low and smelly and loud with the groans of the ship. Although he was in many ways a most unusual jotunn, Sagorn had a typical disregard for the perils of the sea. He was sleeping like a very long baby in a wildly swaying hammock. The darkness was complete, and Rap risked a flash of power to light a lantern. A chorus of protest in the ambience complained that he was breaking the ship's rule against using sorcery.

"*Sorry! We haven't much time!* Doctor?" he said aloud, shouting over the tumult of wind and waves.

The old man opened his eyes and blinked.

"We have to leave," Rap said.

"Our position?"

"About half a league off Dragon Reach and sinking."

"Oh?" Sagorn pulled a smile, which for once seemed genuinely amused and not scornful. "That doesn't seem very efficient for a shipload of sorcerers!"

"We could correct the situation, but the power required can better be applied otherwise."

"How?" The old jotunn twisted expertly in the hammock and planted his feet safely on the deck. Had he been a sailor at some time in his many shared lives, or was that a racial skill?

Dreadnought heeled over at a dangerous angle and this time seemed reluctant to straighten. Timbers groaned menacingly. A sea chest slid gratingly across the deck and slammed into another.

Rap offered the old man a hand to help him straighten. "You and I will be transported to Ilrane. The others will go ashore on Dragon Reach."

Sagorn banged his head on a beam and cursed. "When you say me, you mean one of my associates?"

"Andor, I think. He has been to Ilrane before."

"And you can do this without alerting the Covin?"

"With thirty-seven of us in concert, we have ample power."

Sagorn nodded and rubbed his eyes. "And the vessel will be left to sink alone? I see. Of course your journey will be wasted or even suicidal if Zinixo has already located Warlock Lith'rian. So you must assume that he hasn't?"

"Olybino mentioned him and Zinixo did not produce him, which suggests that he is still at liberty."

The ship heeled again. The old man swayed unconsciously to remain upright. "You risk a lot on a mere suggestion. And just how do you intend to locate the missing warlock when the Almighty has failed?"

"I shall look in the obvious place, of course."

Sagorn's eyes glinted in the gloom. With the barest hesitation he said, "Isn't that too obvious?"

"Then—knowing elves as we both do—doesn't that make it certain?"

The jotunn chuckled. "Well, you may be right there."

"I'm glad you agree with me." Rap had a great deal of respect for Sagorn's acumen. "Time is pressing, Doctor."

"One question before I depart. When are you going to start the war?"

Rap shrugged. *Dreadnought* was listing badly now and shipping water at an alarming rate.

"I don't know. I'm not sure it's up to me to sound the trumpet. Three weeks to Longday, roughly."

The old man looked hard at him, frowning. "The Midsummer Moot? The imperor was going to Nordland?"

"That was the plan, and Raspnex had some scheme he wouldn't discuss, remember? I think it may have involved the thanes. I doubt that there are very many sorcerers to be garnered among the jotnar, but it's worth a try, I suppose. We're not sure that Olybino was loud enough to be heard in Nordland."

"I see. That's why you think Longday matters?"

"Not really," Rap admitted. "This afternoon Thrugg announced that it felt important, and Thrugg's the most potent sorcerer on the ship. Now his mother and Tik Tok are agreeing with him. Grunth and the others will need time to deal with the dragons. Three weeks will be cutting it very fine."

"Of course." Sagorn smiled grimly and held out a frail hand. "Then I shall call Andor in my place and wish you luck of him. I also wish you luck with Warlock Lith'rian!"

"Thanks," Rap said. "I'll need it."

5

The post inn at Yugg had no name and would never rank stars in any travelers' guide. Shandie had met worse in his time—but not often. Nonetheless, as dawn brightened the rain clouds outside he tackled a greasy breakfast with an enthusiasm he would probably regret as soon as the stagecoach began to move. Last night's meeting with Oshpoo had encouraged him greatly. He had enlisted a substantial, if unknown, number of sorcerers to battle the Almighty; he had also solved the Guwush problem that had baffled his grandfather for thirty years. If you can't win give up! What could be more obvious? The Senate would howl, of course. Shandie looked forward to that struggle with pleasure. It would certainly beat fighting sorcerers.

The sooner *that* war was fought and won the better!

He recognized the feeling: It was time for battle to commence. This was not a campaign like any other he had ever fought, but there came a point in all conflicts when the opposing forces were arrayed and preliminary skirmishing gave way to the main event. Time was now on Zinixo's side, for the Covin must still be tracking down and enlisting sorcerers. The counterrevolution would rot away if it was not soon shown some leadership.

Raspnex and Inos were crammed in beside him at the little corner table. He cleared his throat. Neither paid any attention.

The dwarf was picking grumpily at a bowl of some darkly anonymous gruel. He was grouchy at the best of times and venomous at breakfast. So far he had not said a word.

Inos had abandoned her food altogether and was apparently writing a letter. She had steadied a paper on the back of a book and was holding it up to the uncertain light from the window, chewing her tongue and frowning as she doodled.

Shandie started over. "We shan't have a chance to talk until noon at the earliest. Has anyone got any suggestions about where we go from here?"

Raspnex continued eating, his chin barely higher than the dishes. "Out of this flea-ridden swamp, posthaste."

"Granted. I mean after we meet up with Wirax and the others." The other sorcerers were rounding Guwush by sea, due to rendezvous at Randport—two dwarves, two goblins, and a jotunn. "When does the war start?"

"Longday," Raspnex mumbled with his mouth full.

"What! Midsummer? How do you know that?"

The warlock glanced up blankly, seeming surprised. "Dunno. Just feels right, somehow. Hunch."

About to bark a scathing comment, Shandie remembered that he was talking with a sorcerer, whose hunches might well be reliable. Longday was still three weeks off, though. "Then what do we do next?"

Again the dwarf filled his mouth with gruel. He looked up sourly and said, "We wait for the leader's signal, of course."

"Meaning Rap?"

"Who else?"

Mm! It was Shandie's impire that had been stolen. He was a soldier and Rap was not.

"Much as I respect the king of Krasnegar as a man—and I agree completely with Ishist's remark that he 'stands out of the light' as few other—"

"I suppose you want to go on the offensive?"

"Yes I do! Now that everyone knows about—"

"And attack what?" Raspnex growled.

"The Covin, of course."

"Where?" the warlock demanded, scowling. "How? You're thinking like a brainless musclebound legionary. Find the enemy and stick a spear in him, I presume? Well, that doesn't work with sorcery."

Inos whistled a small tune and continued with her writing, not looking up.

"Perhaps you should explain," Shandie said coldly. "I am feeling unusually musclebound this morning."

"Obviously." The dwarf pushed his bowl away and dragged a sleeve across his mouth. He fixed a stony glare on the imperor. "Sorcerous warfare is different! Reinforcements can move instantaneously. When armies are overpowered they're not destroyed, they turn on their friends. Once battle is joined, there can be no withdrawal, no retreat, no regrouping! That's only some of it. It's not the kind of fighting you know. For one thing, it's much faster. If you sound the charge and rush into Hub, you may find no one there. You are only a mundane, and a mundane can't fight this sort of war."

Shandie made a point of never losing his temper. Sometimes that was not easy. "Can Rap, though?"

"We're going to find out, aren't we? He's our leader. Who else could be? Olybino should have been, but he ducked and now he's dead. Besides, the other races never trust imps. Grunth is a troll—for all her snarling and big teeth, she's a rabbit at heart. Are you suggesting that *elf*?" Raspnex raised a fist like a stonemason's hammer.

Dwarves and elves went together like water and quicklime. Raspnex and Lith'rian might both accept Rap, but neither would ever accept the other.

Shandie said, "No."

"Good. Rap invented the new protocol. Rap beat Zinixo once before. Rap refused a warden's throne—three times he refused. Rap is the only sorcerer other sorcerers will ever trust! In fact . . ." The warlock glanced thoughtfully at Inos. "There are rumors that he could have been a God and he turned that down, too."

The queen glanced up and met his stony glare. "Are there really?" she said coldly.

The dwarf chuckled, as if he had just confirmed a suspicion. "*Rap is our leader.* Any more bright ideas, imp?"

"None whatsoever," Shandie said grimly. There had been no word from Rap in months. Was he even alive? He could well be dead, even if the Covin were not aware of it.

Raspnex leered. "Good. It's what Olybino said and no one argued. There's no one else for the job."

"So we are waiting for him to sound the attack?" Inos asked, squinting again at her paper.

"Yes."

"But how long do we wait?" Shandie asked.

"Dunno. Long as he wants. But don't make any plans for Longday. Or after," he added glumly.

"I dunno, either," Inos said. "Have you ever seen anyone like this?"

She passed the paper across to Shandie. It was not a letter, it was a sketch.

"I didn't know you were an artist!" he exclaimed. And a

good one—he turned the sheet to the light. The queen of
Krasnegar was a woman of infinite surprises. She had drawn
four youthful male faces, one frowning, the others smiling.
Yet there was something about the smiles that smacked of
nightmare and raised his dander.

"Elves?"

"No."

No. The noses were wrong. The ears were certainly wrong.

"Then who?"

"I asked if you had ever seen anyone like them."

"*Pixies?* These are the pixies you met in Thume?"

"As well as I can recall. It was twenty years ago, remember." She shivered. "But I still meet them in dreams."

Shandie nodded excitedly. "It could be! The old woman
who told me about the preflecting pool? Rap and Doctor
Sagorn both suggested she might have been a pixie."

"Well?" Inos asked patiently. "Was she?"

"I didn't get a very good look, but—yes! Yes, I think so.
The nose is right. The eyes are certainly right. They were not
elvish eyes."

Inos smirked, pleased at his reaction. "Does that answer
your original question, Sire?"

Raspnex glared up at her. "Are you suggesting what I think
you're suggesting?"

"Yes," she said sweetly. "We'll meet up with the others at
Randport. If the war hasn't broken out by then, well, it would
only take us a day or two to sail across and take a peek."

The dwarf was looking more astonished than Shandie could
ever recall seeing him. "Go to Thume? Woman, you are out
of your mind!"

"Indeed?" Inos cocked an eyebrow. "Why? Tell me why?"

The warlock just stared, speechless.

At that moment the post horn sounded.

"Time to go," Shandie said, hiding his amusement. "Let's
think about it and talk it over this evening."

6

A good-looking young couple in their very early twenties,
possibly accompanied by a female child aged about two.

The description had not done them justice. In fifty years of
service, Mother Iffini had seen no lovers to match them. The
girl had the fragile, innocent purity of fine porcelain, the boy

a winsome sparkle of devilry, but it was their physical beauty that impressed her most—and the way they glowed when they looked at each other.

"Shorter than most and thinner than few" was how Mother Iffini liked to describe herself. She knew of no reason why an elderly cleric need be athletic, whereas a comfy maternal portliness was often an advantage in putting people at ease. With her baby-pink face and soft white hair, she felt that she represented the exact ideal of a wise, tolerant, venerable counsellor. Her appearance certainly deserved the honorific of "Mother," and she tried to make her behavior equally worthy.

Her little chapel stood in the fruit country east of Gaaze, at a crossroads amid the orchards. It had a name on the maps, but no one ever referred to it as anything but the White Temple. At some times of the year the countryside swarmed with migrant workers, and she would fill the place four or five times over on every feast day. Between harvests, the countryside dozed off to sleep again, and even the most popular God would not merit a congregation of more than a dozen. As the bishop admitted, the area could not have supported a permanent temple at all without the inheritance Mother Iffini had received from her grandparents.

The fig season had not begun yet. Orchards stretched out sleepily under the summer haze with the Qoblè Mountains a spectral backdrop to the north. At this time of year her duties were light. When callers came, she preferred to meet with them outdoors, although she was always careful to ask if they minded. She would show them the little courtyard behind her house and explain how completely private it was, even better than the house really because sometimes servants overheard without meaning to, and she would sit them down in the shade of the vine trellis, next to the bougainvillea, so magnificently purple. There was an ancient stone table there, well embroidered with lichens, and some comfortable wicker chairs. When there were children, as now, she would provide a bag of crumbs and point out the gleam of golden scales gliding under the water lily pads.

Thus Mother Iffini put her unexpected visitors at ease this breathless summer afternoon. She told her groom to attend to their horse, had cool lemonade brought for them, showed the little girl how to feed the carp. She moved the parrot's cage to a safe height so there would be no nipped fingers, and finally got down to business, setting out inkwell and quill and parchment certificate on the table. Next to a naming ceremony, she enjoyed weddings more than anything.

Good-looking young couple in their very early twenties, indeed! The girl was an enchantress, unforgettable, the sort of stunning beauty one saw only once or twice in a lifetime. But then the boy was, too, although one normally did not use the same words for men. She could not recall a more romantic couple, nor a couple more obviously besotted. When they looked at each other the sun dimmed.

"Oh, do stop talking nonsense, you feather-headed bird," said the parrot.

Mother Iffini decided that she had a problem.

Never in her born days had she doubted her own loyalty to the imperor, Gods bless him. Gaaze was not so far off that she had no contact with the legion there, the XIIth, probably the best in the army. Many a local boy had gone off to join the XIIth and come back all shining and proud in his bronze to brighten her little temple. She had married legionaries, named legionaries—future legionaries, of course—and buried legionaries. She was a loyal subject of his Majesty and a strong supporter of the army.

But before anything, she was a sworn servant of the Gods. The two duties had never come into conflict for her before. Perhaps they were not in conflict now, but she would have to make sure of that. After all, the legionary who had come calling yesterday had not shown her any formal warrant, as happened once in a while when there was a criminal loose. He had named no crime. He had merely read out a memorandum. That was not quite the same, was it, as showing her a document with the lictor's seal on it? It was certainly no reason why she should not perform a marriage if her conscience said she should, whether or not she reported her visitors afterward.

She dipped her quill in the inkwell. Date . . . "Why, this is Mother's Eve! You are quite sure you don't want to wait until tomorrow?" She beamed at them to show that she was not serious, but she was rather hoping they would agree to a delay, so she would have time to think.

The visitors looked deep into each other's eyes and shook their heads. "No," the woman whispered.

She should have seated them a little farther apart. They were almost close enough to touch fingers across the table if they stretched out their arms. They were having trouble not doing so.

"Actually I have two weddings scheduled for tomorrow anyway. Don't know I could stand the excitement of three. I am sure the God of Motherhood will bless your union even if you do not choose Their day. Your name, my dear?"

The woman spoke the name the soldier had spoken.

Iffini wrote it down with a sigh—not that she had been in any doubt that these were the ones. "That is a very unusual name. It used to be unusual, I should say. Now, of course, it is enormously popular, the name of our dear new impress. I am sure half the girls I have named this year have been Eshialas."

She was surprised to see the shocked reaction in the girl's face, a look of . . . of fright? How odd! Surely she was not seeking a marriage ceremony under a false name? Apart from the insult to the Gods, the procedure would be useless to her. The whole purpose of a wedding—the secular purpose—was to give a woman a legal hold over the father of her children so he could not disown them. That legal hold was the certificate she was now drawing up. It would be invalid if the information on it was perjured.

"Widow?"

"Yes."

"And your name, sir?"

"Ylo. Bachelor."

The legionary had not given Iffini the man's name. Now she had heard it, it seemed oddly familiar. She was sure she had heard that name in the last year or two in some connection or other.

Young Master Ylo was grinning rather naughtily at his bride-to-be, who was trying not to show any reaction. The word "bachelor" sometimes brought out a sense of guilt in some of the racier ones.

"Oh do stop talking nonsense, you feather-headed bird," said the parrot.

Mother Iffini dipped her quill again. "Now, your late husband's name, ma'am?"

Sudden, shocking pallor . . . Silence.

"Is this information necessary?" the boy asked.

That cleared away some of the smoke. Mother Iffini placed her pen in the inkwell and left it there. The legionary had been vague as to why exactly the two persons were wanted for questioning and perhaps had not known the reason himself. She had suspected that just possibly the law and the servants of the law might not have been on quite the same bearing.

Once in a very long while even the law itself might vary a little from what the Gods required. On a matter of bigamy, however, there could be no divergence and no doubt.

"You did not bring the funeral certificate?" she asked.

The girl shook her head and looked in horror at the boy. His expression was bleak—as well it might be—but he was obviously not about to give up. He had probably anticipated that this might happen and he was going to try to bluff it through.

"The man was lost in battle and his body was not recovered, Mother."

Iffini folded her plump, soft fingers together on the weathered old stone table before her. "Then the army issues a special certificate of presumed death. It is not valid for remarriage until three years have passed."

"The circumstances are unusual, Mother. You are aware of the goblin invasion?"

She nodded, wondering if she was about to hear some inspired creative fantasizing. If he had a glib tongue to go with his looks, this Ylo would be irresistible to impressionable young women. She was no impressionable young woman, yet she did not think he was faking his own infatuation.

"Indeed I have," she said. She had conducted several special prayer services on the subject of the goblin invasion.

"There was no formal battle and the man was a civilian, so the army would not be directly involved. He and I were ambushed by the goblins. I escaped, but only just, and his horse fell. Even if he was taken alive by the goblins, Mother, his chances of surviving the day were absolutely zero."

Iffini shivered and muttered a prayer. "There were no other witnesses?"

"No, Mother. I swear this is truth." The lad's eyes were steady. If he was lying about this, he was as accomplished a liar as she had ever met.

"Then you should have sworn an affidavit before the lictor of the district or the military autho—"

"Mother!" he said reproachfully. "The countryside was in chaos! There were no authorities at all, military or civil."

She sighed and stared down at her fingers again while she pondered. A convenient story! The boy moved his chair slightly so he could reach out and grasp the girl's hand.

Mother Iffini looked up. "I suppose I could accept your affidavit on the subject. It would be very irregular, though."

The girl started to smile and then froze. Her pallor seemed to grow more intense.

"I will swear any oath you wish," the boy said calmly, "but I will not reveal the man's name."

The chaplain removed her quill and wiped it. She closed the inkwell. "I think we must discuss this matter further."

"There is no alternative, is there?" he said bitterly. "If we seek out another chaplain and my fiancée claims to be a spinster, then the marriage would be invalid?"

Mother Iffini nodded. "And she would require signed permission from her father, or a brother. I do not make the laws, Master Ylo." *Master* Ylo? Again that vague memory! No, there had been a title. Tribune Ylo? Legate Ylo? Something military.

At that moment the child dropped the bag of crumbs into the fish pool and screamed in frustration. The man jumped up and hurried over to her.

"Maya!" he said . . .

Iffini's heart missed a beat. Two beats. No! It couldn't possibly be! Of course a woman with the same name as the future impress might well have chosen to give her child the same name as the future impress's child. Quite possible! The alternative explanation was untenable. There would not have been a solitary legionary coming around calling on inns and temples, there would have been an Impire-wide hue and cry.

Wouldn't there? Or would the sheer magnitude of the scandal have made that course of action impossible even to consider? *The impress herself?* And the heir to the Imperial throne?

The girl was staring down at her hands on the table, avoiding eye contact. She was worried now, but she had been worried earlier, though trying to hide the fact. After fifty years of marrying people, a priestess could recognize that anxiety with her eyes closed. Either this Eshiala was pregnant or she strongly suspected she was.

Mother Iffini decided that she had not merely a problem, but a very serious problem.

The boy returned, carrying the child. "I am afraid we have wasted your time, Mother. Come, darling."

"Sit down," Iffini snapped. "I need to think a moment."

He sat. The little girl squirmed down from his lap, demanding the fish food. He gave the dripping bag to her, and she trotted over to the pool again.

One possibility was just to ask them if the dead husband's name had been Emshandar, but that would close off any other avenue of escape. Either they would lie or Mother Iffini would have to pretend to accept extraordinary coincidences. She certainly could not believe that the imperor had been killed by goblins while traveling incognito with a single companion. So she must assume that the incident had not occurred at all or that the man had not been named Emshandar. Why, then, was she so reluctant to ask that simple question? Pretty-boy's tale of ambush was a very convenient way to cover up abduction or even viler deeds.

She would not sign a certificate she believed to be false, nor would she perform a bogus wedding ceremony in her temple. Her clear duty was to report this pair to the authorities. No doubt they would then be forcibly separated—but the girl's fear showed that she desperately needed some hold on that slippery beguiler, and had come to ask the help of the Gods.

Hesitantly Mother Iffini said, "There is another possibility. It would require that you both swear a solemn oath that you are not committing bigamy."

The girl looked up at once, hope shining brightly behind her tears. "I will swear!"

"I, also," the boy said.

Well! Mother Iffini relaxed. She had never doubted where her first loyalties lay. Love should be sanctified even if it was legally irregular.

They were holding hands again.

"Yes, Mother?" the girl prompted.

"There is a very rare service called a Blessing of Union. It may be used when a regular legal marriage is impossible—when documents are missing, for example, or when parental permission has been refused. If you feel compelled to live together as man and wife under such circumstances and are willing to swear before the Gods that you will do so for the rest of your lives, loving and being faithful as if united in legal matrimony, then I may witness your oaths and provide a certificate to that effect. I warn you, though, that it has very little validity in law."

She watched as they exchanged smiles and nods and squeezed hands.

"Oh, thank you, Mother," the girl said. "Thank you! That is exactly what we need."

Mother Iffini sighed. "Then I need another piece of parchment." She wondered if she was growing soft-headed in her dotage, or if she was carrying her mothering instincts to absurdity. "You are continuing your travels after you leave here?"

The girl started. The boy's eyes narrowed.

"We are," he said. "Why do you ask?"

"Recent information. The hostelries around here have developed a very poor reputation. I would advise you to seek accommodation in private dwellings. Farmhouses might be best."

"A recent development?" He had a gorgeous smile. "We suspected that, but it is good to have it confirmed. The main roads are very busy and unpleasant, too, I believe."

"So I understand."

"Oh, bless you, Mother," the girl said. "Bless you!"

"Do stop talking nonsense, you feather-headed bird," said the parrot.

To the appointed place:
>   With equal mind, what happens, let us bear,
>   Nor joy not grieve too much for things beyond our
>   care.
>   Like pilgrims to th'appointed place we tend;
>   The world's an inn, and death the journey's end.
>   Dryden, *Palamon and Arcite*

⫷ THREE ⫸

Merely players

1

The watery space between Sysanasso and the Keriths had many names on the charts. Some called it Middle Sea, or the Midsummer Sea, and others No Man's Sea because three races claimed it. To the merfolk it was always Death Water. They made jokes about those who tried to make a living on Death Water, but humor that could turn so fast to sorrow had a bitter bite.

Ko-nu-Al was a sailor from East Kerith who had played the odds on Death Water all his life. The God of Chance had granted him favor, and he had risen in middle age to be master and part owner of the trader sloop *Seaspawn*, carrying a crew of ten and trading to Sysanasso. The ten now included his three sons: Mu-pu-Esh, Po-pu-Ok, and Wo-pu-Al.

Wo-pu was sixteen. This was his first voyage and his last. The God of Chance had claimed Their due; the boy would never see his mother again.

Most merfolk trading with other races was done at sea, at times and places established by long tradition, by vessels known to each other. Their crews were all male. There were also a couple of small trader islets where no woman ever set foot. If such simple precautions were observed, mermen could meet in friendship with fauns, elves, imps, or men of any other race, even jotnar, and do business together.

55

Seaspawn, though, dealt in a cargo that could not be easily moved from one vessel to another, black sand from the southern coasts of Sysanasso. Such sand lay free for the taking; it was greatly prized by the potters of East Kerith for making their famous green glazes. Although the petty faun princes often tried to tax the trade, there were too many beaches to guard and too many princes to collaborate. Since time forgotten, the merchants of the Summer Seas had merely helped themselves. Ko-nu had prospered by choosing deserted shores and honoring the Gods.

Until this voyage, he had avoided trouble. This was the first on which he had brought young Wo-pu, last of his children and perhaps the dearest. Now the boy was dying in agony, his screams audible at all hours. His brother Po-pu was going insane with guilt and might well take his own life.

It was for those reasons that Ko-nu abandoned the caution of a lifetime and sailed into a foreign port. He did not know its name and would not have cared if he had, but the Gods decreed that it be Ysnoss.

The harbor was impressive, a gorge notched back into the cliffs, safe haven in any wind. The village itself was only a mishmash of ramshackle shanties plastered over the steep hillside, many of them supported on stilts. The hot and breathless afternoon stank of sewage. Belowdecks, Wo-pu had fallen silent, perhaps already into his final coma.

Seaspawn drifted in with her sails displaying the blue spiral emblem that proclaimed she hailed from the Keriths. Even before she dropped anchor in the center of the still harbor, people could be heard screaming and running. Dogs barked. Parrots and macaws rose shrieking into the air—faun settlements were invariably rife with livestock. As soon as the hands could stand down from their labors, they began a doleful melody on their sitars, chanting an old lament. Merfolk had songs for all occasions, and this one told of lonely death far from home.

A dory put out from the shore. Ko-nu stalked forward and waited in the bow. The fact that the vessel was holding her stern to the sea suggested that the tide and fragile current would carry her out again when given the chance.

The dory was manned by four husky youngsters. A shriveled, elderly man in the stern was probably the village headman. None of the five was clad in more than a scrap of loincloth, the illusion that they were all wearing black woolen stockings being merely a characteristic of fauns. As soon as *Seaspawn* reached hailing distance, the headman cupped his hands and began screaming at the intruder to go away before she was the death of everyone, interspersing those instructions with improbable profanities.

Ko-nu had expected such a reaction, and he knew enough about fauns to know that mere logic would have no influence on their behavior. He had therefore thought to bring a speaking trumpet. Now he raised it and drowned out the ancient's shrill wails.

"I come in peace and in the name of the Gods."

"Go away! Begone! Lewd menace, you will—"

"I am Ko-nu-Al, master of *Seaspawn*."

"I am Shiuy-Sh. Your rotten plague ship is fouling—"

"Have you a doctor in town?"

The old man paused in his invective long enough to say "No!" and then continued without drawing breath. The young rowers rested on their oars, smirking and nodding as they appraised their leader's tirade.

"An herbalist, then, or one who can provide relief to the suffering?"

"None, scum of the four oceans . . ."

"A priest, then? I must have a priest."

"We have no priest, either!"

Ko-nu's heart sank. It was entirely likely that so wretched a hamlet might have no priest. On the other hand . . . "Then who is that man in black dancing up and down on that balcony?"

The old faun did not even glance around. "He is no priest. He just dresses like one. Now take your bilge-infested barnacle factory out of our harbor before we cleanse it by burning your pestilential—"

Ko-nu glanced around at his crew, nervously clustered nearby, still humming the dirge. "Does he look like a priest to you?"

Pale faces nodded.

"Aye, sir," said Gi-al-Esh, who had eyes like a jotunn. "And he's no faun. He's an imp."

"I wish to speak with the man dressed as a priest," the captain proclaimed.

Shiuy-Sh became hysterical and incoherent. Apparently the request was unthinkable, for reasons obscure.

"If you will not bring him to me, then my men and I will come to him!"

The sailors' dirge lurched and grew louder. They all knew that their captain was threatening a massacre.

"Fool!" the headman screamed. "Imbecile! We have no roads out of town. Our women cannot leave!"

"Then bring me that man dressed as a priest!"

"Never! We have fire arrows . . ."

Ko-nu knew when he was beaten. Fauns were notoriously men of ideas—one each. Threats impressed them no more than arguments and they had called his clumsy bluff, for he knew what would happen if he went ashore. Apparently the priest would not be brought to him. Reason and logic would not change that decision, nor appeals to mercy, either.

The man on the balcony had disappeared indoors. He now returned with a large wooden chair, which he hurled over the railing. It struck the harbor in a fountain of water and garbage. Then he went after it. This time the fountain was even higher.

After a suspenseful pause, the man's head reappeared beside the bobbing chair. Using it as a float, he began to swim toward *Seaspawn*. The journey would take him all day, even if he did not die of overexertion on the way.

"Your imp is apparently intent on coming to me," Ko-nu said firmly. "Now, will you fetch him, or do I come and get him?"

"You will give him back to us?"

"Of course. I merely want him to comfort a dying boy."

"Well, why didn't you say so?" Shiuy-Sh demanded shrilly.

The priest was brought in the dory and passed up like baggage to *Seaspawn*'s waiting hands. He was small, elderly, exhausted, and reeking of untreated harbor. He collapsed in a dribbling heap on the deck and all attempts to raise him failed, for he merely flopped back to his knees. When he had finally caught enough breath to speak, he lifted both hands to Ko-nu in supplication.

"Save me!" he wailed in cultured Imperial tones. "Take me away from these lunatics, from this pesthole! I have gold. I will pay, but for the sake of all the Gods, I beg you to take me out of here."

Ko-nu could not recall swearing any oaths to Shiuy-Sh. To succor a priest might appease the Gods and preserve the ship from any further harm on this ill-omened voyage. Most important of all, the holy man would be able to spend a decent amount of time with Po-pu and Wo-pu.

"Up anchor!" said the captain.

And so it was done.

2

Sir Acopulo had not attempted swimming since he was a child and had been very unskilled at it even then. His condition when he was hauled aboard the ship was not improved by the large quantities of indescribable harbor fluid he had ingested. Nevertheless, by the time the ship had cleared the headlands he had disposed of that and been rinsed off with buckets of seawater and begun to feel better. Not even the onset of inevitable seasickness could dampen his exultation at having at last escaped from Ysnoss.

He had never met mermen before and had never quite believed that their hair could be truly blue. It was though—a very pale blue, but unquestionably blue. Their eyes were silvery. The crew was entirely male, of course, about impish height, slimly built, with skins as pallid as fish bellies, and about as smooth. There was not a hairy chest aboard. He wondered why the sun did not tan them, and why such bleached wraiths should hold such a notorious attraction for women of other races. They seemed a strangely morose bunch, more like a convocation of undertakers than any other sailors he had ever met.

He was offered garments like theirs—cloths tied at the waist, hanging to the calf. They had a pearly shimmer as if made of fishskin and they clung like wet cobweb, although they did not seem to restrict their wearers' freedom of movement at all. He declined them graciously and retained his soaked clerical habit. Imps, he had always believed, should dress like imps. Furthermore, he did not wish these primitives to see the money belt and dispatches he wore around his waist.

With his damp garments clinging to him in clammy embrace, he was conducted to the captain's cabin. It was cramped, with barely room for a table and two chairs, although admittedly clean and cozy enough. It had an odd, musky odor, sweetish but not unpleasant. He refused the chair offered him; he moved some books and instruments from a dresser to the bunk and then sat on the dresser. There he was alongside an open window and could breathe deeply of the cool sea wind. Already his stomach registered every dip and roll of the ship. Upstairs, men were singing a jigging chantey that kept time with the motion. He wished they would stop; it didn't help.

"A draft of yam rum, Father?" the captain inquired, producing a flask and two mugs.

Acopulo's stomach knotted, perspiration prickled on his forehead. "That is very kind of you, my good man, but thank you, no. I may have to go and lie down very shortly. I just want you to know that I am extremely grateful to you for rescuing me from that pestilential lunatic asylum."

The merman's pinched face displayed shock. "You were being held against your will, Father?"

"I was indeed! Some neighboring village recently acquired a resident priest and Ysnoss wished to emulate it. I was bound for Zark on a matter of urgency and must now make up all the lost time I can. I am prepared to pay well for your assistance . . . plus extra for superior accommodation, if available." Acopulo glanced around thoughtfully. Presumably the captain's own cabin was the best aboard. How much should he offer for it?

The merman frowned with eyebrows as blue as his hair. He must be well into his forties, yet there was no spare flesh on him at all—ribs showing, belly as flat as a boy's. At first sight, Acopulo was prepared to think well of the seaman. He had a sober, businesslike attitude; he had given orders to the crew sparingly, efficiently. Just because he was not imp was no reason to look down on him; his breeding was not his fault.

Now Captain Ko-nu turned to replace the flask in a chest and produce another. "If the motion of the ship troubles you, Father, then my grandmother's sea urchin cordial is a proven remedy."

Again Acopulo declined, and this time he thrust his head out the window and sucked in all the cool air he could find. The Evilish coast of Sysanasso was already fading into the distance. Gods be praised! Free at last!

Seven months ago the imperor had entrusted him with letters to the Caliph. Even in winter, seven *weeks* should have sufficed for such a journey. Weather, elves, and finally the odious fauns—all had conspired to block his progress. Obviously the Gods were punishing him. He had assumed clerical dress only as a disguise, but They must have taken it as an affront, an irreverence. Well, now his penance seemed to be over. He would resume lay costume the moment it became available. The Gods could not be so enraged that They would consider a fishskin loincloth adequate for a man of his eminence.

Acopulo had even wondered, in his more desperate moments in Ysnoss, whether the Gods were rebuking him for straying from his youthful ambition to take holy orders. He would have made a fine priest, of course. Possibly in a few years, when Shandie was safely established on his throne and in less need of Acopulo's guidance, that old ambition might be reconsidered. The church would welcome such a recruit, and probably appoint him a bishop in record time.

He discovered that he was staring glassily down at very unruly green water. He resumed his seat on the dresser and straightened his hair with his hands as well as he could. There wasn't very much of it these days, although what there was required cutting.

The captain was hunched over the table with his face in his hands. He looked up with a glum expression. Come to think of it, this did not seem to be an overly jolly ship. The singing in the background was becoming quite depressing. Well, Acopulo was not going to be long aboard.

"Now, Sailor," he said cheerfully. "Where can you let me off?"

"We head home to the Keriths, Father." The captain's accent was strange, although he was obviously trying to speak proper impish in place of the crude patois used on deck.

Acopulo opened his mouth to explain that he was not a priest, but the merman continued, "I hope we shall meet up with some trading vessels to which we may transfer you." He smiled sadly. "We cannot enter any port outside the Keriths, of course."

Mm! Acopulo had overlooked that restriction. "You can put me ashore at some deserted spot, then?"

The thin man frowned. "In Ilrane? The elves have a poor regard for strangers."

"No! Never Ilrane!" Not elves again! Acopulo shivered and wiped his streaming face. He really must go and lie down. His growing nausea was making it hard for him even to recall basic geography—of course there was only Ilrane between Sysanasso and Kerith, nowhere he could acquire respectable layman's garb, even.

The merman tried to smile, although the result was more of a grimace. "And we cannot take you home with us, obviously."

"Oh, I think I should be safe enough at my age." Acopulo spoke modestly, but he knew he would have been safe enough at any age. Even in his youth, he had never been susceptible to storms of passion. No woman had ever interested him much; his only experiment in intimacy, at the age of fifteen, had brought him nothing but embarrassment. He had shunned messy affairs of the flesh ever since. Other men's inability to do so he regarded with tolerant contempt. Chastity was merely a matter of willpower and self-discipline.

The ship was rolling harder and the chanting had taken on a slower, melancholy tone. Suddenly someone shrieked, as if being tortured. Acopulo jumped. The captain groaned, but seemed unsurprised. Then came another, longer cry.

"We shall do what we can for you, Father, even if we have to take you on to Zark ourselves. In the meantime, our need for your services is very great."

"Actually I am not—" The sweat running down Acopulo's face seemed to cool markedly. "Services?"

The gaunt sailor sighed. "The Gods may ease great suffering with small mercies. Evidently They brought us together in our mutual need, Father."

Another scream, louder . . . Unspeakable torment!

"Er, need, Captain?"

Blue eyebrows lifted. "Only in dire distress would a merfolk ship ever visit an outlander port, Father. It was to enlist the aid of a priest that we took that risk."

Acopulo stammered, appalled that he had not seen that possibility.

The merman shifted his feet, as if about to rise. "The Gods in Their wisdom have brought misfortune upon us. We have a young man aboard who is dying and in need of solace."

Acopulo babbled something appropriate while his mind turned cartwheels. He should have realized that the presence of a band of mermen in Ysnoss had threatened orgy—sexual madness leading to homicidal jealousy between the mermen and the faun males, and also among the women of the village. He should have seen that a responsible master would not expose himself and his entire crew to such danger for any trivial reason. To inform the captain now that his venture had been in vain might be extremely unwise.

Staring fixedly at his knees, the merman said softly, "My son! My youngest child!"

"The Good is everywhere," Acopulo mumbled, *"only our sight is lacking."* Given a few minutes he could find a hundred better texts than that to comfort a grieving father.

"You will come to him now, Father?" The sailor stood up.

"Tell me the details, please," Acopulo said, and almost added, "my son."

The captain sat down again, not looking at his guest. The silver of his eyes seemed to shine brighter, as if laved in tears. "The hands were ashore, loading sand. It was a beach I have visited many times without ever meeting anyone, but this time a woman came wandering out of the woods." He shook his head mournfully. "There was nothing special about her. She was not young or beautiful, just a faun come to dig clams, but she was a woman. The men dropped tools and ran toward her, of course."

"Er, of course." Acopulo schooled his face not to show his revulsion.

The captain bowed his head and stared at the glittery cloth covering his thighs. "We were fortunate, I suppose. Such encounters rarely leave survivors. We were saved by the wind."

"I don't think I understand. Wind?"

"It is rarely talked of," the merman told his knees, "but wind can be a factor."

Acopulo became aware again of that curious musky odor he had noticed earlier. Was that the cabin or the merman himself? If Acopulo were a woman, would he find that scent attractive? Would a merwoman be drawn to him because he smelled otherwise? How utterly disgusting!

"She saw her danger," the sailor said, "and turned to flee. The wind was blowing strongly from her direction, or of course she would have run the other way. She escaped into the woods. Once she was out of sight—and out of the wind, I suppose—the older hands managed to regain control of themselves and tried to restrain the youngsters. In the struggle, my youngest son was knifed." He covered his face. "Oh, Father, he is only sixteen!" He choked, and began to sob into his fingers. "What do I tell his mother?"

Acopulo wanted to scream. Why should he be involved in such a sordid disaster, just because a gang of savages had succumbed to a frenzy of animal lust? Yet he should not even be thinking that way, because the insane jealousy provoked by the presence of merfolk was not a sin in the eyes of the Gods. Neither church nor Imperial law condemned crimes committed under such circumstances. Whatever his personal feelings on the subject, he must not reveal them.

"And his brother!" the captain mumbled. "He needs you even more, Father."

"What's wrong with him?" Acopulo demanded, feeling worse by the minute.

The sailor raised a tearstained face. The rims of his silver eyes were raw wounds. "In his madness he thrust the knife into his brother's back!"

Acopulo very nearly yelled, "And you expect me to tell him to cheer up?"

But that was what a true priest would do. It was what he would have to do. The captain had risked his entire crew to obtain a priest and if the supposed priest admitted now that he was an imposter, he was going to be swimming again in no time.

So the charlatan would have to maintain his clerical masquerade, ministering to the invalid and the tormented culprit. That would be sacrilege, a crime much worse than mere imposture. His sin would be infinitely greater than that of the murderer he must absolve.

Cold as a winter tide, the awful truth flooded into Acopulo's heart. It was not true that the Gods spoke in riddles. Very rarely in his life had he ever had difficulty in choosing the correct course of action, or felt doubts that he had done the right thing afterward. To those with the will and courage to listen, the Gods spoke plainly. Their message now was clear.

He had angered Them by wearing a costume to which he was not entitled. They were demanding that he end the deception—not by discarding the clerical habit, but by retaining it. He had thought his penance over, but it had barely begun.

Clasping his hands, he bowed his head in acceptance. He spoke a brief prayer. He made a vow. As soon as he reached safe landfall—preferably within the Impire, if They would allow him that mercy—then he would return to the ambition of his youth and enter into holy orders. Meanwhile, he would do what good he could on this stinking boat.

And with that resolve, he suddenly felt better. His conscience and his gyrating gut seemed to steady together. He let himself slide into the role he must play as a hand slides into a glove.

He looked up. "Take me to them now, my son," he said calmly.

3

Hub was in turmoil. For months, the capital had been crammed with refugees fleeing the goblins' atrocities. Terror and famine ruled its streets, crime and disease spawned in its alleys. The entire XXth Legion had been brought in to reinforce the city watch and was still unable to maintain order. Every night was brightened by fires, every day blackened by riots. Men cursed the wardens and the new imperor; they spoke darkly of the coming of the millennium; already some prayed for a new dynasty.

The Festival of Law was a very minor celebration, but that day in 2999 was destined to be long remembered in the history of the great city. It began with hope of victory. Hasty rumors told of a prophecy made the previous evening by the imperor himself, that the goblins' destruction was imminent. The hungry multitudes took heart and spoke excitedly of returning to their wasted homelands.

The sky was cloudless, promising another fine day. Yet, shortly after dawn, an enormous blast struck the junction of Arave Avenue and Basketmakers Street. Scores of pedestrians were fried or smashed and many buildings collapsed. Moments later, an even greater explosion flattened the botanical gardens near the Opal Palace. Then a bridge over the Old Canal was blown to dust, and its occupants, also.

The barrage continued for several minutes, bolts of destruction raining upon the city without reason or pattern. Temples and mansions collapsed; pillars of smoke rose into the sky. Hysterical mobs rampaged aimlessly, wreaking more havoc than the sorcery itself. The torment ended as suddenly and inexplicably as it had begun. The final death toll was estimated to be somewhere around five thousand, but was never reliably established. Efforts to dig victims from the ruins continued for many days.

No official explanation was forthcoming, but sorcery was the obvious cause. Thus the wardens were the obvious culprits—if they had not caused the devastation, they had not acted to prevent it. The population cursed the Four, and some braver souls demonstrated outside their palaces.

Late in the afternoon, the imperor and impress made an inspection of the worst disasters. The Imperial couple rode in an open landau drawn by eight pure-black horses, escorted by an entire cohort of the Praetorian Hussars. Whatever the back-alley mutterings, imps were invariably loyal to the imperor in public, and the cheering was very nearly as loud as usual.

Although old Emshandar was still mourned, young Shandie held the loyalty of his people. He was a striking figure in his golden armor and purple-crested helm, but it was the beautiful young impress who swayed the crowd. Slim and gorgeous in a simple black dress, pale and sad, Eshiala won the heart of every man who set eyes on her, and most of the women's, also. The Imperial couple made no speeches. They never alighted from their carriage. They looked over the devastation, they spoke to some of the officers in charge of rescue efforts, and then they went on their way, but that was enough. Their mere presence showed that they cared, and they left few dry eyes behind them when they departed.

Two of those dry eyes belonged to a very obese man clad in incongruously soiled finery. His eyes were not merely dry, they were stretched wide with horror and terror.

Lurking well back in the crowd around the collapsed Temple of Love, Lord Umpily had come upon the Imperial inspection by mere chance. He had been working his way home on foot to the palace after attending the sumptuous birthday party of Senator Ishipole the previous night. He had been abducted from that glittering function to experience a harrowing interview with the long-lost Warlock Olybino. At dawn he had been released to his own devices. Within minutes he had been relieved at knifepoint of all his valuables—some money, a few rings, even his boots, the golden tracery ripped off his doublet. He had been more than content to part with all of those in return for being allowed to retain a whole skin. Since then he had wandered in his socks, in agonies of indecision.

Better than most, he knew that the wholesale destruction could be blamed on the wardens, or at least on one warden, the deposed Warlock Olybino. Even Umpily did not know the details, though—much as he would like to. The former East had certainly been planning some challenge to the Almighty. One or the other had caused the devastation, or they both had. One or the other must have died in it, and Olybino was the most likely loser. What he had achieved or even hoped to achieve was beyond Umpily's utmost imagining.

He had too many problems of his own to worry very much about the former warlock. The city swarmed with starving peasantry. Even after he had been looted, other thugs had accosted him without success. Sooner or later some such band would take out their disappointment in random violence and kill him from spite. He was penniless and friendless. The only refuge open to him was the palace itself, yet even worse danger lurked there.

He was no longer bewitched by the Covin. Olybino and his companions had removed his occult delusions. They had laid some sort of protection spell on him instead, but had warned him that it would not bear close inspection. How long could he hope to survive in the palace before being closely inspected?

Typically, he had wandered to and fro until growing hunger stiffened his resolve. At least in the palace he could eat, and anything was easier to face on a full stomach. Thus he was heading homeward almost resolutely when he came upon the smoking ruins of the Temple of Love. It had been one of the largest and richest shrines in the city, easily the most popular. Even by day it had usually been crowded. Legionaries were overseeing gangs of workmen removing bodies, laying out rows of mangled corpses that almost blocked the roadway, many of them women. The death toll must have been enormous.

For some time Umpily stared in horrified fascination at this gruesome spectacle, making mental notes that he could later transcribe to his journal. He was still there when shouts and cheering alerted him to the arrival of the Imperial visitors.

It was then, cowering back in a doorway, that he had his worst experience of that whole dreadful day. Even through the cordon of guards, he could see the royal couple in their carriage. He also saw the officers and officials standing stiffly alongside, answering the royal queries with solemn respect. He watched as the parade moved on, but he heard the cheering through thick walls of solid fear.

Shandie and his wife. Emshandar V and Impress Eshiala. Umpily had seen them quite clearly—royal and gracious, somber and concerned.

At the same time and in the same places, he had seen her sister and his cousin, Ashia and Emthoro. They had been wearing totally different clothes, and he had seen both sets of garments, just as he had seen both sets of people.

He had known for months that those two were impersonating the imperor and his wife. Then, for other months, he had been deluded into not knowing it. Last night he had been forcibly disillusioned.

He had wondered—in his periods of sanity—just how the deception was being worked. Did Emthoro really believe that he was Shandie and Ashia that she was her own sister? Or were the two of them merely puppets, willing or unwilling?

Now he had the answer: They were puppets. They knew what was happening and could not prevent it, could not stop their lips and limbs from obeying orders that came from outside themselves. Their treason was not of their own choosing, but they were aware of it. They were to be pitied, not despised! They had looked sick, disgusted, terrified. Their mouths had spoken the words he had heard, but their expressions had been conveying totally different messages. The wildness in their faces suggested they might both be close to madness now, and that could hardly be surprising.

Moreover, one of the coachmen had been a dwarf and another a jotunn. They had been imps at the same time. Two of the mounted guards closest to the carriage, although genuine imps, had displayed twin personas also. All four, in fact, must have been sorcerers, members of the Covin. That dwarf might even have been the Almighty himself.

Umpily staggered away, trembling. Now he could see through the deceptions. That was Olybino's doing! The warlock had given him defenses against delusion and told him to go away and record events as they truly were.

Fine! From now on Umpily would see events as they really were. But when the fake imperor summoned him to a dinner party or a reception—as he still did sometimes and would probably do much more often in future, with the official mourning almost over—then Umpily was going to see both the Shandie illusion and the Emthoro reality inside it. How could he possibly conceal his own knowledge? There would always be sorcerers nearby, and he would not stand close inspection.

He might even run into the Almighty himself in a corridor when the dwarf was being invisible. His reactions would give him away at once, wouldn't they?

Lord Umpily had spent most of his life at court. He had learned very well how to conceal his true feelings.

But he wasn't that good an actor!

Was he?

If he wasn't, then he wasn't going to last very long.
Was he?

4

The ever-restless ocean had fallen strangely still; a sad wind
sighed gently. *Seaspawn* lay hove to, hardly rolling, and even
the inevitable creakings of a wooden ship were barely audible.
The waning moon hung low in the night, painting a silver ladder on the Summer Seas. A single small lantern cast an orange
glow over the priest's breviary as he read the service. The
hushed crew listened without a sound. Captain Ko-nu let his
tears flow unashamed, knowing they would not be noticed in
the darkness.

Then the priest closed the book and doused the lamp. His
black-draped form disappeared. After a moment's silence, his
voice continued.

"Now we usually call for the eulogy." He was speaking
slowly and distinctly, so that his audience could follow his unfamiliar accent. "But you do not need anyone to tell you of
your lost mate. Even I can testify to his quality, who only
knew him for a few hours. I saw him bear his pain with courage beyond his years. I heard him freely forgive the hand that
struck him, conceding that there was no sin to forgive."

Someone began to sob.

"I tell you all," the priest said, "that the Good has been increased because he lived, and that the Gods will scarce need to
use Their balance to judge Wo-pu-Al. He goes to the last
weighing as we shall all go there in our time; we shall do well
indeed if our souls increase the Evil no more than his does, or
prosper the Good as much."

Waves slapped gently at the hull. Ropes creaked.

The priest spoke a soft cue. Gi-al's sitar sounded a chord,
and the crew began the final dirge. Ko-nu wiped his eyes to
watch the muffled shapes of his two surviving sons lift the
locker door on which their brother's shrouded body lay, bearing it between them to the rail.

"Farewell, brother," Father Acopulo said loudly, in the last
words of the Burial at Sea. "Go to the Gods; we shall follow
in our time."

Mu-pu and Po-pu tilted the plank. The chant surged louder,
hiding the splash as Wo-pu-Al departed on his last journey, one
more victim of the merfolk's ancient curse. The two pallbear-

ers stood with heads bowed for a moment, then Mu-pu took the shutter and laid it on the deck.

The priest moved over to them and laid his hands on their shoulders. Whatever he said was inaudible through the singing, but Ko-nu was confident that the words would be appropriate, and reassuring.

Truly, Father Acopulo was a fine priest! Like any imp, he was prone to seasickness, but he had ignored it. He had spent many hours with the dying boy, and with his guilt-laden slayer, also. He had greatly comforted Wo-pu's passing and had already worked a vast improvement in Po-pu, restoring his faith, easing his load of guilt. The family would not lose a second son.

And now the imp had conducted a wonderfully moving service also. Finding him had been great good fortune.

The Gods had been kind.

Merely players:

> All the world's a stage,
> And all the men and women merely players:
> They have their exits and their entrances;
> And each man in his time plays many parts.

Shakespeare, As You Like It, II, vii

‹ FOUR ›

Impossible loyalties

1

Again the sun was setting in Qoble.

A solitary crow, homeward bound to its nest in Thume, thumped its way high over the Brundrik River—flying, of course, as the crow flies. The two girls standing on the western bank joined hands and disappeared.

Time stopped for Thaïle as she ran into the sorcerous barrier. She gathered power to force an entrance and was accosted by a man she knew, Archon Raim. They faced each other in the still nothingness of the ambience. He smiled. She glared angrily, prepared to wrest her way by him, and then was stayed by the color of his emotions.

"Welcome home, Thaïle," he said softly.

He meant it, too. He was square-shouldered and solid, but the muscle was all genuine; so was the thick curly hair and the smile. He had bright gold eyes. There could be no deception in the ambience, no concealment of mind or body. Thaïle had not been a sorceress long enough to grow accustomed to unrestricted perception, and the last time they had met, she had slapped his face.

"Thank you." Knowing that she was displaying embarrassment, she glanced at her companion, but Kadie was frozen in timelessness—as was the crow, suspended over the midpoint of the stream.

"You are a sight for worried eyes," Raim said. He was amused by her reactions, but he was also flattered by them, and starting to respond himself. He could not have been a sorcerer long enough to have forgotten how it felt to a newcomer. Without a word, he passed an apology for his earlier offense and accepted hers for the slap; the incident was mutually discarded.

"I thought my return would be prophesied?" Thaïle said.

He nodded, surprised. "Of course it is. So is your nonreturn. You have not seen the *Revelations*?"

He was an arrogant young man, but perhaps he had much to be arrogant about. He was very young to be an archon.

"I saw it. I was not allowed to read it."

"I am sure that will be permitted now. You will find it confusing."

"It mentions me."

He nodded again and laughed. "And many other people, also, most of whom have not happened. It mentions you twice by name. Once it prophesies that Thaïle of the Gaib Place will save the College. Elsewhere it says that Thaïle of the Leéb Place will destroy it. That is fairly typical."

"Oh." Thaïle had assumed that prophecies might be obscure or ambiguous, but she would not have expected them to be directly contradictory. "Then why is the book important?"

"Because it spends much ink explaining how the Chosen One is to be recognized. Because you seemed to fit about as many of the clues as could be hoped for." He shrugged those husky shoulders. "Because even such apparent nonsense may turn out to be accurate. Much of the *Revelations* is very, very old, you see."

They could stand here in nothing forever, without wearying or losing a moment of their lives. Kadie remained a statue.

"Old is good?"

"In prophecy it is," he said. "Mountains are best seen from afar, yes? Close to they are obscured by foothills or even trees. For great events, the oldest prophecies are the most reliable." He chuckled, pleased by his own metaphor.

"And it prophesies my return now?"

"It also said you might not return, which would be disaster." Raim hesitated, then grinned and went on, because he could not conceal the rest. "And you have not been having romantic adventures."

"That is important?"

"Apparently. Several verses warn of the coming of a woman with child, as harbinger of Cataclysm. That was why . . ."

Why my baby was murdered!

Raim flinched and nodded. "Er, partly. Certainly why you were not brought in sooner." With less brashness than usual he turned his attention to the petrified Kadie. "And you bring a guest? Only one? The *Revelations* say the Chosen of the Chosen One are to be granted succor—'Chosen,' plural."

Thaïle glanced with relief at the petrified mundane, that piteous, ill-used princess. "She will not be harmed, then?"

"No, I am sure." He frowned, obviously intrigued. "Only a mundane? That sword is a cunning piece of work, but she has no power of her own. Pretty little thing . . . been through some hard times? How and why did you find her?"

"It is a long tale, but she seems to be important, or her family does. Her father is the leader of the resistance to the Covin."

"They do not concern us!" Raim's anger flared up in blue-white auroras. "What the Outsiders do to one another is no concern of Thume."

He was wrong—Thaïle was certain of that, although she did not know how. "That may not be true any longer. He was a demigod once. He knew five words."

The archon started nervously. Had he been standing in the real world and not the ambience, he would probably have glanced over his shoulder. In either case, there was no way to know whether the Keeper was listening. She almost certainly was. "*Was* a demigod? And now is not? How can this be?"

"He told four of the words to the girl's mother, the queen of Krasnegar, his beloved."

"*Four?* His beloved, and he stopped at four?" Perplexity writhed around him like purple flame. "That is contrary to all the lore of magic!"

"Evidently. And the woman broadcast them to her assembled people, diluting them to background words."

Raim shook his head in bewilderment. "An incredible couple, then! It seems our wisdom is deficient. Such things should not be."

Thaïle could not resist the opportunity. "So perhaps these people do concern us?"

He sighed. "Perhaps. I should not presume to instruct you, Archon Thaïle. Your power belittles us all. I am greatly comforted by it, and by your return."

His honesty reassured her. Raim was not jealous of her power, or frightened of it, as Teal and Shole had been.

"Her Holiness is expecting me, I assume?"

Raim laughed, and it was the equivalent of a warm hug. His pleasure at seeing her was completely genuine. "If I could keep your return a secret, I would. I shall humbly suggest that you be granted a few days to rest and relax. You know where to find each other when you are ready."

"And I am to be an archon?"

"You are an archon! You overshadow us like an elm amid seven daisies. Of course you are an archon! But the daisies can cope without you for a while yet. The duties are not taxing, you know, or we should delegate them to someone else!"

Whom do we serve? Yes, Thaïle would be an archon, because that was her duty. All pixies must serve the Keeper and the College, because the Keeper and the College preserved them all against the demons of the Outside. She had walked the Defile and seen the horrors of the War of the Five Warlocks. Now she had sensed the evil of the Covin and witnessed the Almighty's atrocities. She was mighty, perhaps the mightiest since Thraine. With such a Gift, how could she refuse to serve?

"Welcome home," Raim said again.

"It is good to be home," Thaïle admitted.

He nodded and lifted the occult veil to let her pass. Instantly sorceress and friend arrived at the Thaïle Place. Time lurched back to life.

Kadie uttered a yelp of pleasure and approval at the sight of the trim cottage under the trees. She clapped her hands.

Thaïle recoiled in dismay. Oh, it was the Thaïle Place, all right, a luxury version of the Gaib Place where she had been born, set amid much the same upland pines and scrubby vegetation, the same sort of rocky outcropping and taxing mountain air. No one had been near it since she left. To her eyes it was exactly right, to her heart all wrong. A pixie returning home should be overcome with joy, but this was not home. The Leéb Place, now—wattle walls on the banks of the great slow river, the heavy scents of the lowland, the hum of insects; heron and parrot and flamingo, and memories of Leéb . . . Her soul was rooted there, not here, but the Leéb Place was no more; she herself in grief and rage had blasted it to ashes. A pixie with no Place of her own was a flower with no stalk, a snail without a shell.

A few moments later, far away at the Brundrik River, the crow settled contentedly onto its nest.

2

"The rascal is certainly mobile," Tribune Hodwhine remarked cheerfully. "Wassailing down by the docks in Gaaze, getting married out in the fruit country, attending the races over in Forix—and that was all in the same afternoon! Must have wings."

He tossed the whole wad of reports into a basket beside his chair and took a long draft from a misted goblet. Even on a day so hot that the air was hard to breathe, a tribune lived very well in the XIIth's permanent barracks at Gaaze. Officer quarters included private courtyards, like this one, with flowers and cool willows for shade and a small stream running through it. The ranks were convinced that their betters passed off-duty hours sailing paper boats to one another. That did not seem too incredible in the case of Tribune Hodwhine.

Centurion Hardgraa paced from outer gate to trellis. The trouble was, in Qoble he had no real authority whatsoever. He would have more standing back in Hub—at least he would have until he was noticed by the Covin or the imposter imperor. Then he would be turned into a mindless tool, he supposed. He shivered. Still, that was probably no worse a fate than being a legionary grunt, and his duty would probably lead him to it, once he had recovered the rightful impress. He must return the child to court, no matter what sacrifice was required of him personally.

He turned about and headed back to the gate. He could influence events only secondhand, through this aristocratic ninny. He had persuaded Legate Ethemene of the urgency of the case—lying like a camel trader, of course. Sensing scandal and political quagmires, the legate had quickly distanced himself, assigning Tribune Hodwhine of the IIIrd Cohort to "assist Centurion Hardgraa in making certain discreet inquiries in accordance with the imperor's personal wishes." On that slender scaffolding rested all of Hardgraa's hopes and perhaps the future of the Impire until the end of time.

"Do stop trudging up and down, old man," the tribune said

petulantly. "You're wearing a rut in my lawn. Sit down, fergossake! Have another drink."

Very likely Legate Ethemene had selected Hodwhine to handle the Ylo affair because he was a Hathino and the Hathinos had been mortal enemies of the Yllipos for centuries. Hodwhine appeared to be completely unaware of that, or else he considered the feud obsolete. In a sense it was, since the old imperor had wiped out the Yllipos. Ylo was the only one left, and there was no effective way to carry on a feud with one man when that one man was—or seemed to be—the new imperor's most trusted confidant. Now Hodwhine ought to be grabbing the chance to spike Signifer Ylo, but so far he had shown a lamentable lack of motivation.

Hardgraa eased himself grudgingly into the other chair. He preferred hard stools, if he had to sit at all. As a matter of course he wore full uniform, chain mail and all, and he was sweating like an eel. He disapproved of Hodwhine's nudity. The tribune had stripped down to a towel.

"Now, old man," Hodwhine said, prodding the document basket with an elegant aristocratic toe, "we have at least two dozen sightings, from all over the place—"

"Thirty-one sightings, sir, of which eight were in Gaaze itself. The rest were almost all scattered at random, one to a site."

"Well, then! So weight of numbers suggests the rascal's holed up here in Gaaze?"

No, it didn't. If Ylo were in Gaaze he would have been seen more often than that, but centurions did not contradict tribunes, or at least not directly.

Hodwhine smirked inanely. "Better start interviewing all the pretty girls in town, eh? The lads'll enjoy that!"

Gods, the influence his family must have boggled the mind. Very few could have palmed off this dunce on the army as a tribune. Obviously he was not taking the Ylo affair seriously enough. Obviously he had some sort of sneaky admiration for the young lecher. Obviously Hardgraa must clear both of those obstacles out of the way promptly.

"Start with the married ones, sir."

Hodwhine sniggered. "Finds those safer, does he? Someone else signs the nine-month report, what?"

"That's it, sir." Hardgraa smiled.

It was a calculated smile, because he very rarely smiled, and he had no real inclination to smile at this limp parody of an officer. But it was technically a smile and after a moment Hodwhine frowned at it.

"What's funny?"

"Oh . . . Nothing, sir. Just thinking of something Ylo said once about . . . Well, no matter."

Hodwhine's asinine face was already pink from the heat; now it turned slowly scarlet. "Are you suggesting . . ."

"Just gossip, sir. Just common bazaar gossip, no importance. Now, that report from the priest . . . priestess. I think that one's genuine."

The tribune was still glaring, not listening. He was very minor grit in the aristocratic mill—youngest son of a baron, or something. In Hardgraa's experience, the more senior a noble, the easier he was to deal with. Shandie himself had been the best example; they came no higher than the prince imperial, which was how Hardgraa liked to remember him, and as man and officer Shandie had been without flaw. Grass-roots aristocrats like Tribune Hodwhine were obsessed with protocol and social standing and correct behavior and decorum. But of course those concerns could be exploited.

Which was why Hardgraa had just hit this one below the belt.

"I want to know why you were smirking that way!" Hodwhine stormed, almost purple now.

"Nothing, sir."

Veins bulged. "I order you to tell me!"

"Yessir. Ylo bragged more than once that he'd been . . . had slept with every officer's wife in the legion. All those he could get his hands on, he said. A couple were not in Gaaze, of course."

"He's a lying bastard!"

"I'm quite sure he is, sir," Hardgraa said, and he was, although as far as he knew Ylo had never made the boast just credited to him. "Now, this report from the priestess. I think it's the most reliable we've had."

Hodwhine licked his lips and ran a hand through his sweat-soaked hair. He was still wild-eyed. "Why?" he barked.

"Several factors, sir. The fact that we had to enlist the help of her bishop before she would talk. The fact that clergy dislike lying. The fact that she heard the child named."

"Mm? Missed that. What name?"

"Maya, sir."

Even a minor aristocrat could catch the implications. "You

mean short for Uomaya or some such name? Well, this woman Ylo's supposedly abducted has been using the name of the new impress, so it would be a joke to use the name of the princess imperial for her dau . . . Wouldn't it?" the tribune asked uneasily.

In the ensuing silence, color faded from his face until he was pale as a jotunn. He made a choking sound. "Whose wife did you say she was, Centurion?"

"I am not at liberty to say, sir. Obviously the matter has potential for scandal, or his Majesty would not be so grievously concerned."

"But if . . . The child would be the *heir presumptive*!"

Hardgraa shrugged. "Can't comment, sir."

Tribune Hodwhine grabbed up his goblet and drained it. Then he set it back on the table with a shaking hand. "What do you want me to do?"

That was more like it.

"Well, I suspect the target is heading eastward, sir. I can line up most of the best sightings. He's obviously avoiding military personnel, so he may not know yet that the XIVth's been withdrawn and the XIIth's sector extended to include Angot." Hardgraa eyed the tribune's glazed expression and decided he need not waste time on explanations. "I want the guards on the passes tripled. I want maniple signifers assigned to those posts and at least one of them on duty at all times. None of them can claim not to know him by sight. Double-check all shipping."

"We're already undermanned! How can I possibly requisition men from other cohorts without a—"

"Shall I ask Legate Ethemene to assign someone else, Tribune?"

"No! That will not be necessary, Centurion! I'll speak to him. What else?"

"Post a reward."

"How much?"

"A thousand imperials. Any more and we'll be flooded with false sightings."

Hodwhine grunted. "Getting that sort of money out of the bursar would be like skinning hedgehogs." A sly gleam brightened his normally vacuous eye. "My fa— I mean, I could put up that sort of cash personally . . . ?" His voice trailed off in appeal.

"A very noble gesture, sir. I shall see his Majesty is informed of it."

The tribune brightened considerably. "Anything else?"

Hardgraa rose and paced over to the trellis. "Someone tipped him off." He spun around and headed back toward the gate.

Hodwhine opened his mouth to protest and then closed it again. Whether he was concerned about the accusation or his lawn remained unclear.

"It had to be the messenger at West Pass. Target did not go through Pinebridge."

"What do you want?" the tribune said uneasily.

"Seventy lashes."

"Flog him to death, you mean. Bad for morale."

Hardgraa stopped beside Hodwhine's chair and looked down at him with all the contempt he had been hiding hitherto. "I am not playing games, *sir*. The imperor is not playing games, *sir*. But some of his legionaries *are*, sir. I want them to know that this is not a game! Sir."

Hodwhine pouted. "We'll bring him in, then, and do it here in Gaaze. Full muster of the legion, as far as we can. Proclamation?"

"Just general, dereliction of duty. No need to mention Ylo by name—they'll find out." Hardgraa realized he had dug his nails into his palms. "If the target's heading into the eastern foothills, we'll need at least two more cohorts. We must continue to downplay the child, sir. But as you have so astutely guessed, the child is the key."

"Gods!" the tribune said.

The idiot did not know the half of it. Sick at heart, Hardgraa resumed his pacing. Whatever his moral shortcomings, even Ylo would not mock the Gods with bigamy. That marriage ceremony buried the last shreds of doubt. The tale he had told at Yewdark must be true—Shandie really was dead. So the infant was the rightful impress of Pandemia, and Hardgraa would stop at nothing to get her back.

3

"Tell me more about Keef," Kadie said.

She was sitting outside the cottage with Thaïle. They had just finished eating and started telling stories. They both enjoyed stories. It was Kadie's second evening in Thume—a soft, warm evening with pink clouds. The air was drowsy with the scent of trees and flowers, and the clearing so full of peace that she could almost see it.

"There isn't much more to tell," Thaïle said, nibbling a strawberry. "It was a thousand years ago, remember. She was certainly a pixie, and the first Keeper. She overthrew Ulien'quith and founded the College."

"Killed him?"

"Probably."

"How?"

"I don't know." Thaïle's golden eyes twinkled. "Nastily, I hope."

Kadie frowned. True stories were always full of annoying gaps like that. "But if he was such a powerful warlock and had an army of sorcerers . . . like Zinixo?"

"Very much like Zinixo."

"Then how did Keef manage to kill him?"

Thaïle hesitated. She glanced in disapproval at the dirty dishes on the table between them, and they all vanished. "Keef was what your father was once."

"And what the Keeper now is? So she can kill Zinixo?"

"She says she can't." The sorceress smiled oddly. "You know, Kadie, you are almost the only nonsorcerer in the whole world who knows that five words make a demigod! I couldn't tell you if you didn't, because it hurts me to talk about such things to a mundane."

"My mother told me."

"Yes. If she could then it was only because she isn't a sorceress anymore! I'm sure the Keeper could defeat Zinixo if they had a straight-up fight, just the two of them, but he is the Almighty and has his Covin to aid him."

Kadie wondered if she was being too nosy. She did not want to hurt her rescuer and friend, but it was an important subject. "Don't talk about it anymore if you don't want to."

"I'll tell you if it hurts." Thaïle sighed. "Won't tell you, I mean!"

She was very pretty, with her golden eyes and curly brown hair. Kadie had decided she approved of pointed ears. Standard ears were a ludicrous shape, when you thought about it. Were all pixies as trim and graceful? One day she would like to meet more of them—but not yet. No, definitely not yet. For the present, a quiet life at Thaïle's cottage was what she wanted, what she needed. Eat and sleep and exchange stories.

"Well, the Keeper has an army, too. Scores of sorcerers in the College, you said."

Thaïle shrugged. "We are not bound by the same sort of loyalty spell, although of course we are all loyal and we would fight to the death. There just aren't enough of us. The usurper's been gathering votaries for twenty years, all over Pandemia. The Keeper says if he ever finds out about us there will be a battle and we shall lose."

That was a subject Kadie would not pursue any further. To the rest of the world Thume was the Accursed Land. The tiny piece of it she had seen so far seemed more blessed than cursed, a secret paradise hidden for a thousand years behind an aversion spell. Zinixo would never think about Thume unless something drew his attention to it very strongly, Thaïle had said. But Kadie could see now that she was probably going to be a prisoner here for the rest of her life.

Well, it was a wonderful prison. She loved the romantic little cottage in its private glade. It held all sorts of magical wonders, like spigots that put out scalding hot water and lamps that lit when you asked them to. In two days there had been no visitors except squirrels and jays. But never to see her parents again, or Gath, or Eva, or Holi . . .

"Thaïle? Is there any way to find out what is going on Outside? My family, I mean?"

The pixie shook her head sadly. "Nobody ever goes Outside. Well, a few do. Sometimes the Keeper will send out appraisers. Spies, I suppose, is what they are. That is rare. And the Keeper herself, of course. That's her main duty. She can walk the world undetected. No one else can."

Kadie did not like the idea of *spies*. Skulking around everywhere, being invisible, listening and watching and then reporting back to Thume? Perhaps they even came to Krasnegar sometimes! Who knew what they might not have pried into in the last thousand years?

"So tell me more about Keef. She was a demigod, too. She did not destroy her words?"

"No. Keef killed her—" Thaïle stopped and shook her head. She looked appealingly at Kadie, inviting her to finish the sentence.

"Killed?" *No!* "You don't mean her husband, er, goodman? Her lover? She killed her *lover*?"

Thaïle nodded again, but she was very tense now, her face pale and screwed up with pain.

"Let's talk about more cheerful things," Kadie said quickly. She did not like the way the Keef story was going. "My mother escaped from Thume on a magic carpet."

Thaïle relaxed gratefully. "That was during the reign of the last Keeper. I expect it's all recorded in the Library somewhere. We can go and look it up sometime, if you want."

Thaïle had mentioned the Library before. It sounded as if there would be all sorts of interesting storybooks there. Kadie wondered if she could borrow some.

"Not now!" she said firmly.

Thaïle laughed. "Kadie, you are turning into a real pixie! You just want to stay here, at my Place, hiding out in the forest, never going anywhere—don't you?"

Kadie nodded guiltily.

"You've had a hard time," Thaïle said sympathetically. "You'll get over it. I expect you'll become ghastly bored soon."

That might be true one day, but it wasn't true yet.

"I don't mind," the pixie said. "I'm happy to be back." She did not look happy, though. "This is my Place and no one will disturb us here. I was just thinking that it might be fun to introduce you to some people and watch their reactions."

"Your friends?" Kadie asked uneasily.

"I don't have any real friends. I was a novice until just a few days ago. Now I'm a sorceress, I'll have to make new friends. How would you like to go to the Meeting Place?"

The answer was "Not at all," but Kadie felt ashamed of that reaction. She was perfectly safe here—in spite of the nasty experience Mama had gone through when she had visited Thume—because she was the guest of a sorceress. And she couldn't hide out in the woods forever. That would not be princessy behavior at all.

She nodded nervously. "If you think it will be all right."

Thaïle smiled a very thin smile. "It should be fun, watching their faces. You're the first visitor in a thousand years! The language has changed, but I can give you that with sorcery, and most of the people you'll meet are sorcerers anyway, so they could understand you."

"Can I wear my sword?"

The pixie laughed aloud. "In Thume? What do you plan to kill, Great Warrior?"

Kadie felt herself flush. Mama had met danger in Thume! Mostly, though, her rapier had been her constant companion for so long that she could not bear the thought of being without it. It had been her sole comfort among the goblins. It was a reminder of Gath, her twin, and Krasnegar. It was the only thing she had that had come from Krasnegar, and it had saved her from the ravens.

"Let me see it." Thaïle held out a hand.

Kadie drew the sword reluctantly and passed it across the table. The pixie took it and closed her eyes for a moment.

"It's very old. Very subtle. It was made for someone called . . . Olliano? No, Ollialo."

"Inisso's wife! He was the sorcerer who founded Krasnegar."

"And a very powerful warlock. Almost the only warden who ever resigned his throne." Smiling, Thaïle passed the sword back. "It's all recorded in the Library."

"Is everything recorded in the Library?"

"Just about everything. Keeps people busy."

Kadie gasped, seeing the rapier changed. All its silver filigree was clean and shiny, and the one blind dolphin had a ruby eye again to match its sisters. "You've mended it! Thank you!"

"I restored it, too," Thaïle said, standing up. "You almost wore it out killing ravens." Her smile faded. "I can prophesy something about that sword, Kadie."

"What?"

The pixie frowned, as if puzzled. "It will draw blood again soon, but not in your hand. Someone else wields it."

"You?"

"No, not me. Someone I have never met—and who has never yet touched the sword. You give it to him . . . I think it's a him."

Kadie said nothing. She could not imagine herself ever giving her sword away to anyone, anyone at all.

Thaïle shrugged, and smiled. "There are strange times coming soon, times I cannot foresee. It would not be good manners to take a sword to the Meeting Place, I think."

And what use would a sword be against sorcerers, anyway? Kadie reluctantly unfastened her belt.

4

The two of them had barely started along the white gravel path before Thaïle began to realize that she might be making a real error in dragging Kadie away from the safety of the

Place. Her guest was a badly wounded fledgling who needed time to heal, and apprehension was burning up around her like a thicket of purple fire. She had taken Thaïle's hand, and her own was damp and shaking.

"This is the Way," Thaïle explained cheerfully. "It goes everywhere in the College, one road to anywhere. All you have to do is think where you want to be, and it will take you there."

"Oh."

"And that's even more wonderful than you might think, because the College is scattered all over Thume. To go from my Place to the Meeting Place would take you a week on a horse."

Kadie said, "Oh!" again, not sounding at all comforted.

"But it's really only a Way Back, because it will only take you to somewhere you have been before. Notice how the vegetation has changed already?"

Time to heal . . . but that time might not be available. Old Baze, the former archon, had predicted that Thaïle would not be an archon for long. She could probably foresee such things for herself now—although not while shrouded within the Way's shielding—but she had not done so and did not intend to do so. Prophesying one's own future was a dangerous and ill-advised thing to try.

Then the Way emerged from the trees and into the Meeting Place. The clearing was hot and bright with sunshine, a dell of flowered park land enclosing a small lake at its heart. Green was greener here, among the Progiste foothills on a summer evening, setting off the myriad bright colors of blossoms and tropical birds, of gay-clad people sprawled on the grass or conversing on benches and in shady cabanas. White swans floated among the water lilies and wading herons. A herd of small deer grazing on the bank jerked their heads up in alarm, apparently registering the arrival of a mundane. They had been oblivious of their human company until then.

Kadie stopped dead. "Pixies!"

"Of course." Thaïle decided not to inform her young friend that she was one of the dark-haired demons mentioned in the Catechism. This intrusion was probably very unwise all round. Seeing the cold stare on every face, she realized that the few fragile friendships she had begun to build as a trainee were all lost to her. Archons could befriend only other archons.

Well, if she couldn't woo them, she could awe them.

"Come! I'll introduce you to some pixies."

Kadie dragged her feet as she was led forward along the path. "They're beautiful!" she muttered.

Perhaps they were, to her mundane eyes—graceful, youthful, tanned, all clad in fine garments of soft colors, mostly golds and greens. Few were less than full sorcerers, though, and Thaïle could see their true ages and shapes. Why did they bother to pretend? Only the lowly trainees would be deceived.

Talk had ceased all over the Meeting Place. A hundred golden eyes stared disbelievingly at the newcomers. Closest was a group of two women and three men, standing. One of them was distinctively clad in blue, instead of the forest shades most others preferred; he strode forward a couple of paces, flickering with anger and indignation.

"Trainee Thaïle?" he barked. Then he became aware of the solidity of her presence in the ambience. He stopped with a flash of alarm.

Give Teal his due, he made no claims to youth; he projected an image of fatherly middle years, silver hair and a mature figure. To sorcerer vision he was repulsive—old and fat, bald, curvaceous body coated with white fur. Despite the fur, he made Thaïle think of snakes. That he should be the first to greet the visitor might be pure coincidence. If not, it boded ill for Kadie's chances of ever leaving Thume.

Thaïle flashed him an ominous smile. "This is the Master of Novices, Analyst Teal. Master, may I present Princess Kadolan of Krasnegar, a visitor to our land?"

Teal froze. In the ambience he flamed green terror. "An imp?" he croaked. "A *demon*? And you? *Trainee* Thaïle?"

"Archon Thaïle."

Teal vanished with a wail. An instant later, the ambience blazed with occult power and the Meeting Place was deserted. The departure of so many people simultaneously created a clap of thunder. The deer took off for the safety of the surrounding forest. Ducks skittered across the water into flight; swans reared and flapped in white spray.

Kadie jumped and squealed: "Oh!"

Startled herself, Thaïle flinched, and then she began to laugh. "There!" she said. "I told you you had nothing to fear! They're far more frightened of you than you are of them."

Kadie's pale face forced itself into a sickly smile.

"Thaïle, Thaïle!" a reproving voice murmured. *"You'd better bring her with you, I suppose."*

"What's wrong?" Kadie demanded.

Thaïle shivered. "We have to go and meet the Keeper."

Rain was falling on the jungle. Little could penetrate that great ocean of foliage, but the air itself was wet, dense with odors of vegetation and rotting humus. The Way snaked dimly between giant trunks, barely visible to mundane vision. Kadie clung fiercely to Thaïle's hand, whimpering nervously as trailing moss brushed her hair. Together they walked down into the blackness of the vestry, then through into the cold gloom of the shrine. Twice before Thaïle had seen this ancient ruin, and yet the Chapel had lost none of its power to awe her. Empty expanse of flagstone floor, high shadowed roof, ill-placed and odd-shaped window openings, the two black corner doors, and the absence of an altar—all seemed wrong and sinister. Again she sensed the mourning centuries.

Even a mundane could detect the outpouring of grief from the farthest corner. "What's that!" Kadie shrilled, pointing a tremulous finger.

"Keef's grave," Thaïle muttered, and was annoyed to hear herself whispering. "The dark patch is ice, frozen tears." For a moment she considered taking her visitor over there to pay her respects, and then decided not to.

This whole visit was folly. Her return to Thume itself had been. The thought of meeting the Keeper again was starting to hammer pulses of fury in her throat. *She killed my lovely Leéb! She killed my baby!* Hatred and loss! Raw, bleeding, unquenchable loss. Could even Zinixo surpass such evil?

The fourth corner was empty. To reach the Keeper, Thaïle must make that odd *sideways* move to the other Thume, the Thume that existed on the same plane as the rest of Pandemia—and she was not sure how to take Kadie with her. To leave her here alone would terrify her beyond reason. Even as Thaïle wrestled with the occult problem, the Keeper solved it for her. She did not seem to appear, she was just present, as if she had been standing there all along, a darker shadow in the darkness.

Kadie saw her a moment later and shied.

"It's all right!" Thaïle said—adding *I think* under her breath. Nothing was all right where the Keeper was concerned. A demigod was not, strictly speaking, still human. Thaïle bit her lip as she stared over the barren floor at that eerie cowled shape, motionless as a draped pillar. She felt her hatred straining for release, for action. All the power she could summon was useless against the Keeper. She knew that in her mind, and yet her heart urged her to try again.

Hand in hand, the two women approached the ominous figure. Kadie's trembling was likely from fear, Thaïle's from abhorrence. They halted at a respectful distance. Instinctively Kadie sank to her knees, then glanced up in surprise at Thaïle, who remained defiantly erect.

"I will not kneel to you!" Thaïle could not penetrate the darkness within the hood. She could remember the ravaged, wasted face it concealed, but she could not see it now.

The Keeper sighed, and that one faint sound dismissed her visitor as trivial, her rebellion and disrespect as meaningless. Her suffering, that sigh implied, was as nothing compared to what the Keeper endured and must continue to endure. Only her enormous Faculty could withstand the burden of five words, and then only at terrible, superhuman cost.

"You are forgiven. You are welcomed back." The Keeper spoke aloud—for the benefit of the mundane, perhaps—but the voice was a tortured hiss, a sound like rain on dead leaves.

Despite her brave show of defiance, Thaïle felt a cold wash of relief at the words, and despised herself for it. Why, when she felt only contempt for the Keeper and indeed the whole of Keef's grandiose sorcerous design, must her pixie heritage so disgrace her as to make her feel relieved? Now that their cruelty and oppression had been revealed to her, why could she not shuck off the lies and indoctrination of her childhood?

"You are the Chosen One," the Keeper said. "There is no doubt now."

Shudder!

"Then may I read what the book prophesies about me?"

"No. I have destroyed the book."

"Of course you remember what was in it?"

The Keeper did not deign to reply, leaving Thaïle shivering with frustrated rage.

The venomous whisper came again. "Your duties as archon begin now. You are assigned the western sector, as that is where the greatest peril lies."

"I do not know what is required of me."

"You will understand when there is need."

The cowl tilted slightly, as if its wearer had moved to study Kadie, and Kadie, who had been staring up with green eyes big as tiger mouths, doubled over to press her face against her knees.

"You were not prophesied, child," the scaly murmur said, "but I foresaw you."

Kadie's head jerked up in astonishment. "Me?" she squeaked.

There was a pause. "Not you personally, no. But someone yet unborn. You have your mother's eyes."

What sort of mockery or trick was this? Before even Thaïle's occult reflexes could react, Kadie cried out.

"You know my mother?" She half rose, then stopped.

Could that have been a hint of a *chuckle* within that cowl? "I was an archon when she came to Thume."

Kadie blurted, "That was nineteen years—" And stopped.

The Keeper seemed to nod. "I reported the intrusion to my predecessor. I advised him to take a hard look at the young woman in the party. His Holiness commended my acuity of prevision and confirmed my premonition. It was for your sake that your mother was allowed to depart in peace. He let the others go, too, which I would not have done."

"So the princess may remain with me?" Thaïle demanded.

"You sound," the Keeper hissed, "like a child asking for a kitten." Then she was gone.

The audience was over.

Impossible loyalties:

> ... home of lost causes, and
> forsaken beliefs, and unpopular
> names, and impossible loyalties!
>
> Matthew Arnold, *Essays in Criticism*

❦ FIVE ❧

Word in Elfyn-land

1

Crunch!

Mm? Andor stirred, feeling the ache in his back.

Crunch! again? Where was he? Feet cold, back stiff as planks, lying on something very hard . . . *Crunch!* What *was* that infuriating noise?

He opened a reluctant eye and saw sky, pale blue, framed all around in impossibly green fronds. Sleeping outdoors? Wrapped in his cloak?

Crunch! He opened the other eye and turned his head.

The king of Krasnegar sat cross-legged beside him, eating an apple. *Crunch!* The oversized faun looked down with a mocking grin on his ugly, unshaven face and his big jaw moving in a rhythmic chewing. His clothes were laborers' castoffs, as usual. His hair resembled a neglected woodlot—as usual.

"Good morning, Sleepy-head!" Rap said. "I needn't ask if you slept well. You certainly slept long enough."

Fornication! More than dawn dew chilled Andor. Every time he got involved with this accursed ex-stableboy, he landed in trouble, big trouble. Now he remembered: being transported by Evil-begotten sorcery in the middle of the night from that stinking, sinking hulk to . . . Oh, *Gods!* . . . to Ilrane, elf country. Big, *big* trouble!

He returned the smile cheerfully. "Good morning, your Majesty! I trust you also slept the sleep of the just?" He heaved himself into a sitting position.

"No, I just sleep. Don't stand up! You might be seen."

Whatever the troll-sized grass was, it was only waist-height, admittedly, but why should a sorcerer care? Andor yawned and stretched. "Can't you use your farsight?" The first time he had met this big rustic lout, years ago, had been beside a bonfire on an arctic beach. Farsight had been the issue then, he recalled, and he had wanted to scream at the kid not to reveal his talent. He had gone right ahead and done so, of course. There had been "duty" involved, and the faun had always been one of those idealistic idiots who rallied to Calls of Honor. That was a dangerous trait, one that had subsequently landed him in innumerable perils. He was no kid anymore—he was a lot older than Andor himself now—but he had never learned sense. Unfortunately he seemed to have a gift for dragging Andor's neck into the noose with his own.

Now he shrugged casually. "I haven't been outside the shielding yet. I chose this bivouac because it was shielded, remember?"

The faun had breakfast all spread out on the trampled herbage between them. Andor pulled a face and reached for the water bottle. He would prefer not to be reminded of the events of the night. He had an instinctive dislike of ships, especially sinking ships.

"Why would anyone put shielding in the middle of a hay field?"

"This ain't hay, City Slicker! Likely there was a house here once, a sorcerer's house. I think I was lying on some of the foundations, as a matter of fact." The king grinned as if he had not a care in the world. Good humor early in the morning was a revolting vice; good humor in the face of hazard was utter insanity. He would be more malleable if he did not know how Andor felt on the topic, though. So Andor smiled again.

"I had the fireplace! What's the program for today, Rap?"

The faun nodded in a direction behind Andor's back. "We head for that."

Andor turned his head to see. In spite of his grouchy, early-morning feelings, he felt the impact. The first rays of the sun had just caught the summit, blazing in crystal glory, a blur of rainbow high against the pale dawn blue. The sky tree was obviously very far off, the rest of its familiar pinecone shape still an indistinct shadow.

"Valdorian?"

"Valdorian," Rap agreed. He tossed his apple core away and reached for a pear.

See one sky tree and you've seen 'em all. Andor glanced over the choice of breakfast, realizing he was hungry. The last meal he'd eaten had been an excellent dinner at Casfrel Station. The fact that it had been three or four months ago was of no importance. What did matter was that he had been called back into existence last night and had built up an appetite in his sleep.

The menu was entirely vegetarian. "I suppose one of the trolls magicked up this for you?"

Rap raised a quizzical eyebrow. "You'd rather I'd asked an anthropophagus?"

"Er, no!" Andor chose a mango and reached for his dagger to peel it. Big, big, big trouble! He was not only an illegal intruder in Ilrane, he was supposed to accompany this faun maniac on a visit to a warden, an *elvish* warden, an elvish ex-warden, an elvish *fugitive* ex-warden. Crazy, crazy, crazy! Somehow, he must detach himself and head for safety. Even getting out of Ilrane might not be easy. The yellow-bellies were deeply secretive about their ancestral homeland; they hated strangers trekking around in it. Their ports and border crossings were infested with guards, who had loathsome habits of throwing nonelves in jail at the slightest provocation.

Call another of the Group? That seemed impractical under the circumstances. Darad and Jalon would probably collaborate with the faun. Sagorn certainly would—besides, the old fool was too frail to be exposed to hardship and danger. Andor couldn't call Sagorn or Darad at the moment, anyway.

That left Thinal. Funny, in any tight spot, Andor's first thought was always to call that no-good fast-fingered little vagrant. It must be some sort of throwback to their childhood, when Thinal had been his big brother, leader and protector, fearless hero. Changed days now! Thinal did have a rat's instinct for self-preservation, and he would share Andor's sentiments about this present idiocy, but he would have even less chance of escaping from elf country, because at least Andor could usually talk his way out of trouble. How had he ever fallen into this cesspool?

"Valdorian? That's Lith'rian's ancestral enclave?"

The faun nodded, gray eyes twinkling as if he could read Andor's thoughts. He could, of course, but he had some stupid scruples about reading thoughts. So he had always said and he was always moronically truthful.

Andor bit messily into the mango. "Isn't that an absurdly obvious place to look for him? Surely the Covin's been hunting him for months?"

Rap wiped his fingers on grass, apparently finished with breakfast. "I discussed this with Sagorn and he agreed. You must remember that."

Andor hid his annoyance in a laugh. "Rap! Recalling Sagorn's mental processes is like trying to recapture a nightmare. You explain to simple old me, huh?"

The faun frowned, puzzled. "I don't understand that, you know! If you share memories of events, why can't you remember what he was thinking?"

Why didn't he mind his own accursed business? "Because, old friend, I'm just plain dumb compared to him. He jumps to conclusions so fast that he doesn't even notice how he gets there. So he doesn't remember the steps—and then neither do I."

"I see. Well, it's not simple, I admit."

"We're talking *elves*, Rap. Nothing is ever simple around elves."

The faun laughed agreement. "Precisely! That's the point. When Lith'rian fled from Hub, everyone's first thought was that he would head back to Valdorian. Elvish instinct—go home to the tree. But Zinixo is hunting him with the Covin, so the obvious place is the last place he would be, right?"

"Right!"

"So that's exactly where he will be." Rap smirked, and began packing the rest of the food away.

Andor hastily chose two more mangoes and some grapes. "Surely that's too obvious?"

The smirk widened. "Therefore that makes it even more likely!" He turned serious. "It's a gamble, of course, but Zinixo is a dwarf, and you can't have two ways of thinking more different than elves' and dwarves'. I've had a taste of both sets of mental processes in my time, and I tried to apply them as well as I can. As I see it, to Lith'rian the only place he can possibly hide is his own sky tree, Valdorian. Honor and dignity require it! To Zinixo, anything as obvious as that can only be a trap. And there's two other reasons to start there."

"Tell me!" Andor could see that worse was coming, but he smiled as if he were enjoying this craziness.

Rap began buckling up the pack. "First, we don't have any other leads at all, and Ilrane is just too evilish big to search. The elves will never tell us where their beloved warlock is hiding, and he's a very powerful sorcerer—we can't hope to find him by ourselves in a thousand years. It's Valdorian or nothing. Second . . . how do you think Warlock Lith'rian is feeling now?"

"I haven't the foggiest," Andor said cheerfully, thinking that there was nothing in the world he could care less about. Then he guessed, and a moderate size iceberg settled in the pit of his stomach. "Oh! Defiant? Suicidal?"

The faun nodded somberly. "Glorious last stands are an elvish tradition. It fits the present situation, somehow. Lith'rian has been a warden for almost ninety years and probably expected to have another century or so. But now he's facing defeat by his old enemy, a detested dwarf. The millennium has come and brought total ruin to everything. My guess is that he will have rallied his votaries in Valdorian, planning to go down gloriously, with all flags flying." He shrugged. "It's not much, and if you've got a better idea, I'm certainly willing to listen."

Andor had a thousand better ideas, and Rap would never accept any of them. If the big mongrel wasn't a sorcerer, Andor would talk him out of this in minutes. And if there was anything worse than a warlock, or an ex-warlock, it must be a *suicidal* ex-warlock. God of Horrors!

"Sounds good to me," he said.

Rap smiled gratefully. "Sky trees are heavily guarded. You'll be a great help if you can just charm the elves into admitting us."

"No problem, Rap. Elves are about the easiest people I know." He was a sorcerer—let him do his own damned charming! "I can handle elves! Dwarves, now, or fauns . . . Ugh!"

Rap laughed aloud, completely unoffended. "We've had some grand adventures together, old friend, haven't we?"

"We sure have, Rap," Andor said. *And none of them was ever my idea!* "But this one beats them all." Gods get me out of here!

Rap chuckled and rose to his knees, then more cautiously to his feet, looking around him all the while. "All clear," he said.

Then came pulling on of boots and buckling of swords. Andor scowled at his cloak. It would be a dreary weight to lug around, and Ilrane near to midsummer was certain to be hot. The only use for a cloak was as bedding, and he did not intend to repeat this sleeping-out-of-doors nonsense. There was no need to argue that point now, though. Eventually he rose also. He hoisted the second pack, grunting at its weight, although it was substantially smaller than the one the faun had taken. He slung it on his back, and it made him stoop, putting his eyes about level with the king's collarbones. There was something obscene about a faun bigger than an imp. It was contrary to nature.

Waist-high all around them, the lurid green foliage rippled in the breeze. A line of tall hedgerow showed where the road ran close by. Southward, the sky tree of Valdorian was all ablaze now in the rays of the rising sun, a crystal artichoke two leagues high. Thin cloud streamed eastward from the summit.

"Isn't it magnificent?" the half-breed said in an awed voice.

"Fantastic!" It would take days to reach that monstrosity on foot. "Why didn't your sorcerous friends put us closer?"

"Oh, we were afraid there might be magical boobytraps set up around it."

Oh, great! Just wonderful!

"And we must give the others time to get things organized in Dragon Reach," Rap continued, wading off into the greenery. "Lith'rian," he said over his shoulder, "is going to explode in streaks of fiery fury when he hears what we're up to."

Even greater! A *furious* suicidal elvish ex-warlock!

Other plans were needed, and soon. If Andor's mastery was going to be used to charm him into elvish places, those places were not going to be any urinating sky trees, they were going to be *bedrooms*. Come to think of it, there was one bright spot in this mess, and that was girls. Since elves never showed their age, elvish women were all nubile. And lovely. And inventive. And extremely susceptible. They could often be talked into interesting group exercises. So the first fork in the road would see a faunless Andor heading for the nearest convenient port, but on the way there he would certainly refresh his memories of elvish hospitality and intimate—

"God of Fools!" the faun roared. He turned and grabbed Andor and spun him around and rushed him back the way they had come by sheer brute strength, until they reached the trampled patch where they had spent the night. There he stopped. "God of *Misery!*" he added.

Andor hurled himself to the ground to hide. Realizing that the faun was still standing, he peered up—and greatly disliked what he saw. He knew Rap was heavily cursed with the sort of unimaginative stupidity often referred to as "courage." He had very rarely seen Rap look frightened. He had never seen him look like he did now. But if such obvious danger threatened, why was he still on his feet, in full view of the whole world?

"What the Evil is wrong?" Andor bleated . . . demanded.

The king swung his pack off and dropped it. "The Covin!" he growled. He sat on the pack, put his elbows on his knees and his chin on his hands, and scowled homicidally at the distant sky tree.

"Rap—"

"Shut up and let me think!"

That remark shocked Andor more than he liked to contemplate. That remark had not represented Rap's usual stubborn insistence on ignoring trouble. That remark had sounded *scared*. Andor wondered if he ought to make a break for it while there was still time.

"Sorry," Rap muttered, still pulling faces. "I let it startle me."

"Let what startle you?"

"Eyes. Zinixo's eyes."

Andor clenched his teeth to keep them silent.

Rap paused a moment longer, then sighed. "I think I see. I'm not near as wise as I once was, you know, but I think I see what he's doing; how he's doing it. He's . . . well, just because I understand doesn't mean I can explain it." He straightened up and ran both hands through his thicket of hair. "The Covin's mounting a *personal* search for me. It started to home in on me as soon as we left the shielding."

"It didn't *find* you, did it?"

"Obviously not."

"Why obviously?"

"Oh—because we're still alive and at liberty. But it's like being hunted by hounds, I think. Every scenting or sighting will bring them closer."

"Just you?" Andor licked his lips, wondering how to suggest tactfully that he be allowed to leave—alone, of course. A week's start would be only fair.

"Just me. I saw Zinixo's eyes . . . Big as mountains, cold as stone." Rap shivered. "It's sort of like the sending he used on Shandie at the beginning. It's not the same as the hunt for magic he tried on us in the Mosweeps. This is personal!"

And obviously dangerous. "Why now?"

"I don't know!" the faun muttered, scowling. "Perhaps be-

cause of Olybino's performance. Perhaps the dwarf didn't realize I was involved in the Mosweeps thing. Perhaps he still
feared I was a demigod, and didn't dare risk personal
contact ... He's a horrible coward, you know? Worse than,
well, worse than anyone else I can think of. If I was," he
growled, "was still a demigod, I mean, then I'd accept the connection and burn him to a crisp! Even if I had to fry half the
Covin to get to him, I would!" He groaned and returned to his
concentrated brooding.

Andor struggled to regain control over his teeth. "Rap?" he
whimpered. "Rap, if any one of us five ever dies before he can
call another, then the other four will be lost forever, won't
they? That means effectively dead, doesn't it? The first death
will kill all five of us!"

"I suppose so," the king murmured, seemingly still engrossed in other matters.

"Well, then?"

What Andor meant was that it wasn't fair to expect him to
risk five lives all on his own. He had more to lose than other
men, didn't he? How could he put that into words?

"Ha!" Rap grinned. "Got it! At least, I think I have."

"Oh, good."

"He's hunting for my, er, my magical signature, I suppose is
the best way to describe it." He scowled, briefly. "Never mind
the details. What matters is that he's looking for me as a sorcerer. If I cloak myself in a shielding, so I don't react with the
ambience ..."

For a moment he twisted his ugly features in a grimace.
Then he jumped up, smirking. "There! Done it!"

Andor clambered warily to his feet, dusting himself. "Done
what?"

"I just shielded myself." Rap chuckled and ran his hands
through his awful hair again. "No sorcery in, no sorcery out!
So as far as the Covin's concerned, I'm a mundane, and thus
I won't show up to their search! So it's all up to you, now,
friend Andor. Lead the way!"

Not a sorcerer?

Well, in that case ...

A hurricane hit Andor at full force, slamming him into the
ground, knocking all the wind out of him, rolling him over.
Then the great ox was on his back, crushing his lungs, twisting
his arm up until his shoulder was almost dislocated.

"Rap!" he gurgled, through a faceful of greenery. "What the Evil are you doing?"

"Thought you saw your chance, did you?" a gruff voice snarled in his ear. "Thought you'd settle a few old scores, did you?"

"Rap! Never! What in the world are you talking about? We're old buddies, you and I! Ever since I gave you your first lesson in bookkeeping—"

"That won't work, either!" the jotunnish accent said. "This shielding will keep your occult charm out, too! I saw where your hand was heading."

Damnation! "I don't know what you're talking about!"

"Oh, yes, you do! So now I know I can't turn my back on you, Andor, old snake. Too bad, because you'd have been really helpful."

"You're making a horrible mistake," Andor told the vegetation under his nose. It was hard to breathe with that load on top of him. "I was just scratching a bite."

"You were just drawing your sword! And we both know who's the better swordsman. Going to finish our long-ago duel, were you? Well, I think we'll have Jalon in your place, thank you nicely. He can't help as you could have, but he does look sort of elvish at a distance. And I can trust him at my back."

"Rap—"

The pressure on Andor's arm increased mercilessly.

"Rap!!"

"Call Jalon!" the faun roared. He sounded more like a jotunn when he wasn't visible.

The bones in Andor's shoulder creaked and burst into flame. Oh, God of Vengeance! He swore a silent oath and called:

2

Jalon lifted his face out of the mush and said, "Ouch!" The pressure on his arm eased immediately. "This is not easy for a jotunn, you know!" he said. "If I lose my temper, I may start using really vulgar language."

With a hoarse chuckle, the weight vanished from his back. A moment later two big hands grabbed him under the arms and hoisted him bodily upright. He spun around and was enveloped in the big fellow's hearty embrace. They thumped each other and laughed.

He backed off, wiping sap and leaves from his cheeks.

"Good to see you again, Rap! Hope I can stay around a little longer this time, though."

"Hope so, too! It's good to have you back." Puffing slightly, the oversized faun grinned down happily at the undersized jotunn.

"And great to be in Ilrane!" Jalon said. Immature sugarcane rippled all around—oh, that green! He inspected his hand, which was bright with the same green. "You know, I've never found a stable pigment to capture this color? Not close, even! It's almost glauconite, but with less blue in it. Do you think you could magic up some for me some time?"

Inexplicably Rap bellowed with laughter. "If that's all I have to pay for your assistance, then I'll be more than happy to oblige."

"You will? Oh, thanks, Rap!" Jalon rubbed his shoulder. He must not get lost in thinking about painting, though, or singing. He must remember that they were here on very important business, and not go wool-gathering. Then he recalled the sky tree and swung around to take a proper look at it.

God of Beauty! Glorious! The nimbus of color on the sunward side, a spiky kaleidoscope of pale hues, contrasting with the low-value gentian blue of the shadowed face, and the cerulean sky beyond—he drank it in, memorizing the play of light.

"I said," Rap repeated, "that if your shoulder hurts, I can take off my shielding for a moment and fix it for you, while we're here."

"Mm? No, it's fine." Even the clouds took on pearly tints near the tree.

"You've seen a sky tree before, haven't you?"

"What? Oh, yes. Andor visited Valdostor years ago, and he called me to do some of the climbing for him." But Jalon had never really had a good chance to study a tree at a distance, in its proper setting. The land rose in irregular waves to it—the root hills, elves called them—and here they were blotched with orchards and vineyards in malachite and shamrock green, streaked with deeper cypress. Might even be real cypresses.

"What? Oh, thanks." He accepted his pack from the faun and let himself be led across the field toward the road. The air was honey and wine. Ilrane! At last! He had always wanted to visit Ilrane and had always let himself be diverted somehow. There would be songs to learn, too, because everybody knew that the elves had music they saved for homeland and sky trees.

"Aren't you going to put that pack on?" Rap asked as they scrambled through the hedge.

"On? Of course!" Jalon hauled the straps over his shoulders. They were set for Andor, and loose on him, but they would do for now. Meanwhile he was far more interested in—

"This road!" the faun said. "I didn't notice in the night—it's colored!"

"All roads are colored in Ilrane, Rap. Elves don't like bare gravel or rock. The pictures tell a story to speed your journey. Two stories, depending which direction you're going. Let's see, this one seems to be—"

"We have to go this way."

"Oh. Well, that's all right. This way it'll be better. The best tales lead to the trees, of course. Yes, this looks like the tale of Puil'arin. She was the daughter of Zand'arin, War Vicar of the Senior Sept, and she fell in love with . . ."

In a few paces, the ballad came flooding back. Wishing he had a lyre or a lute with him, Jalon raised his eyes to the road ahead and began to sing. Rap strode along at his side, listening contentedly.

There was something magical about the light in Ilrane. It made a man's heart tingle. It roasted every warm color and froze every cool one; a million tints of green vibrated all around. The most banal motifs were transformed into marvels—willows over brooks, cattle under trees, cottages drowning in billows of flowers. Jalon's head ached with the effort of storing up memories he would express in pigment when he returned to Hub. He would try watercolor first, he decided, then oils, but would he manage to capture that enchantment? Probably he would dash off a dozen or so landscapes in a few days, working in a frenzy until he was ready to drop. Thereafter they would lie around his studio until Thinal sold them off for a fortune to rich imps, or Andor gave them away to women. That was what usually happened. He didn't care; it was the act of creation that mattered.

Sometime on that first morning, he lost his pack. Rap was annoyed. He said he'd been watching, and it had still happened, and how the Evil could a grown man lose a backpack without even remembering taking it off? Jalon apologized and promised to pay better attention in future. Yes, he *did* know how important this mission was. But why did they need packs at all? The climate was much like a warm bed all the time, and the hedgerows alone were laden with enough berries to feed them, even without having to raid the orchards.

Rap didn't believe that, so Jalon marched over to the nearest hedge and began filling his hat with berries—some people just couldn't see what was in front of their eyes! He would have collected a dinner in minutes, except he got distracted by a spider spinning a web. He wanted to see how she would finish it, but Rap came and said it was time to move on.

That night they bedded down in a copse by a stream. Jalon insisted on choosing the spot, because he wanted a good view of the sky tree. It seemed bigger now, towering over the hills. It reflected in the foreground pool, glowing begonia pink against the cobalt and manganese twilight, and sometimes fish set it rippling in circles. It was so beautiful it hurt. Perhaps an underpainting of madder scarlet, overlain with glazes of burnt umber and ultramarine . . .

"Just like old times, isn't it?" Rap said wistfully. "Like you and me and Gathmor marching across Dragon Reach."

Yes, Jalon agreed, just like old times. They talked about that for a while. It didn't seem all that long ago to him, but Rap had certainly been much younger then, so perhaps it was. Gathmor had been a likable guy for a sailor; short-tempered, of course. Fortunately Rap was more understanding—Jalon was almost certain he had started out the morning with a sword, and now he didn't have one, and he felt guilty about that. Not that he was any use with a sword, but he might have to call Darad. He wondered if Rap had noticed its disappearance yet.

"I suppose it would be safe to have a dip in that pool?" Rap said suddenly.

"Why not? I expect at least a dozen girls will appear as soon as we get our clothes off."

"Will they? We haven't seen many so far."

"Then why did you keep pulling me into hedges?"

Rap hauled off his shirt. "Three times. Only three times all day have we seen people. No livestock, nobody in the fields! The farms all seem deserted." He pushed off his boots, and then stayed sitting, frowning. "Where is everybody?"

"Fled, I expect."

The faun scratched his head. "Or taken refuge in the sky tree?"

"No. We'd see lights up there if it was inhabited."

"Barnacles! Why didn't I think of that?" Rap stared at the

great bulk of Valdorian, slate blue now against the emerging stars. The play of starlight on it was unforgettable, but not a lantern nor a torch flame showed.

"Because you're not an artist," Jalon said, feeling rather pleased at having been useful for once. "And you can't swim worth a spit."

"Oh, yes? Think you're better? Want to prove it?"

It was too bad there were no elves around. They might have been difficult with strangers, of course, but Jalon wanted very much to talk with real Ilrane elves. Later, when he and Rap had enjoyed their swim, had eaten, and were lying on heaps of ferns, bone weary from their long trek but not quite ready to sleep, they fell to talking about elves. And Jalon found himself telling a little of himself, and what it was like to be a mixture of such impossible opposites as elf and jotunn.

Apparently he had already told Rap once, long ago, that he had elf blood in him, although he did not recall doing so. Normally he never mentioned it. Apart from his size, he was so completely jotunn on the outside that no one would ever guess. Only the inside of his head was elvish.

"You must have had a difficult childhood," Rap said sleepily from the darkness.

Jalon stared up at the star dust above the branches and said yes, he'd had some troubles then. "As long as I stayed away from jotnar, it wasn't too bad, though. Imp boys didn't mess with me, on account of my looks."

"But elf boys would have nothing to do with you?"

"There weren't any elf boys in our part of town." He did not mention his mother, because he could remember so little of her. Whether she'd been raped by a jotunn or had acquiesced in his conception, he had never known. The fact that she had lived apart from the elf community in Malfin suggested that she'd been driven out. Certainly an elf woman who had gone into domestic service must have been in sore straits. He liked to assume that she'd died of a broken heart. "I lived with Darad's family. He was a younger brother to me, although he was always bigger. He used to defend me from the others— mostly so he could beat me up himself."

"Sounds like friend Darad," Rap murmured. "Did he have more wits in those days, before they got banged out of him?"

"Not that I recall. And I used to stay close to Thinal as much as I could."

"Thinal? The Thinal I know?"

"Yes. He was older than the rest of us. He took good care of us, too. We worshipped Thinal!"

Rap snorted but said nothing. It was certainly curious that the boyhood hero had turned out so despicable. Yet Thinal had always had his own standards. Inos's father had liked him, but that had been long before Rap was born.

"I suppose being a faun in Krasnegar wasn't exactly cream buns either?"

"Oh, I was jotunn enough to get by. Besides, no one sneers at mongrels there because most people are, especially the royal family."

"The present king, you mean, and Inos? What are your kids like?"

Rap sighed.

"Sorry!" Jalon said. "Shouldn't have asked."

"It's all right. I think of them every day, so why not talk about them? No fauns, thank the Gods. The twins are the oldest, Gath and Kadie. Kadie's pure imp, except she has Inos' green eyes. She's a little minx! No need to worry about Kadie. Gath and Eva are jotunn in looks. Holi's turning out a sort of blond imp—or he was when I last saw him. He may get picked on when he's older, I suppose."

Jalon prepared to change the subject, but Rap went on, speaking softly to the night breeze.

"Gath bothers me a little. He's a jotunn on the outside, like you, although he's going to be tall. Inside . . . I don't know! I can't figure Gath out at all. He's placid and unassertive and sort of dreamy. Not stubborn like a faun or aggressive like a jotunn. Not greedy and meddlesome like an imp."

"My sort of guy."

"Almost. But he shows no artistic vices, so I can't accuse Inos of having an affair with an elf."

"Will he be king after you?"

"If we win this war . . . Well, who knows?" Rap sighed again. "For all I know, Zinixo has leveled Krasnegar to the wave tops."

Jalon stumbled over hasty words of comfort. "You'd have felt that happen, wouldn't you? Grunth would, at least, or Tik Tok! Someone on *Dreadnought* would have told you if anything like that had happened."

"Probably. I just hope Inos had the sense to go into hiding with the kids. I told her she should."

"Where could anyone hide near Krasnegar?" Jalon demanded, thinking of the bleak tundra.

There was a long pause, then the king said, "She could have gone south. There's a way. Trouble is, the goblins were down in Pithmot, right? How did they get there?" His bedding rustled as he rolled over. "Well, Lith'rian will know. Think I'll catch me some shut-eye."

Guided by Grunth, who had once been there, the meld of sorcerers on *Dreadnought* had set the intruders down about two days' ride from Valdorian—or so they had thought. They had not anticipated that there would be no horses to be found. So Rap and Jalon were forced to walk, and a long trek it was. In the root hills the land was heaved into a maze of ridges and steep-walled canyons. Elvish roads never led directly anywhere, but always took the most scenic route possible.

Jalon lost count of the days, because he was enjoying himself so much. He rarely worried about time, anyway. Rap was fine company—humorous, soft-spoken, even-tempered. Despite his apparent clumsiness and his homely looks, the big fellow was as good for a chat as he was in a brawl. He was impatient to achieve his purpose, yet he never let his frustration show, except for an occasional obscure mutter about Longday.

The land was an artist's dream, prosperous yet beautiful, a blend of garden and apparently virgin nature that only elves could have achieved. It seemed uninhabited because elvish buildings, no matter how picturesque, were always tucked away out of sight. Rap said that the amount of agriculture in the district showed it must normally support a large population and he debated where all the people had gone, and why. Since the first day, the intruders had seen no one at all.

There were advantages to that, of course. Soon they began a little discreet looting—eggs from the farmyards, fish from the ponds, smoked hams from the larders. They took to sleeping in elvish beds. About the third night Jalon discovered a lute on a high shelf. It had been so coated with dust that he felt justified in taking it with him when he left the next morning, certain that its loss would not upset its owner. He would never steal a musician's favored instrument, but this one had obviously been superseded. After that he could play upon the road, and the leagues seemed even lighter.

As Rap pointedly pointed out, he did not lose the lute as he had lost the pack and the sword.

The land rose steadily. Far to the south, two more sky trees came into sight like ghostly pinecones and then vanished again behind the bulk of Valdorian. Valdorian itself grew ever more enormous, day by day, until it obscured the sky and overhung the world. Its summit was no longer visible, only the ribbed undersides of the great petals. At their fringes they shone bright as diamond, darkening inward to the trunk in rich translucent tones, like a glass mountain.

Then one day, just as Jalon finished the "Lament of the Lonely Sisters" and was adjusting the tuning on his E string, Rap said, "Hold it a moment."

Jalon said, "Mm?" and took stock of his surroundings. There was nothing especially interesting in sight, even the road itself, which had just reached the sad end of ill-starred Loah'rian and was doodling in arabesques and chinoiserie before starting another tale. The scenery was concealed by high grassy banks. A dull patch like this invariably hinted at something spectacular just around the next bend; it was designed to clear the palate.

"Let's take a brief break here. Come and sit down."

Uneasy, Jalon followed his companion to the verge and settled beside him on the grass. They traveled light now. Rap had retained only his boots and sword and long breeches, abandoning all baggage. Jalon wore cerise elvish shorts and mauve bootees, while his third layer of skin was coming in tanned. His slim build and fair hair might escape notice at a distance, but elves were golden, not red and peeling.

Oddly, Rap never wore short pants. Funny guy—you could tease him about his hair or his face, you could even address him as "Master Thume" because of the word tattooed on his arm, and he would smile tolerantly—but breathe one word about his furry faun legs and a dangerous jotunn glint would flare in his gray eyes. It was nice to know he was human enough to have tender spots.

A faun and a jotunn in elfland—add a sword and a lute, and you had the makings of a ballad; like "The Minstrel and the Knight," for instance. He hadn't sung that one since . . .

"If you don't mind?"

Jalon started. "Sorry, Rap. You said?"

Rap smiled fondly. "Is the sun bothering you, then?"

"No." Jalon looked upward. "Oh!" They sat in shadow. The

noon sun was almost vertical and the underside of Valdorian's first petal completely overhung them, a pellucid roof whose depths gleamed in indigo and parrot green.

"We're almost there, Jalon."

"Yes . . . I didn't hear what you asked, Rap."

"I would like to consult Sagorn, if you don't mind."

"Of course I don't," Jalon said, with an outward smile and an inward sigh. He had been so much looking forward to another visit to a sky tree, hopefully a much longer visit than those few hours he had enjoyed in Valdostor, years ago. Now he must go, and the next time he was called he might be a thousand leagues from Ilrane. Still, this mission of Rap's was important, and he must settle for these few idyllic days he had been granted. Without argument he called:

3

Sagorn screwed up his eyes against the pink glare, wincing as the seams of his breeches exploded and his toes were crushed—why did that moronic artist never learn to *think*? Why did he never consider that he was the smallest of the five of them, except for Thinal? Sagorn never called *Darad* without loosening his clothes first—not that he ever called Darad unless he had to. All it took was a little foresight. Knowing he might be returned in daylight, he always closed his eyes if he had to call a replacement when he was in a dark place, like *Dreadnought*'s fo'c's'le.

He risked a peek through slitted lids and saw the prognathous smile of the king of Krasnegar. After a moment he blinked his eyes fully open and strained awkwardly to remove the boots.

Rap said, "Morning, Doctor! Or possibly good afternoon."

"Have you tried lifting your shielding at all?"

"No!"

Mm? That dangerous? "You did not explain the hazard very clearly to Jalon, or if you did he didn't listen."

With the unconscious suppleness of the young, the faun rolled back to lean his elbows on the grass. "It's quite simple. Zinixo had melded with the Covin, or some of them, and was hunting for me in the ambience—me personally. It's almost impossible for a sorcerer to hide there."

"But you don't know if he is persisting in his endeavors?"

"And I don't intend to investigate. One clear glimpse and he'd have me."

"He can utilize this technique to locate any sorcerer known to him?"

"Undoubtedly. At these distances it requires enormous power, but he has that."

"So Witch Grunth and the two warlocks are likewise in danger?"

The faun pulled a face, which made him look even more grotesque than usual. "Yes. I just hope they were as lucky as I was, being within easy reach of shielding when it happened. *Making* a shield is a very conspicuous use of power."

"But shielding is not common as crabgrass, surely? We must assume that most or all of the wardens have now been apprehended and perverted." The enemy continued to grow stronger.

Rap nodded in glum silence. Sprawled back with his shirt off, he looked like a common quarry worker, but he was more than mere brawn. He had worked out the evil tidings and chosen not to burden Jalon with them.

"So why hasn't the Almighty—"

"Please, Doctor!"

"All right," Sagorn said sourly, thinking that the name seemed more appropriate all the time. "So why hasn't Zinixo tried this before? No, never mind." There were at least four possible reasons, and the point was moot anyway. "This occult cloak of yours—it is substantially identical to the immurement you once imposed on him?"

"You do like big words, don't you? Yes, it's the same, except that mine I put on myself, so I can take it off. When I shut him up, years ago, I was mightier than he was, so he couldn't break out of the shielding."

"You explained that adequately back in Hub. But he must be out of it now, if you saw him in the ambience?"

The faun scowled. "I saw only his eyes, but yes, it was him. You're right, of course."

The deduction was satisfyingly obvious and yet Rap had apparently not realized the terrifying corollary that could be drawn from it. Sagorn decided to save that insight for later.

He glanced around at the hollow. There was nothing to see except scrubby grass—which was why the spot had been selected, of course, for privacy. The underside of the sky tree loomed overhead like a ceiling. He would not have believed that any mineral growth could support its own weight over such a span, but he noted how the ribs were cantilevered to channel and direct the stress. The great vaulting swept downward steeply and obviously must reach ground level just over the rise. The road would end there.

When the next question did not come, he glanced down to meet the intent gaze of the recumbent faun. "You called me to ask how to get in, I presume?"

Rap nodded morosely. "I'm not even a beetle-sized sorcerer now, Doctor. I'm more of a mundane than you have ever known me—more of a mundane even than you. I need your insight." He plucked a blade of grass and tucked it in his mouth, playing yokel. His flattery would be more effective if it was sincere.

"Well, I cannot assess the occult defenses. We may even be within shielding here."

The faun shook his head. "I don't dare take the risk of trying to find out. We'll have to chance the sorcery—occult alarms may ignore mundane intruders, you agree? But I can't guess how to avoid even mundane alarms, or guards. I assume there will be guards, and locks, and so on. Valdorian has a resident warlock to defend it, but most of the trees must rely on ordinary precautions, so I expect it has those, also."

Logical! The former stableboy had always possessed a clearer mind than his appearance led one to expect, and he had learned the value of ratiocination from associating with Sagorn himself.

"The guards may have fled with the civilian population," Sagorn remarked cautiously. He stretched and yawned, only too aware that he had been roused from a deep sleep just a few minutes ago, in his time. "The fact that you have been able to approach so near without being observed would suggest that the entire tree is abandoned. Getting in may be both elementary and pointless."

"If the population has fled!" Rap said. "Perhaps all the people have taken refuge within the sky tree itself; in which case it will be packed like a herring barrel and we have no hope of entering unobserved. I do not wish to be thrown into an elvish jail, comfortable though they may be. Or a herring barrel," he added solemnly.

"Oh, come! Women and children and old folk? That would be carrying Suicidal Last Stand to extremes, even for elves."

The faun had not worked that one out yet. "Why are you so sure?" he asked, frowning to concede the point.

"Oh, I'm not certain! But we do not prognosticate mundane armies laying siege, and I'm sure the elves don't, either. If the Imperial legions were coming, yes, they would take refuge. The trees can hold out indefinitely, for they have their own sources of food and drink. But in sorcerous wars they are notoriously vulnerable. Jalon displayed unusual tact in not singing you any of the ballads about Valdobyt Prime."

"What of it?"

"It was the greatest of them all. Is-an-Ok overthrew it in the Second Dragon War, spreading destruction for leagues. That's why the outlying population has fled, of course. They don't know which way Valdorian will fall."

"This is the sort of intelligence I need," Rap said humbly. "This is why I asked for you. How do I go about getting in?"

He seemed gratifyingly sincere, but he was talking utter rubbish. Was he up to something?

From what he had said earlier, the war was to all intents over. The Covin had won—Zinixo had won; he had earned his self-bestowed honorific of the Almighty. As the brains of the Group, Sagorn had a duty to his associates to set strategy, and the only sane strategy now was a speedy withdrawal from King Rap and his lost cause; the farther the better. There was no point in continuing a fight once it became impossible.

He glanced around again. There was no point in his lingering here, either. The altitude was already oppressive and the shadow of the tree made the air uncomfortably cool on his bare skin. If he stood up, the remnants of Jalon's garment would fall off him, and he was much too old to go parading around in the nude. He must call one of his associates in his stead and depart. First, though, he should unravel the faun's childish scheme, whatever it was; and a wise man tested his hypotheses against all available evidence.

"Zinixo was a very powerful sorcerer in his own right, was he not? Even before he became warlock?"

"Extremely. A once-in-a-century sorcerer." Rap stuck out his jaw. "But I bested him!" His fists clenched, apparently of their own volition.

"Only just, as I recall your admitting once." Sagorn smiled encouragingly to hide his perennial irritation that the finest scholar in the Empire should have to elicit magic lore by interrogating a semiliterate laborer. "But when you gained a fifth word and were a demigod, then you had no trouble dealing with him?"

Rap sat up and removed the grass stalk from his mouth. "None whatsoever. Why?" he asked suspiciously.

"Give me the facts, please."

"The facts are obvious." He grimaced. "And just because I'm shielded doesn't mean I don't hurt like hell when I talk about them! Every word brings a new level of power. A demigod is as much above a sorcerer as a sorcerer is above a mage . . . or an adept above . . . a genius . . . I rolled out Zinixo like a wad of pastry and . . . thumped him back again."

He wiped his forehead. He was chalky pale and streaming sweat, as if seized of a very serious disease. Stubbornness had its uses sometimes. Still, there was only one question left now.

"And when you wrapped him up in the shielding spell, did you put all your demigod power into it, or only a fraction?"

"I gave it every glimmer I had!" Rap shouted. "I tied that little turd in a bag that I thought the Gods Themselves would not have gotten—" He stopped abruptly, gagging.

So there it was: hypothesis confirmed.

"You all right?" Sagorn inquired, not much interested in the reply. The faun groaned in agony, clutching his head.

Indeed, there it was! The cause was lost, and the only question now was how best Sagorn could extract himself and his associates from it—also how far and how fast. He had been called by Jalon; last time he had called Andor. That meant he now had a choice of Darad or Thinal.

Darad's animal mind would not comprehend the change in allegiance, and would not care if it could. That human polar bear had long ago decided he approved of Rap. That meant he gave him the unquestioning devotion of a dog.

Thinal, on the other hand, was even more protective of his own skin than his brother Andor. Being still young, Thinal would have a chance of outrunning King Rap in a fair, mundane foot race starting right here, and that might well be necessary. Thinal, despite his limitations, was still the best of the five of them when knives began to glint in the shadows. He had resources all his own. He could be relied upon to move himself as far from Valdorian as possible, as soon as possible, and as safely as possible, in effect taking the other four with him.

Thinal it would have to be.

"Why?" Rap moaned.

"Why what?" Sagorn thought back to the conversation.

"Why was I asking those questions? Merely to confirm the obvious, as you surmised."

But if it was all so obvious, then why had the big faun consulted him, in turn? Why had he asked Jalon to call Sagorn here at all?

Just to confirm the obvious, also?

What was he up to?

"What obvious?" Rap asked, still breathing hard from his ordeal.

"The obvious fact that you—er, we, I mean—have lost! If Zinixo is now free of the shielding you put upon him, then the Covin must have released him. Therefore the Covin has finally enlisted enough sorcerers to be collectively stronger than you were as a demigod. Add to that strength Zinixo himself now, plus the three wardens, and it is obvious that there is no force in the world that can ever hope to withstand the Alm . . . the dwarf."

Rap snorted. "You are too ready to grant him the wardens! I admit Grunth may have been vulnerable, out there in Dragon Reach. He may have nabbed Grunth. But Warlock Raspnex is probably down a mine somewhere in the Isdruthuds, and I would bet that Lith'rian has spent the last half year under a shielded bed in some safe hidey-hole."

Sagorn shrugged. "A warden or two here or there hardly matters. The odds were never auspicious. Now they are infinitesimal. I was never sanguine; now I see the cause as hopeless."

"I do not intend to give up!"

"I fail to see what you can do, even where you can start."

Rap had recovered his composure and was glowering. He jerked a thumb at the overweening mass of the sky tree. "I start by getting into Valdorian and finding Warlock Lith'rian."

"How?"

"That was what I called you to inquire! Thinal is the finest burglar in all Pandemia. If anyone can get me in there, he can. But the question is, how do I motivate him?"

Sagorn shook his head in disbelief. "The last time he was called, on the ship, you damned near throttled him! You expect him to cooperate with you now?"

The faun ran fingers through his gorse-bush hair. "I'm truly sorry about that! I will apologize sincerely. I will kiss his toes, if that will make him forgive me."

It would certainly impress the mean-minded little guttersnipe. Few things would please him more than having a king grovel in the dirt for him. Sagorn felt a twinge of worry—could he absolutely trust Thinal to abscond, as he had presumed? Thinal had a sneaking admiration for the stableboy who had stolen both sorcery and a kingdom.

There was another problem, too. Almost a year ago, Thinal had begun organizing an elaborate conspiracy to filch certain priceless artworks from the Abnila Museum in Hub and replace them with forgeries. Appalled by the risks involved, the rest of the Group had cooperated to keep Thinal out of harm's way. Unfortunately their abilities in that regard were limited by the terms of the sequential spell, as amended once by Rap himself, which required Thinal to exist for about a third of the time, so that he might catch up in age with the others. By the night of Emshandar's death, when this madcap venture had started, the little thief had been seriously behind in his quota of real life. The others had been experiencing difficulty in calling one another, instead of him.

Then Rap and Shandie had appeared and dragged them away adventuring. Thinal had regained some ground, but lately he had fallen behind again. At his last appearance, on *Dreadnought*, he had managed to call a replacement only with a great effort, when Rap had threatened him. That must have been eight or nine days ago. Now he would probably find it impossible. When Thinal arrived, Thinal would have to remain. He would be unusually vulnerable without his customary escape hatch available.

"What I was thinking of," Rap said hopefully, "is professional status. I mean, who in all history can ever have managed to break into a sky tree? I'm sure a warlock's enclave is packed with valuables, too. It would be a fabulous heist! Do you think an appeal to his vanity would have any success?"

Sagorn resisted a need to smile. The chances of Thinal falling for that argument were significantly less than zero, absolutely inconceivable. His entire mindset was against it. In fact, Sagorn himself had explained that aspect of Thinal's psychology to Rap twenty years ago, in Faerie, on the occasion of their third meeting. If the stablehand had forgotten it, then that was his lookout.

But had he forgotten it? Or was he playing a double game? If he truly wanted Thinal, then why had he not asked Jalon to call him directly?

Why had he summoned Sagorn at all?

Just to ask such footlingly stupid questions?

Ah! Of course!

Rap did not want Thinal! He wanted Darad!

Obviously Rap believed that he would have to fight his way into the sky tree and needed the warrior to assist him. But Jalon could not have called Darad for him, because Jalon had called Darad the last time. Jalon could have called only Thinal or Sagorn. Believing that Thinal would bolt in short order, the faun had asked for Sagorn instead. Now that Sagorn had demonstrated reluctance to cooperate further in the fruitless struggle against the Almighty, the faun was pretending to want Thinal in the expectation that Sagorn would seek to balk him by calling Darad instead. The yokel was trying to double-cross him!

Nicely tried, Master Rap, your Majesty!

"I do believe your reasoning will impress Thinal," Sagorn said blandly. "So perhaps we have completed our discussion and I should now call him for you?"

"I would be grateful," Rap said, completely straight-faced. "May the Good go with you, Doctor."

"Very well, then. Until we meet again!" With a quiet snigger to himself, dearly wishing he could be present to see the faun's chagrin when Darad failed to appear, Sagorn called:

4

Thinal coughed, rubbed his throat, and pouted reproachfully up at Rap, who sat on the grass at his side.

Rap twisted his big mouth in a rueful smile and whispered, "Hi!"

Thinal made a choking, rasping sound.

Rap said, "I'm sorry I was rough with you. I was under a lot of stress, but that was no excuse for losing my temper. It isn't like me and I'm ashamed of myself. Will you forgive me?"

Thinal swallowed a couple of times, making it seem harder than it really was. He'd known much worse. "Truly sorry? Gonna show me like you said?"

The king nodded solemnly. "If that's what you want. Will one on each foot do, or all ten?"

Oh, temptation! Knowing him, the big lout probably meant it. If he didn't—if he was just testin' to hear the answer—then he might turn Thinal inside out instead. He warn't in Darad's class for sheer size, but with his shirt off he showed meat only a jotunn would argue with.

"All ten—but I'll take a rain check."

"One rain check!" Rap said cautiously.

"Awright, ten toes, one rain check."

"It's a deal." Rap held out a hand to shake. He didn't do the jotunn thing and crush, either. Thinal found himself grinning a bit, in answer to the big guy's smile. He was dumb, of course—rustic, honest, hardworking—*yucch!*—dull, courageous ... *trustworthy!* In spite of all his faults, though, there was something likable about the faun. He'd sneaked his way from muckin' out stables to restin' his ass on a real Evil-take-it throne without changing his hat size. So what if he'd climbed the royal bed sheets to get there? Maybe queenie-doll had a thing about sailor arms, but there'd be lots of thick arms in a port like Krasnegar, and she'd gone for these arms. Small-time boy makes good! Up the workers!

Thinal reached down and pulled on his boots, Jalon's choice of boots. They were loose, but he could run in them if he had to. His breeches were a joke. The drawstring still held, but Sagorn had split all the seams. It was a pukey weird garment, but it wouldn't slow him, either, if he had to make a break. And then he remembered more of what the old man'd been thinkin'.

"You expectin' Darad?"

Rap looked blank and shook his head. "No, I asked for you."

"Sagorn thought you really wanted Darad."

Rap looked even blanker. "Don't have any bloodbaths planned for this afternoon, why'd I want Darad?" He scratched his head. "And if I'd wanted him why'd I've asked for you?"

"The old coot gets funny ideas sometimes."

The faun snorted. "His trouble, he's got more wits than he has brains to hold 'em. Never mind. Look, you know why I need you. The door into Valdorian is round that bend there. It may be guarded, in which case I'll just go up and tell the elves that the king of Krasnegar wishes to pay his respects to the warlock, all polite-like. It may be wide open and deserted. If it is, then I'll walk in and start climbing."

"Have a jolly time."

Rap chuckled, but his eyes were watching Thinal very carefully. "If it's locked and deserted, though, then I'm stumped. That's when I'll need your help."

Thinal shivered. "*Weed a warlock's sky tree?* Not Evilish likely! I learned my lesson there a long time ago, Rap! You know that!" He heard the shrillness in his voice and it scared him.

The faun nodded, looking puzzled. "You burgled a sorcerer's house. But that was a hundred years ago!"

"Hun'red thirty." Shriller.

"So? You needn't take anything, just open a door or two for me."

"No!" Thinal knew he was in a shaky sweat already.

Rap had seen that and was curious. He scratched his hair with both hands. "Sagorn told me once you still felt guilty about what happened that night, but it turned out well in the end, Thinal! The sequential spell wasn't a curse, it was a blessing. When I took it off you all wanted it back. You were the first to ask, too!"

"Old Sagorn doesn't know everything!"

"No? I thought you five shared memories?"

Pause.

"Well?" Rap prompted gently.

"Only of what happened after Orarinsagu put the spell on!" There! Now he'd dunnit. *Pothead!* Change the subject, talk about something else, anything else—

"Ah!" Rap studied Thinal for a moment and then shrugged. "None of my business."

"No, it ain't."

"A long time ago . . . ever talked about it with anyone?"

Thinal shivered and shook his head.

Rap lay back and rolled over to rest on his elbows. He poked a finger idly at the grass in front of him. "If you ever want to, any time . . . I mean, not necessarily now, but maybe some time. It can help to get things off one's chest, you know. What friends are for. I wouldn't repeat anything you told me. You know that."

"It doesn't matter," Thinal muttered. "Don't matter a spit if I told you or not, or if you told anyone."

The big faun just lay sprawled on the grass, not saying anything, not looking around. He pulled up a grass stalk and tucked it in his mouth.

"No reason why I shouldn't tell you," Thinal said uneasily. There was no reason why he should, either. "You wanna hear?"

"I'll listen if you wanna talk."

"Well, we was just a bunch of kids. I was the oldest, right? The leader." Sixteen. His teeth interrupted him, chattering wildly. He got them under control again. "Sagorn was the youngest. I put him in through a transom and he opened the door for the rest of us and we started lookin' around and then right away we saw that there were odd things in there and Andor said we oughta leave and I said awright and we headed for the door and then Orarinsagu appeared, all fire in the dark, and we couldn't move."

Green fire. He tucked his hands under his arms to stop them shaking. They were cold as a sexton's boots. He was hunched, his gut all knotted up. He'd never told anyone about this and the horrors that came after.

"Go on," Rap said to the grass. "You've started, so you'd better finish. You'll feel better when you get it over with."

Thinal sniffled. "You won't tell anyone?"

"Not a word, I promise."

"He said it was all my fault! He put the other four to sleep and . . . There was just me and him. And . . . And he played with me!" *Gods! I was only sixteen, Gods!* "I doan wanna talk about it. He broke me! Crawlin' on the floor . . . gibberin' and crawlin'. He played with me like a kid an'a beetle. I can't tell you what he did, what he made me do. I kept beggin' to die and . . . Gods' bollucks, I doan wanna talk about it!"

He hadn't been conscious of either of them moving, but Rap was sitting up and holding him, crushing him tight, hugging him like a baby, and he couldn't seem to stop talking, even while he was blubbering like a kid, weeping on Rap's shoulder, talking, talking, and sobbing, too.

"He said I was the criminal. He said the others were just my dupes. Said I owed him some fun, said I owed them, too, for leading them astray. Bugs an' bones an' things inside me. Toes 'stead of fingers. Things crawling inside me. I doan wanna talk about it!"

But he couldn't stop talking about it, not until he had detailed every agony and humiliation and terror of that night. Even things long forgotten came bubbling up and got spat out—everything. Only then did the pauses grow longer, the words scarcer, the weeping quieter. He fell silent. Rap maintained his rib-bending hug, and gradually the indignity of that position seeped through to Thinal.

"I wish you'd left the spell the way it was," he muttered hoarsely. "Living isn't what it's cracked up to be."

He tried to pull free, but was held as by hemp cables.

"Living is all there is!" the faun said softly in his ear. "Don't ever think about what follows. You listen to me now. Did you never wonder how Orarinsagu managed a matched set? You five are not just a random handful of men! Scholar, lover, warrior, artist, thief—did you never wonder how he was so lucky, to find one of each?"

Thinal pushed free. He blew his nose, wiped his fingers on the grass, and mumbled, "No."

"Sure?" Rap said. "Sure you never wondered? There was more to that sequential spell than I expected. Lots more. I only discovered it all when I took it apart. Orarinsagu robbed you, Thinal! Sagorn's brains, Andor's charm—all those great talents the others have—they come from you. Oh, the word of power helps, of course, but the basic talents are yours. The spell strips them from you and gives them to the others, so they get a double dose. You sure you never knew that?"

Thinal grunted.

"Mm," Rap said suspiciously. "You must have been quite a youngster with all that ability. In time you'd have been a great man. A great criminal, maybe, but certainly great. The sorcerer divided you up to make the matched set. Darad's thuggery is his own, but basically the others are all just shadows of what you might have been. Without what they steal from you, they'd only be shadows of what they are now."

"Why'd you put the spell back then?" Thinal mumbled.

Rap thumped a big hand on his shoulder and squeezed. "Because you asked me to. You, not them. It was your idea! Oh, partly because I thought it was too late to undo the damage; it would have ruined them to lose the use of your talents, and I didn't think those talents would do you any good then. You'd been a guttersnipe so long, I didn't think you'd ever learn to be anything else. I've often wondered if I made the right decision. And if you tell me that you didn't know where the others get their skills, then I'm going to feel an Evil of a lot worse about it."

"I . . . I maybe guessed some," Thinal admitted. He'd known. He could remember the sorcerer's exact words: *Your larceny I leave you, but all the rest is forfeit.* It wasn't fair, though. The others had grown since that night, gone on to manhood and achievement, and he'd shrunk, gotten less. He'd been a leader before that night and since then he'd been nothing.

"So why'd you ask me to put the spell back?" Rap asked.

Thinal wiped his nose and eyes with the back of his arm. God of Sewage! Why'd he gone and spouted all that crap to the faun? What must he be thinking? "Doan wanna talk about it anymore."

"Then don't," the faun said cheerfully. "And I'm not surprised you don't want to help me break into the sky tree! I understand. I don't hold it against you."

Sniff! "Rap, it's hopeless! The dwarf's beaten you. He's won. Sagorn knows. Give up, Rap!"

The faun doubled over, putting his arms on his knees and his head on his arms. He looked all weary and beat, but when he spoke he didn't sound that way. "I can't, Thinal! You can quit, if you like. Everyone else can quit, but not me. He'll hunt me down somehow. He'll go after Inos and the children. The God told me I must lose one of my children, but They didn't say which one. And They didn't say it would be *only* one. I don't care how hopeless the cause is, I must soldier on."

Silence.

Crazy, stubborn faun!

Thinal snuffled, "Whatcha gonna do? Whatcha wan' me t'do?"

Rap looked up with a smile sad as death. "I'll go and take a look. If there's no one there, I'll come back. We'll talk some more. If I don't come back in a little while . . . You get your ass out of here, okay?"

Thinal nodded and sniffed again. "I'll wait."

Rap thumped him on the shoulder and stood up. "Thanks, old buddy! You must have been quite a kid."

He stepped back onto the road and walked away, not looking around.

The wind blew cold through the gloomy gully. Thinal sat and shivered, hugging himself. Bare grass and bare road, and that awful roof up above, threatening to fall on him all the time. He was being a fool. He ought to make tracks back down the road, real smartish. Lotsa empty houses—even Jalon had managed to break into those. In a few more days Thinal'd be able to call one of the others, probably Andor. Andor'd know which way the sea was, and he could head there and talk his way onto a boat.

The war was lost. The dwarf had won. That was no skin off

Thinal—no skin off any of 'em. The five'd get by whether four wardens ruled or just one Almighty.

Waiting was hell, but he'd told Rap he'd wait. How long? What was the guy doing, all this time?

And if Rap did come back, and asked him, what was he going to do? Crib a warlock's shop?

He stood up and relieved himself—second time—and moved a few steps and sat down again. Right away he wanted to pee again.

Why'd he gone and blabbed all that stuff about Orarinsagu to Rap? What must Rap think of him, a grown man blubbering?

What *was* the guy doing?

Thinal wasn't going to go and see.

Rap must be dead. He wasn't going to come back.

Thinal was going away.

Now!

Well, very soon.

He sort-of tried to call Andor, and knew it wouldn't work. He wouldn't be able to call any of the others for days yet. Curse Rap and his meddling around with the spell! They'd never had this trouble before he changed it.

He was a city boy. All this grass-and-sky-tree crud was not his gruel. He'd never had much truck with elves—no elf in the Impire ever owned anything worth lifting.

Rap wasn't coming back. He would count up to a hundred and then go.

Behind him, someone coughed politely.

Thinal's heart flew away and the rest of him twisted around so hard he near broke his back.

Half a dozen elves stood in a semicircle. They all wore silver chain mail and they all had drawn bows trained on him. If he made one false move, he'd be a human forest.

He called—*Darad! Darad!*

Nothing happened.

So Thinal did what he always did in moments of stress. He screamed in terror and peed in his pants.

5

The elves closed in on their prisoner, babbling in high-pitched voices with an accent he could barely decipher.

Two were men, four women. They were all about his size,

yet they seemed like adolescents and he had seen enough of the underlife of cities for that illusion to frighten him even more. Their golden faces were contemptuous, with big opal eyes flickering in impossible shades. Their silver-link tunics were prettied by bright-hued belts and baldrics and lanyards; their half-boots and helmets were equally gaudy. Their legs and arms were bare, except for dainty greaves and vambraces. Even their weapons might have been chosen for appearance, but he did not doubt that they were real and deadly.

They twittered a few commands at him, ignoring his pleas and questions except to tell him to be silent. They tied his hands behind his back with a silken cord. They put a noose of the same cord around his neck. Then they formed up and began trotting along the road to the tree, cheerfully singing a fast-paced, complex round.

Thinal followed. He had no choice, for the tether ran easily through a silver ring and would choke him if he allowed it to tighten. They ran him on a very long leash, so he must trail far behind them. Somehow that position felt designed to humiliate, as if he were something unpleasant they did not want to be associated with. Trotting along with his soiled rags flapping against his thighs, he preferred not to think about that. If he tried to catch up, then he would step on the cord and strangle himself. He feared that they would just drag him if he fell down.

Guard and captive rounded the bend and the entrance to Valdorian was straight ahead. The trunk itself was still some distance away, a rugged cliff meeting the ground in an untidy, unelvish jumble of broken rock, stretching off on either hand until it disappeared in the far distance, and *leaning outward*, rising to meet the roof. The road ended at a freestanding spiral staircase of red and white polished stone. The guards continued on up the steps without pause, although they stopped their singing. There was no sign of Rap, or anyone else at all.

The stair soared in an impossible spiral to vanish into an aperture in the roof. Halfway up, Thinal was gasping for breath and shaking sweat out of his eyes. He had no time to look around, for he must concentrate on the curve of the snaky cord rising steadily ahead of him. He could tell that he was falling behind when the cord no longer touched the steps. Relentlessly it grew straighter, then darkness closed in as the stairs entered a shaft. He ran harder and harder, yet slower and slower, lungs bursting, legs sheer blades of fire. He could no longer see the tether, but he felt it tighten around his neck—at first with the gentle touch of a teasing lover, then sternly, urgently, murderously; briefly it took some of his weight to haul him up the steps, until he choked and fell, battering himself on the hard edges.

Voices warbled above him like furious birds. He could see nothing. The rope jerked repeatedly, tugging at him until he managed to scramble to his feet, his throat feeling as if it had been beaten with a hammer. He resisted the pull, holding himself to a walk. The noose yanked harder and he fell again, hurting himself in a whole new set of places. Again he rose and again he refused to run; with much angry chirping, his captors acquiesced to his slower pace.

He hoped they knew that he wasn't being stubborn, that they would not be angry with a poor weakling who could run no more. He was beyond speaking, even had they seemed inclined to listen. He plodded grimly upward around the spiral.

Gradually light filtered down the tunnel, and it emerged onto the first layer of the tree. He was vaguely aware of mossy greenery and shrubs, of dripping sounds and a scent of flowers. The ground rose gently from the cliff until blue sky showed over treetops far away. High above those the sloping underside of the next petal roofed the glade like a low cloud, but it was shiny crystal, not dark as the outside layer had been. Light reflected in a million spars of color on ribs and facets.

He had neither time nor desire to admire. His guards hurried him along a brief road, to yet another stair, this one narrower and carved into the side of the trunk. They began to climb again. How far were they going? Valdorian was two leagues high, higher by far than any mountain. He would freeze at the top of it—there would be no air to breathe!

And where was Rap?

The stair turned into the rock and again there was dark. Despite their mail, the elves moved in silence. He could not tell how far ahead of him they were except by the tightness of his noose. He fell only once on that stair, but he cracked his head hard enough to see a million stars.

Back into daylight they came again, into a dim ferny forest, and at last his captors took a break—Thinal just crumpled to the moss at the roadside. A small stream of water cascaded down the cliff, ending in a free-falling jet. One by one the elves stepped under it to drink and be soaked. They jabbered and laughed among themselves, ignoring their prisoner. When they had all finished, they called Thinal over. He heaved himself to his feet and lurched forward; he sank on his knees in the pool, lifted his face. The cold wetness ran over him and down his throat like pure bliss. It was the best thing he could ever remember.

His guards had been joined by another group—three male, three female. For a moment they all chattered together, apparently discussing a cluster of red birds singing in a nearby copse. Then the original six departed back the way they had come.

"Up!" cried a boyish voice.

Thinal leaned back until his groping fingers found the tether under him. He wrapped it in his bound hands as well as he could. When the jerk came it did not reach his neck, and the guards looked back in surprise and annoyance.

He heaved himself unsteadily to his feet, his legs wobbling with fatigue. He could not tell which of the six was the leader, so he spoke to all of them.

"Where are you taking me? Where is my friend?"

The smallest stepped forward, holding up a very shiny, very skinny, very slim dagger. Her eyes twinkled amber and pale green in the dimness, but there was no smile on her face.

"Let go that rope, imp!" she said in a piping treble.

Thinal had never known himself to defy anyone before—not since that night in Orarinsagu's house, anyway—and he knew it could not be courage that made him defiant now. It must just be sheer terror.

"Not until you answer my questions!" His voice was as shrill as the elf's.

The guards all burst into twittering laughter, like birds. "If you do not let go of that rope," the smallest one said, "we shall take it off your neck and put it around your ankles. Then we shall make better time."

Thinal released the rope.

He lost track of the layers. Staircases and ramps went by in an ordeal of mindless trudging. He knew only the cramps and stitches and the bruises he gained in his falls. When he was granted a rest he fell to the ground and usually passed out. He was aware of being given water, and even food, which he could not eat. He was offered liniment for his legs; he knew vaguely that someone massaged it in for him, and more than once; his feet were tended and clad in better shoes.

Higher and higher he went, step after step after step, every one a calculated agony.

He was passed from squad to squad up the tree. The soldiers were not consciously cruel, as goblins would have been. They were not malicious like imps, or even callous like jotnar. They sympathized with his suffering, in their alien way, although they could not help but regard an imp within a sky tree as a pollution. They pitied him after their fashion, but they had been given the task of conducting this prisoner up this tree and elves were fanatical about performing duties.

Somewhere his bonds were removed, but he was never unguarded and he had no hope of escape. He obeyed and endured in sick despair.

He lost track of the days, for after a few hours' rest he would be taken on again, in daylight or by the amber glow of lanterns. As the temperature fell, his escort provided him with warmer clothes, fine silks and light woolens. His lungs strained in the thinning air.

Mostly the way clung close to the central trunk and often followed shafts cut within it. At times, though, it veered away from the cliff, and then he traveled by spidery ladder and perilously narrow catwalks with the petal landscape spread out below him like a map: lakes and forests and fields, tiny picture-book cottages nestling among the meadows. His captors kept careful watch over him at those times, but they need not have worried. Thinal had no fear of heights. Heights were the only thing he did not fear.

Days came and went—weeks, perhaps—and the ordeal grew no easier.

He gathered from some chance remark that Rap was traveling ahead of him. Thinal had never been to Krasnegar, but the others all had, and he remembered the stairs. Rap would be managing better.

He became aware that the soldiers were the only inhabitants, that the tree had been evacuated, like the surrounding countryside.

Time and again he tried calling the others—Darad, Jalon, Andor, or even old Sagorn. The spell never worked for him. He had to put in more living, even if he wore out his heart in doing so. The elves were determined that there be one of two possible outcomes—either he would arrive at his destination or he would die. He could barely remember a time when he had not been climbing stairs.

6

He was in a big, bright hall, whose walls and pillars of intricately carved cedar were barely visible through clouds of scented steam. Someone had just told him to strip. He fumbled helplessly with buttons, then golden hands came to help him, moving swiftly, urgently—two elves undressing him. He did not know what sex they were and did not care. As his pants fell around his ankles, a gentle push sent him toppling backward into a pool of scalding hot water. When he surfaced, spluttering and choking, two soaked male elves were having hysterics on the brink, holding each other up in mutual convulsions of mirth.

After that they spared no more time for jollity. They jumped right in beside him, scrubbed him, shampooed him, ducked him, and then hauled him out to dry and clothe him. He could not stand unsupported, so they fetched a chair.

"Whasall the burnin' hurry?" he muttered, and one of them took that opportunity to shove a foamy toothbrush in his mouth and scour his teeth.

"The High War Chief awaits!" exclaimed the other, lathering Thinal's face for shaving.

He relaxed. He had been afraid it might be the warlock. He dozed off during the shave.

Clad in fine wool garments of silver and burgundy, he was hastened out to a chill morning. The low sun blinded him, blazing in over pine trees, reflecting also from a sky of carved diamond far above, glittering on the frosty grass beside the path and the film of ice on the lake. Steadied by hands on his arms, he stumbled along obediently. The air was much too thin to breathe. He was surrounded by elves, but none of them wore mail or helmets; sunlight flamed on the spun gold of their hair and the myriad colors of their garb.

Then he registered a stranger, a head that stood clear of all the others and was topped by riotous brown thatch. Rap! He was clad in white and gray, the same gray as his eyes, a whale among a school of goldfish—Thinal wondered whose idea that outfit had been. In a moment, Rap glanced around and saw him. His ugly faun face lit up like the sunlight.

What? Pleasure? Relief? In his fog of fatigue and hopelessness, Thinal wrestled with the amazing thought that the king of Krasnegar seemed glad to see him. Had even been *worried*, maybe? It was an incredible notion, a mind-crippling astonishment, a sensation so unfamiliar that his mind could not grasp it. He knew what the other four thought of him. He knew who his friends were back in Hub, and they were no more trustworthy than he was; any of them would sell him for a copper groat. Somebody *cared*?

No, that was ridiculous. It must have been a trick of the light.

He stumbled up the steps into the great wooden hall that stood on the lake shore, barely noticing the ornate carvings, the bronze-studded doors, the ankle-deep rugs within. Then his gaze was caught by a figurine on an onyx table. It was Kerithian workmanship, undoubtedly, but of a style he had never seen before—a horse rising on its hind legs, spreading butterfly wings. The porcelain was so fine that it was transparent and the colors richer than rubies. He had not known that the merfolk crafted for elvish tastes, but of course why shouldn't they? And the thought of the price that piece would fetch from the fences of Grunge Street made his head ache.

Then he had gone by that wonder and was being hurried past a portrait of some elvish beauty, unquestionably the work of the legendary Puin'lyn. No one else had ever mastered her technique of setting gemstones in crystal. With breathtaking artistry, the mosaic face smiled back at him mysteriously, as if challenging him to assess her worth. God of Greed! Of course he'd have to melt it down and job the gems by the cupful, but he'd still pocket enough to buy a palace.

More, and more! Everywhere his eyes turned they found wonders and treasure. The itch in his hands was driving him crazy. Jalon's head would explode if he ever saw this, and his own was like to. Thinal gave no spit for beauty; it was the value that stunned him. He had not known there was so much wealth in the world. This room would buy the Impire and leave enough change for a couple of Zarks.

The sky tree's leaves were narrow, up here near the summit. High and vast and airy, the hall was set on the very brink, its great windows overlooking a mauve sky. All of Pandemia lay below, curving away into a vague fog where the horizon should be. Thinal did not notice any of that. He stood in a fog of gold and riches.

The solitary chair on the dais before those windows had its back to the chamber. Thinal had been placed beside Rap, flanked by a small group of elves. Two were token soldiers, the rest civilians. Everyone was waiting respectfully for that chair to do something—everyone except Thinal. He was estimating tapestry by the square cubit. He was assessing the diamond and crystal chandeliers, the sculptures and paintings. He was wondering if he could sidle closer to some of the jewel-encrusted bric-a-brac on the side tables. It was torment.

The chair pivoted slowly to face the assembly. A youth in white velvet lounged upon the carmine satin of its cushions.

Even Thinal noticed the drama of that quiet move. A quiver of warning raced down his spine. He had seen that lad somewhere before. No, Jalon had. Jalon's recall of events was usually a blur, but his visual memories were acute as razors.

A waiter? No, a dishwasher.

How could that be? Why should even Jalon remember a juvenile dishwasher of no exceptional beauty, at least by elvish standards? Thinal's knees buckled. That long-ago flunky had turned out to be *Warlock Lith'rian himself*!

Fortunately everyone else was bowing, and he converted his involuntary curtsey into a bow more or less like theirs. When he straightened up, he pushed his knees hard together and tucked his sweating hands out of sight behind him.

Rap spoke first. Surprised, Thinal glanced up. He saw no smile to accompany the words, but there must be a smile intended, or they would be outrageous.

"I am Rap, son of Grossnuk. I come in peace. Your foes are mine."

Surely no elf in all history had ever heard that greeting spoken in his sky tree, but the warlock's expression did not change by an eyelash, for there was no expression on his face at all. If he made a signal, it was not mundane. Two young pages hurried forward, one from either side, each bearing a silver tray. Warlock and king were tendered goblets.

Lith'rian took his with graceful golden fingers and raised it in salutation. "Safe haven and good sport," he said softly. It was, of course, the correct response, but he did not drink. The opal eyes shimmered to new shades. "Chieftain Rap, you are welcome to our hearth and spring. We offer what we have, and may the Good be prospered by your coming. May your stay be joyful and your leaving long delayed."

Rap glanced down, met Thinal's worried stare, and flickered him a wink. Probably he was taking a moment to nudge his memory, but when he replied to the warlock he did not stumble: "May the Good grow within your house and the Evil diminish. May your men be strong and your women fertile, your children wax in beauty and your elders in wisdom. May your crops flourish, your herds increase, and all your arrows fly true."

The wink had produced a very odd sensation in Thinal's throat. It had said, of course, that Rap remembered who had taught him the faunish salutation, and where, in days that were gone. But it might have said more than that—he would have to consider . . . Why had the warlock not touched crystal to lip yet? He wasn't waiting on *Thinal* to do something, was he? Panic!

No—Rap seemed puzzled, also. "Your Omnipotence, I confess I am ignorant of the correct elvish greeting."

The youth sprawled in the chair made an inscrutable gesture with his free hand. "Strangers within sky trees are so rare that we have never developed one. In most places it is customary for the guest to drink first."

As the men drank, Thinal felt a strange rustling among the closepacked elves at his back, almost as if they were commenting on the score so far. Suddenly he realized that they might all be sorcerers, Lith'rian's votaries. He suppressed a wail, shivering all the way to his toes.

The pages were departing with the goblets.

"Your Omnipotence," Rap said, "may I have the honor—"

Opal eyes turned on Thinal in gleams of red and blue. "I don't care *who* he is. I can see *what* he is. Your choice of companion is insulting."

"You invited him, not I," Rap said softly. "He would depart gladly, by your leave, I am sure."

"With full pockets, no doubt."

The faun smiled faintly. "I would recommend a body search at the door, yes. He has involuntary reflexes in such matters."

The warlock showed no signs of appreciating the humor. "Minstrel Jalon would be a welcome alternative."

He was speaking to Thinal. Thinal opened his mouth and made a croaking noise, like a squeaky wagon wheel.

Rap glanced at him quizzically and then spoke for him. "My young friend is temporarily rendered speechless by the grandeur of your collection. I am sure he appreciates the incongruity of his presence as much as you do, but he is presently unable to call any of his associates in his stead."

A tiny crease between the elf's golden brows boded earth-quake and cataclysm. "Very well, your *Majesty*," Lith'rian said icily. "He may remain for now. Tell us why you disguise yourself as a mundane. Do you seek to guard yourself against us?"

Rap bowed again in his usual clumsy fashion. "No, your Omnipotence. I seek to hide from the dwarf."

The elf curled his golden lip. "Then you came to the wrong place. This hall is shielded, of course, but the mole watches it day and night. He knows who enters and who departs." The voice was soft, but it filled the breathless hall.

Rap frowned, as if doubting. "Why, then, does he not act?"

"Surely you are not so enfeebled as that, Sorcerer? Can you not smell the blood upon Midsummer?"

"Our time is short, I agree."

"Short for what? You come to join us in our final stand against the self-styled Almighty?"

Rap folded his arms and paused a moment before replying, studying the warlock. "If you plan to resist him, yes. Then I am your man. If you merely plan to die in a romantic, histor-ical catastrophe, I will have no part of such buffoonery."

The warlock frowned. The warden of the south was dis-pleased. The world chilled. He was only a slim youth in white, with the usual opal eyes and golden hair, but there was terrible danger in his frown. None of the other elves had spo-ken a word yet. Thinal eased closer to Rap's comforting bulk.

"Indeed?" Lith'rian sneered. "Two weeks ago that unla-mented idiot, my former Brother East, attempted to raise a banner of resistance. He named you his leader, in fact. He quoted a deal of drivel about reforming the protocol and do-mesticating sorcery—unprecedented populist idealistic clap-trap, which he attributed to you. He uttered a pathetic rallying call and nobody rallied. He was struck down in the gutter, alone and unaided."

Muscles tensed under the faun's fresh-shaven cheeks. "The time was not auspicious. Had we risen then, the Covin in op-posing us would have released the dragons. We could not risk such a disaster."

Lith'rian's eyes flamed. "And what makes you think the mole will not call out the dragons again?"

Rap drew an audible breath. "We have taken steps to see that this will not occur."

"What?" The monosyllable cracked through the hall like a

whip. Everyone jumped. Thinal very nearly . . . but regained control in time.

"With respect, your Omnipotence," Rap said loudly, "when the Covin subverted the dragons from your legitimate control, we construed that to mean that you had abdicated your prerogative as warden of the south. Consequently, certain of my followers—"

"*We?*" the warlock roared. "Who is *We?*"

"Witch Grunth and—"

"Grunth has been coerced into the Covin! Her presence within the meld has been established beyond doubt."

Rap winced. "I am indeed sorry to hear that. Nevertheless, there were others whom Zinixo would not know. I am confident that they will have taken the necessary steps."

Lith'rian sprang up from his chair. His face had flushed to a deep bronze; he was shaking with fury.

"What *steps?*"

"To destroy the dragons if they rise again."

"*Idiots!*" The warlock blazed with fury. The sorcerer onlookers cried out and staggered back in unison. Thinal uttered a shriek of terror and instinctively called:

7

Darad whirled around before the sound of ripping cloth had ended. He snatched the sword from the closer soldier's scabbard and cut his throat with it on the way by. Scarlet blood shot out in a very satisfying spray. Everyone else was still frozen. He leaped past Rap, who was just starting to open his mouth, and swung the sword overhand, slamming it down on the other soldier's helmet. Good dwarvish steel, it split prettyboy's head apart to the neck. A gorgeous fountain of gore and brains erupted over the onlookers. That took care of the professionals, pansies though they had undoubtedly been.

Furniture crashed over, clattering and tinkling. Screaming began.

The kid in the chair was the key—hold a blade at his throat and none of the little darlings would as much as raise a finger. Darad chose a girl at random and grabbed her by the throat to use as a shield. Holding her out at arm's length before him, he rushed for the warlock. She was a pretty little thing, except for the way her eyes bulged. Just on principle, he thrust the sword into her belly on the way and spilled her guts. Conscious of the few fluttering rags still trailing from his nudity, he thought what a waste of a nice rape that was. He leaped for the edge of the platform.

In midjump, he froze. His foot made contact, but his muscles turned to mush. The girl shot from his grasp with a scream and he toppled over on the kid in the red chair. By rights they should have all gone down in a heap, but somehow he seemed to slide off something invisible. He rolled helplessly, slithered off the platform, and ended lying on his back on the floor, completely limp.

Sorcery! Evil-begotten sorcery! *"Rap!"* he bellowed—or tried to. Not a sound emerged.

God of Slaughter! He strained mightily and could not move a finger. The hall was full of shouting. It should be full of screaming. Rap was a sorcerer—why didn't he do something? Rap! Still no sound. All he could see was a big candleholder hanging from the ceiling right above him, a clutter of glass. Then he discovered that his eyes would move.

Sorcery! The yellow-bellies had mended the first soldier. The kid was pale as tin, his helmet off and his too-pretty curls all awry, but he was standing and obviously alive, in spite of the blood all over him. The other one would not be put back together so easily. Not likely! Most of the rabble had gore on them, and they were all twittering at once.

He turned his eyes the other way, to see if the girl had been mended, also. She had. She was standing up, and the warlock kid had an arm around her. Fornication! Only one? He'd taken a blade to a herd of elves and gotten only one of them? That was disgusting! That was humiliating! Convulsed with fury and frustration, he tried again to break free of the sorcery, but again to no avail.

Rap appeared right above him, haggard with shock.

Darad tried to grin. Once Rap got this evilish spell off of him, he'd kill 'em all. He thought of the hall smeared with blood and littered with parts of elves, and it was a thrilling idea. But he could not speak to Rap.

"Oh, Thinal, Thinal!" Rap muttered. "Why did you have to do that?"

Darad flicked his eyes the other way. The kid in white was standing on the edge of the platform, glaring down at him.

"This is intolerable!" the elf squeaked. "One of my guards slain in my own hall? The man must die!"

Have a fit, maggot!

Rap sighed. "I cannot deny that he deserves to."

Rap! Rap, his old friend? He couldn't mean that!

"He is a mad beast," Rap continued. "But if you execute him, you kill his associates, also, by default. He cannot call them back if he is dead. If he calls another first, then he himself is beyond the reach of justice, even your justice."

Darad chortled silently. That's tellin 'em, Boss!

"You underestimate me!" the elf snarled. "That spell is an abomination! It bears your hand. You are equally to blame, faun!"

Aha! Now Rap would settle the pretties' hash.

Pale-faced, Rap ran a hand through his hair. "I am not guiltless, I admit. I did not invent the spell, though. It dates back more than a century. The five of them had aided me, I was in their debt. I released them, but then they asked me to replace the sorcery. I fear I was wrong to do so."

"You were certainly wrong to include this vermin. Without the ability to disappear at will, he would have been apprehended and destroyed years ago!"

Rap nodded sadly. "But I was in his debt, also. He had saved my life—how could I desert him? I hoped, I suppose, that the others might restrain him."

"They did not do so now!" the warlock snarled. "He will be thrown to the winds."

The gaggle of pretties all cheered, and Darad could not even grind his teeth at them. He strained uselessly.

"You had best do it soon, Omnipotence," shrilled one, "or I fear he will burst his heart with anger." The little yellow-asses all laughed. Only Rap stared down sorrowfully at Darad.

He would kill them all. He would cut their guts out and watch them die. He would rape the women and then slit them open.

"And the one who called him is equally to blame!"

"No!" Rap said sharply. "He did not plan this. You startled him, and he invoked the spell without thinking."

"He should have thought!"

The elves twittered loudly in agreement, but Rap held up a hand.

"When you dismantle that spell, your Omnipotence, observe carefully how it is constructed. See what it does to Thinal. When a man is startled, he reaches for the courage within him, correct?"

"So?" the warlock asked warily.

Rap nudged Darad with a foot. "There is Thinal's courage."
The warlock shrugged. "I will look."

Rap! What sort of a shipmate are you? Get this triple-accursed spell off me and let me fight!

"You brought this evil upon us, faun!" the warlock said grimly.

Good! If Rap was threatened he would need Darad, and then he would do something. Rap was a sorcerer, too.

"Not I! Thinal was brought in by your orders."

"Ha! You told us he could not call a replacement."

"I'm sure he could not, not consciously. But you terrified him. A man should not be punished for an act of desperation. The fault, again, was yours."

The elf snarled. "Did I not fancy having Minstrel Jalon's art to enrich our vigil here, I would have this brute dealt with as he is, and let the others fall with him. But I can think of no reason to desire your presence, faun. You will go now—freely, or by force."

Rap set his big jotunn jaw. Here it came! Good old Rap!

But no—"I had hoped to remind you of past glories, Warlock. Pandemia has known no greater heroes than those of Ilrane. Zuik'stor and your own forefathers, Danna'rian and—"

The elf reddened. "Silence! We need no halfbreeds here to lecture us on honor."

"Indeed, I think you do!" Rap shouted. "Not two years ago, seven thousand elves prepared to lay down their lives on Nefer Moor to protest the Imperial invasion. And now you will just give in to a dwarf? A dwarf? I wonder the trees themselves do not fall down from shame!"

"The cause is hopeless!" The little elf could roar like a bull when he wanted. That had to be sorcery. "Your followers are a tiny, scattered rabble. The Covin outnumbers them manyfold. There is no power in all Pandemia can stop him now. Thus we shall—"

"There may be!" The faun's voice cut through the outburst like a razor.

The elf stopped. That had shaken him! Didn't want to show it, but it had.

"Where?" The hall fell silent.

Rap hauled up his sleeve to show his tattoo. "Thume. There is a spell of inattention upon the Accursed Land." Sounds of protest swelled and Rap raised his voice. "You know such an enchantment could not have prevailed unattended since the

War of the Five Warlocks. What power maintains, it, your Omnipotence?"

"Rubbish! Utter nonsense! There is nothing in Thume!"

The onlookers twittered in agreement.

"There must be something in Thume!" Rap said stubbornly.

"No! I will not believe it!"

"I believe it."

"Then you may go and seek this chimera for yourself!" the warlock yelled. "Vice-armiger Fial'rian—remove this mongrel from our presence and evict him!"

Rap seemed to sway backward. "Wait!" he shouted, and straightened. "You said the Covin is watching this place. Do you throw your guests to their enemies? Is this what elves understand by hospitality, Omnipotence?"

Glaring, the elf teetered on the edge of his platform. "Very well. Armiger, convene enough power to evict our unwelcome guest unseen."

Again Rap shouted, "Wait! I may thus escape notice leaving, but I shall be observed arriving at wherever you send me."

The warlock laughed, high-pitched. "I fancy not! We shall send you like a parcel to the destination named on your label. If there is a conjuration upon the place as you claim, then all will be well with you. Begone!"

Rap spun around and marched away without a word.

Rap! Rap was leaving him alone? What sort of a shipmate deserted a comrade? Just because he'd swatted a lousy, yellowassed elf? What did one puky elf matter? He'd killed hundreds of better men than that in his time.

The warlock scowled down at Darad. "Now," he said, "you."

Word in Elfyn-land:

> But, Thomas, ye maun haud your tongue,
> Whatever ye may hear or see;
> For speak ye word in Elfyn-land,
> Ye'll ne'er win back to your ain countrie.

> Traditional: *Thomas the Rhymer*

⚜ SIX ⚜

When days were long

1

While her husband and minstrel Jalon had been strolling the sunlit roads of Ilrane, headed for the sky tree of Valdorian, Queen Inosolan of Krasnegar had been leading a donkey through the blighted hills of Guwush. The weather had been inclement, the landscape drear, the experience odious. As she had remarked more than once to his Imperial Majesty Emshandar V, the thing that bothered her most was his constant hysterical good humor. Shandie, who tended to brood, would then smile thinly and explain that it wasn't the music that upset him, it was the rich food.

They took turns trudging along in the mud at the donkey's cheek strap, while the other sat on the bench, gathering bruises at every pothole. The donkey steadfastly refused to move at all unless it was led.

"Frankly," Inos remarked one mosquito-infested evening when they had both chosen to walk, "you disappoint me, Emshandar. For a man whose ancestors have been imperors for millennia, your appearance is sadly lacking in the poise and polish I should have expected."

"Unfortunately," the imperor said, "I take after my maternal grandfather the centurion. He was extremely fortunate to escape being branded a common felon in his youth. But you, Queen Inosolan? Your forebears have ruled your peanut-sized realm for centuries. They are mere upstarts compared to my family, of course, but I could have hoped for a little more regality in your mien."

"Alas! Like you, I take after the wrong side of the family."

"Which side is that?"

"Thane Kalkor."

"Oh. Pillaging and rape?"

"Pillaging certainly. I find rape too tiring."

Some humor! The strain was telling on both of them, Inos thought.

The road was a quagmire; the countryside looked as if it had been sacked by three or four armies in quick succession—broken fences, weed-filled fields, dilapidated hovels sunk in mud. The inhabitants were gnomes, though, and probably liked it that way.

Shandie had named the spavined, ill-natured donkey Zinixo, perhaps because of its drab gray color. It was unworthy of the honor. The cart was ancient, noisy, ramshackle. It bounced endlessly and could be detected downwind for leagues. From the look of the sky, there would be more rain before sunset.

The imperor of Pandemia was gaunt, unkempt, and filthy. Inos knew she looked no better. Because of the cargo they carried, they dared not stop at the official post inns. They had slept under trees or in barns for several nights now, and their money was running out. A solid square meal had begun to loom even larger in her imagination than a hot tub and clean clothes.

Stagecoaches sprayed past them several times a day. Squads of Imperial cavalry would gallop by without even a curious glance. This area was more or less law-abiding, officially classed as "pacified." Inos' term was "crushed," and although she rarely taxed the imperor on the subject, she was sure that he now agreed with her.

A long silence ended when she asked, "Tell me again how many more days to Randport."

The muddy gargoyle beside her shrugged. "Two. Perhaps three at this pace."

"Will he live that long?"

"I think so." He sighed. "We have done all we can, Inos."

"The Gods award no badges for effort!"

Shandie did not answer.

Days and weeks were creeping by and the rebels' battle against the Covin seemed doomed to perish of sheer futility.

All they had achieved in Guwush was a half promise of assistance from an unknown number of gnomes—hardly an accomplishment to illuminate the history books of future generations. Meanwhile the Almighty must be steadily tightening his grasp upon the world.

They crested a slight rise. Surprisingly, the road snaked out ahead of them in almost a straight line, sloping down to a blighted plain. Normally it twisted like a knotted snake.

"Solitary rider?" she said.

Shandie peered, screwing up his eyes. "Apparently. Why is that of interest?"

"Nothing. Just unusual." Despite the relative peace prevailing in this sector of the Guwush theater, a few gnomish terrorists still roamed the woods. Inos and Shandie had not been molested—at times they had almost wished that they would be, in the hope that they could thereby pass word of their plight back to Oshpoo—but danger had been part of their troubles. A solitary traveler was a rare sight. Even Imperial couriers were escorted. Of more significance to Inos, though, was the fragile hope of rescue she had nursed for days. If help was to come, it must come in the form of a solitary rider.

She told herself not to build castles on the clouds. A few minutes later, though, she felt a faint pulse of excitement as the lone horseman—or, please Gods, horsewoman—drew closer.

"Fair hair?"

"Oh, come! You can't possibly make that out at this distance."

"I think I can! Even djinns compliment me upon my eyesight. You forget I am half jotunn."

Shandie peered curiously at her around the donkey's ears. "They both look the same to me. Which one is the jotunn one?"

That was better! She rewarded him with a smile. "The greener one."

"They are equally beautiful," he said solemnly, and returned to watching the lone rider. "Yes, you're right. Fair hair. And a woman! Praise to the Gods!"

Dwarves could not ride horses. Goblins would be apprehended on sight. Of the five fellow outlaws due to rendezvous with them at Randport, only one could possibly come in search of them, to find out why they had been delayed.

And Jarga it must be, for she was kicking her mount to a gallop. Big and raw-boned, leather britches caked in red clay, she was an ungainly rider. She could never have been beautiful, even in her youth, but she had the strength and competence of a jotunn sailor. She was the most welcome sight Inos had seen in months. Inos knew hundreds of her kind in Krasnegar, and knew their worth.

Flaxen hair streaming, Jarga arrived in a shower of mud. Her attempt to leap from the saddle almost pitched her to the ground. Horse and donkey flashed teeth and temper at each other and were brought under control.

By that time Jarga had hauled back the leather cover on the cart to peer at the unconscious dwarf on his straw. His cheeks were hollowed under the iron-gray beard. His breathing was shallow, and yet dangerously labored.

She looked up, face flushed by the wind—and perhaps by anger. "How long has he been like this?"

"Five days," Inos said.

"It happened on the coach, the morning we left Yugg," Shandie explained. "He just keeled over on the bench. He was at the front, I was at the back ... We don't know if he was struck down by the Covin, somehow, or if he just had a stroke, or ..." Realizing that further detail was unnecessary, he fell silent, waiting hopefully.

"He is old," Inos added. "And he wouldn't dare use sorcery to keep himself hale." That, also, need not be said. Nor was there need to explain why the conspirators had been reduced to buying a cart and donkey to transport the warlock. Adventuring in real life was never as glamorous as it was depicted in the romances Kadie had enjoyed so much. An invalid of any description might carry infection, and a man in a very deep coma was a disgusting, smelly companion. Inns and coaches would not accept such a patron, so imperor and queen had taken on the unpleasant chore of transporting and tending him. Inos had insisted that her experience of raising babies qualified her to cope; Shandie that he had nursed wounded in field hospitals. They had taken turns.

Apart from keeping him clean and warm, though, they had achieved very little. They had managed to force no nourishment into the sick man, and not much water. Every day he was weaker. That a powerful sorcerer could be brought to such a pass was a sad commentary on the current state of the world.

Jarga straightened up bleakly and replaced the cover. "It is sorcery, minor sorcery—a sleep spell, is all."

Shandie bellowed, *"What!"* and turned a look of fury toward Inos. "Those accursed gnomes have betrayed us!"

"I think not." Jarga glanced around the landscape. There were no houses in sight, and no gnomes, either, in these daylight hours. There was no life to be seen, other than a few pathetic sheep grazing the wet grass of the fields.

"I am a sorcerer, not a medic," the sailor said in her harsh Nordland voice. She hesitated. "Hub is noisy now, but I have detected no sorcery close at hand for days. That is both good and bad. Even a little power may betray us."

Shandie nodded. "You must be the judge. But I think our friend is worth a risk or two."

Jarga smiled gratefully. The concern on her leathery face was oddly touching, and also puzzling. Any hint of tears in her eyes must certainly be a trick of their extreme paleness, closer to the color of winter fog than to blue. A jotunn sailor, even a female jotunn sailor, was no more sentimental than a goblin, and the idea of one feeling attachment to an elderly dwarf was absurd. As well match a walrus and camel.

But Jarga did look worried. "It is dangerous for a man of his years to lie flat for so long. There is fluid in his lungs, but surely a couple of hours more can do no great harm. A league or so back I detected shielding in a gully."

"Excellent!" Shandie said. "Let us take him there and see what you can do."

"Would my horse pull your cart faster, do you think?"

"Not without a horse collar." Inos was surprised how much the sorceress's arrival had eased her mind already. In this bleak, alien world of the millennium, she felt vulnerable without sorcery close at hand. Although neither Jarga nor Raspnex dared exercise their powers very often, they could observe and report on what was going on, and just to have them around was reassuring.

"Would you like to ride awhile, my lady?"

"Not in this dress." Inos winked at the sailor. "Surely it would be more fitting for us humble womenfolk to walk and let our lord take the horse?"

"When you adopt that tone," Shandie said, "I feel a need for a cohort or two to defend me."

"Cavalry, I suppose? And Jarga and I would still walk."

"Undoubtedly. Allow me to demonstrate equitation." Shandie sprang nimbly into the saddle.

A moment later he dismounted. As he stooped to shorten

the stirrup leathers, Inos and Jarga shared smiles of satisfaction at the noteworthy redness of his ears.

A donkey might scorn an imperor. It could even ignore a queen regnant, but a jotunn armed with a rail was a serious matter. Soon the little beast was displaying more enthusiasm for work than it ever had previously, and the cart jangled forward at a pace it had not approached before, with both women riding on the bench. The lessons had been effective, but brutal. Inos probably felt much worse than Zinixo did.

"What did you mean when you said 'Hub is noisy'?"

"Sorcery," the sailor said. "We think the Covin is dismantling all the shielding. That makes waves."

It also made sense. Zinixo—the two-legged Zinixo—was notoriously nervy. Shielding anywhere might conceal enemies. When he had removed all of it, there would be nowhere in the world for opponents to hide.

Jarga was a woman of few words. She addressed most of them to the donkey, periodically wielding her club. She would brook no slacking.

Inos wondered again what feelings there could possibly be between a middle-aged jotunn and an elderly dwarf. Even for friendship they had nothing in common except the cause of the counterrevolution. They would make an absurd-looking couple, for Jarga was almost twice his height. Inos had assumed that the warlock, in adopting the principles of Rap's new protocol, had released all his votaries. She had never asked him, though, and she very much doubted that Shandie had, for the crusty old dwarf was not the sort of man to tolerate impertinent questions. Of course there was no way to find out from Jarga. If she was still bound to the warlock, she would lie about it.

Jarga's concern for the old man might stem from nothing more than friendship—Inos herself was anxious for him to be restored to health—but it might have darker roots. Votarism was rank evil, a slavery of the soul. Rap's hatred of it was much in character and nothing new. If Raspnex used his powers to gain sexual satisfaction, he would merely have been following an ancient tradition. If he did, Inos decided, he would not impose his wishes by force, he would make his victim willing. He would make her love him. That was well within the powers of a sorcerer, and only marginally less evil than outright rape. On the other hand, the grumpy old scoundrel did seem to have mellowed in the past few months. What had caused that?

They had all changed. Minutes ago, Shandie had praised Inos' eyes in an easy, offhand compliment that he would never have managed when she first met him. It had been a meaningless pleasantry, a social grace like a smile, valued only for its own sake. The Shandie of last winter would not have seen the need for such flippancy, would not have attempted it if he had, and would certainly have stammered and blushed if he had tried.

And she? She was not conscious of change in herself, and yet there must be some. She had lost her husband, her kingdom, her children, and had no hope of regaining any of them unless Rap could somehow overthrow the Covin. Such burdens must change anyone.

"Faster!" Jarga roared, bringing her rail down hard on the donkey's back. It brayed and lurched wearily back into a canter.

About to utter a protest, Inos stopped herself just in time. Gods! she thought. Am I learning patience?

Or am I just growing old?

The gully was so gentle that it would have escaped attention had there not been a stream and a ford. Trees closed in on either hand. It was a shaded, gloomy spot, and rain had begun to fall again.

"Here?" Inos said as the cart rattled to a halt. "Where?"

"All around," Jarga said, dropping the reins. "The road runs right through it, or I wouldn't have noticed, because I wasn't consciously farseeing."

"Why would anyone ever put shielding here?"

"Ambush," Shandie said. He was standing by the horse, letting it drink. He frowned at the murky tangle of undergrowth. "How far back does it run?"

"Quite a way. Would hold a cohort or two."

"Let's hope it isn't occupied at the moment."

"It isn't," the sorceress said. She had twisted around to haul the cover away from Raspnex.

"How long?" he asked in his familiar deep growl.

Inos gasped with delight, seeing his eyes open. He was upside down from her viewpoint on the driving bench, but he looked better already.

"Five days, they say." Jarga was smiling happily at the results of her sorcery. She very rarely smiled.

Sorcerers did not need long convalescence. Raspnex sat up and already his color was returning, changing from clay buff to his normal gray sandstone hue. Glowering under craggy brows, he flickered his pebble eyes from Inos to Shandie, who had come to stand by the side of the cart to grin.

"I owe you my thanks," he muttered. Dwarves were as effusively demonstrative as glaciers.

"You owe us an explanation!" Shandie said. "Who did it?"

"I did. It was the first thing that came into my head."

The imperor shot Inos a glance of exasperation and then tried again. "Why did you do it, then?"

The warlock heaved himself to his feet. Even standing, he was barely taller than the two women sitting on the bench, but the cart rocked under his weight. "My nephew tried something new. He came looking for me in the ambience."

"Zinixo himself?" Shandie said, startled.

"In a meld of the Covin. It was a personal thing, though. I recognized him—heard his voice, you could say. I had only seconds before he located me. I had to disappear fast, so I slugged myself." His ugly face twisted in pain. "Even that was a risk. Sorry."

How often did one hear a dwarf apologize?

"Any risk was better than having you perverted! What do we do now? How can you leave this shielding without being caught? Unconscious again?"

Rain pattered faster in puddles below and trailing branches overhead.

"He can shield himself," Inos said. "Mundane disguise."

The warlock bared his teeth. "You're very free with advice today, aren't you?"

"It would be torture!" Jarga roared. "He would be blind and deaf and crippled."

"He'll get used to it! My husband hid his sorcery that way for years."

Now the jotunn looked even more dangerous than the dwarf. "And he will be conspicuous! We have an advantage in that the enemy's loyalty spells show up. A body shielding will show, also. It is unthinkable!"

"No, Jargie," Raspnex growled. "She's right, as usual."

Jargie?

Shandie had been scratching his black-stubbled chin. "If the

Almighty can pull this personal-tracking trick, then why hasn't he done so before?"

"Because it requires one-on-one contact, and normally that could be dangerous if . . ." Raspnex winced.

"If the one you seek is stronger," the jotunn said. "It is much like hand-to-hand combat. But of course the Almighty wields the power of the Covin, so he can be in no real danger." Pain wrenched her face, also.

"It will work on any sorcerer?" Shandie asked grimly.

"Anyone known to him personally." She took a deep breath. "And I suppose any sorcerer known personally to any member of the Covin. It is a serious development!"

"Powers preserve us," Shandie muttered. He glanced apprehensively at Inos.

So did the warlock and the sorceress.

Rap? Oh, Rap!

"Why has he—Zinixo—not done this before?"

"Perhaps because of Olybino," Raspnex said. "It happened the next day, remember? When he saw that the opposition could not save Olybino, he decided he had the edge."

"What odds would satisfy Zinixo?" she demanded, her voice louder than she had intended.

The warlock grunted. "About a thousand to one, maybe. Come on, let's be on our way." He sat down on the straw and hauled the wagon cover over his shoulders to deflect the downpour.

"Wait!" The world had darkened for Inos. If even Zinixo was satisfied with his advantage, then it must be overwhelming. "He may have caught Rap the same way?"

Shandie was avoiding her eye. Had Rap been quick enough to react as Raspnex had done, and hide in unconsciousness? Even if he had, did he have comrades available to tend him, or was he lying helpless in some forgotten jungle? For six days she had believed that Rap was alive, and now that hope had been stolen away again.

"He may have captured Rap," Jarga said brusquely. "This is not a game of *thali*, this is war. Sitting here wailing won't solve anything." She jingled the reins and screamed abuse at the donkey.

Inos grabbed at the side as the cart lurched into motion. "Oh, that's easy enough for you to say! I'm concerned about the man I love!"

"So am I," said a silent voice in her ear, Jarga's voice.

"Huh?"

"Move, you spavined, illegitimate latrine washing! *He has been a sorcerer for a very long time, and this privation will distress him greatly.*"

Inos looked blankly at the sailor, who was apparently engrossed in her bullying of the weary donkey.

"Yes, I love him," the voice whispered again. *"Sometimes I think he loves me. We do not talk of it. He took pleasure of me once, long ago, but only once. After that we never dared."*

"Oh!" What to say, with the warlock himself so close? "Love does complicate life sometimes."

"Faster, you barnacled, brick-brained son of a pig! *Better off without it. Forget what I just said. I was joking. Sorcerers can never love other sorcerers, only mundanes—you should know that better than any, Queen Inosolan.*"

2

Randport was a sleepy but prosperous outpost of Impire, a naval base, and, also, a favorite retirement town for officers and civil servants. Its buildings, climate, and nightlife were agreed to be harmonious, monotonous, and picturesque, the order of application depending on the speaker. A few elves down on their luck lived there, prostituting their art to the imps' notions of culture; gnomes were allowed to enter after dark to remove the garbage; all other races were *strongly discouraged.* To the military, that meant *evicted on sight.* Inos saw nothing of Randport proper and had no wish to.

Just over the headland lay Old Town, a major port crushed between a cliff and the battlements of the naval base. The army preferred to stay out of Old Town, even in daylight, and imps were a minority there. It claimed to be the only city in Pandemia where jotnar lived in peace together. Indeed there was surprisingly little fighting in the jotunn quarter, but the jotunn quarter adjoined the djinn quarter, the boundary being marked by a line of fresh bloodstains.

To a jotunn, a djinn was an irresistible challenge. To a djinn a jotunn was a barbarian maniac best knifed quickly. A jotunn might concede djinns to be the second tallest race in the world and the second best fighters, but he would insist that they cheated. What the djinns said about the jotnar has no easy translation. Trolls, who were larger than either, worked as porters and stayed out of the fighting. Imps ran the businesses, both honest and dishonest, with djinns close behind. Fauns were rare, but not unknown. Procurers would promise genuine mermaids. Dwarves were quite common, because of the nearby lead and silver mines, and they traveled in packs. Gnomes were everywhere out of the light, and no elf would ever dream of setting foot in Randport Old Town.

Inos had been hoping that a glimpse of the sea would cheer her up, but Randport depressed her. Its residents were too alien, too numerous, and too surly. The familiar tang of weed and fish made her homesick. For the first time in her life, she was happy to board a ship.

Northern Vengeance was berthed in a remote corner of the crowded harbor. Throughout her long career as the river trader *Rosebud* the little ketch had been based in Urgaxox, but she seemed to have survived her ocean voyage around Guwush unscathed. She still bore her original name on her stem—as a *nom de guerre*, of course.

Wirax and Frazkr were standing watch on deck when the land party trooped down the ladder from the quay. Even allowing for dwarvish solemnity, their greetings were subdued and curt. They scowled mightily as they observed Raspnex's shielding and realized that the most powerful sorcerer of the group had been nullified. He marched past them without a word and disappeared belowdecks. As Jarga had foreseen, he was chafing within his occult imprisonment. He had hardly spoken for two days.

"I think we must be about to hold a council," Shandie said. "After you, ma'am."

Inos clambered down the companionway and went into the dingy, cramped cabin. Raspnex was already sitting at the far end, his head barely visible above the tabletop. Without speaking, she sat down on the bench and hotched herself along it until she was sitting beside him. Then she watched the others enter and repeat the process.

No dwarf could ever appear frail, but old Wirax was silver-haired and stooped. Frazkr was younger, soft-spoken and at times almost polite. He could never go so far as to be cheerful or optimistic, though. At least those two were predictably stolid and durable.

The continuing ordeal was starting to tell on the goblins. They were farther from home than any goblins had ever been, stranded in a culture utterly foreign to their simple forest upbringing. The sea voyage would have been a trial in itself, and in port they must stay hidden at all times. Moreover, they must know of the disaster that had befallen their king and comrades. No official news of the great occult battles at Bandor had yet reached the mundane population, although rumors were rife in the alleys of Old Town, but sorcerers knew of it.

Pool Leaper was as jumpy as a cricket; his face had taken on an unhealthy turquoise tinge. He was quite young, around twenty, and only a mage, not a full sorcerer. Once or twice in the past Inos had detected a genuine sense of humor in Pool Leaper, a hint that someday his people might outgrow their barbarism and develop a civilization based on something more rewarding than torture. He was not jesting now.

Moon Baiter was considerably older. At first sight Inos thought he was in better shape, but then she noticed that he had chewed his fingernails to the quick, so that they had bled. Both men must be mourning brothers and friends lost to the Almighty's sorcery; they must be wondering how their homeland fared. If they could ever find their ways back to the taiga, they would encounter a blighted society of women and children with few males and no babies for many years to come.

Jarga and Shandie arrived, also, to complete the company. Jarga sat, having trouble fitting her knees under the table, as always. Shandie leaned back against the door, folding his arms. For a moment there was glum silence.

Two mundanes—three in fact, for the crippled Raspnex must now be counted as a mundane—four sorcerers, and a young mage. Against them, the all-powerful Covin. They could not be sure that they had any allies left, anywhere in the world.

The crusade was leaving its mark on Shandie, also. He was gaunt now instead of slim; his dark hair hung lankly, often flopping over his face like a youth's. He seemed to burn too bright, a lantern in winter's blast, his eyes shining with a dangerous zeal. For a mundane to take charge at a conference of sorcerers was paradoxical. He did not even ask the others' consent, but then leadership was his business.

"First the bad news," he said. "Warlock?"

Gruffly Raspnex explained what had happened.

Shandie barely let him finish. "The good news is that we may have found some sympathizers. We talked with Oshpoo. He promised to tell his sorcerers—and he may have a lot more than we expected—but he would make no commitment beyond that."

He was being modest, Inos thought, making no mention of his own promises to the rebels. But that was Shandie. He would want to talk about the future, not the past. He surprised her.

"The winter before last," he said quietly, "I cornered the Ilranian army on Nefer Moor. I outmarched them, outthought them, outmaneuvered them. I brought them to bay and laid my blade at their throats. I had all seven thousand of them totally at my mercy. Then I offered them the most generous terms I could conceive of, in direct breach of my orders. My grandfather would have called my actions treason.

"They turned me down. They said they would rather die where they stood than accept their lives at the cost of their principles. I cursed them for a gang of illogical nitwits. I derided their infantile elvish fancies.

"And now I understand. Now I sympathize."

His voice grew even softer. "Now the tables have been turned. My enemy has harried me from my capital to Julgistro, from Julgistro to Dwanish, from Dwanish to the shores of the Morning Sea. Beyond that water stands my deadliest mundane foe, the caliph. Soon, very soon, I must turn at bay, for I have nowhere left to run. My strongest ally, Warlock Raspnex, has been effectively removed from the battle, at least for now. Our chosen leader, King Rap of Krasnegar, may very well have suffered the same fate or worse; Witch Grunth and Warlock Lith'rian likewise. My wife and child may be taken—I have no way of knowing. Every day the enemy grows stronger and we grow weaker. We have no intelligence, no reserves, and no viable plan."

He unfolded his arms and slammed a fist against the door. Inos jumped.

"And I will be damned to the Evil for Eternity if I will give up!" He glared bleakly around the faces, seeking agreement or argument.

"How's a man to get any sleep if you make so much noise?" The satirical reply came from the youngest of them all, Pool Leaper.

It was the most ungoblinish remark imaginable. Shandie blinked, and small patches on his cheekbones flushed against his pallor. Then he saw that everyone else was smiling or chuckling.

He relaxed, and laughed. "Well spoken, lad. I got carried away. I take it you agree with me, then?"

"I got nothing to lose, Imperor." The goblin showed his fangs in a nervy grin.

"We all have something to lose," Inos said. "We can lose our freedom to be ourselves. I would rather die than be a tool of Zinixo's evil."

Nobody disagreed.

Shandie nodded, satisfied. "Then where do we go from here?"

"Longday," old Wirax said in his raspy voice. "The Evil comes at midsummer."

"You, too? Raspnex said the same."

Everyone looked to the warlock, who shrugged angrily. He was a blind, deaf sorcerer, who could add nothing new.

Wirax scratched his white beard. "Two weeks until Longday. We have two weeks."

"Can you tell how it comes?" the imperor asked. "In what form? Or where?"

"No. It's just everywhere."

"Can you see beyond it, then? Can you say if the Evil prevails or is thrown back?"

The old man shook his head. Shandie interrogated the other sorcerers with his eyes and they all shook their heads—Jarga, Moon Baiter, Frazkr.

"So what do we do in the meantime? Do we go fishing? Do we cross to Zark and throw ourselves on the minuscule mercy of the caliph? Or do we try to throw in our lot with Oshpoo and his rebels?"

That Shandie would even utter such words was incredible—he certainly could not mean them. Inos opened her mouth and he caught her eye, stopping her words unspoken.

"I know what you're thinking," Raspnex growled, "and what the woman was about to say—that we should take the chance to sail over to the Accursed Land and investigate Thume."

The other sorcerers looked shocked, amused, bewildered.

"I reacted that way, too," he said, "when she first suggested it. Now I think she may just have a point. Something Evilish odd's going on over there, and has been going on for a very long time."

"A thousand years?" scoffed another dwarvish voice.

"There is nothing going on in Thume!" Jarga protested from the doorway.

"That's what you're meant to think."

"Tell us about this Accursed Land," Moon Baiter said. "We have no history of it in the woods."

So Shandie began to describe the War of the Five Warlocks and Inos remained silent. Obviously he was steering the meeting the way he wanted. Obviously *Northern Vengeance* would set course for Thume, simply because there was nowhere else to go. However thin the hope of finding a miracle in Thume, it was the only hope they had left, the only port in the storm.

It was Inos' idea, she should be pleased.

The Morning Sea was a notoriously fickle stretch of water and Inos was the world's poorest sailor. Yet far worse than the prospect of seasickness was the memory of the last time she had visited Thume. She had come within minutes of being raped by four men. She and Aunt Kade and Azak had almost died there. One thing she could not expect to find in Thume was a welcome.

3

"Do you believe in destiny?" Eshiala asked with a gleam in her eye.

"Of course. Why?" Ylo already had an arm around her, so he just squeezed it a little tighter. He carried a blanket over the other.

"Mm. Saw something. Come this way."

The wood was eerily still in summer heat, as if all the birds and insects were sleeping or had flown away, the afternoon heavy with mingled scents of wild flowers. Leaving the path, Eshiala began pushing through the trailing branches and tall weeds. Ylo was forced to release her and follow behind, watching the play of sunlight and shadow on her blouse. She had pinned up her hair again with the tortoiseshell combs he had given her. A few fragments of dead leaves were caught in it, but he was not about to tell her so.

"Where in the world are you going, wench?" Twigs swung back at his eyes. "Ouch!"

"Through here. I thought I saw—yes. See? Yellow iris!"

"Very lovely. You want to pick some?"

"Ylo!" she said in mocking reproach. "You're not concentrating on important matters!"

Trouble is, he was. He was drowsy and content from making love, and yet his previous worries were returning stronger than ever from their temporary banishment. He ought to be sharing them with her, but he hated to spoil the romantic perfection of this wonderful summer day. He ought to be saddling the horses and leading his love and her child out of the path of danger posthaste. He had already wasted half the afternoon and should not . . . No, those hours had emphatically not been wasted. They had been two of the most precious hours of his life. Perhaps the knowledge that they were foolish hours, stolen hours, had made them all the sweeter.

He put his arm around her again and glanced around the glade of golden iris with a smile only skin deep. "Are you implying that I can't tell an iris from a daffodil?"

"Oh, no, darling, never! But perhaps the preflecting pool was a little vague on details? And you must admit that you might have been distracted by the rest of the vision you saw."

"Distracted? I was driven insane. I still am insane."

"Good! Spread out the blanket then."

He laughed. "Eshiala, Love of my Life, I will do anything for you—anything you wish, anything mortal man can do. But what you are asking for right now is a miracle." *In fact, I thought the last time was a miracle.* He tried to kiss her, and she slipped away.

"A destiny." She took the blanket and spread it out, ruthlessly crushing irises. "Naked, I believe you said? Naked, on a blanket, smiling?"

Gods! "Listen," he said. "Nettles . . ." he said. "Er, wasps?"

She was unbuttoning her blouse.

"Maya will be awake now," he protested. "She will be upset to find you not there."

"It's a cruel world," Eshiala said airily, stepping out of her skirt. "Mistress Ingipune promised to feed her candy cakes. I have been waiting for months for some serious lessons in outdoor lovemaking and that callous little brat has perversely frustrated me every time."

"Lessons? Serious? You're an instant expert! And you do not think your lovely daughter is a brat. And . . ."

His lady tossed away the skirt and began removing lesser garments. Gods! He moaned. No, it wasn't possible, not so soon.

"Now," Eshiala said. "How do I look?"

"Perfect! But . . ."

But perfect. The proud line of her breasts, slender limbs, the sweeping curves of hip and belly—never had the Gods made such a woman. Not a mole, not a freckle.

"How was my hair in the vision?" Without waiting for a reply, she pulled out combs she had so painstakingly replaced not twenty minutes before. She shook loose a torrent of black tresses. Dark eyes gleamed at him, appraising his reaction as he stood and gaped.

Drooled. Time was short if they were to make their escape today. He hadn't told her the news. How could he tell her now?

"There!" She sank down and stretched out on the blanket. "What posture, my lord? On one elbow, like this? On my back, like this? Legs together? Apart? How wide a smile? Come here, you big lummox."

The vision!

He dropped to his knees at her side, and his hand moved unbidden to caress her. Soldiers had been asking questions in the village . . .

"The man is half-witted," Eshiala muttered, and raised a hand to unbutton his shirt.

His hand stroked her arm, her shoulder. Her breast. Firm, heavy, smooth. Oh, God of Love! He had expected to be safe, here in the east, but now he had learned that the XIVth Legion had been withdrawn from Qoble and the XIIth was everywhere, even in Angot, so he dare not go there now.

With no recollection of moving, he was kneeling over her, tongue stroking nipple. When had that happened?

He could no longer trust their hostess, Mistress Ingipune, because a reward had been posted. Neighbors would talk in a little place like this. Eshiala had pulled off his shirt and was struggling one-handed with his belt buckle.

They must saddle up and leave, and head up into the foothills . . .

"Do take off those stupid breeches," Eshiala said crossly. "You will manage much better without them."

Shock! He released her breast and ran his hand over the firm cream-smoothness of her belly. Then he turned his head to stare into her eyes incredulously. He made a gibbering noise.

A marvel of dimples appeared beside her mouth. "I was wondering when you were going to notice. I understood you were an expert on the feminine body." Despite the banter, there was concern in the deep blackness of her eyes.

"Oh, my beloved!" he said, choking. "My dove! My darling! My love!"

He might have kept maundering like that for hours, had she not said, "Then you're pleased?"

"Pleased?" He grabbed her face with both hands and kissed her wildly. His child! She was going to give him a child!

What legions? There were hours of daylight left yet. His child, too.

Somewhat later he paused breathlessly. "It still isn't possible!"

Her hand slid around from his back and down to more intimate places. She knew all the tricks now. "Of course it is, see? And we are not leaving here until you do it."

If she had loved Shandie like this, she would never have been his.

But she was his, all his. And it was possible. His love, his child. Anything was possible, even miracles.

4

Before *Northern Vengeance* cleared the bar at Randport, Inos arranged a spare sail on the forward deck as a makeshift tent. She had furnished it with a water bottle and a straw-filled mattress and prepared to make the best of things. The spot lacked privacy, but it did have plenty of fresh air, and the rail was within reach when she needed it. Saying he preferred to suffer out of sight, Shandie had gone below.

Two days later she was still in her tent, ignoring the voices and activities of the others. The sun was hot and the wind fair. Gulls crying, ropes creaking, the ketch rose and fell over the green hills of ocean. Perhaps the swell was barely visible to the eye, but it felt like mountains to Inos. Until she arrived at Thume she would be useless; she could do nothing but endure life and curse the impish side of her inheritance. Her jotunn ancestors might be ashamed of her, but the other half would all sympathize. Shandie would be in no better condition than she was.

Dwarves did not admit to feeling seasick and apparently the trait was a personal thing in goblins, for Pool Leaper had been felled, but Moon Baiter had not.

When she could ignore the rolling, yawing, and pitching, her thoughts were mostly of Rap and the children. She had no hope now of ever being reunited with any of them. She could not even believe that she would ever know what had happened to them, far away in this cruel world, and that ignorance proclaimed her failure like a blast of trumpets. Kadie dead; Rap dead or taken; Holi and Eva perhaps destroyed in a ruin of all Krasnegar. Only Gath, she thought, might still have a chance. She had been furious and bitter when he slipped his leash and took off adventuring on his own. Now she was profoundly grateful that he had. At least he was not here with her, sailing to the Accursed Land.

Perhaps Gath would survive somehow in Nordland, provided he was not betrayed to Thane Drakkor—or betrayed himself to Thane Drakkor. *Was* Gath aware of the blood feud? She thought so, but could not be sure. And what sort of a life was she wishing on him there? At least he would never become a bloody-handed raider like his grandfather Grossnuk. She had shared Rap's doubts that Gath would ever become assertive enough even to rule Krasnegar—Gath as a raider was an idea that would never float. At best he would be a lowly churl, a slave. At worst . . .

"My lady!" That was Jarga's voice.

Inos opened one bleary eye. As long as she kept her head still, she might be able to hold a conversation. "Mmph?"

The sorceress dropped to one knee. "We have problems."

"My husband always says that every problem is an opportunity."

The big sailor rarely appreciated humor. "First, the Covin is scanning the area. We are agreed—Wirax, Frazkr, and Pool Leaper."

Inos opened both eyes. "Searching for whom?"

"No one special, we think. Just watching, and especially watching for magic. We can sense the attention. I dare not try to ease your suffering." The jotunn's face was against the sky, so that her expression was not very clear. Sunlight and blond hair painted golden glory around her head.

" 'Sawright," Inos murmured, and closed her eyes again. Let the Covin hunt all it wanted!

"The second thing is, we have company, much company."

Seasickness took a step backward. Eyes flicked open again.

Jarga's worried face swam into focus. "They may wish only to establish who we are." She neither looked nor sounded convinced. "You will have to stand up, my lady."

Before Inos could explain how utterly impossible that was, cold logic stilled her tongue. Dwarves at sea would be as com-

monplace as whales in a desert; goblins even more so. Her
blond hair would look jotunnish at a distance, and a ship of
this size would have a better chance of passing a hasty inspection if it had two hands on deck instead of only one. What
could they do about her green face, though?

"Help me up," she said.

Truly the Gods had cursed her.

It had been common knowledge for years that the caliph
would launch a war against the Impire as soon as he had
united all Zark under his banner. Even back in Urgaxox, the
markets had known of his sudden interest in chartering shipping. The imposter imperor had withdrawn forces from the
eastern shores, giving him his chance. So now the war had
come, and Inos had fallen right into it. All around her, the sea
was spiked with sails. Few of them resembled Imperial vessels.
Most were Zarkian dhows, lateen sails slanted like the wings
of gulls. This could only be the caliph's navy, on its way to
Ollion and invasion.

"How could you let this happen!" she croaked.

Jarga shrugged impassively. "They have our wind. They are
faster."

"I apologize. My remark was unjust."

"Come aft, my lady."

As Inos reeled aft behind the sailor, she saw that some attempt had been made to give *Northern Vengeance* the looks of
an ordinary fishing vessel. Very smelly nets were heaped
around the deck, and every cask and barrel aboard was in evidence. But where was the mythical crew? At least half a
dozen flaxen-haired giants were required immediately.

Frazkr yielded the wheel to Jarga and hurried below, leaving
the two women alone. The panes of the cabin skylight were
open. No question that the rest of the motley crew would be
standing directly under it, attending very carefully to whatever
transpired on deck.

The vessel bearing down on them was many times their size,
and resplendent. Her two triangular sails curved to hold the
wind like a lover's hands, white against a sapphire sky. The
high stern gleamed in gold and many colors, while the long
pointed bow cut through the blue-green sea with flashes of
foam. She had a bone in her teeth and she was closing relentlessly on the tiny ketch. She represented danger, but she was
a magnificent sight.

All the other vessels in view must be her allies. There was nowhere to hide, for the coast was a vague brown line dirtying the southern horizon. Above it and very close to invisible, distant peaks peered through the haze, pale ghosts of mountains. Inos knew that range of old, although she had never seen its northern limits before. Those were the Progistes, and west of them lay Thume.

She swallowed the vile taste in her mouth. "The Covin is still watching?"

"Yes, my lady." Clutching the wheel in her big hands, Jarga eyed the dhow appraisingly.

It was obvious why the Covin would be watching: The caliph's fleet had put to sea. Zinixo would want to know where it was headed, and what sorcery might be aiding it.

"Then we have a choice," Inos said bitterly. "We can escape the djinns at the cost of falling to the Almighty. Or you and I can look forward to a career in a seraglio. Which fate do you choose, Jarga?"

"I will take the djinns."

"I suppose I will, too."

The dhow was only a few cable lengths away now, but her bowsprit was still aimed at the ketch. Amid the elaborate carvings and gilding on her prow the name *Arakkaran* was inscribed in angular Zarkian lettering. Still she came! Did she not flaunt her finery like a vain harlot, she might be suspected of planning to ram. But she was beautiful.

Inos realized with a shock that her nausea had gone. Could that be from fear? Or was it from anger? For the first time in her life, her jotunn half had prevailed at sea. Yes it was anger, but not directed at the dhow.

How *dare* the Gods play such tricks upon her? Rap, were he here, would make one of his blasphemous remarks about Their taste in irony, and for once she would agree with it. Nineteen years ago he had rescued her from vile captivity in Arakkaran—well, almost rescued her—and now the Gods were spitefully throwing her back in again. She was still east of the mountains, technically in Zarkian waters. Women in Zark had all the rights of dairy cattle.

What of her male companions? What cruel end awaited them? Raspnex and the other dwarves might choose death over the Covin, but the goblins had no reason to do so. If they loosed their powers to escape the djinns, Zinixo would pounce on all of them.

Suddenly Jarga spun the wheel. *Northern Vengeance* came about, spilling wind from her sails. In a few minutes she was hove-to, and *Arakkaran*, having matched her maneuver, was drifting close. Scarlet dolphins, blue gannets, and golden squids writhed on her sides amid weeds and stylized waves. She towered over the smaller craft, and she bore some complex banner at her masthead. Red Djinn faces peered down under white turbans.

"She must be the flagship!" Inos said, but Jarga was staring, lost in wonder of this glorious floating palace.

A line snaked down. Jarga ran to take it, snapping at Inos to hold the wheel. At the last possible moment fenders fell into the gap and the two vessels came together with a gentle bump. Like a shower of apples from a tree, a dozen sailors leaped down, thudding bare feet on the ketch's deck. Clearly *Arakkaran* was a well-run ship, no mere showpiece.

After months of consorting with dwarves, Inos had forgotten just how big men could be. They wore white breeches and white turbans with nothing between. Shiny scimitars flashed at their waists; ruddy skin rippled over muscles and red eyes gleamed with amusement as they registered the sex of the two crew members present.

Their leader swaggered aft to confront the women. White teeth shone in his red beard as he sneered.

"All alone? What sort of craft is this?"

"We are simple fishing folk, Mightiness," Jarga mumbled, with a most unjotunnish humility. "We mean no harm."

"Nor we. Indeed we shall brighten your lives considerably! Go aboard." The big man gestured to a rope ladder, which had just unrolled itself down the dhow's side.

Somebody yelled a warning overhead and a barrel crashed to the deck. It exploded on impact, spilling black fluid everywhere. At once the djinns began throwing nets on the mess.

"Pitch!" Jarga cried.

"Pitch." The officer glanced contemptuously at the open skylight. "We are about to torch you. The ladder will be removed in a few minutes. Stay and fry if you prefer."

The expression in Jarga's blue eyes caused his hand to jump to the hilt of his sword—she was very nearly as tall as he, and jotunn. Inos stepped between them and pushed the sailor toward the ladder. Jarga went reluctantly. Passing the skylight, she called out, "Abandon ship!"

Feet drummed on wood as the men hurried up the companionway.

Minutes later, when *Arakkaran* came under way again, *Northern Vengeance* was already a smoking inferno upon the sea, sails and rigging dissolving in yellow flame. The eight prisoners huddled together on the dhow's deck under the amused and puzzled gaze of at least fifty huge djinns. In the bright light of the open sea, their eyes were the color of dried blood.

Inos had never seen a finer craft. Every scrap of brass shone like gold. Every plank was waxed and gleaming, every cable smooth and new. Bright-hued lacquer traced out exotic carvings on any surface that did not need to be flat. This, she supposed, was Azak's doing. He was a perfectionist. If Azak built a fleet, it would be the finest fleet the Gods had ever seen.

She glanced at her companions. Jarga seemed to be in a trance, bewitched by the splendor of the dhow. The dwarves just glowered, out of their element. The goblins were shifty-eyed and jumpy; Shandie's face was almost as green as theirs. Raspnex was imprisoned in his self-imposed cocoon.

The imperor was too ill to think, and all the others must be concentrating mightily on not using sorcery within the occult inspection of the Covin. With her newfound sea legs, Inos was in better shape to cope than any of them, but a woman was no more than a domestic animal to djinns. Nothing she said would be heeded, even were it credible: *I am Queen Inosolan of Krasnegar, this is the imperor, and may I present Warlock Raspnex . . .*

The cordon opened to admit a portly man of middle years. He was weather-beaten, his unfastened blouse displayed grizzled chest hair. The blouse, his turban, and his voluminous pants were blue; he wore a jeweled scimitar and ornate shoes. He could be assumed to be the captain.

"A motley catch!" he boomed in the metallic accents of northern Zark. His red-and-white brows rose ever higher as he inspected that catch.

Inos turned away from his arrogant gaze and her eye was caught by a movement up on the poop deck. Her heart stopped in its tracks. She stared in disbelief. It could not be! That was nineteen years ago, woman!

"By the beard of the caliph, what are these two?" the captain demanded. He addressed the question to Wirax, the oldest male.

"They are goblins, eminent sir."

"Goblins? Got a bad case of seasickness, have they?" The unjustified mirth this remark generated in the onlookers confirmed that the speaker must be the commander.

But the one up on the poop? The young one leaning on the rail and staring down at the play? Exceptionally tall, even for a djinn . . . impossibly wide shoulders and narrow waist . . . a nose like an eagle's beak, face weathered to a rosewood red, and an arrogance to face down Gods . . . *green* clothing.

He was far too young, but the likeness was uncanny.

"Your names?" the captain barked. He was clearly puzzled now. He had probably never even heard of goblins before. "And stations, if any."

"Jarga, sir, master of *Rosebud*."

"Frazkr, iron founder."

"Yshan, merchant," Shandie mumbled.

"Inosolan, widow."

But Inos was distracted, wrestling memories. That huge young man wore green, royal green! Which of them? They had all seemed so alike in their childhood and she had never paid them much heed anyway.

And none of them had ever seen her face!

The litany of names and lies had ended. No wiser for it, the captain scowled. "And what business brings goblins and dwarves and the rest of you to the shores of Zark?"

Wirax launched into a wild tale of seeking opportunities for mining ventures. As the noble lord was doubtless aware, goblins were exceptionally skilled at detecting ore bodies . . . But the goblins were becoming steadily more nervous. Any minute now, Inos thought, young Pool Leaper would crack. He would unleash magic and the watching Covin would swoop down on the ship. Then everything would be lost. Better the djinns than Zinixo, but how could she justify or explain that to the goblin?

What was his name, that arrogant prince on the poop? That prince who looked so astonishingly like his father? Like his father had been, twenty years ago. The oldest. Name! Name! Name!

"I don't believe a word of it!" the captain roared, ending Wirax's fantasy. He turned away. "Throw the men overboard and give the women to the crew."

"Wait!" Inos shouted. She had it! And that one *had* seen her face! "Prince Quarazak!" she called. "We have met before, your Highness!"

A beefy djinn at her side lifted a fist to silence her, and stopped as her meaning penetrated. All eyes swung to the dandy on the poop deck. Inos expected a summons, but he reacted exactly as his father would have done—instantly and dramatically. He vaulted over the rail and landed on the main deck like a giant cat. Then he stalked forward and sailors backed in haste out of his path. He stopped in front of Inos and stared down at her with deadly red eyes. Like his father, he wore his beard trimmed to a narrow fringe; it was darker than she remembered Azak's, though.

"Not likely. I have never had a woman as old as you."

No one laughed, because the remark was not intended to be humorous. The only female faces he would have seen since his childhood would have been those of his daughters and his concubines. Perhaps daughters. Daughters were failures.

Inos was familiar with the attitude and did not let it distract her. "You bore a golden chain on a cushion. When the ceremony was interrupted I lifted my veil. You saw me."

The red eyes widened and the young man seemed to grow even taller. His reckless intervention had landed him in a confrontation so unpredictable that it might cause him to lose face before the crew and the ship's officers, but his composure did not waver. His response was calculated and prudent. "What name do you go by now?"

"I am Inosolan of Krasnegar. You know where we met. And you know who my husband is."

That last he might not know, if he was not in his father's confidence, but the rest he did. Oh, yes, he knew. He had been only eight years old, but he would not have forgotten the day his father married the foreign queen. No one who had been present in that hall would ever have forgotten the battle when one lone horseman overcame the entire palace guard.

He looked over the captives, the goblins in particular. Then he made an instant decision, just as his father would have done. He turned to the captain, who somehow contrived to grovel without moving a muscle.

"Strike my flag. Signal my brother to raise his. Break out of line and set course for Quern."

"Aye, Prince Admiral!"

"Send the woman to my cabin. Put the rest in irons until I decide what to do with them." With that, Admiral Prince

Quarazak ak'Azak ak'Azakar of Arakkaran, oldest son of the caliph, spun on his heel and stalked away.

Inos was roughly shoved after him, knowing that now she must play a part as she had never played before.

5

In Thume, on a snoozy summer afternoon about a week and a half before Longday, Kadie and Thaïle were lounging in the woods, weaving baskets. It was not, as Thaïle had explained, necessary to weave baskets. Weaving baskets was no great feat of artistry or skill. The finished product would be singularly useless in the College—it was just a pleasant way to spend an afternoon.

Kadie was perfectly happy to weave baskets with her friend. She was quite content to do anything in Thaïle's company. She knew she would never have woven baskets in Krasnegar, even had suitable withes been available. In Krasnegar she would probably have denounced the whole procedure as an idiotic waste of time; she might have gone so far as to describe it as peasant's work and thus provoke a sermon from her mother, but in fact it was a pleasant way to pass a hot and sticky afternoon.

Facing her, Thaïle sat on a mossy root, legs crossed within her loose skirt of gold and brown, sandals lying nearby, discarded in the grass. Her white lace halter was very nearly transparent and she wore nothing under it. She seemed like part of the woods themselves, a wild flower.

Kadie wore identical garments, except that the stripes on her skirt were gold and a green that Thaïle said matched her eyes. It was very suitable costume for a deserted forest on such a day as this, but the blouse would cause a revolution in Krasnegar—she tried to imagine Papa's reaction and thoughts failed her. The mind boggled, whatever boggling was.

Poor Papa! How she had enjoyed teasing him! Never again would she be able to outrage him. Never again would she smell burning peat, or run panting up the interminable stairs of the castle, or lick snowflakes off the end of her nose—a trick that always annoyed Gath, who couldn't. Oh, Gath! He and Mama had gone off with the imperor, never to be seen again. Probably never to be heard of again. Thaïle could not help, for she did not know what had happened to the king and queen of Krasnegar, or to Gath. The Keeper might know, because the

Keeper knew everything, but apparently no one ever asked questions of the Keeper. *Nasty old witch!* Papa had never come to rescue his dutiful, beautiful daughter from the goblins, so he was probably dead, just like Thaïle's baby and husband. The world was cruel. Blood Beak was dead; Death Bird and all the goblins were dead. The legions had been burned up by the dragons . . .

"You all right?" Thaïle asked softly.

Kadie sniffed. "Oh, yes! Quite all right. Perfectly all right. Nothing wrong. Well, my fingers are a little sore, maybe."

Thaïle laughed and threw her half-finished basket over her shoulder. "Then forget about the footling baskets!" Her big gold eyes sparkled.

"But I want to! I want to be able to make them round and smooth and even, like you do, and not all lumpy and squished."

"It doesn't matter."

"It does to me!" Kadie said crossly. "You're so good at everything and I'm so hopeless!"

"I expect there are lots of things you can do that I can't. Not without using sorcery, at least."

"I don't know any. And even if there was something I could do, then it would be a Krasnegar thing, a princessy thing, and those things aren't going to do me any good at all here in Thume. I'm no good for anything here!"

Thaïle pushed her feet out of the hem of her skirt and scrabbled over on her hands and toes, gangly as a newborn colt. She sat down next to Kadie and put an arm around her.

"Berry brain!" she said softly. "Of course you're good for something! You're company for me. I don't know what I'd do without you, Kadie!"

"Really? Truly?"

"Really! Truly! I have no friends, no family. I can't make friends with the other archons, I just can't! Not anyone here. I miss Leéb horribly! I know why the Keeper and the archons and the College did what they did, even if I can't tell you. And yet I can't help blaming them. You're the only one who doesn't remind me of Leéb, and I really, truly think I'd go mad if I didn't have you here with me."

Kadie blinked a few times. Then she wiped her cheeks with a finger. "I feel a fool, weeping all the time like this."

"You don't weep all the time. You don't weep any more than I do."

They had this conversation, or one like it, far too often. The next bit was where Thaïle told her that all those months with the goblins couldn't be wiped out in a couple of days, or a week—and now it was more than a week. That was nice to hear, but in truth she was not behaving at all like a rescued princess should. After all, it wasn't as if the goblins had ever actually hurt her. Blood Beak had only threatened to rape her, so he hadn't ever meant what he said, and no one had ever subjected her to any of the awful tortures they had used on all the other prisoners, filling the nights with howls of torment and bellows of mirth from sunset to dawn. Just being terribly frightened for a very long time was not much of an excuse for a princess to behave like a ninny.

"Let's keep that first basket of yours," she said. "It's too good to leave behind."

Thaïle nodded vaguely, golden eyes staring at nothing.

"We can pick some plums and strawberries on the way back to the Thaïle Place."

"Mm."

Kadie felt a twinge of alarm. "And will you let me try cooking again tonight?"

"What?" The pixie looked around distractedly. "Sorry. Er, I have a job to do."

"Job? You're going to leave me here?" Kadie heard her voice quaver into shrillness. "All alone?"

"We can go back to the Place first, and I won't be long."

"How long?" What if Thaïle never came back and Kadie was left in the cottage all alone, a stranger here in Thume . . .

"Steady!" Thaïle squeezed her hand. "No need to panic! No need for me to leave you, either. I'll take you with me. Come!"

She jumped up in a flounce of skirt and ran to her sandals. Kadie fumbled in the grass for hers.

"It's all right—you taking me, I mean?"

The pixie grinned. "And who's to complain? I'm an archon, I can do anything I want. Come, give me your hand."

"Where are we going? Why? Who're we going to meet?"

"We're going to the coast. Close your eyes, it's bright."

They joined hands. Kadie felt no sense of movement, but at once pink light glared through her eyelids and a shivery wind enveloped her. Its clammy embrace raised every goosebump possible. She said, "Eek!" loudly. She was certainly no longer in a shady forest. She heard a familiar unending rumble, scented a familiar smell. Gulls shrieked appropriately in the distance.

In a moment she forced her eyes open against tears. She stood on a sand dune, knee-deep in coarse grass that danced in ranks before the breeze. Below her lay a silver beach and beyond that, of course, the sea her nose and ears had detected. It had never been so blue in Krasnegar, nor the sky so wonderfully deep.

"Oh, I love the sea!" she said.

"It's all right, I suppose," Thaïle agreed doubtfully. "It's so restless and noisy!"

"It does bump things around a lot."

"It repeats itself all the time."

"It steals things and litters."

"But I suppose it is useful. If it went away, all the fish would fall down."

They laughed together.

"Where are we? Sea of Sorrows or Morning Sea?"

"Somewhere in the west. This is my sector, and someone's coming."

Kadie took a long, careful look around the bay, from headland to headland: waves, wet shiny sand, dry golden sand, dunes, trees, and sky. There was no one in sight at all—no boats, no ships, no cottages, no livestock, just a few white birds. About a furlong away, a small stream emerged from the woods and slunk across the beach in a shallow, sinuous channel. Each new wave sent ripples exploring up it, but that was about the limit of the excitement hereabouts, as far as she could see.

"Where? How do you know?"

Thaïle was studying the sea, and perhaps she was seeing sorcerous things, because she spoke distractedly. "I know because it called me. The coast called me, to say there were strangers." The sun chased golden highlights through her hazel-brown hair.

Kadie waited a moment for more explanations. None came. "The coast called you? The waves or birds? Or all the little sand grains jabbering at once?"

"Just the coast. I'm attuned to it, like the mountains speak to Raim . . . Yes, truly!" Thaïle smiled.

"I believe you!"

"Your face didn't! All right, I wouldn't have believed it, either. I didn't know, but it's true. More of Keef's work, I assume."

"Oh," Kadie said doubtfully. "And where are the strangers?"

"They're here! Watch the trees."

In a flash, the trees changed. Most of them disappeared. Those that remained were different, and in among them lay fields, and a couple of distant cottages. Turning, Kadie saw that there were more cottages spotted along the course of the stream, and the stream's path across the beach was different, too. Four dories lay above high water mark.

"This is the other Thume," Thaïle said. "The one the people . . . Ouch! I'll try and explain sometime." She pulled a face, as she always did when she tried to talk about sorcery.

"Pixies?"

"Pixies. Not typical, though! This would rank as a pixie slum. Most pixies won't tolerate a Place that has another Place in sight. And there are the strangers."

A sailboat lay offshore. A dinghy had almost reached the shore. Kadie stared in astonishment at the four men in it—their hair!

"What . . . I mean, *who* are they?"

"Mermen," Thaïle said softly. She chuckled. "Fishermen, I expect. They've come ashore to fill their water casks. See them in the boat?"

"*Blue* hair?"

"Yes, merfolk."

"Can they see the cottages?"

Again the sorceress chuckled. "No. They would if they went inland a little way—but they won't, because of the aversion spell. There's a spell on that water, too. Watch what happens."

The dinghy grounded near the stream mouth, and the men jumped out to heave it farther up the beach. Then they all straightened up and looked around warily. They had very pale skin. Their hair was long and light *blue*, the color of a jotunn's eyes. They were bare-footed and bare-chested, their loins and legs swathed in long wraps that glittered silver in the sunlight. They were about imp height, but they lacked impish chubbiness.

"They're only boys!" Kadie realized her hand was gripping the hilt of her sword and released it. What good would a rapier do her against four youths? And what harm could come to her with Thaïle here? "They look fairly harmless." Quite nice, in fact.

"They're not just boys. Merfolk are all skinny like that. Do you think they're good-looking?"

"Well, yes . . . Yes, they are, in spite of that blue hair." Kadie glanced suspiciously at her companion's grin. "What's funny?"

"If I weren't here, you'd be in serious trouble, Princess. Those are mermen!"

"At this distance?"

"Easily!"

"Then I am very glad you are here!" Kadie said uncomfortably. Everyone knew what happened with mermen. It was not nice!

Having made their dinghy secure, the four sailors set off in a group across the sand. Kadie shied, then realized that they were not heading for her. They had not seen her and probably could not see her. Thaïle was with her, she had nothing to fear.

In a moment, too, the sailors' path began to curve seaward. Soon they had reached the waves again. They lined up and together knelt to cup hands and drink. Kadie burst out laughing as each in turn jumped to his feet. Faint sounds of cursing drifted across on the wind.

"What in the world are they doing?" she asked.

Thaïle was grinning. "Drinking the sea, of course."

"But why? What do they *think* they're doing?"

"They think they're tasting the stream, and they think it's bad water."

The four sailors marched farther along the beach and tried again. The sea was just as salt there, apparently.

It really was very funny. At this distance, the men did look like boys, or at least adolescents, and they were obviously furious. As a group, they began retracing their steps over the sand, angrily chattering and waving hands.

Kadie put an arm around Thaïle and hugged. "Are you doing this?"

Thaïle responded with a matching arm. "No, dear. The stream is spelled. One of my predecessors must have laid a curse on it. Don't feel sorry for them! They know they're not supposed to come ashore in Thume. I probably ought to give them all a dose of footrot, or something."

"Don't! You wouldn't!"

"Well, I probably should," Thaïle said doubtfully. "But I don't suppose this lot'll ever be back."

The mermen were heaving their boat back into the surf, their casks unfilled.

"No need to bother the Keeper over them," Thaïle said with obvious relief. "There's some big fat trout in that stream. If I coax them out, would you like to try cooking them tonight?"

"How about a bathe in the sea first?"

"Why not? Race you!"

6

Where the morning sea laved the foothills of the Progistes Range stood the bastion of Quern, around whose towering walls the tides of men had surged for centuries. It had withstood sieges without number, been sacked times without number, been betrayed and looted and rebuilt, again and again and again.

Years ago, the caliph had taken Quern without a struggle, on the strength of his reputation alone. Had it resisted, he would have starved it into surrender and put every living creature within it to the sword, as he had at Shuggaran and Zarfel and Mi'gal. Instead he had offered mercy and delivered it.

Quern was the last outpost of Zark. Westward lay Thume, and the Impire. Now the caliph had returned to Quern at the head of an army such as Zark had not seen in generations. His fleet patrolled the coast to maintain security and guard the massed shipping in the harbor. All other vessels were being seized and sunk. The war had begun.

He stood in full sunlight on the battlements of the fortress, with his sirdars around him. They were watching Fourth Panoply drill on the dusty plain below. The men were good, but not good enough. Gurrak had sworn by the bowels of his sons that he would have the Fourth licked into shape before the army moved out. He had come close, very close. But not close enough. So now Azak must either pretend a satisfaction he did not feel, or select a replacement for Sirdar Gurrak.

Replacements were always a problem, and they seemed to be needed ever more often now as his original lieutenants died off, for one reason or another. Each new appointment shifted all the subtle balances of power and intrigue around the person of the caliph. They changed the balance of the army itself—ten years ago Fourth Panoply had been the cream, the staunch reserve that could turn the tide when all seemed lost. Now it was saber fodder, the trash he rolled in first to tire the enemy's arms.

Still, he had a good staff of sirdars. A couple were cousins of his, three were survivors of other royal families, and two were so far removed from any throne as to be almost commoners. One and only one was a son. To give a possible successor command of thousands of crack troops was not the act of a prudent man. Too much prudence, of course, might be interpreted as timidity. Nuances were important. Thus one son a sirdar and only one—so far. Admirals were less dangerous.

Tomorrow they moved against the Impire. Everything Azak had done for nineteen years had led inexorably to this. Historically, the Impire's invasions of Zark were beyond counting. Only three times had the djinns ever seriously returned the favor, and never as a united people. Unity came hard to a land that was basically a chain of isolated cities around a waterless waste, and only a need to evict invaders had ever united them in the past. Now Azak had done it for them. From Ullacarn in the south all the way around to here, Quern, the continent acknowledged the rule of the caliph. The Caliphate of all Zark, his life's work.

Far below, a bugle called. The camel corps exploded into a charge. Ah! Now that was better! One moment lines of stationary mounts and riders like statues—barely ant size from this height—the next a rolling cloud of dust and potential death. Perhaps the camels' performance could be allowed to ransom the wretched Gurrak. Some of the sirdars muttered appreciation as the camel corps wheeled around the infantry squares.

"That is good," Azak said softly. He did not look; he could feel Gurrak's spasm of relief at this hint of praise. He could also smell the rankness of fear on the man.

"The credit must go to my emir of camels, Sire," Gurrak said hoarsely. "But he has done no more than we expect of an ak'Azak."

Others murmured quick agreement.

Fear and flattery. Flattery and fear. They were all the same—sirdars, sultans, princes—all terrified, all sycophants, all sickening. On the other hand, there must be some truth in what the craven said. Those camels were doing better than the First's had yesterday, much better. So young Tharkan might really be as good as he thought he was. How interesting! How old now? Azak made a quick count. Almost eighteen, of course, because Tharkan had been one of the first among his second family, the crop of sons born to him after the hiatus created by the meddling sorceress Rasha. Tharkan ak'Azak ak'Azakar, borne by . . . what was her name? The thin one from the hills. She'd produced nothing but daughters after Tharkan.

A mutter from the sirdars and a stifled sob from Gurrak drew his attention back to the massed specks of humanity moving on the earth far below. The horse corps was in turmoil, their mounts panicking as the camels charged past. Men were being thrown and trampled; the entire corps was on the point of stampeding. *Execration!* That was unforgivable! What sort of trash was he supposed to lead into battle?

Order was being restored, but he could not pretend to overlook that debacle. So now the problem was to choose Gurrak's replacement. To have to change sirdars on the very eve of departure, that was infuriating! He must promote someone within the panoply itself, a man who would know the other emirs. After that camel demonstration, the choice was obvious. Of course it would set up young Tharkan as a potential challenger, but that might slow the others a little in their endless plotting. Tharkan probably thought of himself that way already. At his age Azak had kept four assassins on his personal staff and had known as much about poisons as all of them put together.

The archers would be next. Fourth Panoply had been noted for its archers even back when Kirthap ran it. If Gurrak had let them slip, then he would have to suffer for it before he died.

Azak blinked in the intolerable sun and wished he could wipe the sweat from his eyes. Nineteen years. Nineteen years of blood and struggle. Fifteen battles, three long sieges, four massacres, seven rebellions, innumerable executions. After the first year or two he had been sorely tempted to give up and just hold what he had already collected, but that would have been certain suicide. And the same again, two years ago, when he had been routed at Bone Pass and nearly died himself. In the end he had always just pressed on, because he had never had any real choice. Nineteen years ago he had mounted a tiger. He was still aboard and the tiger was still running. Tomorrow he would ride it westward at last. He could never dismount from the tiger alive.

The single target was ready. A flag waved. A line of arrows flew, invisible from this height. Then they seemed to congeal like a rush of smoke and the target leaped backward under the massed impact. The sirdars sighed in approval. Azak waited for the misses to be counted and signaled. Every arrow bore its owner's mark, of course.

The archers swung around and prepared for the rapid-fire demonstration. He raised his eyes to the hills, black with men and tents and livestock. The city in the distance was packed from wall to wall. The harbor beyond was floored with shipping, all of it just a . . .

Arakkaran! His eyes were not what they had been, but that could only be *Arakkaran* entering port. What was that idiot Quarazak up to? Why had the admiral deserted his fleet?

Azak's mind floundered through a dozen possible explanations and could find none that would stand up to a second thought. He realized that he had clenched his fists and gently opened them again. Some of his companions must have noticed the dhow even before he did; they must be wondering as he was. He would not give them the satisfaction of knowing that he had not expected this.

"Well, who are the true djinns amongst us, sirdars? Can you see? Is that my dilatory son at last?"

A chorus confirmed that the vessel was indeed the flagship.

"About time!" Azak snapped his fingers and a herald ran forward. "See that the prince admiral is admitted to our presence the minute he arrives."

The man bowed head to knees and was running before he had even straightened up again.

What was Quarazak dreaming of? Had he brought news of a battle, perhaps? Had he sunk the Imperial Navy? No, he would have sent a dispatch boat.

The rapid shoot was completed. The drill was over. At Azak's side the massed sirdars waited in frozen apprehension to hear his decision. Probably they all knew what it must be. Those horses! Who could he put in Gurrak's place at this late date?

For some reason he thought of Krandaraz, and sighed. In almost thirty years of breeding sons he had produced only one Krandaraz. Krandaraz had been the only diamond in the shingle. Krandaraz should be here now, first among the sirdars—he would outshine them all.

He would also outshine Azak.

The caliph turned to his tense associates. They could guess what was about to happen. They waited to hear his choice of victim. He selected the youngest, Azakar, Sirdar of the Sixth, the only one of his sons to command a panoply—at the moment.

"Ak'Azak? What do you think of Fourth's performance?"

The lad pursed his lips. Had he licked them, his father would have struck him.

"Much improved, Sire." He blinked garnet eyes warily. His beard was oddly forked and still notably thin, although he was one of the first family and no longer a boy. Gods! He must be twenty-three or so, older than Azak had been when he proclaimed himself ruler of the continent and set out to prove it.

"But not," the sirdar continued, mouthing each word with care, "quite up to the standards of . . . others . . . we have seen here in the last few days."

Not bad. Not bad at all. It did not commit either way. Which was as it should be.

"Not up to expectations, you mean?"

Azakar grabbed at the hint thus offered. "Disappointing, really, Sire."

Azak nodded.

Gurrak made a curious coughing noise.

Azak looked at him sorrowfully. He quite liked Gurrak, a splendid horseman himself, an excellent man on a hunt. The terror in his face now was heartbreaking, but his voice remained remarkably steady.

"I commend my sons to your service, Sire."

"I judge men by their deeds, not their fathers, Sirdar."

Sweat was streaming down Gurrak's face, but he knew he had been given all the guarantee he would get. He bowed. Then he scrambled up on the parapet and stepped off.

Azak snapped his fingers twice, for two heralds. "Inform Prince Tharkan ak'Azak that Sirdar Gurrak has met with an accident and he is to assume command of the Fourth . . ." He glanced at Azakar, but saw nothing in his eyes to contradict the pleased smile of the mouth. ". . . temporarily. And you— direct the Secretariat to issue the necessary commissions."

The men ran.

Yes, another contender would give little fork-beard Azakar something to think about. There was always the chance that the two of them would gang up on their old man, of course, and bring a quarter of the army against him, but ganging up required some minimal amount of trust and trust did not run in the family. Never for long, anyway. And this appointment would be a general message to the first family that their innumerable younger brothers were now to be taken seriously. Tharkan must look to his own safety from now on.

Azak walked away, eager to go in out of the sun and start work on the mountain of documents awaiting him. And in a little while he would find out just what that idiot Quarazak was dreaming of in disobeying orders and returning to port.

Zark might very shortly be going to need a new admiral, as well as a new sirdar.

Azak approved of the fortress of Quern, which was barren and functional and nondecadent. The room he used as a presence chamber had probably been a mess hall in the past, perhaps other things, also. It was eminently plain, a stone vastness full of hollow echoes, dimly lit by windows that were mere tunnels through walls several spans thick. Even now, just ten days or so short of Longday, it was cool. The secretaries swarmed like black insects over the document tables by the entrance; he sat at his desk at the far end. There was another door at his back, just in case.

As a further advantage, the room was shielded against sorcery. Furkar had seen to that many years ago. Furkar had shielded a chamber for the caliph's use in every one of the many palaces he used on his travels about Zark.

Quarazak was eerily sure of himself. Even as his son came in through the wide doors and began marching across the slabbed stone floor toward his desk, Azak registered that curious absence of fear. He waved the secretaries away, and they scurried off like beetles, their black kibrs swirling around their ankles. They bowed to the prince in passing and then settled in around the tables of documents at the far end of the shadowed hall. Dung beetles.

So now caliph and eldest son would have a private talk, overseen but not overheard. Quarazak stopped and bowed turban to knees.

Amazingly sure of himself, he was, for an admiral who had flouted his orders when at battle stations. In the last hour a large portion of Azak's nimble brain had been wrestling with that problem while the rest of it attended to the endless edicts and requisitions and proclamations. He had found no conceivable explanation.

Mutiny at once suggested revolution, but he could not believe that it would be done like this. Now, on the very brink of war, he was probably safer than he had ever been since he first laid the sash of Arakkaran over his shoulder twenty-one years ago. And when it did come, it would be done with a blade or a vial, not a ship—not when he was half a league from the sea.

It might be done by sorcery. Just for a moment he let his eyes shift to the ominous black-clad figure sitting alone in the farthest corner—Furkar, court sorcerer. If Furkar ever changed sides, then everything would be over very quickly. Yes, Furkar might do it like this.

But not with Quarazak. The eldest prince was good, but not good enough, and he knew it. Furkar knew it. By the standards of ordinary men Quarazak was outstanding—tall and handsome, ruthless, quick of hand and mind. He was very nearly a duplicate of his father as he had been at that age, but not quite. Compared to Krandaraz he was nothing. He knew that, too. More than anything else in the world, perhaps, Quarazak would like to know where Krandaraz was. It was the last thing in the world Azak would ever tell him.

Quarazak was waiting now for permission to speak. Azak did not tell him to take the solitary chair. Only Furkar ever sat in that chair.

"This," Azak said softly, "had better be good. Very good."

"It is, Sire. You will approve." Ruby eyes twinkled.

Play my own game at me, will you? Oh, he was sure of himself! He was afraid, of course. They all were, always, but Quarazak was much less afraid at the moment than he usually was, or ought to be.

"You have thirty seconds."

"I brought a prisoner, Sire, one you will wish to interrogate yourself."

Azak spread his hands on the desk. He should have done that sooner. "A prisoner? I can think of no prisoner who would justify your presence here at the moment except perhaps the imperor himself."

His son chuckled very softly, deep in his throat. "Hardly."

"Or perhaps the sorcerer Rap of Krasnegar." Now there would be an ally!

"No, Sire, but you are close."

The old wound in Azak's leg twinged as all his muscles stiffened at once. "Who is this prisoner?"

"His wife." Quarazak smiled in triumph. "*Your* wife, of course, by the laws of Zark."

7

The Inosolan problem ached in Azak's mind all the rest of the day, throbbing like a festering wound. Had he been asked beforehand, he would have said that the chances of Inosolan ever returning to Zark were so slight as to be nonexistent, like loyalty among djinns. The timing was so suspicious that coincidence could be ruled out absolutely. What did her arrival have to do with his invasion, though? He could not even guess who had instituted this: Rap himself, or the imperor, or the Almighty? Where did dwarves come into it, or goblins? There was certainly sorcery involved somewhere. Motive, means, culprit—all of them enigmas.

Several times he found his mind wandering away from the endless flood of detail flowing across his desk. Inosolan! How could it be Inosolan? It must be an illusion, a trap of some sort.

Quarazak had been sure. He had insisted that she was the woman he had seen at the wedding, so many years ago. On the ship he had questioned her closely, but he said he had used no violence, only threats. He had threatened to have her raped by every man in the fleet, but he had not shaken her story. She was Inosolan. She had business with the caliph, which she would divulge to no one else, and the caliph had a triangular scar on his ribs, about *here*. Which he did, although it was almost invisible now.

Sorcery! It had to be sorcery.

Azak had sent Furkar off to investigate in person and had then attempted to push ahead with his work. The day before launching the largest war of the century was no time to be woolgathering about a marriage twenty years old, a marriage that had never even been consummated.

Yet, whispered a small voice of temptation.

Quarazak had made the correct decision. Azak had told him so—that he could not fault anything his son had done in a very unexpected situation. As wife of the sorcerer, the woman was of vital importance; as former wife of the caliph, she must be treated as a state secret, concealed from public knowledge. Surprisingly, Quarazak had made a difficult decision correctly, which Azak would not have expected of him.

And Quarazak had replied, "Thank you, Father," in a very

annoying way. Then he had bowed and withdrawn to return to his post.

It wasn't exactly the way he had spoken that had been so accursedly annoying, it was the way Azak himself had reacted. He had been very tempted to call the boy back and give him command of the Sixth Panoply instead of Tharkan. That would have been a breach of security, for the enemy must continue to think that the navy was doing something important enough to require the personal attention of the eldest—imps were much more impressed by eldest sons than djinns were.

It would have been also a breach of personal security. Throughout Zarkian history, any ruler who had ever begun to feel sentimental about his sons had arrived early for his appointment with the Gods. A firstborn had very little advantage over his brothers, but he did have some, and to provide him with any opportunity at all for military glory would always be rank suicide—the kid would be checking out the seraglio by nightfall. No, Quarazak must do his duty afloat. They also serve who only block the light.

Paperwork! Why must a man who had conquered a world spend all his time chained to a desk when he would rather be out hunting, or reviewing the troops, or dallying in the women's quarters? To top off all the requirements on the caliph's time that day came news that his viceroy in Charkab had been assassinated. The culprits would be assuming that the forces he had left in the south were not adequate for massive reprisals. Well, that was true at the moment, but Quarazak's deception would not be needed for more than five or six days.

Azak dictated orders for the fleet to proceed to Charkab thereafter. After due consideration, he stipulated that the town be razed and the surviving inhabitants enslaved. That would keep all the other cities quiet until he returned.

At noon, as was his wont when he was not hunting, he retired for a rest. Usually he enjoyed a woman at this time, but today he did not feel in the mood even for that. Doubtless that was the reason he was unable to sleep. Grumpily he ordered his handmaids to prepare his bath. After that, he went back to work.

Inosolan! The only woman he had ever taken to wife and he had never even kissed her.

Yet, said the little voice.

What folly was this? She must be forty.

Thirty-six. Six years younger than you.

He had never made love to a woman older than thirty. He retired them then if they had been fruitful, or else gave them to his sons.

A trembling herald from Third Panoply reported that half the water skins had been filled and one-third of them were leaking already. Azak sent queries to all other panoplies and ordered requisitions of barrels, wagons, more draft animals.

Furkar returned at last. The woman was telling the truth, he said.

Azak leaned back in his chair and stared blankly at his court sorcerer while he thought about that. Furkar was the only man in Zark who was not afraid of him. Probably Azak ought to be afraid of Furkar, but he wasn't. Partly that was mere fatalism—he would die when the Gods decreed, like any other man. Partly it was because he knew Furkar to be utterly dedicated to the cause.

Long ago, impish soldiers had killed Furkar's father. He detested the Impire just as hotly as Azak did. They had made common cause against it. Furkar had made it all possible, Furkar and his votaries—Azak did not know who they were or how many of them there were, and he never asked. Without that sorcerous assistance, Azak would long ago have died as an obscure sultan. He would never have made reality out of his empty claim to be caliph. He knew that and Furkar knew that. Probably no one else did, though, and certainly no one in Zark would ever dare whisper it.

Furkar had not taken the visitor chair reserved for him alone, so he did not intend to stay long. He wore black, always—a trailing black kibr, and even the agal binding his black headcloth was itself black. Azak had never seen anything of him except his hands and face. They were paler than most, but otherwise unremarkable, except that he was clean-shaven. He looked about twenty-two or -three, but he had looked like that when Azak had first met him, nineteen years ago. He was a sorcerer.

He never smiled. He seemed to have no outside interests, no friends, no interest in women or boys. He never, ever smiled.

"You understand, Majesty," he said in the soft tones of the desert men, "that I used a bare minimum of power. The Covin is still probing."

"I do understand. We agreed. What of her companions?"

"They are in the lowermost dungeon. It is shielded."

Azak nodded. "Then there are sorcerers among them?"

Furkar's face did not change expression. "If you wish me to take the risk, I shall do so."

"Risk?"

"I did not enter the shielding. Together they could be strong enough to overpower me."

Azak pouted. He detested sorcery, but it was a necessary evil. "Of course. No, I do not wish you to take that risk. Our entire venture depends upon you and your, er, associates. I shall see the woman as soon as I have time. You have no clue as to her purpose in coming here?"

"No, Majesty. Only what you already know—that Warlock Olybino named her husband as leader of the opposition to the Covin. That does suggest she may have been sent with a message."

"How about her emotional state?"

"Yes, that is curious. Agitated. She is understandably frightened, but hiding it better than I should have believed possible. A tentative diagnosis, that is."

Azak sighed. That sounded like Inosolan. "Well, we shall see. I shall expect you to watch our encounter, of course."

Furkar inclined his head respectfully and walked away.

Azak shivered, and went back to work.

The work kept coming to Azak. Forage, water skins, arrows, horseshoes, bandages, medicines ... He was surrounded by morons. Any detail he did not check himself would inevitably explode into a problem during the campaign. He owed his success to his infinite capacity for taking pains.

He had always done his best work by night. He revived after the sunset meal and a new phalanx of secretaries arrived to help, but it was well past midnight before he felt able to send for Inosolan. By then he was bone weary, aware that he must snatch a few hours' sleep before he led out the army at dawn. Still, if the woman had been nervous before, then the long wait would not have calmed her fears.

He had dismissed the beetles, although their tables were still loaded with documents. His desk was lit by lanterns hanging from the high ceiling, but otherwise the room was dark. Furkar sat like a graven replica of himself in the far corner, a disembodied face, and even that invisible unless one knew where to look.

She stepped in through one flap of the double doors, and it

closed behind her. Then she began to walk across the wide expanse of barren stone toward the desk. She was not as tall as he remembered, but of course there was imp blood in her. She had been garbed in plain white, the all-enveloping chaddar of Zark. As she drew close he saw the green of her eyes and he remembered their wedding night, the one time he had seen her unclothed.

Ransom? She had been stolen away from him by the imperor himself, all those long years ago. Was it possible that she had been sent back as a peace offering? Did they really think he would call off his war now, for this?

And yet . . . He had possessed hundreds of women, probably thousands. Why then must his heart labor so shamefully at the sight of this one?

He spread his hands before him on the desk.

She did not prostrate herself or even curtsey. She dropped the veil from her face and pulled off her head cloth, spilling honey hair loose about her shoulders.

"Hello, Azak," she said airily. "Been a long time, hasn't it?" She sat down on the chair unbidden and smiled at him. Her face was no longer that of a girl, but he would have guessed ten years short of her age. Northern sun was kinder, perhaps. The lines on her face were faint, certainly not to be classed as wrinkles. Her eyes were still as green and bright as the emeralds in his baldric.

"I was not expecting you."

She chuckled. "I don't suppose you were! The years have been kind to you, Big Man. More weight? Quite a lot more weight! But you have the bones for it. You look good."

She was lying, of course—he had proof of that—but the words raised his chin anyway.

"They have been kind to you, also," he said huskily.

"Flattery! I have borne four children."

"I have bred a hundred sons."

"It's easier for you."

Had not Furkar himself told him she was frightened, he would not have believed it. He would have sworn that she was the only person in Zark, apart from the sorcerer, who was not afraid of him—how unlike the fawning, shivering maidens who served his needs in the seraglio! She seemed totally at ease, her smile was perfectly composed. He had seen that smile before somewhere . . . Oh, yes, her aunt.

"Princess Kadolan?"

A shadow darkened that golden face. "She passed away a few years ago. Very peacefully. How about Prince Kar?"

"He developed ambitions."

"I am sorry to hear that."

Again the pearl on his index finger darkened momentarily.

"Zark is the only place I know," Inosolan said gaily, "where ambition is so swiftly fatal. And Mistress Zana?"

"She, also, has been weighed by the Gods."

"I am truly sorry to hear that."

The pearl stayed white.

This was women's chatter. She could keep this up all night! What would it take to make her show her fear?

"And what dread purpose brings you to our domain, Inos?"

She raised a golden eyebrow. "I do not think you should describe your eldest son as a 'dread purpose,' Azak! I had no intention of violating your borders until he insisted. I was on my way to Thume."

White, still—but Azak's heart chilled.

"Why? What is there in Thume?"

"You don't know?" the queen said coyly. "You mean you will just march in without knowing?"

"We embark tomorrow to sail to Ollion."

The old familiar grin. "Azak! Really! Those ships in the harbor are deserted. The hills are thick with soldiers and livestock. If you were planning to embark all of them tomorrow, the harbor would be a madhouse. It's not. It's a morgue. Your shipping may fool the imps, but it doesn't fool me."

He had forgotten the root of her appeal—the deadly combination of beauty and brains. To match wits with a woman was a stunningly unfamiliar sensation for him, and it aroused him as he would not have believed possible.

She seemed to guess his thought, because she grinned mischievously at him. "I'm not one of your broodmares, Azak. I never was."

"No. You never were. After what happened the last time, I do not know why you should wish to return to Thume."

She frowned, and white silk rustled as she crossed her legs. *God of Lust!* He remembered those hard, slim legs, the honey-colored down where they met, the skin more fair than any in Zark, the firm breasts and rose-pink nipples. Never had he laid a hand on her!

"We know," she said, "you and I know that there is some unfathomed power in Thume, even now. It seems to be unpredictable, and it is apparently masked by some sort of inattention spell that selectively discourages sorcerers. But it exists."

He nodded. The pearl in his ring remained white.

"I hope to enlist that power in my husband's war."

Furkar's voice whispered in his ear for him alone: *"She is talking nonsense, Majesty!"*

But the pearl had stayed white. What she said might be wrong, but she believed it to be true.

"I love you," Inos said.

"What?"

"It's the pearl? I wondered why you kept staring at your hands. It changed color then, didn't it?"

He glared at her and she smiled.

"Not a broodmare, Azak!"

He raised his hand, crooking his fingers to display the pearl. "I think I still love you!" he said thickly.

The pearl darkened.

"Lust after you," he corrected.

The pearl turned white again.

Color poured into her face and she dropped her eyes to her own hands, clasped upon her lap. Yes, now she understood her danger. Better!

He waited, and waited, until finally she broke the silence.

"Our adventure in Thume was an ordeal. It was hateful. And yet . . . I admit . . . Those were the days of our youth, Azak. The horror has faded. The joy has not!" She looked up appealingly. "Do you remember how we rode through that romantic forest, so full of enchantment, and you lectured me on dog scats? I am grateful for the help you gave me then, Azak. I am grateful that you came to say good-bye to me in Hub, and sorry I was not there to receive your farewell. Let us cherish those memories, forget the harsh words, and go forward as allies."

Still he did not speak. The big room was silent, except for the buzz of mosquitoes. Moths whirled crazily around the lanterns.

Now her apprehension was obvious. No color in her face now. "Am I still your wife, here in Zark?"

He shook his head. "I signed a decree of divorce as soon as I returned."

She nodded gratefully. "It must have been a difficult time for you."

"The court was amused that I had lost my foreign bride. The

imperor's treaty I brought back with me helped. And I declared war on Shuggaran right away."

She closed her eyes for a moment. "Then I was responsible for what you began then? That was the start of it?"

"It was. A scorned sultan does not rule long, but a war will bind the factions, at least temporarily."

Golden fireflies played over her hair as she shook her head. "I am glad you managed to survive, but I dislike the means you employed. And now you carry the war to the Impire? You realize that you are walking into a trap?"

Ah! "You had best explain that remark."

A tiny crease appeared between her eyebrows. "Rap came to see you once, long ago. Apparently he detected power being used within the palace, although he never mentioned that to me. I assume that you had some sorcerous assistance in your climb to power?"

"You know how I detest sorcery."

The quirky smile returned briefly. "You were always good at evading questions. All right, how much do you know of the present situation?"

"What should I know?"

"Rap and Shandie sent you letters."

"I never received them."

The frown returned, stronger. "That's strange! The messenger was reliable, I was told. Well, they wrote to you last winter. Things have changed ... If you have sorcerous counsel, you must know that the imperor in Hub is an imposter. You must know that Zinixo, the former warlock, has overthrown the wardens and calls himself the Almighty. And you know that my husband is leader of the counterrevolution."

"Ah, Rap! He is still alive, then?"

"As far as I know," Inos said cheerfully.

The pearl dulled briefly.

She hopes so, Furkar whispered. *She is not sure.*

Unaware, Inos continued with apparent confidence. "The mundane world knows nothing of this. The fake imperor has withdrawn forces from the frontiers. You see your chance to invade. So, doubtless, do Dwanish and Nordland. Guwush will rise in revolt. That is the plan."

A woman talking military strategy! Why should this obscenity, this perversion, make Azak's blood race so? How dare she lecture him? He struggled to hide his rising fury. "And the payoff?"

"The Almighty will step forth to reveal himself as savior of the Impire and smite you all."

Furkar had mentioned this possibility.

"You know what he did to the goblins?" Inos added.

"You are suggesting I postpone my campaign?"

"I would, if I were you."

"If you were me, you would not be here."

She smiled another of those heart-stopping smiles. "True. But you do see the risk? It is the only possible explanation for the Impire's present vulnerability."

"No, it isn't!" Azak said grimly. "Yes, I know about the Almighty. I rejoice to see the wardens overthrown. I rejoice to see the imps suffer—and I think dwarves do, also. And jotnar and goblins, too. The Almighty is a dwarf. I think he is telling us we can now take our revenge for all those centuries of aggression!"

Clearly she had not considered that explanation. It shook her. When she spoke again, she was far less confident. "Then why did he destroy the goblin horde?"

"And all those legions, also? That was hardly the act of a savior, loosing dragons on the legions! I think that both massacres were merely a show of strength to impress the free sorcerers. It was followed by orders for them to enlist, as I understand."

Inos nodded, biting her lip.

Azak chuckled. "I remember that misshapen runt as well as you do, and I am an excellent judge of men. He is spiteful, vindictive. He is malevolent. I say he revels in the mischief he can create."

"That's worse," she muttered. "Evil for evil's sake?"

Ha! She could not disagree when he pointed out the truth. He had bested her arguments as easily as he could overcome her physical strength if he chose to do so. The prospect was enormously exciting. None of his women ever put up a convincing resistance, even if he ordered them to.

"The Impire is vulnerable, Inos, as it has never been. It lies before us, naked and helpless. It is weak and we are strong. We can inflict what hurt we want and take any satisfaction whatsoever, any retribution we choose for past humiliations. It is mine to take!"

And so was she.

Her green eyes narrowed as she appraised the threat. "But what of Thume, Caliph? What happens in the Accursed Land?

Many armies have invaded Thume in the last thousand years, and they have vanished without a trace."

"Not all of them. Some have marched through without harm, seeing not a living soul. Yes, I have sorcerers to aid me. I lead a well-disciplined force that will do no damage to whatever spirit rules that land. We seek only to pass through and be gone. It is a risk, but one I have determined to take."

"I think you are crazy," she whispered.

He laughed. Crazy? He would show her what crazy was! His laughter grew louder, echoing through the chamber. She cowered back in her chair, and that amused him even more. "Perhaps I am," he said when he recovered his breath. "But you should not apply the standards of ordinary men to me. I am one of the great figures of history."

She seemed to have shrunk. She must know what he was thinking of now. "What did you do with the others who were captured with me?"

"Threw them in a dungeon."

"A shielded dungeon, I presume?"

He nodded. "So there are sorcerers among them?"

He glanced quickly at his magic ring, but her reply did not darken the pearl.

"Yes. And they are worried about the Covin's scrutiny, so a shielded dungeon may seem like a welcome refuge to them."

"Rap himself?" Dwarves, goblins, one jotunn, one imp—there had been no report of a faun, but he might be disguised.

"No, not Rap."

Furkar: *She is holding something back, Majesty!*

Let her! It could not matter. Her associates could lie in that dungeon until they rotted. When he returned, Azak would investigate them. Until then, Evil take them!

Silence fell, silence broken only by the hum of insects. Dawn could not be far off, and he should sleep. Already the panoplies would be starting the first preparations—cooking food, harnessing the draft animals. He really ought to sleep, and put off whatever satisfaction he might find in this woman until another night. But why should he? His strength had not deserted him yet. He was thoroughly aroused now. Nineteen years ago he had begun this war because a woman had been stolen from him. Now he was ready to consummate all his plans and preparation by invading the Impire, and lo!—here she was, within reach. Utterly in his power. How wonderfully appropriate!

"You say you were on your way to Thume?"

Green eyes studied him, and then she nodded.

"Then you shall go to Thume, and in a style befitting your station. You will go with me, as you went there before, but this time at the head of many tens of thousands."

She frowned, seeming to consider the matter as if his words had been an invitation and she had a choice. "I trust you will not be expecting me to share your tent, Azak?"

Oh, that was superb! She had style. She would be worthy. "You will do whatever I say, like everybody else."

"It will not be my preference."

"No? Will you choose death before dishonor?"

She colored at the mockery and raised her chin in pathetic defiance. "No, I do not expect to become suicidal. If you make advances, I shall not submit willingly, and I warn you, Azak Ak'Azakar, that my husband is a sorcerer and will hold you to account for your treatment of me."

He sprang to his feet. "Threats? You dare to threaten me?" He moved swiftly around the desk, shivering with joy and anticipation. "No one threatens the caliph!"

She rose, but he reached her before she could run. He grabbed her robe, hauled her to him, folded her in his arms. She struggled, but she was only a woman, small and puny. Not even a djinn! He crushed the breath out of her, caught her hair, twisted her face around to his. He sniffed the scent of her fear, saw the sweat shine on her forehead. No pretense now. Real, real fear.

"Threats?" He was panting and salivating so hard that speech was a real effort. "No one has threatened me since the night my wife was stolen from me. No more threats now, Inosolan?"

"Let me go, you brute!" She twisted vainly.

"Oh, that is trite, really trite. I would have expected better of you. Now let us see some passion!" He pushed his mouth on hers, crushing her even tighter.

She kicked at his shins and bit his tongue. He howled at the sudden pain. She squirmed, she screamed at him.

Bitch! She would scream to more purpose in a moment. He was past speech, past caring, more inflamed than he had felt in years. He took the neck of her gown with both hands and ripped it open. He forced her down on the desk and held her there easily with one hand on her chest, ignoring her efforts to punch and kick. She struggled uselessly while his other hand tore away her garments, exposing her breasts, her belly, then her thighs. Revenge! Justice! He would tame this yellow-haired bitch if it took him the rest of the night. Let her flat-faced sorcerer lover undo it then.

When days were long:
> In summer, when the days were long,
> We walked together in the wood:
> Our heart was light, our step was strong;
> Sweet flutterings were there in our blood,
> In summer, when the days were long.

Anonymous, Summer Days

⬱ INTERLUDE ⬱

The long days lengthened in that dread summer of 2999, and men spoke grimly of the coming of the millennium.

Death Bird himself was dead, but the destiny the Gods had given him still echoed through Pandemia. News of the Bandor Massacre spread across the Impire faster than any mundane couriers could have borne it. No one could say where the rumors came from, but they were everywhere and never denied.

In Julgistro, Ambel, and Pithmot, armies of shocked and ragged survivors wandered the wasteland left by the horde's passing. At first the wake was as sharply bounded as the trail of a tornado; of two towns that had once stood almost within sight of each other, one might be unharmed and the other only ashes. Inevitably the damage spread like a stain, for there were no legions to maintain order. Starving refugees began looting and destroying their more fortunate neighbors. In all the western Impire, no harvest would be gathered that year except the harvest of death. Famine and disease were the reapers now.

Shimlundox, the eastern Impire, had escaped the goblins. It was ravaged by the imps themselves.

Refugees, starving and desperate, had swept out of Hub in a horde outnumbering the original goblins manyfold. They stripped the land like locusts.

West and north toward them came the many legions the imperor had summoned from the borders. As the armored columns trudged along the great highways, civilians stared in amazement and then turned to gaze back where all these troops had come from, wondering what enemy might enter by those now-unguarded doors.

Had anyone known the true situation, the legions might have stabilized matters enough to allow some sort of crop to survive to harvest. Only in the south was there contact between the army and the rabble, and some skirmishing broke out when individual tribunes attempted to restore local order. Before the main forces could collide, Imperial couriers broke through the swarm and delivered new orders—the goblin crisis was over, the legions were to return to the bases they had left months before.

The legionaries cursed and turned around to begin retracing all those wearisome leagues.

Doubtless that recall had seemed like a wise move to whoever issued it, but a legion consumed many tons of food a day. The Imperial Commissariat had worked miracles in assembling depots along the road to Hub; it had not anticipated the sudden about-face. Refusing to watch their men starve, legates turned off the highways to follow lesser roads and began to requisition what they needed. Soon great swathes of the Impire were being looted at swordpoint by its own troops.

Official mourning for old Emshandar had ended at last. The court was engrossed in preparations for the coronation. Fifty years had passed since the last coronation, and Shandie had decreed that his must be the grandest in the history of the Impire.

The aristocracy, which would normally have retired to its country homes before the hot weather turned Hub into a fever pit, had mostly chosen to remain in the capital. The city exploded in a riot of salons and garden parties, making up for the loss of the previous social season. Although Lord Umpily attended many of these functions, he was believed to be in poor health. Not a few of his acquaintances remarked on his pallor. He was certainly jumpy. There were even unconfirmed rumors that he had lost his appetite.

In Guwush the rebellion raged with ever-greater fervor. Oshpoo had been given a promise for the future, but he had not agreed to stop his war before the unlikely Imperial pretender made good on his side of the bargain—if he ever could.

Triumphant gnomes swarmed on the depleted Imperial garrisons like piranha.

Ollion was a ghost city, haunted by fearful sentries waiting for the djinns. The Imperial Navy had every available ship patrolling the shore, ready for the Zarkian fleet's attack.

The dwarf army had returned to Dwanish. Furious, the Directorate deposed General Karax and dispatched its forces down the Dark River to carry the war to Urgaxox.

Every raider on the four oceans was homing on Nordland, where the thanes had run out their longships. Every male jotunn who could find a lord to swear to was headed for Nintor, for the Longday Moot. No one doubted that this year it would be a war moot. Oarsmen chanted battle songs in time to the racing waves.

A strange occult campaign was being waged in Dragon Reach. Many of the anthropophagi sorcerers had been betrayed by Witch Grunth and those of her trolls who had been captured with her, but tiny bands still roamed at large, attempting to set their snares under the dread eye of the Covin.

Sir Acopulo reached a trading rendezvous off the western coast of Kerith and transferred to an impish merchantman bound for Zark, sending *Seaspawn* on her way with his blessings.

Rap climbed a sky tree, and then departed from Ilrane much faster than he had expected. Ylo and Eshiala wandered the hills of eastern Qoble, lovers in search of sanctuary, wishing only to be left alone.

The djinn army marched along the coast under the beetling crags of the Progistes Mountains.

In far-off Krasnegar the harbor had been free of ice for a month. Herds and workers swarmed over the hills in their customary summer business, but this year the merchants waited by the docks in vain. The world seemed to have forgotten Krasnegar. No ships came from the sea, nor traders from the woods.

⊂ SEVEN ⊃

Hope never comes

1

The lowermost dungeon at Quern lay far underground, an odious cavern carved out centuries ago from the living rock. The darkness was absolute, the air unbreathable, and water dripped constantly. Sanitation was left to natural seepage. Once a day a squad of soldiers delivered food under the direction of the chief jailer. It was the most unwelcome assignment in the fortress.

Torches sputtered, emitting foul fumes and casting evil shadows on the rough walls. The chief jailer peered cautiously through the iron bars of the gate, making sure the corridor beyond was unoccupied. Then he jangled keys and set to work on the rusty locks—five of them. At his back, soldiers were gagging already in the stench.

The gate creaked open unwillingly. With swords drawn, the squad advanced through it and then halted while it was locked behind them. And then they advanced again, down the slanted passage, until they reached the dungeon itself.

The chief jailer peered around appraisingly in the flickering light—two djinns, three dwarves, two of those green monsters, one imp, one female jotunn. All correct and accounted for. All lying on their backs, their legs held upright by fetters in the walls, all unspeakably fouled. They all had their eyes closed against the unaccustomed light.

"Move if you can!" he growled.

Hands moved. They were all still alive.

He moved cautiously around the cell with his basket, precarious on the slimy footing, staying as far as possible from the cesspool in the center. Every day he came to distribute stale loaves and scraps of vegetables to the inmates. For water they could sit up and lick the rock. It was something to occupy their time.

A few groaned. Nobody spoke. But all still living! They were a tough bunch, this. Three days was standard life expectancy in the lowermost dungeon.

The squad moved out again and he followed. Locks and bars clanged. Darkness returned. Silence returned.

"It's a dull job but somebody has to do it," Raspnex remarked.

A cool breeze brought scents of pinewoods and fresh grass. Sunlight or something like it shone bright on leather chairs and lavish carpeting, potted flowers, a sparkling fountain in a marble pond. Paintings and stags' heads ornamented the timbered walls; the wide windows looked out on meadows and snowy peaks, or seemed to. The dungeon was not merely much larger than it had been a few moments ago, it was now transformed into a comfy saloon, combining varied hints of ship's cabin, men's clubroom, village meetinghouse, and officers' mess hall.

Moon Baiter and Frazkr resumed their game of *thali* on a table of ebony inlaid with ivory. Shandie picked up his book. Raspnex poured himself a tankard of ale at the bar.

The two djinns set to work sharpening their scimitars again. The sorcerers had promised them the chief jailer.

Shandie tossed his book aside and heaved himself out of his armchair. "Did you learn anything new?"

The dwarf paused in his departure, tankard in hand. "Not much. Those nonentities won't be told anything significant. The army has left and not returned. The town's a graveyard."

"Arrgh! How much longer must we endure this?"

Raspnex frowned ominously. "Until Longday. You know." The little man was better dressed than Shandie had ever seen him, in a dark suit with colored piping on the lapels and trousers, silver-buckled shoes. By dwarf standards, he was an astonishing dandy. Even his iron-gray beard looked neat and trim. "Anything more you need, your Majesty?" he inquired sarcastically.

Shandie gritted his teeth. "I have a horrible suspicion that I am imagining all of this! I am convinced I am actually chained to a wall by my ankles."

The goblins were leering at him. Even the dwarves seemed amused. The two djinns were listening intently, though. Like him, they were mundane.

"Well, you're not!" the warlock said with all his old grumpiness. "What you see may not be all real, but it's a lot closer to reality than what the jailer sees. If you want anything, just ask—wine? Roast pheasant? A woman, maybe?"

Before the imperor could answer, the taller of the two djinns roared, "Is *that* possible?" His red eyes shone like hot coals.

Raspnex turned a sour gaze on him, having to look *up* although he was standing and the djinn was sitting on a soft divan. "Strictly speaking, no. But we can arrange it so you won't know the difference."

Both djinns leaped to their feet.

The dwarf sighed and waved a shovel hand at the door that led to their quarters. "Go ahead, then."

The djinns vanished at a run and the door slammed.

"Last we'll see of them for a while!" Moon Baiter remarked with a leer of fangs.

"You organize it, then," Raspnex growled. "Give you a chance to be inventive! You, too?" he demanded of Shandie.

For a moment the imperor thought of Eshiala, but his heart screamed at the thought of associating her with this vile dungeon, even an illusionary Eshiala.

"No. But I do want to know what's happening to Inos!"

Raspnex scowled and looked away. "She'll be all right! Azak knows her of old and she's Rap's wife. Even the caliph won't dare hurt Inos! Expect she's living in real luxury, not just this occult artifice."

"You don't know that!"

"No. But I know that anything we do about it is more likely to make things worse than better for her. Don't accuse me of cowardice, imp!"

Shandie clenched his fists. "I still don't see why we can't risk sending out a scout! I can walk through the shielding. If you made me some tools I could pick the locks—"

"You'd be the only imp at large in the city and the Covin may still be watching. I've told you—we stay here until Longday. Then we'll break out in force and join in whatever's happening. Until then, read your damnable poetry."

Raspnex turned on his heel and stamped off into the quarters he shared with Jarga. The door clicked shut.

Shandie sat down angrily, avoiding the amused looks on the others' faces.

Come to think of it, what was the old warlock up to with the jotunn? Shandie hadn't seen her in days.

2

Bluerock had been a major city until the hurricane of 2953 caused the Pearlpool River to change its course and find a new mouth several leagues to the south. The harbor silted rapidly. Sailors departed first; merchants soon followed. Finding themselves without clientele, the artists and artisans went, also, and so did the harlots and the clergy. Teachers failed to find scholars, doctors ran out of patients. Within a generation, Bluerock shriveled from a great trading port to a shabby fishing town. Within another it was almost deserted.

Many of its buildings stood empty, inhabited only by bats and vermin, until the great hurricane of 2999 flattened them, and thereby completed the work the earlier storm had begun.

On the morning after the hurricane, Sister Chastity was out gathering windfalls—bananas, oranges, breadfruit, and many others.

The grounds of the convent were a shambles of branches and toppled trees, steaming in the hot sun and reeking of mulch. One chicken coop had disappeared and the dairy had lost half its roof, but the main building had survived unscathed. It had seen many hurricanes, for the Refuge of Constant Service had originally been built as a fortress. Its walls were cubits thick and its roof lead-coated. The Sisterhood had taken it over when shifting tides of politics had made a fortress at Bluerock unnecessary, some centuries ago. Since then the Refuge had served as a home for the religious and a hospice to the needy.

Chastity straightened and rubbed her aching back. To clear up this mess and restore the grounds to tidiness was going to take months. It was a task for an army of able-bodied gardeners, not eight aging women. She stooped with a grunt to lift her laden basket. There must be some good in hurricanes, for Holy Writ insisted that there was good in everything. There must be some good in all this waste and destruction, if she could only see it. Perhaps the exercise would be beneficial. The ways of the Gods were inscrutable. That was what faith was for.

Picking her way through the debris, she headed for the root cellar. The basket seemed to grow steadily heavier with every step. At the gate of the herb garden she paused to catch her breath, resting her burden on the wall.

She was disconcerted to discover that she could see the river from there, as the floral hedge had totally vanished. Oh, dear! The estuary was a swamp of floating wreckage. Beyond it stood the remains of the city. It was too far off to make out much detail, but many temple spires had disappeared. Tragedy!

"It's a mess, isn't it?" boomed a hearty voice.

Chastity turned, carefully not loosing her grip on the basket. Sister Docility was approaching, a rake slung over her shoulder. Docility was a large and energetic woman, with an infectious cheerfulness. She was just a teeny bit *wearing* at times, but no one could *dislike* Sister Docility.

"It is a disaster!" Chastity said. "I keep feeling that we should be over there, ministering to the injured."

Sister Docility guffawed. "And just how do you propose to get there?"

"You don't mean the bridge is down?"

"So Sister Humility says."

Oh, dear! Sister Humility was a mere forty-five, the youngest of the eight remaining Sisters. She had the best eyesight of any of them, and reminded the others of it at every opportunity.

"But . . . Then we are cut off from the city?"

"What city?" Docility demanded, standing her rake upright and leaning on it. "Bluerock hasn't been a real city since I was a girl, and even then it was failing. There's precious little left of it now."

"But if the bridge is down, then there will be no travelers coming by!"

The big woman shrugged. "We had two visitors last year and none the year before. I doubt the difference will be noticeable."

Chastity sighed. What use was a Refuge without refugees, or oaths of service when there was nobody to serve? What good did eight elderly women do when they sang praise to the Gods and nobody heard? The Gods Themselves surely did not need to be reminded of Their goodness. When the sick were out of reach there could be no healing. When no new initiates came there could be no teaching—and there had been no initiates at the Refuge for many, many years. Chastity felt guilt at thinking such negative thoughts, but Constant Service seemed to be serving no useful purpose at all now. If the bridge was down, it was virtually cut off from the entire world on its little headland.

"Why," Docility demanded in a stern voice, "are you out here anyway?"

"Why are you?" Chastity inquired with mild reproof.

The big woman pulled a face. Then her eyes twinkled. "To build up an appetite, I suppose."

Chastity suppressed an unseemly snigger. Docility was not merely tall, she was buxom, also, and she enjoyed her food. Today was Sister Virtue's turn to be Mother Superior. Virtue enjoyed cooking, so she almost always assigned herself kitchen duties, usually with disastrous results. Chastity was the most skilled cook among the eight of them—that was not vanity, it was acknowledged fact. She enjoyed cooking, which possibly *was* vanity. But the Acting Mother Superior had told Sister Chastity to gather up the deadfall fruit before it rotted, so that was what she must do, bound by her vows of obedience.

She must not complain at that, because yesterday she herself had been Mother and had sternly kept everyone at work when they had all been tempted to stand and stare out the windows at the hurricane.

It was seven years since old Verity had died. The sisters had written to the Matriarch of their order, asking her to name a replacement Mother Superior. The letter had perhaps gone astray, but at any rate no answer had ever come, so the sisters had continued to rotate the office among themselves ever since. Seven years ago, each sister had been Mother every fifteenth day. Now it was every eighth. One day there would be only one of them left and she could be Mother Superior all the time.

The arrangement worked quite well and no one ever suggested changing it. If the sisters ever did decide to choose a permanent leader, it would certainly be Docility. She was the only one of them with any real knack for leadership. She always took charge when there was a crisis. Like coping with yesterday's hurricane, for instance—Docility had done all the thinking and planning and then dropped hints to Chastity so she could give the actual orders.

"I was instructed to tidy the grounds!" Docility remarked

manfully. She flexed an ample arm. "Stand aside, lest I rake you up by mistake."

"I shall be very careful!" Chastity promised, smiling. "But perhaps you could begin by clearing a path to the quinces? There must be a million quinces on the ground, and I can't get to them. I can make marmalade with them tomorrow."

"Excellent thinking!" Docility boomed. "Want me to take that load in for you?"

Chastity would love to have her burden taken from her, for her back was already promising to keep her awake all night, but she said, "Oh, I can manage, thank you." She was just about to resume her journey when—

"Sisters! Daughters, I mean!" Acting Mother Superior Virtue came hurrying along the path. Virtue was elderly and petite. Her hair now was as white as her skin, although of course she kept it hidden under her headcloth. She must have been a beauty in her youth, and her face was still striking. At sixty-seven, she was the oldest of the eight, but spry enough that she seemed likely to outlast most of them. During her days as leader, she tolerated no backtalk.

"Mother?" Docility and Chastity spoke in perfect unison.

Virtue was perturbed. There were pink splotches on her cheekbones. Curiously, she was clutching a coil of rope.

"A boat is approaching the headland!"

Docility propped her rake against the wall and rubbed her hands. Her eyes gleamed. "Mariners in need of succor, Mother?"

"That would seem to be a logical presumption!" Virtue barely came up to the large woman's shoulder, but her manner left no doubt that today she was in charge. She had known whose help to enlist when there was trouble, though. Chastity was involved only because she happened to be in Docility's vicinity.

"It has been many years!" Chastity said. No ships called at Bluerock now.

"That is no reason to delay," the Mother of the day said. "You may come, also, in case we need to summon more help." She swept off in a swirl of black cotton robe. Docility followed with long strides.

"But?" Chastity said to the empty air. Rope, yes, but should they not also take blankets and medicines and water bottles? Apparently not, because she was already alone. She would be sent back to fetch them, most likely. She lowered her basket painfully to the ground and hobbled off after the other two.

The cliff path was a morass of treacherous mud. Holding skirts up, the three ladies picked their way down it circumspectly, despite the urgency of their mission.

Chastity could just barely remember the last ship to be wrecked below the Refuge, although such disasters had been common when Bluerock was a busy port. Virtue must have assisted at several rescue efforts in her youth. The danger was Scalpel Rocks. If a vessel struck those, then the crew had little chance of survival. If it cleared them safely, it would be swept into the bay and run aground on the sand. The odds were better there, especially when the tide was out, as now.

Puffing, the three reached the flat grassy lookout at the point of the headland and stopped to take stock. The wind had dropped, but the sea was still troubled. Dangerous green swells marched shoreward, bursting in white breakers below the lookout, hurling spray skyward. Masses of floating brown kelp testified to the violence of the storm; the air smelled clean and salty.

The boat was a tiny dinghy, half awash. It had already cleared Scalpel Rocks and was being swept around the headland, almost directly under the watchers. It contained a single mariner, sitting on a thwart, clutching the bare mast with both arms and leaning against it. From the look of him, he was alive, but in a weakened condition, barely conscious, perhaps unaware that he was about to be shipwrecked.

Chastity held her breath until she almost choked. Then she glanced sideways at the other two. They did not seem to have noticed what she had noticed.

"Excellent!" Virtue said, as if she had arranged matters herself. She raised a hand to her eyes and stuck her neck out, peering. "Er—isn't he wearing black? You don't suppose he could be a priest, do you?"

Neither of the others spoke. A strange flush showed now on Docility's pale cheeks. So she had noticed!

"We must head for the beach, Daughters."

"But—" Chastity said. Her heart was pounding unbearably.

"I do hope he doesn't require medical help," Virtue continued. "Or one of us is going to have a long walk. Come."

"Just a moment!" Docility barked. "We had best decide what we are going to do while we can still think clearly."

Chastity did not think she was thinking very clearly at all. Her head was spinning, her knees trembled. If a mere glimpse at this distance could upset her like this, then what would happen at close quarters?

"What?" Virtue turned to peer in surprise at the big woman.

"He is a mainlander!"

The Mother Superior said, "Oh, damn!"

The three stared at one another in appalled silence. The boat had passed the headland and was into the bay.

"What can we do?" Verity wrung her hands.

A strange gleam shone in Docility's silver eyes. "It will be all right! No other men ever come here! With the bridge down, we shall probably never have visitors ever again!" She glanced defiantly from Virtue to Chastity and back, as if daring them to disagree.

"But our vows!" Virtue whimpered.

"It is not a sin!" As always in emergencies, the big woman had taken command. "The Church recognizes the impossibility of resisting the curse. Or are you ordering us to let the man drown, Mother?"

"No, of course not! But what of ourselves? I mean . . . Well, we shall quarrel! Fight, even! It will be awful!"

Chastity shivered, having a momentary nightmare of Sister Docility wielding her rake against all seven of her sisters. There were butcher cleavers in the kitchen. The possibilities were appalling!

Docility drew herself up to her full height. Cotton seemed to strain over her ample bosom in a way Chastity had never noticed it doing before. "We are not mad children! We are mature women. Holy ladies! It will be a test of our commitment, of course, but we have all lived together in harmony for many years. Surely we can agree on, er . . ."

Even Docility could not quite put it into words.

"*Share* him, you mean?" Chastity whispered.

"We shall have to. Just as we share the leadership."

"Really!" Virtue protested.

"Well . . ." she added.

"Indeed!" she concluded triumphantly. "You are perfectly right, Daughter. We cannot let him drown, and we cannot escape the consequences. The two, er, duties will have to go together, and today I am Mother." She beamed excitedly.

"No, Mother!" Docility said firmly. "Duty and, er, pleasure . . ." She cleared her throat harshly. "I mean, one cannot supervise the work schedules and—*ahem!*—tend the visitor at the same time. We must establish some other rule."

Virtue's eyes flashed. "I think it is my prerogative to settle this matter, as I am Mother Superior at the moment."

"Your responsibility is a grave trial, Mother," Docility said with what seemed to be a severe effort. "But would it not make more sense if we assigned the, er, hospitality duty to another day? Fewer distractions?"

"The following day!" Chastity exclaimed. "The day after being Mother. A reward!"

"Reward?" Her companions turned shocked stares on her.

"Well, er . . . Well, yes! Why not be honest about it?" Chastity was astonished to find herself arguing with them like this, but her heart had not thumped so ferociously in years. She thought she might burst into tears if they refused her now.

"I suppose that does make sense," Virtue admitted, wringing her hands. "I mean, tomorrow is not so very long to wait."

"Six days?" Docility moaned. "I shall be the last!"

"A real test of your commitment!" Chastity snapped.

"Indeed!" Docility bit her lip. "Of course, if he is young and hale . . . and strong . . ."

"Muscular, you mean?" The strange visions floating up from Chastity's imagination were probably cause for a three-day contrition.

"Not necessarily, although I hope, I mean, some men can, are capable of, like to . . . One a day is not necessarily the limit."

Docility's flush darkened as the other two eyed her with open suspicion.

"As long as he plays no favorites!" Virtue conceded.

"Exactly what I was trying to say," Docility agreed with relief. "After all we must consider our, er, guest's wishes, also. If we explain the problem, he may be able to satisfy—" Her eyes widened.

The other two spun around and then uttered shrieks of alarm. The dinghy was very close to the beach already.

"No, wait!" Docility's big hand settled on her Superior's shoulder. "The surf is not extreme. Perhaps Sister Chastity can handle . . . I mean, she will not require assistance. You and I, Mother, should go and warn the others of what we, you that is, have decided."

Without waiting for further encouragement or the results of the argument, Chastity lifted her skirts and ran.

* * *

Hopelessly out of breath, she reached the beach just as the boat did. It slued sideways and tipped. The next wave hurled it over. She saw the occupant fall clear before it turned turtle. She plunged into the water, struggling to run as waves tugged at her skirts, beat against her knees, her thighs, her waist. The boat rolled and bounced, its mast leaping alongside in a tangle of ropes. Chastity went down and was submerged. A wave rolled her and thumped her on the seabed; she swallowed water; choked. Then she sat up and found her head above the surface. She coughed. A big green wave curled up before her.

Strong hands grabbed her and pulled her erect. The sailor! She clung to him as the wave broke around them. Then the two of them stumbled awkwardly shoreward together, holding each other, gazing at each other in joyful wonder.

He was not young—about her own age. Thin silver hair was streaked over his face and scalp, white stubble adorned his cheeks. But his face was a wonderful tan color and his eyes a wild, mysterious black. And he *was* a priest! Any lingering doubts about sin could be forgotten if a priest was involved, and he certainly was involved. He seemed even more frantically eager than she.

"Wet clothes!" she said. She must get him out of his wet clothes before he caught a chill, and apparently he had the same idea about hers. She was fumbling with the buttons on his back before the two of them were even out of the water, then her patience gave out. His clerical habit was tattered already—she ripped it apart. He might not be young and muscular, but he had a wonderfully hairy chest. He wore some sort of packages strapped around his waist, and she had trouble getting them off him because he was busy with her underwear and the two of them kept getting in each other's way. He was moaning with frustration and impatience.

Then it was done, all except for his socks, which didn't matter. He might be scrawny-limbed and pot-bellied, but oh, how beautiful he was! His lips pressed against hers. She clasped him to her, hairy chest against breasts. They sank to the sand together. As her last rational thoughts were swirled away by storms of passion, Sister Chastity realized that the doubts she had felt earlier had been answered.

There was much good in hurricanes.

3

Rap hit the water with an impact that half stunned him. In a moment he became aware that his clothing was slowing his descent into the depths, but already the light had faded to green darkness and he was choking. He tried to kick, fought against panic as his boots resisted, watched the daylight grow slowly, slowly brighter. Saltwater filled his nose and mouth. At the last possible moment he broke surface and gasped life-saving air before he went under again.

He tugged his right boot off; seized another breath, then set to work on the left. After that he took a brief rest, treading water, before he began tugging at sodden garments. By the time he had stripped to his breeches, he already felt exhausted.

He had been a strong swimmer twenty years ago. Now he was twenty years older and had not swum a stroke since. Blue-green swells raised him, lowered him, and there was nothing but sea anywhere. He snorted water out of his aching nose. This might all be some sort of elvish prank, but more likely Thume's occult defenses had skewed the sorcery and deflected him.

How far? If he was as much as a league out to sea, then he would never make it. And which way? North was usually landward in the Summer Seas. Calling up blurred memories of charts, though, he recalled that the coast of Thume trended almost north–south, so he ought to head eastward—unless he'd been bounced right over the land and come down in the Morning Sea instead. The water felt warmish, so he'd best assume he hadn't. The early sun would lie roughly southeast . . . except that he'd gone a long way east and the sun would be higher here.

Time for sorcery! He must remove his body shielding and use farsight—and hope that the defenses, whatever they were, did not make him forget where he was supposed to be going, and also hope that the Covin had not detected a hint of his arrival and set watch for more power in use.

His shielding would not budge, he remained mundane.

That was ridiculous! He stopped treading water for a moment, letting himself sink as he tried again, but again his power failed to operate. No one could make a spell so strong he could not undo it! It was impossible. This must be more

Thumian mischief. No help for it, though, he would just have to swim.

He kicked back to the surface, turned until the sun was over his right ear, and began.

Sometime in the long ordeal that followed, he worked out what had happened to his sorcery. Three of the four words he knew were feeble wraiths of words, words that Inos had crippled years ago by broadcasting them to a multitude of listeners. The only effective word of the four was the one she had never known, the one he'd bullied Sagorn into sharing with him, long ago.

So now he knew what had happened in the sky tree after he had been sent on his way. Obviously, Lith'rian had unraveled the sequential spell in order to administer justice on Darad. *Thrown to the winds,* the warlock had said, and no imagination was needed to understand what that meant in a sky tree. The jotunn was probably dead already. He had attempted a massacre and might have slaughtered everyone present had he not been balked by sorcery. Killing had been a reflex to him, he had been a wild beast. Rap could not find it in his heart to mourn.

He felt no sorrow, only guilt. In retrospect, he saw that he had let personal gratitude blind his judgment. He had been wrong to include Darad in the meld when he replaced the sequential spell. He should have left the jotunn out and transported him to Nordland, where his behavior would have been controlled by others of his own kind.

Yet who could say what Darad might have done then? Free of the time limits of the spell and knowing a word of power, he might easily have won himself a thanedom and led murderous raids southward to ravish the coasts of the Impire. "Might have been" was not a game for mortals.

Lith'rian had not harmed the others. Sagorn, Thinal, Jalon, and Andor must at least be alive, for they were Rap's problem. The word of power must now serve five where it had once served only two. He could not remove his own spell. He was even less of a sorcerer than he had been before.

He was a lot less of a swimmer, too. He kept up a slow, leisurely stroke, telling himself that he was conserving his strength and trying to avoid a killer cramp. In fact, of course, it was all he was capable of.

He was going to drown.

There were worse ways to die. It was better than falling into Zinixo's clutches, for a start. His biggest regret was that Inos would never know what had happened to him. He wished he had been less brusque when they said good-bye, three-quarters of a year ago. He had walked out of her life without warning and she would never know that his corpse had fed fish in the Sea of Sorrows.

He began taking rests, floating on his back. The rests grew longer and more frequent.

He had no memory of the end of the swim. Suddenly he was in surf, and his knees hit sand. He rolled, scrabbling vainly with his fingers to resist the undertow. Then he was lying on a beach with shallow water racing away around him. Behind him, he could hear the next wave coming.

His limbs would not take his weight. They were made of dough. Froth surged over his legs, lifting him, bearing him landward. Again he grounded and dug fingers in the sand to fight against the back flow. He dragged himself a span or so up the beach and the next surge did not move him.

So he was in Thume. Or perhaps the Keriths, or almost anywhere. He was deadwood; he could not lift his head. He needed a drink. He needed shade, for the sun was a furnace on his back. He was going to go to sleep. Sleep was death. Couldn't help it.

A flapping sound made him open his eyes. A large gull had settled near him and was busily tucking its wings back into storage. It studied him with one cruel yellow eye.

"Go away!" he mumbled through salt-cracked lips. "Shoo."

The gull tried the other eye.

Another gull flapped down on his other side, his left side, out of sight.

"I'm not dead yet. Come back in an hour or two."

The first gull waddled two steps forward.

Humiliation! To be so weak that a stupid seagull could peck his eyes out! He wanted to weep with frustration. *"Shoo! G'way!"*

More gulls shrieked overhead. They would swarm over him like flies. If he could only have a drink of fresh water, he might find the strength to move. Drinking seawater drove a man insane, didn't it? He had probably lowered the level of the oceans perceptibly. His head was spinning and his belly was racked with cramps.

The gull spread its wings and began to flap madly. It took off, low above the sand. What had scared it? Over the rumble of the surf, Rap heard a voice, a human voice, shouting.

With a mumble of relief, he contrived to turn his head and look to his left. A girl was running over the sand toward him. She had long black hair, like Kadie.

He made out the word she was shouting as she ran.

He must be delirious already. He was having delusions.

4

"Daddy, Daddy, Daddy, Daddy . . ."

Delirious or not, by the time the apparition reached him, Rap had managed to struggle to his knees. It could not possibly be Kadie, and yet it looked just like Kadie—thinner, perhaps, than he recalled, but a juvenile imp with trailing black hair and emerald eyes. She wore a long striped skirt and a white cotton blouse. And a *sword*? Obviously it was an illusion! But it sounded like Kadie. It stopped just out of reach and regarded him nervously.

"Papa?"

He held out trembling arms and tried to speak her name. What came out was a strangled croak: "Water?"

She backed away a couple of steps and looked around. No, that was never Kadie! Rap slumped limply to the sand. There was another girl . . . woman? Sorcery? No, for magic could not penetrate his shielding. Delirium!

Then a beaker of cool water was thrust at him and hands helped him hold it to his mouth. He drank and drank. He threw it all up and then drank more.

"Why are you shielded?" a woman's voice asked. "If you remove that shielding, I can help you."

"I can't."

"Oh. There isn't much to it. There!"

Occult strength poured new life into him. His pain vanished, his head cleared. He blinked and returned to reality with a rush—gritty sand, baking sun, saltwater, and the rumble of the sea.

Two girls. One could only be a pixie. Her eyes were elvish, big and slanted, but gold. Her ears were even more pointed than an elf's, but her hair was hazel, her skin fawn, her nose wide. She was very young, unless pixies, like elves, did not show their age. The other was either his older daughter or an exact double.

"Kadie! Is it really you?" He scrambled to his feet in joy.

Kadie flinched at his approach. She went rigid in his embrace and did not respond. When he released her, she stepped quickly to the other girl's side, looking horrified.

"Kadie?"

"She has had a harrowing experience, your Majesty."

Only now did Rap register the ambience. It was a ghostly shadow of the ambience he had known, indicating his loss of power, but the pixie was rock solid in it. She must be a very powerful sorceress.

He bowed unsteadily to her. "I am Rap, of Krasnegar."

"I am Archon Thaïle of the College," she said aloud. *"Your daughter was a prisoner of the goblins,"* she added privately. *"They did not harm her physically, but she has not yet recovered from the ordeal. Perhaps more clothes would calm her— she seems to mistrust men with bare chests. May I assist?"*

"I'm very glad to see you, Papa," Kadie said uncertainly. "Oh!"

Rap had said, *"Please,"* to the pixie, and been immediately clothed in shirt and long trousers and sandals, with loose, cool cotton replacing his sodden wool breeches.

"Kadie, my darling!" Again he offered his arms, and this time she seemed more willing to be hugged, now he was no longer a half-naked castaway. Yet again she returned quickly to the pixie, her smile unconvincing and troubled. Where was his little minx, the juvenile harridan who tried to run the entire kingdom? Where was the irrepressible tormentor who battled her wits with her father in make-believe revolutions? Had reality so damaged the starry-eyed storybook princess? Tears sprang to his eyes. Oh, Kadie, Kadie!

"Who did this? And what?"

"She was a prisoner of goblins for many months," the sorceress said sadly. *"Dawn alone will not banish such nightmares."*

"Kadie—your mother?"

Kadie blinked uncertainly and surreptitiously clasped the other girl's hand, as if in need of reassurance. "Mama and Gath went off with the imperor, Papa. I don't know what happened to them."

"Kinvale? The goblins took Kinvale?"

She nodded, edging even closer to the pixie. "They burned

it and they were going to kill the imperor but Gath saved him I mean Mama did because Gath told her who he was and then Death Bird took me as hostage and was going to marry me to his son Blood Beak and the other three were sent off with the dwarves." She blinked fearfully at him.

Marry her? Dwarves? Where did dwarves come into this? Rap clamped a hold on his tongue. As the Thaïle girl had said, Kadie was obviously in a state of distress. Sorcery could heal damaged bodies, but not bruised souls. *Oh, my fledgling!*

"I'm so glad that you're safe, anyway!" he said, forcing a smile.

She returned the smile doubtfully. "And you, Papa. I kept hoping you would come and rescue me but you never did. I prayed to the God of Rescues. Is there a God of Rescues?"

His heart felt as if it were being squeezed. "I don't know, Kadie. But someone rescued you?"

"Thaïle did!"

"She was at Bandor, your Majesty."

"She saw the massacre?"

"She was the only survivor. I detected her sword."

Sword? What sword? Rap peered in bewilderment at his daughter. He remembered that he had seen her wearing a sword a moment ago. Oh! Yes, there was indeed a rapier hanging at her side, but now it was fuzzy and hard to make out. How had Kadie ever acquired a magic sword? And *Kadie* the only survivor of that appalling destruction, his child?

He took a very deep breath. Then he looked around, concentrating. The three of them stood at the water's edge on a long white beach. Inland lay grassy dunes and clumps of trees, and low hills beyond them. The serenity of the land was as palpable as the sunlight. Thume. He was in Thume. With Kadie.

The other girl—woman—was regarding him anxiously.

"So this is the Accursed Land?" he said, trying to believe it. "I knew that there were people still, because my wife visited here, many years ago. I suspect that there was sorcery. I had trouble making anyone else agree with me. The inattention spell is extraordinarily potent."

"I know about your wife. Very few come and depart safely, your Majesty."

"Please call me Rap. And your title—Archon? Are you a ruler here, then?"

The young face was solemn. "Thume is ruled by the Keeper, and I have to take you to her at once."

Mm! His wild hypothesis seemed to have been proved correct. There was sorcery in Thume, much sorcery. That did not mean that he would be a welcome visitor, of course. Kadie had definitely flinched at the mention of the Keeper, whoever she was.

But Kadie was safe, if not quite unharmed, and that was wonderful. Yet, like him, she was an intruder in a closed land.

A long time ago a God had warned him that he must lose a child. Kadie? He had a horrible feeling that part of Kadie had been lost, perhaps forever.

Or Gath? And where was Inos?

Perhaps the Keeper, whoever she was, would have some answers.

5

Like some gigantic millipede, the caliph's army crawled along the coast of the Morning Sea. On one hand rose the barren crags of the Progistes Mountains, on the other white foam washed the cliffs. Only seabirds kept vigil in the vast bleak terrain.

This no-man's land was unmapped, but there were old records of Imperial armies invading Zark across these borders, so a return journey must be possible. At times progress was halted by the need to bridge wadis or scout a passable route, and water was strictly rationed. By and large, though, the expedition was proceeding on schedule.

The caliph was pleased. So Zarga said.

Azak had carried through on his promise to bring Inos back to Thume. She journeyed in a screened wagon with six of his women. It creaked and rocked and tortured her with nausea. Its heavy drapes cut out all view of the world and made the interior insufferably hot. Drawn by oxen, unsprung, the cumbersome vehicle tossed its unfortunate passengers around on their silken mattresses. At times it would lurch bodily sideways and they would all slide together, ending as a screaming heap of cushions and nubile female djinn. And Inos. Often she would wrench her twisted shoulder in these scrimmages, or bang her swollen face, and at such times she was hard put not to express her true feelings about the mighty Azak.

This was one of three wagons used to transport the royal seraglio when the caliph campaigned—a small part of the royal seraglio, apparently. Only the most favored concubines had been selected. They were all greatly impressed by the honor. They were all very young and lovely. Except Inos.

She gritted her teeth as she listened to their inane chatter. She kept her own council when they praised their lord the caliph and congratulated themselves on their good fortune in being allowed to serve him. Inos puzzled them greatly. She answered all their questions—and told them nothing, because they had not known what to ask. They were barely aware that there was a world beyond the harem walls, or people other than djinns.

At times they puzzled Inos. They could be as vicious as adders in their talk, and once in a while would fly at one another with nails slashing, yet there was a strange innocence about them. They were pets, like fish in a bowl. Since childhood they had been taught to believe that their only purpose in life was to please the caliph and breed him sons. They saw no world beyond Azak. He was their God. How could they possibly be happy with minds so stunted? But they were happy. By and large, Inos had never met a group of people so content.

She preferred the company of these juvenile rabbits to that of their supervisor—Nurkeen, keeper of the caliph's women. Nurkeen was almost certainly one of Azak's innumerable sisters, and she was a poisoned prune of a hag. Nurkeen was no rabbit. Nurkeen and Inosolan were fire and oil. Fortunately, at the moment Nurkeen was riding in one of the other wagons.

There had been a brief stop at noon. Zarga, who was all of fifteen, had been summoned to the caliph's tent. Now she was reporting to her companions. He had been very happy with the progress of the army. He had been jovial, also very energetic and demanding. That was always a good sign. She had pleased him and given him great satisfaction. He had said so.

They always said that. Mindless little idiots!

He might even send for her again this evening. They always hoped that—twice in one day was a lifetime triumph.

He had wrapped the emerald sash around her naked body before he coupled with her. That was a very great honor. The others all hastened to claim that he had done that with them, too, many times.

The wagon rumbled forward, tipped, straightened, lurched. Outside, in the fresh air and sunshine, soldiers were singing a marching song as they trudged. Its theme was the glory and invincibility of the caliph.

Zarga glanced pityingly at Inos. "It is very foolish to resist him," she said primly.

"I daresay," Inos retorted through her swollen lips. "It was because I would not resist him that he struck me."

The others all looked puzzled. "But if he told you to resist, then why did you not resist?"

"Just chicken, I guess," Inos said grimly. Her shoulder was the worst, but she had other sore places and few of them were the fault of the wagon. "Is it true he uses magic to maintain his virility?"

Squeals of shocked denial . . .

No one had ever suggested such a treasonous idea in Inos' hearing, but the remark was enough to bring the conversation around to sorcery. She was a captive and must endure what her captor dealt out, but in the process she was taking the opportunity to learn as much as she could about Azak and Azak's rise to omnipotence in Zark and Azak's use of sorcery. Azak would probably have been very surprised to know how much his concubines could reveal of his affairs when Nurkeen was not around.

What use this information might ever be, Inos had no idea, but one thing she knew for certain—some day she would get even with Azak ak'Azakar ak'Zorazak. One rape on a desk and two in his tent, and the tally sheet was likely to grow longer before this journey was finished.

6

For months Rap had lived in a world where sorcery must be handled like gold in a back-street tavern, hoarded and concealed, to be expended only in dire need. Thume was not like that. The Thaïle girl had already flaunted power around him—to restore his strength and clothe him—and now she released it in a thunderbolt.

The sun-baked beach vanished and the sounds of the sea were cut off as if by an ax. He staggered with shock as he found himself within a massive jungle, a giant tangle of ancestral tree trunks and sodden undergrowth. The air was as clammy and heavy as a wet sponge, the light a faint greenish glow in primordial gloom, all sound muffled. He heard Kadie whimper close by and wanted to grab her up in his arms, but he resisted the impulse. Kadie was going to need slow care and love and much patience. At the moment she seemed happier with the Thaïle girl than with him; that rejection tormented him, but he would not distress her more by interfering.

Dimly he made out his two companions, and then a cliff of ancient, crumbling masonry, shrouded in moss. The pixie was already entering down a slippery ramp of humus, leading Kadie by the hand.

Rap followed, into a wet, black crypt. Two corner doorways led through into another chamber, which was brighter only because it was not entirely dark. The flagstones were cold and gritty under his sandals. Blank walls soared up into darkness. He paused, awestruck by the grim majesty of this ancient shrine. Here was sanctity, and sadness, and unutterable authority. Whatever he had expected in Thume, it was not this. He could not have expected this anywhere.

"What is this place?" His voice came out in a whisper, as if afraid to ruffle the dread stillness.

"It is the Chapel," Thaïle murmured. "I think Kadie and I had best wait here, King Rap. You are expected."

Indeed he was. He had an eerie sensation that the building itself was conscious of his presence. Its windows were gaping wounds, irregularly shaped and positioned, toothed with broken fragments of stone tracery. The proportions were all wrong, somehow sinister. As his eyes adjusted to the faint glow penetrating the jungle outside, he saw that there were no furnishings within the Chapel, other than one small chair in a far corner. An indistinct figure sat there, waiting for him. With a conscious effort, he began to walk.

Then he located the core of the mystery, the source of all this sanctity and power. Sorrow poured out from the fourth corner, radiating from the ground itself. His hair stirred as he registered the anguish and undertones of rage. Whatever it was, it knew he was there. It resented him.

With measured step he approached the woman on the chair. Had he not been told to expect a woman, he would not have known her sex. She was muffled in a dark robe and cowl, and she did not show in the ambience at all—strange indeed! He could not explain that, but he remembered Shandie's story of the woman who had appeared to him with word of Wold Hall, and he knew that the circle had closed. That mystery was solved at last.

When he had met Lith'rian they had bantered with the ritual greetings of various races. Who could know the greetings of the pixies, which had not been heard in a thousand years? And who could ever use levity in this awful place?

He stopped a respectful distance from her and bowed low. "My name is Rap. I come in peace." If she was mundane, why did his farsight not penetrate her garb? If a sorceress, why was she not visible in the ambience? What *was* she?

For a long moment she sat silent. Then her voice came like a whisper of wind in trees. "I am the Keeper." She lifted a hand from her lap and laid back her hood.

Instantly Rap knew what she was. The haggard face, the tortured eyes, the raw suffering—he had never seen their like, but he recognized them at once. Things became much clearer.

He sank to his knees and bowed his head in homage.

She sighed. "You know me for what I am."

"Lady, I do. I also knew five words once."

"For how long?"

"A few months." He cringed at the memory. "And you?" he whispered.

When her reply came at last, it was even softer. "Seven years."

He could not imagine what seven years of such an ordeal would be like, nor what they would do to a living being. Her every moment must be torment, a struggle merely to continue existing within the suffering flesh. A demigod never slept.

"You are not welcome here," she said.

"But you know why I have come."

"The follies of the Outside do not concern us."

"You spoke to the imperor, telling him of the preflecting pool."

She sighed again. "It was a misjudgment and it did no good."

"I think mayhap it did, Lady." Shandie had found Sagorn, and Rap. According to Kadie, Gath had recognized the imperor in time for Inos to save him from the goblins. Ylo had remained loyal to Shandie in the hope of seducing his wife and had thereby made possible his escape from Hub—all these things because of the visions in the pool.

"Mayhap it slowed the fall," the Keeper conceded in her leathery whisper, "but it will not change the outcome for the better. I may have incurred the enmity of the Gods by overstepping the limits They set for Keef."

"Keef?" he queried. Then he turned his face to look at the dark miasma of anguish rising from the floor in that other corner.

"The first Keeper lies there. Your presence here awakens ancient malice, Rap of Krasnegar."

"I mean no harm."

"Indeed you do!" The Keeper straightened; fury flamed around her. "You hope to enlist our help in your vain struggle against the one who calls himself the Almighty. You would have us discard a thousand years of sacrifice and renunciation. You would tear down walls that generations have lived to defend."

Rap was shaken by the vehemence of her rejection. "Is not the battle against the Evil a duty for all mortals?"

"Do not presume to lecture me on what is evil!" Her voice rang louder, and bitter. Echoes stirred. "The sufferings that the world inflicted upon Thume cleared any debt—that was the concession Keef wrung from the Gods. We may keep the world away, but never meddle."

"Then you do not know what is happening out there."

"I know very well. The Keeper is allowed to watch—even, in some cases, to send others to appraise. But knowledge must not stray into action."

She was as open to argument as a granite pillar. His cause was hopeless.

"Then tell me how things stand."

At once he wondered if he had been wise to ask that. Her gruesome, wizened face writhed into a cryptic smile. Before he could summon courage to withdraw the question, she answered it.

"They do not stand. They crumble even as you breathe. Every day his power waxes. Even I, with all my powers, dare not venture now beyond the boundaries of my domain lest I be discerned."

"If we can gather all the free sorcerers of the world together—"

"You will not come close to matching the Covin."

There was a dread finality about that judgment. If it was true, then the war was lost. If it was true. Rap felt the cold despair of the Chapel chilling his heart. He struggled against the ancient negation he sensed in this strange place, the stark hopelessness, a thousand years of denial.

"With respect—can you know this?"

"I can. I do. I have watched this evil grow since long before the wardens knew of it, and I have its measure."

"Add to those few sorcerers, then, the many I suspect you

have here in Thume. Add also yourself, the paramount power of a demigod. How then does the balance seem, Lady?"

"Closer," she admitted, "but still not a fair fight. And you shall not draw on our powers. All we have is needed to preserve our security. We will not throw it away in a hopeless cause."

His quest was doomed! Angrily Rap rose to his feet. He was handily the taller, yet so great was her might that he still felt prostrate before her.

"How can you hope to keep your presence secret? You know the dwarf's mind. As his powers grow, so do his fears. If he rules all the world but Thume, then he will feel required to rule Thume, also. He will find you and he will crush you in your turn!"

"The land is hidden from him and will remain so," the Keeper said with icy finality.

"Then may I take my child and depart in peace?"

The Keeper's hollow eyes glittered. "No. I told you I may not meddle. I have answered your questions. To release you with what you know would be to influence events."

He had suspected that. "You lay subtle traps!" he said bitterly.

"But unequivocal. You and the girl will remain. You will find life here tedious, perhaps, but it will be better than the torment Zinixo would impose upon you. And when you die, Sorcerer, you will deed us your words of power in payment for your board."

"But—"

"Such is my decree." The Keeper and her chair faded like smoke into the dark, leaving the Chapel empty. The grave in the corner continued to pour forth its thousand-year lamentation.

Hope never comes:
> A dungeon horrible, on all sides round
> As one great furnace flam'd; yet from those flames
> No light, but rather darkness visible
> Serv'd only to discover signs of woe,
> Regions of sorrow, doleful shades, where peace
> And rest can never dwell, hope never comes
> That comes to all.

Milton, *Paradise Lost, I, 60*

❮ EIGHT ❯

Minstrel boy

1

Stroke! Stroke! Stroke! . . .

Blood Wave II rushed over the gray sea with a bone in her teeth, lifting her head in time to the strokes, riding the long swell. Banked oars moved as one, brawny rowers moved as one, breathed as one: blades up, heads down; heads up, blades down; *stroke, stroke!*

The pace was merciless. Gath had never seen Drakkor drive his crew like this. It seemed impossible that those gasping, sweating men could stand the strain a moment longer. Veins bulged in scarlet faces. Almost every oar handle was smeared with fresh blood, yet not a man aboard would even want to quit, because there was a race in progress. They would sooner die than lose, all of them.

It seemed rather silly to Gath. He was only half jotunn—two quarters, to be exact—so perhaps his mixed blood didn't have the right ingredients to let him understand how plowing a beach ten minutes ahead of another crew could be worth all this torture. More important, his prescience made him quite certain that *Blood Wave* was going to win. That did take the thrill out of things.

The cliff ahead rose sheer from the ocean, its toes standing in a welter of white surf like fleece. *Blood Wave* would pass that reef to starboard, and very close. To larboard, and even closer, *Seadragon* matched her pace. He could hear the hoarse intake of breath from their crew over the cold wind, the cold salt wind that must feel so kind to all the overheated, half-naked rowers.

He was on water duty with Vork, moving down the lines with a water skin, squirting into open mouths as the heads went back at the end of the stroke. Three or four mouthfuls per man, a quick cooling drench on the head, then on to the next. It was infinitely easier work than the actual rowing, but it required every bit as much care. If he stumbled into an oar or even shot the jet into a man's face and threw him off his timing, then all the Gods would not save him from the thane's fury—or the crew's, for that matter. He would be torn apart.

His prescience showed it happening—very faintly, but clear enough to keep him mindful of the danger. The chances that Vork would do it were clearer, quite scarily possible. Still, Gath would not say anything. To mention prescience or sorcery on board this ship brought an automatic whipping, as he'd learned the first day.

The cape was Killer's Head and on the other side of it lay Gark, *Blood Wave*'s home port, Thane Drakkor's thanedom. The island itself was Narp; part of it was Gark and part was Spithfrith, but the division varied from time to time, depending on the respective thanes' skill at denting and perforating neighbors. At the moment almost the whole island was Spithfrith, and *Blood Wave*'s crew had given young Vork a very rough voyage because of that. Gark was the little town that would be coming into view shortly. For the last hour Gath had known what it would look like, and he was not much impressed. He would not say so.

He washed down Grablor and moved to Red, the biggest man aboard, who amply deserved his nickname now. His hair was even redder than Vork's, and today his face matched it. His eyes bulged like onions. Gath wanted to ask why *Blood Wave*'s crew would be so utterly and eternally disgraced if Thane Trakrog's *Seadragon* reached Drakkor's home port first. It made no sense, because they'd sighted Trakrog hull-down two hours ago and made up all that distance already, but apparently it did matter. It mattered greatly.

He gave Red his third squirt, doused his head as it went forward, and then moved to the next man, Gismak, sneaking a glance at the opposition.

Oh, Gods!

He forgot about Gismak, whose open mouth went by unwetted. *Seadragon* was drawing ahead, half a length already—*Blood Wave* was going to be cut off! They were almost under that beetling Killer's Head and the surf was very near. With *Seadragon*'s blades on one side and leaping froth on the other, there was just not going to be room. Positively not. How could this be? Gath had not foreseen this!

For a moment he wanted to shout at the world to correct the mistake. Nothing could happen that he had not foreseen! Nothing must be allowed to. He was accustomed to having life unroll itself in predictable fashion. He depended on it! Now, suddenly, the future was changing itself? His vision of *Blood Wave* riding up on the shingle had vanished; he could barely recall what Gark itself looked like. Had looked like. Would have . . . *had been going to* look like. Unless Vork jostled a rower, *Blood Wave* was going to win—had been going to win—but that was apparently no longer true. What sort of sorcery was going on here? Variable future?

"Awrk!" croaked Gismak as another stroke went by and the waterboy still stood like a dead tree, neglecting his duties. Gath spasmed into action, but between squirts he continued to sneak looks at *Seadragon*, relentlessly edging ahead to larboard, and the pounding fury on the reef to starboard. If the two ships fouled oars, then *Seadragon* might escape, but *Blood Wave* would be out of control long enough for the current to throw her on the rocks. Positively! This was suicide, plain suicide. As he gave Gismak his final douse he glanced back at Drakkor, grim as death, holding the helm.

The thane beckoned him. Gath had not foreseen that, either, but he moved, fast, hurrying along between the two lines of oars, still being careful, stepping warily over bundles, not jostling. The thane did not like to be kept waiting. The thane would like it even less if a dolt waterboy lost the race for him. It seemed lost already to Gath. One thing Drakkor certainly could not do was increase the stroke.

Even as Gath thought that, the thane said something, and the coxswain blew a double pip, indicating a coming increase in stroke. God of Mercy! Their hearts would burst!

A moment later, *Seadragon* matched the new pace.

Panting, Gath reached coxswain and helmsman.

Drakkor was not especially tall, twenty-three years old, looking about fourteen; but he was thick, with arms and shoulders noteworthy even on a jotunn sailor. He rowed a watch every day to keep them so. His baby face was clean-shaven and he bore no tattoos—reputedly in imitation of his father, Kalkor. His ash-blond hair hung to his shoulders. His eyes were as brilliant a blue as eyes could be, and as cold. He had killed six thanes in reckonings; how many lesser men he might have slain was never thought worth mention. At the moment he wore only the customary sailor breeches and an expression of implacable fury.

He was studying the opposition. Then he turned that boyish face with its blood-freezing blue gaze on Gath and snapped, "Watch the rocks, lad!"

Gath said, "Aye, sir," automatically and looked at the rocks, close off the starboard bow now. He could see *Seadragon* at the same time, and she was frighteningly close, closing in so there was less than an oar's length between the two ships' blades. He did not ask why he was supposed to watch the rocks. He had been taught not to ask questions on this ship. If he had to stand there until he died of old age he would not ask. He muttered a prayer. He was sweating like the rowers. Gods, Gods! Images of catastrophe began to grow clearer and clearer.

They were going to hit! His hands started to shake despite all he could do to stop them. *Blood Wave* was going to hit the rocks! Her oars would foul, the current would spin her around, and then the strakes would buckle in near the bows ... He could see the surf blasting up pink, see seaweed, see bodies being pounded on shell-coated rocks that would rip them to shreds in seconds. Gods! He knew it! He knew he was about to die. His prescience left no doubt. Terror won over discipline.

"Sir!" he screamed, and looked around.

Drakkor smiled grimly. "Keep watching!"

Oh! Gath watched again. The image of destruction faded suddenly. Then it returned. "Too far!" he yelled, wiping his streaming face.

Again the threat diminished as the thane eased the steering oar back. Bastard! Filthy, barnacled bastard! He was using Gath's prescience! He'd deliberately set course closer and closer until Gath had told him—

"Say when, boy!"

"Clear now, sir," Gath said hoarsely. "Larboard—too far! A little more ..."

Suddenly *Blood Wave* was within rocks. Foam rushed past, its edges barely beyond the tips of the oars on either hand. The longship swayed uneasily, but her draft was so shallow that the currents hardly moved her. Death reached out, and then withdrew—and reached again.

"Starboard *now*!" Gath screamed.

Then the danger was past. *Blood Wave* hurtled through the reefs and came around the headland. Safe! . . . for now.

Gath felt as if he'd been washed and hung out to dry, wet and limp. He was shaking like a cook's flour sieve. The nerve of the man! The first day, the thane had personally taken a rope's end to Gath's hide just for mentioning that he had prescience—and now he'd used that prescience to win a race! Drakkor had cheated in a race with another thane! Well, perhaps that was not too surprising, but why hadn't Gath foreseen that sneaky little piece of deception?

Then he saw the reason for the insanity. *Seadragon* was still crowding, but *Blood Wave* had gained ground with that suicidal shortcut. Neck and neck the two longships raced toward a massive seastack, its top leaning over as if to touch the cliff, almost an arch. Side by side they bore down on the channel between. Just maybe it was just barely wide enough for one, but it certainly would not take two abreast. Now it was *Blood Wave* that was crowding out *Seadragon*, hurtled straight for that tiny gap. The enemy had the rocks this time. At the last possible moment, *Seadragon* backed water, her crew's roars of fury quite audible. Drakkor bellowed. His men shipped oars, the swell caught the longship and lifted her. She surged forward like a startled horse, out of the sunlight into cold, windy shadow, rank with the tang of seaweed. Rocky walls rushed past on either hand, with blue sky high above and white birds circling. The sailors howled in simultaneous triumph, raising echoes, cheering their thane for that superlative piece of seamanship—and for almost killing the lot of them.

Gath had not foreseen any of this. He grinned weakly at Vork, who was in the bows, leaping up and down in his excitement, almost as red as Red.

A moment later the tide vomited *Blood Wave* out into the calm of a wide bay, enclosed by steep green hills. On shore lay the thorp of Gark itself. *Seadragon* would be delayed by having to detour around the seastack and the rocks beyond, or double back and make another run at the gauntlet . . . she went around, Gath foresaw. She'd take it easy, too, in tribute to the winner, so that Thane Drakkor could be home to welcome his visitors.

Gath's prescience had returned. Obviously there was a shielding on that headland, just like the castle at home in Krasnegar. He couldn't foresee what happened inside shieldings; he hadn't foreseen the seastack or Drakkor's devious ploy. Once inside, he hadn't been able to foresee events outside. Why would a sorcerer put a shielding on a cliff? To discourage visitors coming by night, of course, or in fog. If their pilot had more than mundane vision, he would not be able to use it to find that shortcut.

The rowers ran out their oars again and picked up the stroke, which was fast but not murderous. Gath found the water skin and went back to where he'd finished before. But now he could relax a little and contemplate the immediate future—the thane's tumultuous welcome from his subjects, and his own walk up through the village to . . .

Oops!

There was shielding in Gark, also. The future ended before he reached the end of that walk.

2

Gark was not much of a place, even compared to Krasnegar. It might be better living than Dwanish, though. The surrounding hills were grass and rock, bereft of trees. The houses had low walls of stone and roofs of sod, so that from the bay the thorp hardly showed up at all, just chimneys growing out of grass. Gath decided that either Nordlanders walked around on their knees indoors or their dwellings lay half underground. For warmth in winter, maybe? There were goats cropping those shaggy roofs, although they weren't visible from the sea, either. The only large building stood on a slight rise, and it was a timbered hall with a roof of copper, a paler green than the sod. That would be the thane's palace.

Considering that the men of Nordland had been raiding everywhere else for thousands of years, Gath wondered what they had done with all their loot, apart from putting that copper sheeting on the palace roof. Furthermore, Gark was supposed to be a very strategic thanedom, controlling the south approaches. Garkians pillaged other jotnar on their way home. What did they do with it all?

Squandered it in the bars and brothels of the Impire, dummy! What else would it be good for?

The beach was coming up fast and the population was

streaming down to the strand to meet the returning thane. The cheering was drifting out over the swell already.

Vork jabbed an elbow in Gath's ribs. Gath jerked around and saw that he was wanted astern. Already! He'd been day-dreaming. Again he hurried aft. It was time for the death threats.

Still holding the steering oar, Drakkor had a quizzical look in his inhumanly blue eyes. "Boy?"

"Aye, sir?" Gath said. *You'll keep your mouth shut about that.*

"You'll keep your mouth shut about that."

"Aye, sir!"

Drakkor nodded, with perhaps a hint of a trace of a sugges-tion of a smile on his baby face. "Keep it shut ashore, too."

"Aye, sir." Gath wasn't sure what was meant yet, but here came the threat—

"You say the wrong thing, I'll have to kill you. That goes for your copper-haired friend, too."

"Aye, sir. I understand," Gath said.

You're a good lad and I'd rather not, but I will if I must.

"You're a good lad," Drakkor said with a smile, "and I'd rather not, but I will if I must."

Was Vork not a good lad, then? Still, praise from Thane Drakkor was unexpectedly chest-puffing. He was a bloodthirsty killer, but Gath had spent the last month in the company of fifty men who worshipped their thane's toenails and would cut off their ears to hear those words from him. Good lad, huh?

"Aye, sir." Now came: *I'll have someone explain.*

"I'll have someone explain." The thane turned his attention to the beach.

Twist.

Beaching a longship was a ceremony and a celebration and a job that must be left to the crew. The population of the thorp stood back and watched, cheering. Gath and Vork leaped into the water with the rest of the men, although their puny strength would make no difference. *Blood Wave* went up on the shingle with the rush of the next wave, but she was almost being car-ried by all those brawny arms.

Thane Drakkor leaped ashore dry shod and glanced around. "Gismak? Grablor?"

The two men waded forward, glowering.

"I'll see you two tomorrow."

"I'm ready to do it now!" Grablor snarled. He stood a head taller than the thane, but the betting on board had been that his careless backtalk was going to cost him dearly.

"So am I," Drakkor said, "but I've got visitors coming. Tomorrow. Unless you want to grovel now?"

"No!" both men said at the same moment.

"Tomorrow around noon, then." Drakkor turned away to look at the sea. It was a captain's duty to discipline his crew, and a jotunn captain must do it with his own fists. The thane's hands were twisted and scarred by a thousand such fights. There was not a mark on his face. His nose and ears were their proper shape, most unusual for a jotunn.

Far out in the bay, *Seadragon* was approaching at a tactfully gentle pace, Thane Trakrog coming to call in at Gark on his way to the Nintor Moot.

Drakkor spun around and headed landward. That was the signal. Screaming welcome to the returning sailors, the townsfolk came rushing forward through the upturned dories and the lobster pots, between racks of fishnets and heaps of drying whale bones. Wives dashed to husbands, children to fathers, parents to sons. The men wore breeches and some had boots, as well. The women were in simple gowns of bright homespun. Smaller children ran naked. There was not a dark head among them, and the sight of so much fair hair made Gath feel homesick for the docks at Krasnegar. Half the queen's subjects were impish, but the docks were the domain of the jotunn half.

Vork was looking at him with green eyes wide, wanting guidance. He thought he was Gath's buddy, but he was really his follower.

"We stick close," Gath said. *Until Twist comes.*

Sticking close to Drakkor was not as easy as he had made it sound. Half the population of the thanedom seemed to want to speak to the ruler. He was in a hurry to reach his hall before Trakrog beached, and the result was a mob scene. Only two things were important enough to slow him down. One was a presentation ceremony—every new baby born since he had left was held up by its mother for his approval and blessing. He patted heads and smiled, nodding as he was told the names of his new thralls. The other delay was caused by a limber maiden in a brightly woven gown. She was granted a lingering embrace and a kiss. The noisy onlookers shouted encouragement and lewd predictions.

With an odd sense of unreality, Gath realized that he was actually in Nordland, the home of half of his ancestors. Through his mother he was related to the thane himself, but very distantly. Grandfather Grossnuk had been a humble raider who must have come from some village like this. Even Dad had not known which island he had hailed from, though, nor any more about him, not even the name of his longship. Some of these people might be Gath's first cousins, and that was a very strange notion. He would ask while he was here.

Moving in the midst of clamoring chaos, Drakkor headed up the gentle slope toward his hall. About halfway there, he seemed to remember his two young guests. He stopped and looked around. Before he could speak, Gath elbowed through the mob with Vork at his heels.

Drakkor's blue eyes twinkled briefly as he recognized prescience at work. He scanned the crowd.

"Twist?" he shouted. "Where is that misshapen mongrel?"

People then backed out of the way to make an opening. A strange figure came hurrying forward in a lurching, awkward gait, leaning on a crutch. Children screamed in derision, and not a few adults, also.

He was a hunchback; he dragged a withered leg. He was as jotunn as anyone, but among the horde of healthy golden giants this puny scarecrow was a sorry excuse for a man. His limbs were thin as poles, his hair hung lank, and every bone seemed twisted out of shape. His age was hard to assess because of his thinness, but he was probably not much older than Gath, for his beard was a straggly silver fuzz. He leered up at his thane with teeth that seemed to stick out of his mouth at a dozen different angles.

"There you are, you runt!" Drakkor said, looking down contemptuously. "I thought I told you to grow up while I was gone?"

Everyone laughed.

"You are welcome back, lord!" the cripple said, whining.

"One look at you and I wish I'd stayed away."

More cruel laughter. Twist cringed back, as if expecting a blow.

"See these two?" Drakkor snapped.

The hunchback glanced at Gath and Vork with eyes of a pale gray like sea fog. "I am seeing them."

"Explain things to them. Now!" Drakkor cuffed him across the face. The cripple staggered on his crutch and almost fell. A foot snaked out of the onlookers and caught him behind his good knee. Down he went in the mud, and the crowd hooted with raucous mirth.

Drakkor departed and the mob streamed after him, leaving three youths, one prostrate on the dirt. To mock cripples was perfectly normal. It happened in Krasnegar, too, although Gath's parents disapproved of it. Vork was sniggering, probably to hide his disgust at being assigned to the attention of this runt. Gath stepped forward and helped Twist to his feet.

"I'm Gath, sir, son of Rap. This is Vork, son of Kragthong."

Leaning on his crutch, the cripple beat dust from his clothes with his free hand. He wore a homespun robe of drab brown, a woman's garment. Real men in Nordland never covered their chests until there was ice on the buckets. The gray eyes flickered from one boy to the other.

"Athelings? Krasnegar and Spithfrith?" The grotesque teeth blurred his speech, but there was an odd lilt to it.

"Aye, sir."

"We are not being at sea now."

"No. I mean, yes, sir." Gath realized that the colorless eyes were surprisingly bright and perceptive. He felt they were looking right through him.

"And you are calling me 'sir' you are asking for trouble, Twist being my name. Come, then." He set off at a fair pace, swinging wildly on his crutch so that it was impossible to walk close to him. Soon his breath was wheezing and rattling, but he did not slow down.

Vork sneaked a hand on Gath's arm to hold him back. He looked worried. "What happens?" he whispered.

Gath grinned. "Wait and see!"

Seers had reputations to keep up. He wasn't about to admit that he did not know.

The streets were narrow and wound higgledy-piggledy between the low cottages. Goats grazed on the sod roofs, bleating at the passersby. Once a gaggle of children spotted Twist and jeered in chorus. He ignored them, hastening along in his painful gait.

Here came the shielding.

Shielding could last a long time, Gath knew. Wirax had told him of age-old buildings that had crumbled away and left their occult defenses guarding nothing but meadowland. That must be the case here, for the blankness he foresaw lay right across a street. Once he was inside, he would be able to see the future again. Perhaps in ancient times the thane's hall had stood here.

It didn't work as he expected. His prescience vanished, and stayed vanished. He walked on after Twist and there was still no future, only awkward present. For a moment he almost panicked, as if he'd gone blind, then he gritted his teeth and reminded himself that other people had to live like this all the time.

Twist's house was one of the smallest, a hovel on the edge of the little town. The sod roof was canted at a bad angle, like its owner, as if about to collapse. The cripple plunged ahead down two steps and in through a doorway that had only a tattered old hide to cover it.

Gath followed, stumbling down into a stuffy, earth-smelling dimness, and there was still no future. Vork came in behind him. The flap dropped over the doorway, creating darkness. Twist was bumping around somewhere.

Gradually Gath's eyes adapted. There was only the one tiny room, and one small window, with a covering of bladder or strips of fish skin sewn together. This was summer, so the hearth was bare. He made out a roll of furs that must be bedding, a small table, an ancient seaman's chest, and one rickety chair. Dishes, pots, and a few books were stacked on a precariously canted shelf. On the floor by the fireplace stood a splendid harp, shining like a full moon at dusk.

"You two had best be sitting there," Twist said, waving at the chest, "and trying not to be too heavy. I am at making a cup of tea for visitors, and you will be telling me how the thane got his hands on the two of you."

Vork rolled his eyes and curled his lip, but he went over to sit on the chest. Gath stayed standing. He did not think he could sit down if he tried. He was sweating like the rowers had. A world without prescience was terrifying!

Twist had laid out a candle on the table and was fumbling with flint and steel, balanced precariously on one foot. "Well?"

Vork was going to leave the talking to Gath.

"We wanted to attend the Nintor Moot. We asked Thane Drakkor to let us ship with him. We're his kinsmen."

Twist's pale eyes seemed all white in the dark, as if he were blind. "Sixth cousin in your case. Atheling Vork is being his third cousin, twice removed."

"How do you know that?"

The young cripple smiled bitterly. "I am being his skald.

What is a cripple good for, except being a skald? It is skalds' business to be knowing their masters' families. That is their main business! Shall I be reciting the lists for you?"

"No. I believe you."

The tinder caught. The skald lit the candle and then snuffed the tinder with his fingers, so as not to waste it. He sniggered meanly. "So, athelings, thanes' sons, want to go to the moot? Are you worthy, though? You will be fighting to prove it."

"Fighting?" Vork demanded warily.

"Fighting. Many thanes are coming to visit on their way to the moot and are bringing sons with them. There will be feasting in the hall now until we leave. For entertainment, athelings will fight, much gold being wagered." His odd speech echoed the forms of the old ballads.

Gath should have guessed about the fighting. He wondered if his prescience would work in the hall. If it did, he had little to fear. If not—well, he would have to fight fair. Except that he did not have the arms of a real rower.

"Fists or swords?"

"Fists, heads, teeth, boots."

"Do we have to win?"

"Indeed not," Twist said, with a mean grin. "You had best be fighting a bigger opponent and be getting injured right away. It will be happening sooner or later, so why not sooner? Bleed bravely!"

"What does a cripple know about fighting?" Vork snorted.

"This cripple has been seeing many fights," Twist said. "And knows good losers and bad winners." He lurched over to the shelf and took down a very battered kettle.

"This place stinks," Vork complained. "Tell us whatever it is we're supposed to know, and then we can leave."

"But I am being very honored by having two athelings my visitors! So you were asking a favor of Thane Drakkor? Are you both crazy?"

Gath recalled the thane's words: *You're a good lad and I'd rather not kill you, but I will if I must.* "Er . . . Why do you think we might be crazy?" What was coming? Oh, how he missed his prescience!

The little cripple dipped the kettle in the bucket and set it on a tripod on the table. He placed the candle underneath. "Your fathers did not negotiate this? This was being your own idea?"

"Yes."

"Ah! Well, let us be considering the instance of Atheling

Vork." Twist was very cheerful. Perhaps having visitors was a very rare and welcome experience for such an outcast, but there was an ominous malice behind his amusement.

"What about me?" Vork said grumpily, shooting alarmed glances at Gath.

Twist adjusted himself on the chair and laid down his crutch. "Your father is being thane of Spithfrith and ambassador to Dwanish. As the first he is owner of most of this island, which Thane Drakkor feels belongs to thanedom of Gark. As the second he is being immune to challenge. Am I speaking correctness?"

"Well, er, maybe."

"Is being correct. But my brother is feeling—"

"You're his *brother*?"

Twist grinned at his guests' surprise. "Indeed. And full brother, not half brother. Our father left us many half brothers." He beamed proudly. "We are all athelings here."

Gath made a mental comparison of the two brothers and shivered. Drakkor was masculine perfection, everything a man might hope to be; Twist was a nightmare. What would it be like to have to live in such a wreck of a body—all day and every day? "But he struck you!"

"Of course. Am being a weakling. Is correct behavior for jotnar to be mocking cripples and full of contempt for cripples. If he were not being a big softie, he would be kicking me, also, killing me perhaps. Our father, if returning from his last voyage, would have been having me drowned. Drakkor has been very kind to his puny brother. He was making me his skald."

The strange youth glanced from one visitor to the next, and seemed to think they disbelieved him. "Look!" he said, and fumbled inside the neck of his robe. He pulled out a string, with a glitter of gold on it. "He is a ring-giver. He was giving me this at Winterfest for my singing." He smiled shyly. "He would not be liking me being seen wearing it, though." He tucked it out of sight again.

Unable to find anything to say, Gath walked over to the chest and sat down, elbowing Vork to give him more room. Why had he not realized that Nordland would not be just another Krasnegar? Was it wrong or just unfamiliar? If his homeland seemed more civilized to him, was that just his personal taste, or could he find an argument that might convince an independent witness? If it was more civilized, was that due to the imps there, or his parents' rule? He had a lot to think about. These were things a man had to decide for himself.

"So Thane Drakkor has feud with Thane Kragthong," Twist said, pale eyes sparkling with amusement. "But diplomats are being immune. Cannot make war against ambassadors or challenge to reckonings. Now he has the thane's son?"

"I am his kinsman!" Vork shouted, alarmed.

"Third cousin. He has killed three brothers. Lost count of cousins."

"I am his guest!"

"Is true." Twist glanced at the silent kettle and sighed, as if eager for his hot tea. "But if Thane Drakkor is deciding to blind you, or neuter you and sell you as slave to the djinns, then what will Thane Kragthong be doing?"

Vork made a horrible strangled noise. All the color drained out of his fair-skinned face, leaving only red hair and terrified green eyes, and freckles like sand on white china. Twist obviously found that transformation amusing, and Gath was ashamed to realize that he did, too.

"Would that be honorable behavior toward a guest?" he asked warily.

"Honor is decided at reckonings."

"You're lying!" Vork screamed.

"Oh, surely! I am a runt, and probably being soft in the head, also."

"His father is not coming to the moot," Gath said.

"This year!" Twist smiled his tangle of teeth meanly. "And there are brothers. But Thane Kragthong will have to come next year and challenge for revenge, is not correct? Must be waiving diplomatic immunity then. Or if he is sending up older sons first, then Drakkor is killing them off one by one." He clapped his little hands. "Is no one better with an ax at a reckoning than my brother, not since Thane Kalkor, our father, many years ago." He smirked proudly.

God of Horrors!

Vork whimpered. "Will he? I mean, blind me? Or cut off . . . do what you said?"

Twist chuckled. "Is depending how much your father is valuing you. Good son or not-much-good son? He is aware you are here?"

"Yes!"

"Then am hoping for your sake Thane Kragthong is now

sending message, offering much land and peoples for return of son in good condition."

Vork uttered a long wail. He doubled over and buried his face in his hands. He made muffled sobbing noises.

I did warn him this might be dangerous, Gath thought uneasily. And if Thane Kragthong did ransom his son at some incredible cost, what would he do to that wayward son when he got him back?

"And what about me?" This unforeseen living was very hard on the nerves.

"Ah." Twist eased his crooked body on the chair as if he hurt. "You are thane of Krasnegar!"

Gath's world lurched. "*No, I'm not!* My mother is thane of Krasnegar!" Thanes got challenged to reckonings!

With axes. Against Drakkor? Oh, God of Slaughter!

The silver-faced cripple shook his head. "Holindarn was. Women cannot be thanes. Whether they are able to pass on titles to sons . . . is being argument usually settled at the moot."

Gath should have thought of this! If Dad were still alive—but he had not reported on the magic scrolls for months, so he couldn't be. And to expect the thanes to accept that a faun could ever be a thane was beyond the limits of Gath's imagination anyway. Suppose Drakkor demanded that he surrender Krasnegar to him? He wondered if he'd turned the same milk color as Vork.

This journey had obviously been the worst error of Gath's life, since he was not likely to have time to make many more.

"Vork," he said—and his voice sounded painfully hoarse, "how well can you swim?"

Twist laughed shrilly and passed into a painful fit of raspy coughing. There could not be much room in that shrunken chest for lungs. What a nasty specimen he was! "You are also," he said when he caught his breath—"you are also son of Rap Thaneslayer."

"What do you mean?"

"You are not knowing? Your father killed our father at a reckoning, in Hub."

Vork raised his head and stole a horrified look at Gath, who wondered why the little hovel had suddenly become so cold. His feet felt as if the floor was deep in ice-water.

"That was a formal reckoning! Your father claimed to be rightwise-born ruler of my mother's realm. My father was her champion, and he won!" Somehow that argument did not sound as convincing as he had expected it to.

Twist rubbed his hands in glee. "But reckonings do not set precedents! My brother can repeat my father's claim anytime—only now it will be against you!"

Gath met the spiteful smirk as steadily as he could. "Then obviously he will kill me. I hope it gives him great satisfaction and wins him great honor."

Twist pouted, as if disappointed by the reaction. "He does not need a reckoning. The matter is being a blood feud. Your father is sorcerer and was using sorcery to kill ours!"

Gath straightened up. "Oh, no! If my dad killed yours, then he did not cheat!"

"You were there?" Mockery gleamed in the ice-pale eyes.

"No. But the wardens would have condemned him for using sorcery against a jotunn raider. Warlock Raspnex told me that your father was a sorcerer, also, and it was he who tried to cheat with sorcery and the Gods struck him down!"

"Oh, you talk with warlocks?"

"Yes I do. Besides," Gath shouted, "I knew my dad! He never cheated!"

Twist smiled. "Even to save his life?"

Hateful, warped little *runt*! "No. Never! He never cheated!"

"You speak in past tenses?"

Something took hold of Gath's heart and wrenched.

"I fear my father is dead!" he whispered.

The skald's head moved. His neck was so bent that a nod was hard to distinguish from a shake. It seemed to be a shake.

Hope? Could this agony be hope? "You're a sorcerer!" Gath shouted.

Twist's youthful face contorted in horror and he threw up his hands. "If you are saying outside this house that Thane Drakkor keeps a tame sorcerer, then he will be required to kill you! Or kill you if you are saying our father was, even."

Unbearable hope! Gath could barely spit out the words.

"That's not shielding, you're blocking my prescience! You sing with a harp when you can hardly breathe because your chest is so twisted—*you are a sorcerer* and you are saying my dad is still alive?" Gath leaped across the little room and fell on his knees before the cripple's chair. "Dad's alive? Really? You are telling me this truly?"

Vork shrieked in alarm. "Gath, you're crazy! If he was a sorcerer he wouldn't go round looking like that!"

"Yes, he is!" Gath said. "Aren't you, Twist? You're a real sorcerer and you know about my dad? Please, Twist, please!" He was almost crawling into the skald's lap.

Twist reached out a hand no larger than a child's and playfully ruffled Gath's unruly hair. "King Rap is alive, Thane Gath. He is leading the war against the evil usurper."

The candle winked out of its own accord and the kettle began to boil furiously.

3

Gath had come to Nordland to ask the Thanes to hunt down sorcerers, and he had found an actual sorcerer already. Truly the Gods were with him!

And Dad was alive! Gath never seriously considered that the skald might be lying when he told of Warlock Olybino and dragons. Sorcerers had no need to lie. Two or three days later, Twist commented on that.

The pair of them were back in his hovel and Twist himself was kneeling by his water bucket, washing. Undressed, he looked as if he had been stamped on by a giant in his childhood and ground underfoot. Gath sprawled on the roll of bedding, nursing a very unbalanced stomach and the worst hammering headache of his life. Skuas had been nesting in his mouth.

"You, Atheling," the skald said, "are a most unusual mundane."

Gath groaned, detecting a lecture coming. "Because I'm dead and can't stop suffering?" The backs of his eyes hurt the worst.

"Because you are probably the world's greatest expert on sorcerers! No, I am being serious! You saw Atheling Vork. His teeth were chattering when he learned about me, and yet his own sister is a sorceress. Mundanes are never knowing what you know." Twist grinned, drooling and showing his awful bird's nest of teeth.

"What do I know?"

"How sorcery works. How the sorcerous think. I have been watching. I drop a hint on the water and you yank out a trout every time."

"But I traveled for months in a wagon train with five sorcerers. There were six on board *Gurx*."

The skald chuckled. "And how many mundanes have ever done that? You are without guile, yet keep your own counsel, which is being a most unusual combination! You are having a slight talent of your own. You invite confidences. I say you are the greatest mundane authority on sorcery the world has ever seen!"

Phooey! "When are you going to restore my prescience?" Gath asked grumpily.

"I am sorcerer here," Twist said shrewishly. "I do not like competition. Besides, you are not wanting it back at the moment, Son of Rap. You are much happier not knowing how long you're going to feel like you are feeling now."

Time seemed to stop moving while Gath was in Gark. The sun rolled around the sky without ever setting. Longships came and longships went; the feasting in the mead hall never stopped. Men ate when they felt hungry, drank all the time, and slept when they did not mean to.

By the time Gath and Vork reached the hall, that first day, greasy carcasses sparked and smoked on creaking spits, Thane Trakrog and the crew of *Seadragon* were already two-thirds drunk, and the great sunlit chamber rocked with mirth and boasting. Gulls soared through, riding the wind. Swallows jabbered angrily but unheard from the high rafters. A few goats wandered unnoticed within the crowd, but there were no dogs. Jotnar hated dogs.

With pale face and clenched fists, Vork did as the skald had told him. Head high, arms stiff, he marched the length of the hall, through the lesser folk sprawling on the floor in the sunlight, all the way to the tables where the thanes and warriors sat, until he stood before Thane Drakkor himself. There he proclaimed that he was Atheling Vork, son of Thane Kragthong of Spithfrith, son of as many successive forebears as he remembered, and he came in peace to this hall. In conclusion, he issued formal notice that Gark's enemies would henceforth have him to look out for, also, at which a widespread titter was barely suppressed. With his red hair flaming bright above his skinny pale neck, he looked absurdly young to be playing the role he had assumed, and his voice remained relentlessly treble.

"If he pours you a horn of mead, of course, you're safe,"

Twist had promised. "If he throws it in your face, you're a dead man. If he tells you to go and eat ... well, there's still hope."

Drakkor glowered at Vork as if he had never seen him before, and then pointed with his dagger at the hearths and told him to go eat with the churls.

As for Gath ... "You want to announce yourself as thane of Krasnegar, lad? That's suicide—his father died denying that claim. As son of Thane Rap, a faun half-man? As son of Thane Inosolan, a woman?"

Gath bristled. He thought *son of Rap Thaneslayer*, and discarded that idea quickly. "As his kinsman, then? As the imperor's messenger?"

Twist shrugged his hump. "It would be safer that you not reveal yourself at all."

Gath assumed he meant the athelings' exhibition matches. "I'm not afraid of a fight!"

Twist smiled so wide that he drooled. "With the Covin? It will be sending watchers to the moot, you know. May even have one on *Seadragon*—I haven't looked them over yet."

"You mean I've come all this way—"

"And you want to go all that way back, don't you? So you'll stay just a water boy, and you won't be going to the moot! Which would you rather be: Vork-son-of-Kragthong in Drakkor's clutches, or Gath-son-of-Rap in Zinixo's?" He cackled.

The Covin was the danger. The Covin was the enemy, and for all Gath knew he might have already muddled up some plans of Dad's with his meddling. The Covin might be the real reason why Mom and the imperor had decided not to come. And yet, although royal honors had never meant anything to Gath before, now that he was being denied them, they suddenly felt important for the first time in his life. Growling, he agreed that he would sit among the groundlings, for the moment.

He slunk into the hall to watch Vork's entrance and subsequent humiliation. He felt somewhat better after that, and went to join him at the spits for a slab of roast goat and some cheering up. A couple of *Blood Wave*'s crew spotted their two tyros and decided to fill them both with peasant beer. They were prepared to use force if necessary, but Gath was not in a mood to argue—he needed to assert his manhood, even if it was only by getting drunk. Events blurred very quickly after that. There was much roast goat and fresh black bread, and some singing, and buckets and buckets of green beer. There was a sort of a fight between Gath and a lanky youth from the thorp, but they were both far too blurred to do any damage. There was falling down and throwing up. There was helping to drag out the drunks to make room in the hall.

There was waking up much later in the grass and going back inside again for more goat, and more green beer, and seeing different visiting thanes at the high table, and more useless windmilling fighting, over and over and over. The sun never set.

And in among all this insanity, there were moments of serious business.

After Thane Trakrog departed, and before Thanes Jorvir and Griktor arrived, Thane Drakkor went back down to the beach and hammered Gismak and Grablor into insensibility, one after the other. A captain must discipline his crew.

There were also moments of rapture, when the thane's skald sang for the guests. In the hall Twist wore breeches like everybody else and his deformities were cruelly exposed. He was jeered at, had things thrown at him and tipped over him, but when he sat down and touched his harp and began to sing, then even the snoring stopped.

It was impossible for that crumpled body to produce such sound or those tangled teeth to hurl such words, and yet the skald filled the hall with pearls and rubies of song.

He sang of death and sorrowing. He sang of legendary heroes and great disasters. Most often he sang of Kalkor, Thane Drakkor's father, former owner of this hall, sacker of cities. Gath thought the endless recitals of loot sounded very much like his own father's shopping lists for the spring fleet, but fortunately he was never quite drunk enough to say so.

There were moments of muddled worrying. Twist's news about the goblins was horrifying—*Kadie, Kadie!* Gath tried not to think about that, but there were hundreds of other things he should be worrying about, and most of the time he couldn't keep a thought in his head for more than a few seconds before it drowned.

Yes, he had accomplished more or less what he had set out to do, in that he had made contact with a Nordland sorcerer—

and apparently Warlock Olybino's proclamation had made his trip unnecessary anyway. The moot itself would not be crucial, if Twist would organize the other sorcerers. There must be others, many others. But was Twist going to cooperate? That was something Gath could not establish. The skald was rarely available for talk, and when he was, Gath's teeth and tongue refused to cooperate with his brain.

Probably a wise decision.

About the second or third time Gath heard him, Twist sang a different song. He sang of Thane Thermond, venerable, vulnerable, being challenged at the Nintor Moot. His sons had been delayed by a storm; who would save the noble thane from the challenge of virile Atheling Koddor?

Then stepped forward Atheling Drakkor, exiled by a brother's spite, landless sailor in another's ship; eight and ten years only and untried with the ritual ax. He would be champion for the hard-pressed thane.

The tale could not hold much drama after that, Gath thought. When two men entered the Place of Ravens for a reckoning, one left his bones on the grass for ever. Had the loser been Thermond's champion, then the old man would have had to go forward also and bow his neck for the victor's stroke. In this case the outcome was fairly predictable, with Drakkor himself sitting there in full view. The story unfolded as Gath expected. Axes clashed, gore spurted, and the overambitious Koddor fell headless. Thus venerable Thermond was saved—end of tale.

So that had been Future-Thane Drakkor's first reckoning? He had risked his life for a stranger? Interesting!

"I do not understand," Vork complained, "how a man can be a sorcerer and look like that monster."

The boys were dragging their feet down to the shore. They had been persuaded that the best remedy for a hangover was to dip oneself totally in the Winter Ocean and then run all the way back up to the hall. Gath would have more faith in the proposed remedy if he could see anyone older than himself applying it. On the other hand, he was desperate enough to try anything. He felt as if he was walking on his eyeballs.

"He's a jotunn."

"So?"

Gath didn't want to talk at all. "How do they feel about sorcery? We feel, I mean." When in Nordland be a jotunn.

Vork sniffed. "Sailors are so frightened of bad luck that they won't even talk about it. Warriors think it's cowardice and cheating."

Exactly!

They stopped simultaneously, toes at the water line. Very cold ripples ran up on the shingle.

"So?" Gath said. "If Twist turns himself into a muscle-boy raider like his brother, he's cheating. His friends would spurn him and flee in panic."

"Friends?" Vork shouted in his piercing treble. "They knock him down in the mud and spit on him!"

Why could he not see it as Gath saw it? "But they are still his people. He could live as a king in the Impire, but that isn't what he wants. This is his home. This is his life. And he is his brother's skald."

"What can that mean to a sorcerer?"

"You haven't been paying attention," Gath said smugly.

"Oh, no? See that piece of driftwood out there? I'll race you to it."

"Right! Go!"

Vork plunged into the icy water.

Gath turned around and headed back to the hall.

At some point in that endless feast, he found himself sitting on the sun-warm grass outside the mead hall, talking with Twist.

"Skalds?" he said. "Or women?"

"Or priests."

"But never warriors, never sailors?" Gath peered carefully at the minstrel's shining harp. He had no headache and he could only see one thing at a time, which meant he was drunk again. Idiot! Trouble was, when he wouldn't drink up like a man, the sailors held his arms and poured the muck down his throat. Or turned him upside down and put his head in the bucket, which was worse. "Real men aren't sorcerers?"

"Never. Or rarely. You may be right in saying our father cheated that way. Don't be saying it to anyone else, though."

"Is that why the Protocol . . ." The thought wandered away into the beery fog.

Bodies snored in the grass all around.

Twist chuckled. "So goes the legend. Because the jotnar

would never use sorcery in battle, Emine agreed that no one else might use it against them, and the warden of the north was assigned to defend them from it."

Gath followed that idea around in his head, one word at a time, then nodded. The world rocked sickeningly. "But way back here in Nordland, who could tell who might be cheating?"

"And no thane ever trusts another."

"So the skalds stay home and guard the thorps against sorcery?"

"Purely defensive," Twist agreed, amused by something.

Gath lay back on the warm turf and closed his eyes. He put an arm across them to cut out the pink glare of the sun. That was better. "Who else knows this?" he muttered.

"The thanes and the skalds. Nobody else at all. Not even the warlock of the north nowadays, I suspect."

"And your brother won your words for you by being champion for Thane Thermond?"

"That was the price. I was thirteen. I was dying—the taller I grew, the worse my back curved. Sorcery saved me."

Without any hard evidence at all, Gath had come to know that this human ruin was his brother's counsellor, the brains of the family partnership. Drakkor was only the muscle.

"You will be going to Nintor, Twist?"

"Of course. Every year the thanes meet at the Moot Stow on Nintor. The reckonings are held at the Place of Ravens. But there is always another moot, every year, a secret moot."

"The skalds?"

"The sorcerers. They go to see fair play. They also hold a moot, a moot of their own, at the Commonplace."

"I have to come."

"It is too dangerous for you."

"Stuff that harp," Gath muttered sleepily, and heard a chuckle. "I am coming."

There was another thought, something he must tell . . . Oh, yes. "This is going to be a war moot?"

"The imperor has pulled back his legions from Guwush."

"The fake imperor." Gath yawned mightily. "It's a trap, of course." The sun was pleasantly warm on his chest and limbs.

"Perhaps it is, but no one knows about the fake imperor or the usurper. No one but sorcerers know that the Covin has overthrown the Four."

"Drakkor knows?"

"I have told him. Doubtless most of the other thanes know also. But their followers do not." Twist's fingers stroked the strings and the harp sighed. Then it proclaimed a martial chord. Several apparently unconscious drunks sat up quickly and looked around.

"After three thousand years," he continued, "who will believe that the Protocol no longer operates? Drakkor has been preaching war for two moots now. How can he stop when the Impire is being so vulnerable? You cannot be arguing with a hungry bear!"

Gath sighed as the wind sighed in the grass. "It is a trap!"

"Perhaps it is. What sort of a trap, though? Have you worked that out, Little Atheling?"

"Yes."

"Then tell me!"

"I will tell the secret moot," Gath said sleepily. Silence.

4

The longships had stopped coming. Only one spit held a goat and the hall was almost deserted. The villagers had returned to their wives and their labor. Down on the shore, *Blood Wave*'s crew readied her for departure.

Gath was close to panic. He was going to be left behind! Twist was avoiding him apparently, and who could ever catch a sorcerer who did not want to be caught? Drakkor was unavailable to a lowly water boy. He haunted the thorp and the hall in misery. Once in a while a gang of sailors would catch him and fill him full of disgusting beer again, or match him up in a fight. He was sick of the drunkenness and foolery and juvenile games. There was a war on, and he was being excluded.

Then he saw Twist lurching along the hall in an unusual hurry. Heedless of danger, Gath followed, right through into the private quarters, dark and mysterious and out of bounds. He caught up with the cripple just as he hurtled in through a door.

"*Raven Feast* has rounded the head and Thane Kragthong is on board!" the skald cried.

The little room was dim and stuffy. It was larger than Twist's cottage, but stark and simple as befitted a jotunn's chamber. The bed was made of plain boards covered by a worn fur. On it lay Drakkor, unshaven and haggard from days of unending feasting, and the blue of his eyes was circled by red. He had probably been asleep. In a fast reaction, he threw his goat's-wool blanket over his companion and blinked up blearily at his brother. "I will be there."

Twist turned to go, and discovered Gath.

Gath could tell that this was not the most appropriate setting for discussing business. The girl on the bed was invisible now, but she was certainly not Drakkor's wife, who was out in the hall. She had also been much younger.

"Thane?" Gath shouted.

Twist rolled his eyes and stepped aside.

The look he received almost melted Gath's bones, but he stood his ground.

Drakkor growled. "What the Evil do *you* want?"

"To go to Nintor with you."

"It is too dangerous." The thane rolled over on his side and put a thick arm over the shrouded girl.

Twist tugged urgently at Gath's wrist.

"Since when has that mattered to a jotunn?"

Drakkor tightened his embrace on the blanket, not turning to look at his visitors. "Jotunn? You? Go away, half-man!"

If he was sober he would not be able to do this, Gath thought, trickling sweat. "Sir, I bear a message from the warlock of the north—and from my father the Thaneslayer."

The muscles in Drakkor's back tensed like cables. "Brother . . . Turn him into something horrid!"

"Then I ask Thane Kragthong?" Gath asked shrilly.

"Go away!" Drakkor roared. The blanket jerked nervously.

The grip on Gath's arm tightened with superhuman power, digging into the muscle. He yelled in fury as he found himself being dragged away bodily by that flimsy runt.

"Stop!" the thane said. He rolled over on his back and glared. "We carry no passengers to Nintor. You would row?"

There were only four days left until the moot. If the wind was not favorable, that meant three days of hard rowing. God of Horrors! Gath hesitated, thought about Dad, and said stubbornly, "Aye, sir! I'll row double watch if I have to."

Drakkor groaned. "Take him away, Skald. I'll thump him later."

The mead hall was packed as *Raven Feast*'s crew marched in. Gath sat on the floor amid the massed groundlings. Beside him, Vork hugged his knees and watched with wide green

eyes. His red hair seemed to be standing on end, and all his
freckles showed.

The leader was a hulking thane of middle years, scarred and
battered. A pace behind him walked the passenger he had
brought from Urgaxox, Vork's father. In this land of giants,
Kragthong no longer towered so tall, but there was not a belly
in Gark to match his. It overhung his breeches like a thatched
roof. His face was older and more careworn than Gath remembered, but his forked silver beard jutted forth arrogantly in the
sunlight streaming through the great windows.

Vork seemed to shrink down and down until only his eyes
showed above his knees, like green pebbles.

Smoke swirled from the fires. The visitors paraded along the
hall. They came to a halt before Thane Drakkor at the high table. He was freshly shaven and clear-eyed, as if the feasting
had never happened, young and jubilant. Even the wind
seemed to hush expectantly.

Thane Afgirk of Clarn recited his honors and his ancestors.
"Your foes are mine," he concluded.

"Safe haven and good sport, brother of Clarn! You are welcome to this hall." Drakkor tipped mead into a drinking horn
and passed it across joyously. He filled another for himself.
The two thanes drained them simultaneously. Drakkor waved
his guest to a stool and sat down, ignoring the other visitor.

Kragthong tugged his beard with two hands. Then he
straightened and his great harsh voice boomed out. "I am
Kragthong, Nordland ambassador to Dwanish, and I come in
peace to this hall. Your enemies are mine, Thane."

"By law, all ambassadors are admitted." Without looking up,
Drakkor carved a slab of meat and handed it to Afgirk.

Kragthong glanced around and then spoke out again, louder
than ever. "I travel to Nintor on business, Thane."

Now Drakkor did look up, and he cocked a silver eyebrow.
"What business?"

"In view of my advancing years, I have decided to resign
my ambassadorship."

The assembled Garkians murmured excitedly. Drakkor rose
slowly to his feet, eyes gleaming.

Kragthong's shoulders slumped. "And my thanedom, also!"

The flash of triumph on Drakkor's boyish face seemed to
light up the hall. "Your successor as thane of Spithfrith?"

"My oldest son having declined the honor, I am minded to
offer it to yourself, kinsman."

Whatever was said next was drowned out in the roar. Vork moaned and rose uncertainly to his knees.

"Good luck!" Gath whispered, glad he was not in Vork's breeches. Vork himself would be lucky if he managed to stay in them in the immediate future or sit in them afterward.

Then Gath thought that he would be more than happy to pay that price if he could be reunited with *his* dad.

Beaming, Drakkor filled a horn, passed it across to the ambassador, and filled another. He seemed about to offer a toast, and the excited tumult faded away. But the visitor had not raised the horn to his lips.

"I believe I have a younger son around here somewhere?"

"That is not impossible." Drakkor's eyes raked the hall, seeking that red hair.

Vork tottered to his feet and stumbled forward through the seated groundlings until he reached his father. He hung his head and waited. Kragthong looked him up and down, checking for damage.

Then he turned to his host. "A favor, Thane?"

"Name it!"

"I need borrow a whip for a couple of hours."

The onlookers bellowed with laughter as the two thanes drank. Then Drakkor vaulted over the table to embrace his former foe and the Garkians sprang to their feet to cheer in deafening clamor. The future of the world hung in the balance, Gath mused, and these ruffians were interested only in who ruled the middle of a barren little island.

As he was about to rise, someone tapped his shoulder. He looked around and discovered the contorted figure of Twist sitting in an awkward heap behind him, showing all his angled teeth. Everyone else was standing now, so that the two of them were alone in a forest of legs.

"There is a sorcerer in *Raven Feast*'s crew," came the whisper.

"With a votary spell on him?"

The skald nodded, fog-gray eyes agleam. "Come." He accepted help to stand, and he leaned heavily on his crutch as he hobbled toward the door. At times he could move faster than a cat, but he would give himself away if he used power in the presence of the Covin.

In Dwanish Gath had been a giant. In Nordland he was a youth with promise. Unseen amid all the blond heads, he followed the cripple out. He had been feeling a little hurt that

Kragthong had not inquired after his health as well as Vork's, but that might be a good thing under the circumstances, and perhaps a deliberate precaution, for the fat man was much shrewder than he liked to pretend.

Twist hurried toward his house with his wildly rocking gait, showing no desire to talk on the way. When he reached the cool dimness of the hovel, he flopped on his chair, panting. Gath went and sat on the chest wearily. Red-hot hammers thundered inside his head.

"You are being a reckless, suicidal idiot!" the cripple gasped.

"It's the jotunn in me."

"My brother was right—no one normally takes passengers to the moot. Skalds, or priests, but not boys."

"There's a law?"

"No, but you don't want to be attracting attention."

"I can row," Gath said grimly. Three days to Nintor—it would kill him if the wind failed.

"Fill the kettle." The wood-ash eyes followed Gath as he rose and moved to obey. "For what you did today, he may maim you for life. Pray he uses his belt, not his fists. If I tell him to, though, he will take you to the moot. He may even leave you wearing half your hide. But I need a reason. What use are you, stripling, tell me?"

Gath dropped the kettle and clutched his head to calm its echoes. "The stronger a sorcerer, the better his spells, right?" he said hoarsely.

"Is correct." The skald frowned suspiciously.

"And the Covin is enormously powerful."

"Is also correct."

"Much stronger than just you alone, Atheling Twist." Gath looked around blearily. "But you tell me there is a sorcerer spy among *Raven Feast*'s crew. How are you able to see the votary spell on him?"

The skald's fog-pale eyes glittered. He drew in breath with a hiss. "I am being meant to see this?"

Gath felt a little better. "Maybe. Maybe there are decoy votaries—and also real votaries. Or else the Covin is strong enough to watch you from Hub and does not even need spies. Before you and your friends hold your secret moot, you will deal with the decoys? Then you will feel safe?"

Twist fingered his tangle of teeth. "This is not honest thinking like a jotunn's!" he said angrily. "This is sneaking!"

"I'm not all jotunn. You said yourself I know a lot about sorcery. I know dwarves, too. They think they're straightforward, but they're canny—a dwarf's first offer is never the final price."

That remark made the sorcerer look almost as nauseated as Gath felt. "I am sorry, Atheling. You just may be useful. But I want to know what you plan to do. I want to know what the Almighty's trap is. And don't try to lie to me."

Gath stooped to dip the kettle. His brain seemed to swell inside his head and he straightened up again. If he told everything he might be left behind anyway. But that did not really matter—his own feelings were not important. The snappish little sorcerer was being surprisingly scrupulous in not just pulling the thoughts out of his head regardless. All that really mattered was Dad's war.

"The trap is simple. Zinixo's pulled back legions everywhere on the excuse of fighting the goblins. It won't just be Urgaxox. Jotnar, gnomes, djinns—everyone's going to attack. War everywhere. He'll let the Impire bleed and let the wardens take the blame for not stopping it—ordinary people don't know there aren't any wardens anymore. You said yourself that only sorcerers know what's been really happening."

"Ah! And then?"

"Then he'll step forward as the Almighty, smash the invaders, and declare the wardens overthrown."

Twist tutted angrily. "Of course! If I wasn't a simpleminded jotunn I'd have seen that, too! But what do you think you can do about it? There is no way to stop the moot from launching a war, Atheling Gath! None! You must have heard the thanes who came here—they're spitting blood already. The only argument left now is who shall be leader."

"The rules have changed, Twist. The Protocol is ended. No warden of the north protects the raiders now. They may win to start with, but then they'll be massacred like the goblins."

The cripple thumped his crutch on the floor. "But I just told you! Nobody will listen to you or believe you. If they did believe you, they'd go anyway. They smell blood!"

Gath saw his victory and grinned in glee, headache forgotten. "I don't expect them to listen. Only the other moot, the secret moot. Forget the old songs, minstrel! They've trapped your mind in the old ways, and no matter who wins, those ways are gone forever! How many sorcerers will be there?"

Twist made the clumsy movement that seemed as if his hump was shrugging. "Fifty, perhaps."

"A longship crew exactly."

"What?" The fog-pale eyes widened. "But we stay home and guard the thorps! Always!"

"Not anymore! The rules have changed! This time the skalds go to battle—and we'd better get them there before the main army arrives!"

Twist's mouth hung open. Then he gulped. "Skalds? Priests? *Women?*"

"The lot!" Gath yelled. "All the sorcerers in Nordland. As many as we can get, anyway. The enemy is the Covin, remember? You want the jotnar to suffer what happened to the goblins? You're going to go to war, sonny. To help my dad."

Minstrel boy:
> The minstrel boy to the war is gone,
> In the ranks of death you'll find him,
> His father's sword he has girded on,
> And his wild harp slung behind him.
>
>   Thomas Moore, *The Minstrel Boy*

❰ NINE ❱

Manly foe

1

On a muggy afternoon five days before midsummer, Rap emerged from the Way and strolled across the clearing toward Thaïle's cottage. Before he reached the steps, the pixie came around the side of the house, carrying a bundle of washing. She advanced to meet him, so he stopped where he was and waited for her.

As usual, she wore a long striped skirt and a white blouse; today it was sleeveless. She was barefoot. As usual, he found himself reacting in odd ways to her intent golden gaze. At times she seemed a striking young woman—beautiful, in fact. She wore her hair too short and her figure was almost boyish, but that was true of most of the pixies, for they were a gracile race. He could appreciate her womanhood. Then, suddenly, he would find himself thinking of her as a mere girl, less than half his age and barely older than his daughter. Not yet seventeen, Kadie had told him. But she had borne a child; she had suffered its death and the death of her lover. She was probably the most potent sorcerer he had ever met—Thaïle was an enigma, and he felt clumsy and unsure of himself in her presence.

She dropped her bundle almost at his feet. "You are welcome to the Thaïle Place, goodman." Her voice was musical, her expression solemn.

He smiled and bowed. "I am Rap of the Inos Place, and I come in peace."

If she recognized his attempt at humor she ignored it. "Kadie is washing her hair."

"I think you are lying, Archon."

"Yes." She knelt and began spreading clothes out on the grass, to dry in the summer sun.

Rap sat down to watch. She was not hard to watch.

"Well, this is a chance for us to speak without her."

"Yes." Thaïle continued to deal with the washing. "Be patient. So many months of torment are not discarded easily."

"Is it just me, or all men?"

"All men. From the time she was stolen away from her mother until I rescued her, she did not speak to a single woman. Now she distrusts all men." The golden eyes glanced swiftly in his direction. "It will pass; give her time."

He sighed. "Gladly. But you understand that it is hard for a loving father to find his daughter spurning him."

"She does not spurn you. She weeps because she treats you badly."

His throat knotted. Oh, how he needed Inos! "Tell her not to weep. I love her, and will wait." He had the rest of his life to wait, a prisoner in the Accursed Land. "I forgive, always. I hope my visits do not upset you, also, Archon?"

For a moment the pixie did not reply, but she was almost finished spreading out the laundry. He never knew how to speak to Thaïle. Normally she made him welcome at her Place when he called. She seemed genuinely fond of Kadie, and for that he was immensely grateful, but he knew now that Thaïle was damaged, too. Her husband and baby had been slain in cold blood by the very College she was forced to serve. She must know why. She must know the fate that awaited her, and that knowledge itself would be enough to unhinge anyone. Widow and bereaved mother, Thaïle, also, was an ill-used child.

She adjusted the last sleeve and then sat back on her heels to face him. He thought of a butterfly resting on the grass.

"You do not distress me, your Majesty. Kadie and I complement each other. She has no cause to trust men; I have no cause to trust women."

He winced, feeling awkward and inadequate. "I did not mean to hurt. Please bring Kadie to visit the Rap Place sometime. Take her there, perhaps, when I am absent, and let her see it. Tell her that it is a replica of a house I lived in once in Durthing, on Kith, when I was much the same age you are now, Archon. I was lonely and friendless myself in those days."

"You are lonely and friendless now?"

He nodded. "We live in hard times. Trouble should become easier to handle as we are older, but by then we know that the world is not cruel, only indifferent, and that hurts even more. Give Kadie my love. Tell her I will wait, and I understand."

The child face was remorseless, hardened by burdens beyond its years. "Do you? Can any of us ever understand the sorrows of another?"

"That is what love is for, Thaïle."

She turned away, scrambled to her feet, and walked off in the direction of the cottage.

"Be sure to tell Kadie that I love her!" Rap called. Finding himself alone, he rose and headed back to the Way.

He told the Way to take him to the Meeting Place. He had no desire to go home. After many months of traveling, he had a roof to call his own again, but it was not one he cared for. He had been granted a pleasant site for it, in a dell with a few spindly trees, close to the sea to placate his jotunn half. He had set to work creating a replica of a log cabin he had inhabited once in his youth. The occult tumult he had thereby caused had brought him assistance in the shape of Archon Toom, who had completed and furnished the cabin for him in a twinkling and had also added all sorts of useful magical contrivances that Rap would never have thought of. Knowing four words of power, he was technically still a sorcerer, but his abilities were feeble indeed.

After four days in Thume he was frustrated to frenzy. His war against Zinixo might continue, but he could not know of it. More likely it was just fading away into futility. The Covin was winning by default and he was completely powerless to do anything about that.

The change in Kadie distressed him beyond measure. His haughty, assertive little girl had withdrawn into timidity, and he could not reach her. He fretted about Inos and Gath and even Shandie, all carried off captive to Dwanish. At best they lingered there in a dwarvish jail; at worst they would have been betrayed by some spy of Zinixo's. He worried also about Krasnegar, vulnerable to the Almighty's spite. At times he even found himself worrying about Tik Tok, and then he knew he was going crazy.

Vegetation around him grew lush as he neared the Meeting Place. Thume was more strange than he had ever dreamed. The manner in which sorcery had been organized and domesticated was a marvel that went far beyond anything he had envisioned for his new protocol—magic as a public service, overt, available, and useful. Yet even here the Evil had penetrated and perverted the Good, for Thume could be viewed as one enormous jail. It seemed to exist only to conceal itself. The pixies' lives were regulated and constrained to serve the College, and in the end all effort turned around upon itself and the College did nothing but defend its own existence. It could murder a baby in the name of love.

The pixies themselves were a shy, solitary people, ingrown and reclusive. Almost he could compare the whole race of them with poor Kadie, as if the War of Five Warlocks a thousand years ago had blighted all pixies in the same way her ordeal with the goblins had blighted her. They denied the world. They sat out the dance, and that philosophy was no more comprehensible to Rap the king than it would have been to Rap the sailor, stableboy, or wagon driver.

He sauntered out into the Meeting Place: flowered parkland, lawns, and picturesque lake. He cared little for the oddly skewed architecture of the little cabanas, but the overall effect was pleasant enough—if you liked playgrounds. He came here every day to sit on a bench and watch the swans and hope someone would stop and talk with him. No one had done so yet. Even sorcerer pixies were too shy, too alarmed by this inexplicable "demon" who had been allowed to violate their sanctuary. If he tried to initiate a conversation, his victims would gibber at him. Sometimes they would just vanish like soap bubbles. Perhaps in a few years someone would bid him good morning, or something equally daring.

No, he was being unfair. He had forgotten the two archons—Toom and Thaïle. Thaïle he pitied beyond words; he admired her, also, for her strength and her gentleness to Kadie.

Toom was entirely different. Toom was a solid, genial man of around his own age, slow and deliberate in the manner of a peasant farmer. He even had dirt under his nails. Toom had called on Rap a couple of times, to inquire after his needs. He had conducted the guest around the College, answering every question with apparent frankness. Rap suspected that Archon

Toom had been assigned to him as jailer, but the man was informative and helpful.

Perhaps a dozen pixies now inhabited the Meeting Place. Conversation had stopped, though, while the golden eyes studied the intruder. No one sat alone, available for friendly advances.

He frightened them! He had come to Thume looking for allies in a war. What use these delicate folk in a war? They were porcelain people, soap bubbles. They made him feel overlarge and lumpish; he must seem even more so to them. To press his attentions on them seemed cruel. He must just give them time to adjust, like Kadie. Time? Only five days until Longday. If Armageddon came to Pandemia then, did Thume survive?

He continued walking, telling the Way to take him to the Library. He would find a book of Thumian history and carry it back to his Place and try to read . . .

"King Rap? Do I intrude upon your meditations?"

Archon Toom strolled at his side, peering cautiously up at Rap with guileless golden eyes.

"No indeed, Archon! I welcome company."

"Ah. I apologize for my comrades' incivility. I hope you will make allowances for a thousand years of custom?"

"Gladly. I appreciate the honor of your hospitality."

"The Keeper's hospitality," Toom murmured in his plodding, deliberate speech. "And Archon Thaïle's, of course. There is a prophecy about the Chosen of the Chosen One, you see. But no matter. I wonder if you would spare a little time for a discussion. On a matter of some importance to us?"

Already the Way was leading them out into the forest.

"Time," Rap said with a laugh, "is one thing I have in excess. Gladly, Archon, gladly!"

A matter of importance? He still had enough premonition to sense a major turning point. Something was about to happen.

2

In a few minutes, Rap and Toom arrived at the Raim place, a simple cottage in a grove of willows, close by a stream. Archon Raim himself came hurrying out to greet the visitors, buttoning up his shirt. Toom spoke the ritual greeting; Rap picked up his cue and followed suit.

Raim was little older than Thaïle, a comely youngster, husky by the standards of the dainty pixies. He offered chairs under the trees, he laid chilled mead and a dish of sugared fruits on the plank table. With obvious pleasure he introduced his good-wife Sial, who was even younger than he was, and of course a mundane. Rap sensed that their relationship was a very recent innovation, for they glowed at each other like honeymooners. She blushed and stammered, departing as soon as she decently could, and Raim smiled after her with eyes of gold.

Rap sat back, crossed his ankles, and waited to hear what a matter of some importance might be. His admittance to the Accursed Land was a violation of an ancient tradition; such things did not happen by chance in a society of sorcerers. If he could be of use to the College, then perhaps he would have some scope for bargaining. Of course these two could drag every thought out of his head if they chose, but the use of power seemed to be restricted by custom and good manners in the College. The Keeper would not likely put much stock in etiquette, though, and the Keeper might have instigated this meeting.

The archons inquired after his welfare, and Kadie's. They asked about his journey and means of travel. They frowned when he told them of the dragons and the elves' intransigence. They revealed nothing.

Surprisingly, it was the older, stolid Toom who first grew tired of trivia and came to the point. He flexed his thick peasant fingers, as if longing for the feel of an ax or spade.

"I understand, Goodman Rap," he said cautiously, "that it was you who cut off the supply of magic some years ago?"

"It was. Many years ago."

The archons exchanged glances.

Young Raim said, "There is no chance that whatever you did could be reversed?"

"Why should you want to see it reversed?" Rap asked coldly.

"Oh, I don't!" Raim protested, fumbling with his crystal goblet. "It's just that the dwarf Zinixo has assembled a worldwide monopoly of sorcery. In the past it was the wardens' ability to draw on Faerie for additional words of power that prevented anyone ever doing that."

"So in a sense I am responsible for what has happened," Rap admitted. "But I have very few regrets. I should do the same again, I think. The farming of the fairies was an unthinkable atrocity."

The archons stumbled over each other's words in their haste to agree.

"I was merely inquiring," Raim explained awkwardly, "because I should not like to think of the Almighty, as he calls himself, ever being able to draw on that prime source, also. I was just hoping for that reassurance."

Oh, he was, was he? Or did the archons—at least these two—not share the Keeper's absolute reliance on Thume's immemorability?

"I do not believe that even the Covin can recover what I removed." Rap reluctantly concluded that he must take them into his confidence if he hoped ever to be taken into theirs. "As I understand what you told me, Toom, when the Holy Keef established the College, she moved it to another Thume."

Toom nodded. Then he nodded again, seeing the connection. "That is so. We exist side by side with the real world. The two lands are similar in big things—rivers and mountains, and so on. When Keef made the duplicate, the two would have been exactly the same, down to individual leaves and flowers. Except for the people, of course. You see, the new Thume was uninhabited until she moved her followers here. Now, after a thousand years, they have grown apart. Trees and so on have changed in different ways. The copy is no longer exact, you see."

Rap saw. "I did the same with Faerie. I moved the fairy folk to a land of their own, where they would be left in peace, not slaughtered like animals. I believe I located all of them, both free and captive. Unlike Keef, I then severed the connection."

Toom smiled, apparently pleased. "And by now the two lands will have diverged so far that no sorcerer would be able to locate the replica? Not even Zinixo and his gang!"

"That is my belief," Rap agreed, "and my hope. Even if he catches me and forces me to explain what I did, I do not think the fairies can be recovered." He eyed the two men thoughtfully. "You agree?"

They agreed. They did not seem disappointed, either, which was a relief.

"More mead, your Majesty?" Raim said, offering the bottle. He was young enough to enjoy playing host to a king, even a very minor king in exile. "That is good news."

Perhaps it was, but it had not been the main business of the meeting.

For a few minutes the three men sat under the dappled

shade of the willows while only the brook disturbed the silence. Archons were the rulers of Thume, but they apparently lived very simply. The Raim Place and the Thaïle Place were humble abodes. Gold and jewels were irrelevant to sorcerers, multitudes of slaves unnecessary. Yet Thaïle washed clothes; Raim made his own furniture. As a king who detested pomp and liked to groom his own horse, Rap thought he approved.

This time it was Raim who spoke up. "You are familiar with the occult protection around our land?"

"In a general way," Rap said. "I have never met its like, though."

"The barrier could only have been created by a demigod, for it requires powers beyond sorcery. It is a form of shielding, of course, concealing our use of power, yet more than that. Not quite an aversion spell, for that can be felt. Not a conventional inattention spell, because the existence of the land cannot be denied. The maps would not fit! No, it is mostly a matter of irrelevance. Everyone knows that Thume is here. No one cares. They *know* that it is empty, and they *know* it offers nothing of value."

Curious to discover what provoked this admission, Rap prompted: "And it works most strongly on those with the strongest power?"

Raim frowned. "I never heard that!"

"I do not think so," Toom said. "Not directly. But those who have great power are accustomed to certainty. They tend to reject what they cannot sense for themselves. The ignorant will accept Thume more readily, you see."

Sagorn had been willing to believe in Thume!

Rap felt as if he were playing a part in one of Kadie's romantic dramas. His next line was obvious. "But sometimes people do enter. What then?"

"Imps are notoriously nosy," Toom agreed with a sigh, "and djinns rapacious. Mostly imps, though. We archons detect them—that is our function. If the matter is serious, the archon alerts the Keeper. He or she decides and usually . . . deals with them." He paused uneasily. "Keepers, you see, have, er . . . take a long-term view."

What he meant was that they had few scruples. If every minute was a torment, a struggle against pain and magic overload, if life itself was a coat of fire, the foibles of mere humans would soon start to seem trivial.

"Keepers tend to be ruthless?"

"Er, well, yes."

Raim intervened. "We all do our duty. A few months ago, a party of djinns crossed into my sector, hunting goats. Her Holiness told me to evict them, so I sent them troubles with mountain lions. One was badly clawed, another broke a leg running across a rock slide. This is why Thume is known as the Accursed Land." He grinned with boyish glee. He had enjoyed the sport.

"Keepers are their own laws," Toom said soberly. "Some have allowed whole armies to pass through Thume unmolested. Others have put shipwrecked mariners to death. The uncertainty is part of the mystery, you see."

"No one has ever been allowed to remain," Raim added, "until now." His gold eyes twinkled at Rap.

And Rap was at a loss. He could not tell if this conversation was as innocent as it seemed, or if the two archons were deliberately passing the stranger a message they dared not speak directly. Perhaps he was merely more worldly and cynical than they, jumping to unintended conclusions, or perhaps there was a scent of mutiny in the air. *Delicate and childlike we may seem,* they were telling him, *but pixies have a strong sense of territory, which makes us ruthless toward trespassers.* That observation let a man leap easily to a very interesting conclusion. *The Keeper has refused to participate in your war against the Covin, but she will feel otherwise if our own borders are violated.* Was Rap supposed to make that jump? Was he expected to go one jump farther: *There is a way you can provoke such an invasion?* Surely not!

"You trust this boundary spell to deflect the Covin?"

Both archons nodded.

"Even knowing that Zinixo will live for centuries? Even knowing that he may leave a successor as powerful as himself to rule for more centuries after him?"

Again two nods, less vigorous.

"I am delighted to hear it," Rap said dryly. "What exactly was it that you wished to discuss?"

Toom's plain face registered uneasiness. He passed the question to Raim with a meaningful glance.

"The caliph."

"The caliph? And what is my old friend Azak up to?"

Astonishment! Dismay! Both men spoke at once.

Rap threw up his hands, remembering that he was dealing with an alien culture, was speaking a language that he had been given by Thaïle's sorcery, and was therefore liable to cause accidental misunderstandings. "I expressed myself loosely. My wife was married to him once. I have met him a couple of times. We are not on terms of affection, though. Frankly, I consider him a bloodthirsty barbarian."

The archons nodded their agreement vigorously.

"Caliph Azak," Raim said, "is presently set on invading the Impire. He is leading an army of about sixty thousand along the northern coast."

The population of Krasnegar was about five thousand. Rap whistled, trying to hide an amusement he knew he should be ashamed of. "Into Thume?"

"Into Thume."

Thume had a problem! "And the Covin is watching?"

Raim nodded glumly. "So the Keeper says."

Still Rap struggled against a smile. The outside world was a threat the pixies were warned against from infancy, and it had few worse horrors to offer than a djinn army. A djinn army would worry jotnar, let alone pixies. There was something oddly funny about so terrible a danger threatening so peaceful a people, like a lion squaring off against a rabbit. It would not be funny, of course, if Thume did not have the Keeper to defend it. The rabbit was armed.

But this was the millennium, and perhaps the joke was over.

"I comprehend your concern," he said cautiously. "If you cause the army to disappear, then the Covin may wonder why and start to investigate? And if you just leave it alone—"

"We cannot just leave it alone," Toom growled. "The coast is inhabited. That is where the mundanes live, in the real-world Thume."

"You could—well, the Keeper could—transfer the entire army to this Thume, or some other plane altogether?"

"The caliph's own sorcerers would certainly notice, and likely the Covin, also."

"So you must turn it back," Rap said. He thought that was obvious, but their reaction showed there was another possibility. "I have missed something?"

The archons exchanged uneasy glances.

"The Keeper . . ." Raim said. "I mean, we. *We* are considering the possibility of a, er, natural disaster." He refilled the three goblets and then drained his.

Toom cracked his big knuckles. "An artificial natural disaster, you see."

Rap maintained a skeptical silence. He had not yet fathomed the distribution of authority in the College. Possibly there was no fixed rule, and it varied over the years. The archons seemed to do the day-to-day work of running the College and guarding the borders. The Keeper kept watch on the Outside—that much she had told him herself—but the Keeper must also have the last word in any disagreement. Even eight sorcerers in unison could not stand up to a demigod, any more than a mage could resist a sorcerer, or a demigod defy the Gods. The Gods Themselves must obey the Powers.

"There is a lake in the mountains," Raim muttered. "A very large lake. There is a valley leading down to the coast."

That made no sense to Rap. "I am sure Azak is too experienced with desert campaigning ever to pitch camp in a dry riverbed." Even in Krasnegar flash floods were a hazard in the hills after summer storms.

"A landslide," Raim said. "A minor earth tremor could drop half a mountain into that lake."

Rap shuddered and took a drink.

They were waiting for him to comment. "So the djinn army, or a fair chunk of it, would be washed away by a tidal wave? An *inland* tidal wave! Don't you think the Covin might be just a teeny bit suspicious of this fortunate coincidence?"

Neither archon replied. Neither was looking at him.

He wondered if the Keeper was aware of this twitch of mutiny within her ranks. Or had she set this up? Somebody was having an attack of conscience—who? To wipe out an army with sorcery was a throwback to brutality not seen since the War of the Five Warlocks. And obviously it might alert the Covin.

"What you are telling me, gentlemen," he said—trying to omit any inferences about what they might not have said but had tried to imply, "is that your precious border spell may not be adequate protection if anything draws the Covin's attention specifically to Thume? Zinixo himself is insanely suspicious, right? You are also saying that you cannot stop Azak's army without using substantial sorcery, one way or another. Even if you just let him pass through, the Covin would lose track of him and wonder where he had gone. Have I summarized the situation accurately?"

Toom nodded. "We are not practiced in such matters."

"Nor am I. I assume that you are about to ask me to wander over and kill the caliph for you?"

Their shocked expressions were answer enough. Apparently the idea had not occurred to them.

"We merely wished to pose the problem," Toom protested, "and see if you had any suggestions to make. Your experience has been different from ours."

"I'll not argue that," Rap said. "Have you considered an assassination, though?"

"He has sorcerers in his train to protect him."

"They may be as afraid of the Covin as you are."

Toom pulled a scowl that seemed oddly unsuited on his naive pixie face. "We are not afraid! The Covin does not know we exist and never will. The Keeper has assured us of this."

"Oh, of course," Rap agreed. "Absolutely. Assassination?"

The archons exchanged worried looks. If they conferred in the ambience, though, they managed to conceal their talk from Rap. They seemed almost more upset by the idea of a single cold-blooded murder than they had been at a massacre of an entire army. Murder was personal, massacre beyond comprehension.

Raim said, "What good would assassination do? The army would just elect a new leader and continue its march."

Rap hesitated, but decided not to argue the point. He could try to explain to the pixies that djinns elected their leaders by elimination and that a new caliph would probably race back to Zark to stamp out a hundred rebellions. Even if the archons could understand that, though, Rap must then concede that the army might tear itself apart in the election. The losing half rampaging out of control into Thume would be even worse than the whole sixty thousand with Azak in charge. Cancel assassination.

He ran his hands through his hair, pondering aloud. "That does suggest the right sort of answer—what you want is a purely mundane solution, using no sorcery at all, or very little. If Azak caught a fever, for example. But that isn't too likely, is it? Not to order. How far away is he?"

"Not very."

Rap took a sip of mead. What was his interest in this? The Covin was his foe—not Azak, not Thume. He wanted the College and the Keeper to throw their weight into the battle against Zinixo, and this situation might well trigger an attack on them that would force their hand. But the idea of a djinn army ravaging the pixies' peaceful land was appalling. Djinns would be bad enough by themselves; if Zinixo fired them up to slaughter, they would destroy everything in their path. Rap could not just sit back and let such a disaster happen without trying to help somehow. He could not live with himself if he allowed that to happen. Why was he so cursed with scruples?

Not that he could do very much, but perhaps he could try. The prospect of action was enticing. If he did achieve anything, then the Keeper would be in his debt. Whereas, if he refused to help . . . Could this be some sort of test?

"You think Azak will camp within your death-trap valley tonight? I assume the lake is within the occult barrier and the irresistible campsite just outside?"

Raim nodded—and grinned, looking very boyish again. "The Keeper warned me you might be smarter than you look."

"I certainly hope so," Rap said. "Could the Keeper cloak me in a similar spell?"

The youngster blinked gold eyes in astonishment. "Her Holiness can do anything she wants, I suppose."

"Then let me go and call on Azak tonight."

Both archons flinched.

"And what can you say to him?" Toom demanded.

Not much! "I could tell him to turn back, without saying why. He may heed my advice, because he knows me. If he won't, then you can still drown him. I could try dropping a discreet hint to his tame sorcerers, also. What have you got to lose?"

"Everything," Toom said glumly. "What if his sorcerers have already been perverted by the Covin? I can't see the Keeper taking such a risk."

Raim uttered a sinister laugh. "Unless she appointed him an appraiser."

"What does an appraiser do?" Rap demanded, not sure that he wanted to hear the answer.

"Spies for the Keeper. But if he is discovered, then he bursts into flames."

3

The sheep station lay in the hills west of Castino, in eastern Qoble, under the beetling spires of the front range. It probably saw very little excitement between one century and the next, so Hardgraa had felt no compunction in taking it over for a day or two. There was nothing at the station itself; it just happened to provide a suitably large establishment at a strategic midpoint on the charts, and the owners should feel honored that the imperor needed it. Not that there was an imperor at the moment, but they weren't to know that.

In the hills the nights were evilish cold even close to mid-summer. Some lowly legionary had been told to light a fire, and legionaries were expected to display zeal, so the blaze that roared in the hearth would have roasted twin oxen. Nobody wanted to stand close to it. The cool end of the room was packed with metaled men and the other almost empty. The candles stood tall and fresh, although dawn was not far off.

Feeling frowsy after a mere hour's sleep—the first in two nights—Hardgraa paused in the doorway to glance over his squad. They would not have described themselves that way. Most of them were centurions, with a few optios and a couple of signifers who knew the quarry well by sight. The ineffectual Tribune Hodwhine was present, and nominally in charge. Two more tribunes were out in the field, supervising the sweep, and they were real soldiers, not aristocratic jellyfish.

For a group so giddily honored by rank, this one was singularly failing to live up to the standards of the XIIth. Shandie would have stalked around the room like a jaguar, ripping stripes. If Hodwhine knew his job, he would be slamming down on the yawning, the slouching, and those unshaven chins. A man should not waste time sleeping if his armor needed cleaning, either.

Hardgraa could not interfere in those matters, but everyone knew who was really in control. He marched into the room and a ripple ran through it, turning heads and stopping conversations. Here was the imperor's man. Legate Ethemene had assigned three cohorts to this man's personal command, purely on the strength of his reputation as Shandie's chief of security. He wore the imperor's four-pointed star. One man who had displeased him had been flogged to bare bones in front of the legion. He had their attention now.

He nodded perfunctorily to Hodwhine and snatched himself a tankard of coffee from the mess table. Then he turned to the crowd around the chart table and centurions backed out of his way to make room. He knew by the shape of their silence that there was something new. It couldn't be capture, or he would have been told at once. A good sighting, then. His eyes scanned the green chalk marks that represented sightings, the red marks for his troops. There had been no additions since he went off to catnap. There had been deletions.

He tapped a thick finger on the paper. "The cherry orchard didn't pan out?"

"A priest," Hodwhine said at his back, "and his bishop's wife, would you believe it?"

Just for once, Hardgraa let his sense of humor out of its cage. A priest and a bishop's wife? No wonder they had tried to evade questioning! Yes, that was worth a smile, and of course the smile was being noticed. "An *unfrocked* priest, sir? Would that be an instance of a little bit of good in every evil, or a little bit of evil in every good?"

"Depends," Hodwhine said quickly. "Depends how good the goods are, I'd say." He'd probably been tutored in witty rejoindering.

Hardgraa let the chuckles fade away while he continued to study the chart. The deletion was not enough to explain the new sense of expectancy—not in this exhausted group at this hour of the night. They knew something he did not. Nevertheless, the pattern was clearer now. Without the priest the sightings clustered better. Almost he could feel that the chalk marks were footprints and he was some great sharp-eyed raptor soaring over the foothills of the eastern Qobles, tracking his prey.

You run, Master Ylo. You try to hide, Master Ylo. You double back and circle, Ylo, but you can't shake me. Do you feel my breath on you now, Ylo? Can you hear my claws on the rock?

"He's going east," Hardgraa said. "He'll cross the Angot road about here. Then . . . Then we've got him, haven't we!" He leaned across, but the light was too poor to be certain. "There's no trails marked through the mountains there, are there?"

"No, sir," said the optio at that corner of the table.

Hodwhine coughed. "Oh, Centurion?"

Hardgraa turned. "Sir?"

"Letter here for you," the tribune drawled. "Came a little while ago. Imperial post from Angot."

So that was what was new! Hardgraa accepted the packet and glanced over the inscriptions. The seal was intact. "Thank you," he said, and tucked it away in his pouch.

"You're not going to read it?" Hodwhine said, frowning.

"I have read it, sir. I mean I've got the message, sir. That's Ylo's hand."

The annoyance on the tribune's face showed that he had known that. One of the signifers must have identified the writing.

"Posted in Angot," Hodwhine said sharply. "Addressed to you at the barracks; forwarded here. Posted in *Angot*, Centurion, *yesterday*."

"Yes, sir. That's the message."

The tribune colored. "Centurion!"

"Look!" Hardgraa barked, and turned back to the table. He pulled out his dagger and used it as a pointer. "They're here. Within a league, they're here. One of these fruit farms, likely. And we're all round them, and they must know that now. There's the road to Angot."

"So he slipped by us!"

"No, sir. He did not slip by us. He chose a woman heading down to Angot and slipped her one of his smiles to post a package for him in Angot. That's what he did, sir. That's the message, sir—*Here I am, come and get me!* But it's a lie, sir. He's not in Angot. He's here. Right here!" Hardgraa slammed his dagger into the chart and left it standing there.

Hodwhine bared his teeth. "Read the letter!"

Hardgraa almost shrugged. They must all have been speculating for an hour on what it said, and it didn't matter. "Yessir." He pushed out of the group and marched over to stand beside the inferno on the hearth—alone, with every eye in the room watching him. Only then did he pull out the package and break the seal. The heavy parchment crackled as he opened it. He expected to see cipher, the code that Shandie had used within his personal staff, the old "handful of men" he had trusted: Hardgraa himself, Lord Umpily, and Sir Acopulo, Prince Ralpnie, later Ylo . . .

To his disgust, though, the letter was in clear, its text a shameful breach of security.

Signifer Ylo (retd.)
to
Centurion Hardgraa, assigned to the XIIth:
Greetings!
   We were friends. If the Covin has enslaved you, then I am truly sorry. If you are still your own man, then how can you imagine that our former leader would ever have put any consideration at all ahead of his child's welfare? He always maintained that every individual should have the right—

There was a lot more. Hardgraa tossed the thing into the fire and walked back to the table. He switched to the northeast corner of the chart and, when space had been made for him, he was looking across at a red-faced, glaring tribune.

"Horse piss, sir. The only message was the Angot post seal, and I told you how he did that." Putting the letter out of mind, Hardgraa turned his attention back to the maps.

Got you now, Libertine Ylo! Always knew your lechery would be the death of you. Acopulo said you'd go to the Evil crotch first.

"We can move up here, checking every house, and drive him over there. Then he'll be pinned between the mountains and—"

And Thume. Why did that not feel right?

He looked up, searching the ring of faces until he found the local expert. "Optio? What's in Thume?"

"Nothing, sir."

"What sort of nothing?"

The youngster looked alarmed. "Just trees and stuff, sir. Nobody lives there. I mean, nobody ever even goes there!"

"That's all right then," Hardgraa said. He glanced at the tribune to make sure he was conscious, or as close to it as he ever got. "You can concentrate forces now, sir. We'll pin him between the mountains and the Thume border. Bring up the VIIth Cohort to close off this sector. Then ... Optio, is this river fordable?"

"The Brundrik, sir? I suppose so. But there's nothing on the other side ... sir?"

Hardgraa was about to ask what sort of nothing, and realized he'd asked that before. Gods, but he was tired! And he'd have to head out at first light. *Two days more, Pretty-boy Ylo, and I peg out your hide!* Maybe he could steal a few more hours' sleep. Still, there was something wrong, somewhere, he just knew it.

"Why does nobody ever go there?" he demanded.

"Where, sir?"

"Across the Brun-thing River. Into Thume?"

"Well— There's nothing there, sir." The optio was clearly at a loss, as if Hardgraa's question made no sense.

It did, didn't it? He thought it over carefully and decided it was the sort of question that usually had an answer.

He leaned his hands on the chart and glared at the youngster. "What would happen," he said in his most menacing tones, "if I ordered you to ford that river?"

The optio's chain mail jingled. "I'd-d-d ob-b-bey, sir."

"And what would happen to you then?"

"Dunno, sir. An uncle of mine did it and came back mad as midges, sir. Know of a fellow went hunting and got his face clawed off. Most don't come back, sir."

"Why didn't you tell me about them sooner?"

"I—I dunno, sir."

"Mmph!" Hardgraa looked for the tribune, but he'd wandered away somewhere. He selected a centurion instead—good man, been at Highscarp. "Tiny, line up some elvish trackers, will you? If the target should make a break for it into Thume, we'll have to follow."

To the ends of the earth, Lecher Ylo. To the ends of the earth!

4

To advance up a valley without controlling the heights was normally rank folly, but sometimes a man had no choice. Short of winching everything—including the camels—up sheer cliffs, the caliph had to come this way. He had interrogated his scouts closely and had even ridden ahead to see for himself, escorted only by the horse cavalry of Fifth Panoply. He had returned satisfied. The sides were too steep for a charge, too high for an archery attack. The upper end was closed by a sizable lake, and there would be a steep climb up a tributary valley on the morrow, but that could be managed. Furkar reported no evidence of sorcery at work, except for the Covin's continuing surveillance. Azak set a guard on the exit and moved his main force into the valley for the night. It was an excellent location. The floor was level and wooded, with a stream providing the first adequate water the army had seen since leaving Quern.

Following his custom, the caliph rode around as camp was set up, inspecting, criticizing, and acknowledging the cheers of his troops. Arriving back at his own quarters, he observed that the seraglio wagons had been arranged to form an enclosure by the stream, with the gaps between them curtained to keep out prying eyes. A ring of armed men surrounded this silken bivouac, all standing with their backs to it and ignoring the shrill squeals emanating from within.

So his women were enjoying a bathe? Azak told his bodyguard to stand down and ducked through the draperies to enjoy the view. At his appearance, of course, they all prostrated themselves. The sight of seventeen bare bottoms in the air was intriguing—sixteen? One woman had merely turned her back and sat down. That one was a wench of a different color, of course. He signaled to Nurkeen that the festivities should continue, and he continued to watch with approval as the girls began showing off for him; all but that one, who remained where she was. Her defiance intrigued him far more than all the juvenile gymnastics of the others. He began to feel quite aroused. Inosolan was the only woman who had ever humiliated him. Tonight he would administer another rebuke.

At sunset Nurkeen informed Inos that she was his Majesty's first choice for the evening. Somehow Inos had expected that. She braced herself to endure more hurt, more humiliation. She had absolutely no way of escaping the constant surveillance, and she could acquire no weapon. Her only satisfaction would be to minimize Azak's enjoyment, and so far her success in that direction had been nonexistent. In Quern she had struggled and he had overpowered her. In his tent, two nights ago, she had remained completely passive, so he had thrown her around. The end result had been the same either way—he was just too big, too strong. She could win no points in this game, except to conceal her fear and distress.

She might refuse to obey the summons, of course, but then she would just be carted to his tent bodily, like a parcel. Or he might even come and abuse her before the rest of his women. That would be no answer. When she had been suitably adorned and perfumed, she set off submissively with Nurkeen and an honor guard, walking into the night.

Someday, by all the Gods, he was going to pay for this!

The journey was short. Even in her all-enveloping wool robe, she shivered in the sudden chill of a desert night. Camels bellowed in the distance, and she could hear the thousands of men and horses—but she heard those every night. Scenery she had seen only rarely since her imprisonment. Steep mountains framed the valley; the sky over them was afire with stars. Odors of sage flowed down from the hills to blend with the smoke of innumerable fires. Thume, she recalled, was always beautiful. The evil at its heart was human.

The caliph's tent was very large. The guards remained outside; Inos entered with Nurkeen. Azak was not there. The interior was opulent, with bright-hued rugs and silk hangings, warmed by braziers and lit by lanterns attached to the many poles. Thick quilts had been piled for the royal bedding, and a

meal spread out on a cloth nearby. There were damask cushions and two solid chests for documents; no other furniture.

"Give me your robe," Nurkeen said. "His Majesty will return shortly, I expect. Warm your hands." Filmy red eyes
peered out over her yashmak. "I suggest you strive to please
him this time, and avoid unpleasantness."

Inos said nothing.

The old hag departed, leaving her standing there, garbed
only in a swirl of obscenely transparent gauze. Her face was
still purple from his last wooing; her shoulder still hurt.

As soon as the tent flap fell, Inos stepped over to the display
of food, seeking a weapon. She found nothing more dangerous
than a small silver spoon, not even a knife for peeling grapes.
She eyed the braziers, but they were cunningly crafted of fretted bronze. If they fell over, the coals would not spill. She
might contrive to set the tent on fire, but that pettiness would
not harm Azak and he had a million cruel ways to retaliate.

Shamed by her fear, vulnerable in her state of undress, she
settled cross-legged in a corner and wrapped herself in a quilt.

She had to wait a long, nerve-wracking time. That was probably deliberate. Eventually, though, she heard hooves outside,
and gruff Zarkian voices. Then he entered, throwing off his
cloak. He wore his usual green—loose trousers and shirt.
Across his wide chest the emerald baldric of Arakkaran glittered like a river of green fire. That alone would purchase her
whole kingdom, and he was liberally draped with other jewels.
When she had first known him, he had preferred to sport the
sash as a belt, wrapped many times around his waist. It would
not go many times around now. He seemed larger every time
she saw him, for he had added beef to his great height. He
would be almost a match for the largest jotnar in Krasnegar,
even Kratharkran. He was not sporting any weapons. Azak,
unfortunately, had brains.

His big hands sparkled with rings—they would add to the
pain when he struck her, and she had no doubt he would strike
her. There was white now in his red beard. There was blood in
his red eyes.

"Take off that quilt!" he said, seating himself beside the
food.

She dropped the quilt.

He reclined on one elbow, spreading himself out along the
cushions like a basking walrus. He began to eat, stuffing food

in his mouth one-handed without seeming to notice or care what it was, barely taking his eyes off her.

What had she ever seen in the man? Once she had been sorry for him, she recalled. Once there had been hints of greatness, where now remained only pride and cruelty and debauchery. She remembered wise old Sheik Elkarath prophesying what happened to a sultan who trod the red road of war. In those days Azak had loomed above Arakkaran like a human thunderstorm—dangerous, frightening, but also awesome, full of menace and might and potential. Now he was a blood-soaked tyrant, glutted on twenty years of battle. Now—as she knew only too well—he was physically repugnant, gross and disgusting. She had not felt clean since he first laid hands on her.

Unfortunately, although he now held no appeal for her at all, the reverse was not true. His lusts had more to do with power than sex, although he enjoyed that, also.

"You have worn well," Azak mumbled. "Come and sit there." He pointed to the floor just across from him.

Steeling herself not to tremble, Inos rose and did as she had been told.

"Pour me wine."

She poured. Each tiny obedience ranked as a defeat, and yet each itself seemed too small to justify provoking violence. How far would she pander to his demands? Soon he would tell her to strip. Would she go that far without compulsion? She did not know.

He leered. "More cooperative tonight? Speak. Amuse me."

"I have nothing to say to a turd like you."

His eyes narrowed. "Revenge is very sweet, Inosolan."

I am sure it will be.

The tent flap moved in the background. For a moment she wondered about that, then decided it must just be the wind.

"I have waited twenty years for my revenge," Azak said, still chewing. "And I find it exquisite. Now, stand up and dance for me."

"I cannot dance that way."

He chuckled and reached under one of the cushions. He brought out a coiled whip and laid it on the rug for her to see. "Dance."

Light gleamed on the oiled leather of the thongs. Shivering, unable to take her eyes off that awful threat, Inos clambered to her feet.

Rap put a strong arm around her and became visible.

5

Inos wondered afterward why the shock did not kill her on the spot, but it didn't. She grabbed him in a bear hug—tight, ever so tight, burying her face against his neck. Rap! Solid, breathing Rap! His clothes were still cold from the wind outside, and he smelled faintly of horse. He was panting.

"Oh, Rap! Darling! Rap! Rap! Rap!" She mumbled incoherently into his collar, only gradually becoming aware of the fire in her shoulder.

"It's all right," he said hoarsely. "Safe now."

Safe? Sorcery? Wondering, she stole a look at Azak. He was frowning, peering around the big tent as if he had lost something or forgotten something, but he was clearly oblivious of her and Rap.

"He can't hear us?" she whispered. Obviously he couldn't.

Rap did not answer. He was shaking convulsively. She looked up at his face.

The gray eyes were unfocused, his lips white and curled back from his teeth. She had seen that expression often enough in Krasnegar, that kill-crazy jotunn look. Rap was half jotunn. That explained the trembling and the odd breathing. He was a hound straining on a leash. Oh, Gods! His left arm was clasping her, but his right was between them, and she guessed that he was holding the hilt of a sword.

Die, Azak! You die now, you bastard! No? Why not?

Azak heaved his great bulk to a sitting position. He fumbled with his fingers, muttering angrily.

"I want to kill him," Rap croaked. His eyes bulged. "I've got to kill him. Promised I wouldn't. I must kill him! I want to cut him in slices! Wretch! Scum! How can I kill him, Inos? Tell me how I can kill him!" He was almost sobbing.

"What do you mean?"

"He can't *see* me!"

God of Madness! Suddenly Inos saw worse things than Azak. Rap could not kill a man who couldn't see him. *Must not* be allowed to kill a man who couldn't see him! The memory would drive him crazy. In a fair fight, yes. Even an execution. But to stab a blind man was murder, and cowardice. A jotunn could not kill like that, and Rap could not. After so many years she knew her man. He would never be able to live with his guilt if he violated his own ethics. It was from Rap that Kadie had inherited all her romantic notions, not from her mother.

Gods have mercy! Inos would have to break the news, tell Rap about Kadie and the goblins . . . Well, Rap himself was the immediate problem, still crazy-trembling in an agony of frustration. His teeth were chattering. She must stop him.

She must somehow save Azak, whom she wanted to die.

Ask for the sword? Do it herself? No, she couldn't do it now, either. Simple death was too good for Azak. He must know how and why he died.

But Rap was here and nothing else really mattered. She hugged him even tighter and kissed his cheek.

"Oh, my darling! How did you ever find me?"

Staring hatred at the caliph, Rap licked his lips. "Didn't. Just luck. C-c-came here . . . t-t-talk with that *slime*!"

Azak lurched to his feet. Rap hauled Inos aside, and the huge djinn stormed past them without a glance. At the end of the tent he ripped aside the drape that concealed the privy. Baffled, he wheeled around and strode back again, grinding his teeth. He seemed to know that he had lost his victim, but not how.

Suddenly Rap's grip tightened and his eyes searched Inos's face urgently. "He hasn't . . . I did get here in time, didn't I?" Fury quivered on the brink of explosion again.

"Just in time!" she said quickly. Just in time *this* time. The truth could wait. "You came to talk with him?"

"Get'm to turn back."

"Why?"

Rap opened his mouth and closed it. Then he glanced sideways at her, and she saw that something was distracting the bloodlust.

"Better not say here. The results might be dramatic."

Again Azak stamped by, again fumbling with his fingers.

Eek! "Rap! Those rings! He has magic rings. One of them will summon Furkar! His sorcerer." She had seen the truth ring in action and the women had mentioned the other. Perhaps there were more tricks, too.

"Let him!" Rap snarled. "Sorcerers won't—Ah!"

The tent flap rose and fell.

The young man who had entered was tall and sinister in a trailing black kibr. A black kaffiyeh framed his face, and red djinn eyes gleamed in its shadow. He glanced around the tent

without registering Rap or Inos, and then inclined his head perfunctorily in the direction of the fuming caliph.

"You summoned me, Majesty?"

"I did! I tried calling you earlier, too. Where were you?"

The newcomer must be the sorcerer himself, Furkar, if only
because anyone else would be cringing in terror before the caliph's rage. He was showing no expression at all. "I was inspecting the route we must take out of here tomorrow."

"That is my job. You handle the sorcery and I'll do the
rest." Azak stalked over to the two wooden chests and sat
down.

The sorcerer remained undaunted. "This place makes me
uneasy. And I warned you not to use that summoning while
the Covin may be listening."

Azak glared. "This is important. Did you see the dispatches?"

"No."

"Trouble in Shuggaran. And other places."

The younger man had not moved since he entered. He still
stood just inside the door. He was a talking pillar. "As soon as
your back is turned? Only to be expected. I trust you are not
feeling faint-hearted?"

Azak's face turned even redder than usual. "No. But I was
a fool to leave the Prisoner alive. He is a risk. I want you to
go back and kill him."

Furkar raised coppery eyebrows. "And how am I to travel to
Dreag?"

Azak ground his teeth. "The dwarf still watches?"

"Day and night. I remind you that it is not you that interests
the Covin. It is me and my associates. I would have to travel
by horse, so you might better send one of your assassins. He
would go faster."

"I just may do that, then."

"And if you persist in using those sorcerous trinkets I shall
either take them from you or gather up my votaries and depart." A faint hint of a sneer curled Furkar's lip, but his tone
remained deadly calm.

"I don't think he's lying," Rap muttered. "Looks like the
Covin hasn't got him yet."

Azak choked, growled, and beat his fists on his knees.

"Will there be anything more, your Majesty?" Furkar inquired sweetly.

"Yes. That jotunn woman was here. She must have escaped when my back was turned. Have the camp searched for her."

"I hear and obey, Mightiness." The sneer became more pronounced.

"Doesn't like being ordered around like a flunky, does he?" Rap remarked cheerfully.

Azak stood up. "Go! And tell Nurkeen to send me another. One of the fat ones."

Furkar turned and disappeared out the flap without even a pretence of a bow. Azak stood up and cursed at length.

"Any idea what all that was about?" Rap inquired loudly.

Inos felt a wash of relief. The killer glare had faded. Rap was still enraged, extremely dangerous, but he was rational.

"Yes," she said. "Did you say you wanted Azak to go back home to Zark?"

The caliph had been rummaging in one of the chests. He slammed down the lid and sat on it to begin pawing through a tangled sheaf of documents.

Watching him intently, Rap growled low in his throat. "I want him *dead*! But I can't just kill him. Yes, back to Zark."

"The sash is the answer!" Inos said. "The Prisoner they mentioned is his son Krandaraz. The women talk of him. He almost overthrew Azak some years ago. He's supposedly being held in secret somewhere, to be released if Azak dies. That's how he keeps his other sons in line."

Rap's gray eyes had turned to her as she spoke. Now they began to gleam, seeing where her logic led. "Krandaraz must be quite a lad!"

She would have given half her kingdom for that smile. "He must be. The others daren't move as long as he is alive."

With a muttered oath, Azak threw his papers over his shoulder in a blizzard. He unfastened his emerald sash and tossed it on top of the other chest.

"How obliging!" Rap murmured. He urged Inos forward and they approached the caliph.

Azak pulled off his turban, revealing a hedge of red and white hair around a bald crown. He set to work on his shirt.

"Getting ready for the fat one," Inos said. "I think I'm flattered, but I'm not sure." She was babbling. The sight of the caliph's bulging, red-furred torso was bringing back nightmares.

"Any idea where this Dreag is?" Rap asked, edging closer to the glittering baldric on the chest.

"No."

"Well, I expect the—I mean, I expect certain friends of mine can find it. Thank you, dearest. You've solved the problem. Oh, yuuch! disgusting, isn't he?"

Azak had removed his boots. Now he rose and dropped his pants, sitting down to pull them over his feet.

Rap felt Inos' shiver and bared his teeth. "Hang on to my hand. It's time to deal with this vermin. By the way, do you recognize the sword?"

As she stepped clear to give him room, he drew a slim rapier and flicked it a few times.

"No. Oh! *Rap!*"

"It's Kadie's. I borrowed it for the evening. She wasn't any too willing to lend it to her dear papa!" His gray eyes were shining with pleasure now. "She's safe, Inos."

The tent swayed. The lanterns dimmed briefly.

"You all right?" Rap cried, steadying her.

She nodded. To faint now, after all this? Never! "Yes. Oh, yes! That's wonderful!"

KadieKadieKadie! Kadie safe!

Rap started to turn to Azak and then looked back at her hesitantly. "Gath?"

"Gath went off on his own to the Nintor Moot."

"Oh." His face ran through a whole bazaar of emotions—surprise, disapproval, confusion, alarm, and then pride. "Well! Nintor? On his own? Did he just? Tell me later. Hang on."

He reached out with the rapier and lifted the emerald sash of Arakkaran from the chest. It writhed, an angry snake of green light. Azak twisted around and stared blankly at the empty space. He gave the impression of a very puzzled man—not sure what he'd seen or what he should see or why it mattered.

"There! Always wanted one of these." Rap draped the sash around his neck like a scarf. "Give Krasnegar a bit of class." He bared his teeth. "Now . . . We'll leave a note explaining that the sash has gone to Dreag. I plan to write it in blood—Azak's blood. A fairly serious flesh wound is required, I think. Somewhere appropriate. You want to do it, or shall I?"

"You do it, darling," Inos said. "Husband's privilege. But give it an extra twist from me."

6

After all the potent sorcery Rap had been throwing around, Inos expected the escape from the djinn camp to be a simple matter. Things did not happen quite that way.

Azak's agonized screams brought a mob of guards pouring in. The big man roared like a camel as he stumbled to the door, clutching his groin and trickling blood between his fingers. He vanished into the horde of brown-clad family men in tumult and commotion. Revenge suddenly felt nauseating.

The first problem was the message. There was plenty of blood, but it soaked into the rugs and even the stains were not all within easy reach, especially as Rap was hampered by the need to stay in contact with Inos. By the time he had scrawled a few words with his finger on the back of a discarded dispatch, the guards were carrying Azak over to the bed, while still more men blocked the doorway. The racket suggested a huge crowd gathering outside.

A rapier had no cutting edge. Rap stabbed repeatedly at the side of the tent, cursing as it billowed, unable to make even a hand hole. One of the fearsome guards brushed against Inos and leaped back with a yell, reaching for his sword. Then he stood and gaped all around in bewilderment while his companions demanded to know what was wrong and he could not remember. Everyone seemed to be shouting at once, and Azak was still screaming.

Furkar had arrived, but he was standing back and watching with a cruel sneer, making no move to assist.

Inos made a fast grab for a dagger tucked in a guard's sash. As she made contact, he caught a momentary glimpse of the intruders and in turn made a grab for her. She stabbed at his hand; he fell back, yelling in terror. She swung around and slit the fabric with one long slashing stroke.

Rap yelped gleefully and pushed her out through the gap. She caught her foot and pitched headlong, remembering just in time to throw the dagger away lest she fall on it. In consequence she crashed heavily onto the grass, wrenching her swollen shoulder. Pain flashed like red flame, driving every other thought from her mind. Icy panic followed. She had escaped from Azak's tent, and Azak was injured, and what on earth was she going to do now? The hue and cry was in full spate already. There were tens of thousands of men all around her and they would all be hunting her. Yells from inside the tent told her that the gaping rent had been noticed.

Then strong hands grasped her to help her up and she remembered that Rap was here, also. Oh, good!

Rap set off at a run, dragging her through a darkness full of trees. She stumbled barefoot over the rough and prickly ground. Her garments were nothing to keep out the cold of the night, and the undergrowth seemed determined to strip even those from her. The camp was in an uproar, men running everywhere, and the only light came from the stars and the campfires.

"Had a pony," Rap shouted. "Can't get to it. Can hear horses over here somewhere." He was swinging the rapier like a cane, striking men out of his way like weeds and leaving a trail of near hysteria. He was also blundering through a multitude of branches and shrubs, cursing continuously. Gauze tugged and ripped as she followed.

"You can't see?" Inos said. "Can you do something about my shoulder? Why don't you just zap us out of here?"

He did not seem to hear her, but in a moment he came to a halt and lifted her hand to his lips and kissed her palm.

"Have you still got the dagger?"

"No." She was panting. She was too old for this wild adventuring.

"Then hang on to me. Don't want you to get lost."

In the dark her fingers fumbled at his neck. She felt the prickly coldness of the emerald baldric. A fortune in itself, it was also the title deed to one of the richest states in Zark, and Azak had redefined it as the symbol of the caliphate. As loot, it was a fair start for a career in theft. She felt she had earned it, though. Her feet were slashed to ribbons and her shoulder was lashing her with sickening waves of pain.

What was Rap doing? He was bent over something, muttering angrily.

"Can't you see?" she asked again, shivering as her sweaty skin cooled.

"No. Daren't use sorcery."

"By the Powers! What have you been doing all night, then?"

"That's different. Not me."

What was the use of having a sorcerer for a husband if he couldn't even see in the dark? Then the huge dark shape right in front of her uttered an ear-splitting whinny and she realized that Rap was fumbling with the tether.

"Got it!" he said. "Up!" He lifted her onto the horse's back. Hooves clumped the pebbles. He tried to scramble up after her and almost pulled her off.

"Who's there?" demanded a harsh voice close by.

"No one," Rap said. *"Umph!"* He was aboard. "Lie flat!"

Either he used occult mastery on the horse, or else his faun gift for animals was enough by itself. The beast took off through the night like an arrow, as if the Evil itself were after it, hooves thumping up the valley. Inos sprawled forward, head alongside its neck, clutching its mane with both hands and trying to favor her bad arm. Rap was on top of her, crushing her, clinging madly. Half the jeweled sash was between them, and with every bounce his weight drove it into her back. Branches caught in her hair and slashed at her legs. It was the wildest ride she had ever known, wilder even than the time she had demonstrated her riding skills for Azak and the princes, long ago in Arakkaran. Time and again she thought they were both about to slide off and crash to the ground. Time and again their steed stumbled and recovered, whinnying with terror. Whatever Azak had been planning for her could hardly have been worse than this.

Fires rushed by. Men were shouting everywhere, and camels roaring. The horse could not understand that it was invisible and silent—it was past caring anyway. Unsuspecting soldiers were smashed aside like puffballs as it thundered through the camp. Then the woods were dark and deserted. The exhausted mount began to slow.

With no warning the trees ended, the slope reversed, and the horse clattered and slithered down a shingled incline. It came to a shivering halt.

Rap straightened. Inos straightened. She felt as if she had been dragged behind on a rope, the whole way. Her shins and feet had been whipped raw. Overhead whirled the stars, and before her—more stars. For a bewildering moment she thought the world ended there, until she realized that they stood on the verge of a huge dark lake, reflecting the sky.

Rap slid to the ground and helped her down and held her. She would have fallen without that support.

"All right?"

"No, I am not all right!"

"Fussy! Never satisfied. What's bothering you now?"

"Let's start with my jewel-encrusted spine."

He chuckled and hugged her tighter, even as he applied sorcery. Her pains eased and were gone. She sensed her tattered veils solidifying into warmer, more modest wear, soft wool. Shoes clutched her feet. Relief! Wonderful, wonderful sorcery!

She clung to him, hearts beating together. "Oh, Rap! Lad, I have never been so glad to see anyone as I was to see you tonight."

"I should hope not!"

He kissed her. There was no passion in the embrace—that must wait for later—but there was love beyond measure. Rap, oh, Rap!

After a while he said, "And I to see you. The Gods were good to both of us tonight."

That did not sound like the Rap she knew, but she was not about to disagree. In the background the horse splashed its hooves into the lake and began drinking noisily. Far away down the valley the camels still roared.

"Oh, how I missed you!" Rap said. "You can't imagine."

"Yes, I can. I know exactly."

He squeezed her again. "I have never understood how I came to deserve you."

"The honor is mine, all mine. And Kadie's all right?"

She detected the tiny pause, the hesitation. "Physically she's all right. The goblins didn't hurt her, but she had a very long, very hard ordeal. And then ... you know what happened to the goblins, at Bandor?"

"I heard."

"She saw it. She hasn't quite recovered yet. She needs her mother."

"Take me to her, then."

"In a minute." Rap stepped back, still holding her hands. "Gath went off to the Moot, you say?"

"We were in Urgaxox. The word was that it would be a war moot. We decided it would be useless to go, and far too dangerous, but Gath—"

"Who's 'we'?"

"Shandie and I—"

"*Shandie!* Shandie's all right? He's still with you?"

"Gath saved him from the goblin—"

"Kadie told me."

Of course! She thought of all the things that had happened since she parted from Kadie, then decided they could wait.

"The last I heard, about a week ago, the imperor was in a jail back in Zark. Warlock Raspnex is there, too, I think."

Rap uttered a disbelieving bark of a laugh, almost a cry of despair. "A *warlock* in jail?"

"As far as I know. Gath hitched a ride on a longship going to Nintor." She steeled herself to ask the question that had tortured her for weeks. "Rap, does Gath know you killed Thane Kalkor?"

This time the pause was longer, more worrying. "I think he does, but he can't know all the implications. You don't mean he hitched a ride with *Drakkor*, do you?"

"I don't know who he hitched a ride with. He dreamed it up all by himself."

"But why?"

"Because he thinks you're dead. To help your cause. To be worthy of a father he loves and admires and mourns."

Rap made a strangled, choking noise. His face was a blur in the night. "Midsummer! The moot's held at Midsummer, and the evil begins then."

The God had told him he must lose one child. She felt her nerves beaten raw, and a hundred years old. "How is the war going, Rap?"

"Poorly. Tell you everything tomorrow."

"Take me to Kadie."

He sighed. "I'll try. I just hope this will work." He raised his voice, calling into the night. "Archon, we are ready!"

Everything vanished at once: the stars and the starlit lake, the sounds of the horse, and the cold.

The air was like steamed towels wrapped around her head. It reeked of earth and rotting leaves. Inos sensed thick jungle, drippy and likely dark even in daylight. In the night she could see nothing at all. Rap's arm was around her.

"There's a door just ahead," he said. "The side door. It's level ground."

She let him ease her forward.

"Where is this? Where are we?"

"In Thume. This is the heart of it, the holy of holies, the Chapel." He sounded displeased, as if he had hoped to be somewhere else.

Ancient hinges groaned. She saw something—not truly light, but a different quality of darkness. Rap went first, ducking his head for the archway, and she made that out. She followed.

The inside was vast and blank and still almost dark. In one corner a bluish gleam fell on a group of people, but even they were indistinct, and the rest was all shadow. She could not see where the light was coming from. It seemed like moonlight, but there was no moon. The air was much cooler than it had been outside, and musty like old attics, yet the floor was clean, not heaped with leaves or bat droppings. She walked forward at Rap's side, clutching his hand, that strong, familiar, welcome hand.

Nine people—she counted them—kneeling in a row with their backs to her. They had left a gap in the middle, four on one side, five on the other.

"Who—"

"Sh!" Rap squeezed her hand tightly.

What God was worshipped in this chapel?

They reached the gap, and Inos saw that there was a tenth person present, beyond the glow, a dark, hooded figure standing alone in the corner, holding a long staff. Her scalp prickled. Whatever or whoever that was, it was not a God, for she had seen a God once, and yet the nine seemed to be praying to it. What manifestation of the Evil was this?

And then, to her astonishment, Rap knelt, also, tugging on her hand. Dumbfounded, Inos obeyed. She could never have imagined Rap kneeling to anyone. Even to the Gods he knelt reluctantly.

A voice came from the venerated figure beyond. It sounded like fingernails scratching on pottery, almost too quiet to be heard, even in this enormous silence. It might, just possibly, be female.

"You have proved yourself a friend to Thume, Rap of Krasnegar."

"Thank you, Holiness," Rap said with what sounded like genuine humility. "I think the caliph will depart and take his army with him. He will not be riding a horse, though."

"You did well not to kill him."

"I surprised myself." There was a hint of a more normal Rappish humor there.

The nine worshippers made no sound. Perhaps they were merely stuffed replicas of worshippers. None of them had stirred since Inos entered. Her heart hammered unnaturally, an ache in her chest.

"We have brought back a trophy of war," Rap said softly. "We almost brought two. This one should be delivered to somewhere called Dreag, in Zark, and given to the prisoner who is kept there, and he should be freed. He is what draws Azak away."

"Leave it here when you depart," the rustly whisper said.

"I informed Azak that it would be delivered to Dreag."

"Indeed?"

"And my word is important to me."

Stubborn faun!

"But not to me." The woman, if it was a woman, spoke again, before Rap could argue further. "The threat will suffice. You have earned your sanctuary. We are grateful."

He growled. "Holiness, there are several sorcerers with that army, and it seems the Covin—"

"They do not concern us!" The voice was no louder, yet it seemed to echo through the great hall. Again Inos felt her scalp prickle.

"But, Holiness—"

"*Silence!* The war does not concern Thume. The Covin does not. We will never let ourselves be drawn into the affairs of the Outside. I said you have now earned the sanctuary that had previously been freely given you. Your help was freely given, also, was it not? You did not bargain."

"No," Rap admitted angrily. "But—"

"No buts. You and your loved ones may remain here, in a haven safe from the storm without. That is recompense enough. It is recompense indeed."

The dark figure had gone.

Rap snarled and hurled the jeweled sash clattering across the floor. He sprang to his feet. Inos jumped up, also, wary of his rage.

"Who was that?" she demanded, and then realized that the rest of the congregation was rising from their obeisance. So they were alive!

"That was the Keeper!" Rap said, as if pronouncing an obscenity. He drew a ragged breath. "These, dear, are the titular rulers of Thume, the archons. Archon Raim, my dear wife, Inosolan, the *exiled* queen of Krasnegar." He was certainly making no effort to conceal his bitterness.

"Allies?" Inos said, peering at the indistinct form of the man presented. All she could make out were the oddly angled eyes.

Memories of her last visit to Thume crowded in on her like wraiths and she edged closer to Rap.

"Just friends, ma'am," the pixie said. He sounded young. He seemed stocky. "There is someone who should speak with you first, though."

Inos said, "Who?" and felt a hand touch her arm.

Kadie said, "Mama?" in a small, uncertain voice.

As mother and daughter persisted in their tearful embrace, Rap turned away.

"Archon Toom," he said harshly, "why is it that women weep when they are happy?"

"I don't know, your Majesty," old Toom said, peering at him curiously. "Why do you?"

Manly foe:
   Give me the avowed, erect and manly foe;
   Firm I can meet, perhaps return the blow;
   But of all plagues, good Heaven, thy wrath can send,
   Save me, oh, save me, from the candid friend.

                                   George Canning, *The New Morality*

❬ TEN ❭

A necessary end

1

Sunlight filtered down through greenery. Dew sparkled on every blade of grass as if the world were a virgin bedecked in diamonds and come to her wedding. Fresh scents of summer promised a long, hot, carefree day. Horses grazed nearby with steady crunching, while somewhere on the blue doorstep of Heaven a skylark sang plaudits to the morn.

Roasted, that lark would make a delicious start to breakfast.

Ylo turned his head in a crackle of dry leaves and peered one-eyed at Eshiala. Her jet-black tresses were a tangle of mystery, her long lashes lay on her cheeks like combs. Sleep seemed to have brought her peace, while his had been tortured by nightmares. He could not touch her, for Uomaya lay between them, sheltered from the night's chill.

Now morning had come but the nightmares remained. There lay the woman he loved, the only one he had ever loved for more than a week. She carried his child already. He would do anything to win a smile from his lady. All he possessed in the world—wits, half a bag of gold, a fit body, a certain charm—all those were hers for the asking, plus all the remaining days of his life if she would accept them. And he had brought her to this.

Hungry.

Sleeping under hedges.

Hunted.

You have failed, Ylo. Failed!

Today seemed certain to consummate that failure in disaster. Never again would he waken to see her loveliness beside him. She would be returned to the palace and he dispatched to jail. That was the best that would happen to her and the least that might happen to him. Uomaya would rule the world as puppet for Zinixo.

In a mad chase across Qoble, they had eluded the legion for almost three weeks. That was a triumph for them, especially for Ylo himself, but a humiliation for the legionaries. He had been a hero and he had betrayed their trust, or so they would have been told. He could never hope to make them believe the truth. They might not know his crime, but they would not deal easy with him when they caught him, as catch him they must. His very success in evading capture for so long would count against him.

He felt Maya stir, Impress Uomaya. In its time the Impire had known perhaps a dozen reigning impresses, but surely none of them had ever had to sleep under bushes. Some of the imperors had done so, doubtless, but never an impress regnant. For the sake of the child this chase must end.

And for the sake of the other child, also—his, the unborn babe.

End it must. End it would. Yesterday the fugitives had ridden north, no longer daring to ask directions, but hoping to find a pass through the mountains. The road had petered out at a goatherd's hovel. They had retraced their path, but any prey, when it backtracked, was headed into the jaws of its pursuer.

A league or so down the road lay a hamlet whose name he had not bothered to ask. The legionaries would be there by now, or if not there then at the first crossroads beyond. They would have maps and the Cooperation of Law-abiding Citizens. They must know that their quarry was just ahead, trapped in this dead end. They would be ready to move out at dawn.

Dawn had already come. The day had begun.

He was hungry, filthy, and unshaven. His clothes were ragged and dirty. No longer could he overawe the peasants by playing gentleman. Now he looked what he was, a hunted outlaw.

"Mommy?" a small whine said.

Eshiala's eyes opened. She could not have been as much asleep as he had thought.

"Yes, dear?"

"I'm hungry."

Eshiala looked at Ylo—without reproach, but without illusion, either. Sadness and resignation. Interrogation.

"I was thinking about roast skylark," he said.

She smiled faintly. "We could eat gold."

"So we could," he said, stretching. "We'll go and buy a meal at the nearest farm and linger over it. One, big, satisfying bloat!" He thought about the fare in Imperial jails. That was the second-best way to get rid of an appetite.

Toilet was easy, consisting mainly of brushing leaves off. The two horses looked up reproachfully as their owners emerged from the thicket. Kindly people, their sad eyes said, do not hobble us.

Ylo scanned the landscape, seeing a dismal vista of empty fields and pasture, with no houses close. The Qoble range was a hard white bulwark to the north; he had learned to hate it. He should not have come so far into the hills. Nearer the coast there was cover. He should not have strayed into the countryside at all, for concealment was easier in cities. He should never, never, never have come to Qoble; it had been a trap from the start.

Two arms came around him from behind and hugged.

"You are giving up?" she said softly, her head against his shoulder.

"We must give up. For the children's sake."

"I do not want to give up. Another day will not kill us."

This day might.

He turned within her grasp so he might embrace her also. "Look at us! Bedraggled serfs! Who will trust us? Who believe anything we say? I have run out of credible tales to win assistance."

"If you use gold you can buy anything."

"And risk being knifed?" He sighed. "My darling, I have failed you. The perils grow worse."

"What's over there?" Eshiala pointed to the rising sun.

He had no idea. He was hopelessly lost without a map, but to say so would only worry her more. The land rose gently to a crest not a league away.

"Another valley, I assume."

Eshiala set her jaw. "Let us go and try it, then. It cannot be worse than this one, can it? If they are waiting for us there, then we can give up there. If not, then we have won another day."

Yes, but—

"Mommy, I'm hungry!"

"She is hungry," Ylo said, conceding defeat.

"Those cows have calves."

"So?" he said.

"You think of me as an impress still? Sir, I am but a humble grocer's daughter and granddaughter of farmers. I can milk a cow even if you can't, Signifer Ylo!"

He laughed. "I catch 'em, you milk 'em?" Cheer faded. "We have no bucket."

Eshiala's eyes glinted angrily. "We have two soft leather bags! We can put the gold back later. We can leave it lying in the grass for all I care! Saddle up, Signifer!"

The cows were reluctant and a couple of times Ylo thought he was about to be gored. He had no experience with cattle, but desperation was always the mother of innovation and he was prepared to wage all-out war. The taking of hostages had always been one of the army's preferred strategies, and it worked with calves. In the end the cattle paid ransom of enough warm milk for breakfast and morning showers, also, for the bag leaked. When the day grew hot the fugitives would all reek of sour milk. Nonetheless, the world brightened when hunger was banished, at least for a while.

Maya was very tired of riding. She wanted to go home, she said, although she probably could not remember a home. She became difficult when Ylo wanted to lift her.

"Give her to me," Eshiala said. "You can ride with Mommy for a while today, pet."

Ylo was worried about the roan. The previous evening he had suspected it was favoring its right foreleg, and although he could detect no trouble now, he wanted to keep careful watch on it. He mounted Eshiala on the sorrel with Uomaya before her. He kept the roan for himself, thinking he might dismount later and walk for a while.

Eshiala smiled down at him triumphantly. "Eastward ho!" she said.

"Eastward it is," he agreed, swinging into his saddle. It had been eastward all along—always eastward, as if they were some strange birds that migrated at right angles to all others, as if they fled the sunset.

They set off over the pasture at an easy trot, staying close to a hedgerow as high as a small forest, alive with dog roses, figwort, and golden cinquefoil. Eshiala was an accomplished rider, well tutored by the experts of the palace. She rode without apparent effort, laughing and coaxing her daughter to good spirits. Ylo stole miserly glances at her face. His realization earlier that she must soon be taken from him made him greedy for more memories of it, and yet he already knew every jot of it better than he knew anything in the world.

He had seen that face inflamed with passion and racked by ecstasy. He had seen it gentle, adoring her child. He had seen it kind, winning worshipful aid from peasants. Back in the palace days he had seen it coldly imperious and known that the spirit within was terrified beyond reason, but hiding that terror from all but the most perceptive. In Yewdark he had seen it desperate but unvanquished. He had never seen it sulk, never petty or spiteful or selfish.

And now their danger was greater than ever. He did not say so, and he had not argued against this new course, because their cause was now so hopeless that any risk was worth taking. True, the next valley might grant them a few hours' or days' more freedom. *Yes, but—*

Travelers on the road were inconspicuous to anyone except their pursuers. Cutting across country attracted everyone's attention, and the farmers' ire. To leave the roads was always a fugitive's last resort. This was the final lap.

His concern was well founded. They had ridden hardly a furlong over the pasture before their way was blocked by another hedge, its thorny tendrils reaching higher than a horseman and thicker than a wagon. They turned aside to flank it and with surprising good fortune soon found a place Ylo thought they might break through. He dismounted and persuaded the roan that if he could do it, a horse could follow. There was hawthorn in the hedge, and wild roses, and stinging nettles. Both man and horse got well scratched, but not fatally. The far side was pasture. He looped the reins round a branch and went back to fetch the sorrel.

A flash of light far-off caught his eye and he knew at once that it was sunlight on armor. They were distant, two fields away, but he could make out the dust they were kicking up. He counted eight or nine riders, already spread out as if they had been in hot pursuit for some time.

"There they are," he said numbly. "See, darling?"

Eshiala must have seen. With a wild scramble her horse exploded through the hedge, screaming in alarm. Ylo leaped back out of the way. Maya, clasped tight before her mother, uttered a wail and lifted tiny hands to fend off trailing branches. The sorrel catapulted into a gallop.

Common sense said that the game was over. The hounds had their quarry in sight at last and now they could run it down.

Common sense be damned—Eshiala's maternal instincts had taken over. Her child was in danger.

"Ride, Ylo!" she shouted, her voice fading into the distance. "Ride like the wind!"

2

Archon Raim built his own furniture with adze and chisel. The exiled king of Krasnegar preferred sorcery. Rap had constructed two admirably debauched lounging chairs to adorn the lawn outside his cabin, outfitting them with comfy pallets in an eye-catching purple. They would have swallowed a pixie whole, but they let him stretch out to his full length and degenerate in comfort. They were on the large size for Inos, and she had made some fitfully disparaging remarks about his color sense. If the Gods were truly insistent that he must wither away into senility in this gilded prison, then he would have ample time to do something about such matters.

But not now. Now was still for talking, and smiling, and strange feelings of thankfulness. It was only two days since he had brought Inos to the Rap Place at dawn, feeling much less like a romantic knight rescuing his lady than a plowman carrying his peasant bride home to his hovel. Years ago she had given him a palace; now he had landed her in a two-room cabin. Being Inos, she had sensed his mood and praised the quarters beyond reason. Being Inos, she made that hovel feel more homelike than any castle.

Two days were not enough to wipe out eight months of separation, eight months of not-expecting-ever-to-see-again. Two days were not enough to exchange tales of all their strange adventures. Two days were not enough to erase the feelings of miracle upon waking to find the wanted one lying alongside, or looking up to meet the remembered eyes again. Two days were nothing and yet infinitely precious.

Now they lay under the shade of the elm and smiled at each other in bone-deep contentment.

"What was the worst?" she said suddenly.

He shrugged. "When the sorceress caught me in Casfrel, I suppose. Or when we had to let Olybino die. But he must have known that would happen. I feel guilty that I always underestimated him."

"He probably underestimated himself until he needed to be more than he had been. And the best part?"

"Silly question."

She chuckled.

Later, she sighed. "What happens next, Rap?"

"Here? Nothing. The Keeper will see to that."

"Can she? Can she really keep the Covin away for ever?"

"She thinks so. Or says she does. It is in the laps of the Gods. If anything brings Zinixo's full attention to bear on Thume, he will realize that it is not what it seems. Otherwise . . ."

Otherwise the two of them remain here in exile for ever, moldering away into old age.

"No escape?" Inos asked, knowing what he had not said.

"Not without her consent. I expect she has bespelled us so that we cannot escape. She probably foresaw what happened in the djinn camp, or else she had a prophecy to guide her. She knew I would return. She knew—you can bet on that. I don't think the Keeper takes any risks at all." He glanced around. "We have company."

Kadie and Archon Thaïle came strolling across the grass. One had short fawn hair, one long black hair, but they wore identical skirts of blue and green, identical white blouses, identical sandals. Gold eyes and green eyes, but their smiles were equally strained.

Kadie had elected to remain at the Thaïle Place. She came to call twice a day, but she never stayed long. She was improving, yes, but even her mother had failed to effect a cure. That was going to take time, and Rap had an uneasy hunch that Kadie made those visits only because Thaïle sent her. Today she had brought her instead.

Rap clambered out of his chair and summoned two more chairs from the cabin. He spoke formal greetings to the pixie, and hugged Kadie. He tried to believe that she was less wooden in his arms than before. He thought he even detected a hint of the old Kadie, a faint trace of devilry as she inquired sweetly if her mother had slept well.

"Of course not," Inos said blandly. "Do sit down."

Alas! Kadie was startled by the reply, so she had not been needling. Her green eyes flicked from Inos to Rap and back again. She was of an age to start appreciating her parents as people and not natural phenomena, but she seemed shocked to think they might still do *that* at *their* age.

The four of them settled in a circle, the youngsters insisting that the older folk take the more comfortable chairs. Rap invited Thaïle to provide refreshments according to local taste, and she magicked up a cool and tantalizingly bitter fruit punch. The meeting was all very civilized and fraught with undertones. Was this merely a rehabilitation visit for Kadie, or was there a deeper purpose?

"Papa?" Kadie said with almost the old primness she had displayed when plotting mischief. "Tell us how the war is going."

"I doubt if Thaïle wishes to talk of such somber matters."

"Oh, she does. I mean—" Kadie caught her friend's eye and sniggered. "I mean, I am sure she won't mind."

Deeper purpose!

"She probably knows as much as I do, or more," Rap said cautiously. He was certain that the Keeper had instituted the meeting with Toom and Raim that had triggered his visit to the caliph, but he did not think Thaïle would be so cooperative, not with the woman who had slain her child and lover. Nothing was certain with sorcery, of course.

"The djinn army is still withdrawing, your Majesty," Thaïle said quietly. "The caliph still rides in a litter."

"I am delighted to hear it. Please call me Rap unless you see me actually wearing my crown. I left it on the bedpost today."

She nodded solemnly. "So Thume is out of danger, thanks to you."

"But can it stay that way?"

She shrugged. "Probably, for only sorcery can expose us and we have defenses against sorcery. How does your war go? Have you and, er, Inos had time to compare notes?"

"We have," Rap said, wondering who else was listening to the conversation. "I doubt if we know as much as the Keeper does, but here is what we do know. Of the four wardens, East is dead and West, Witch Grunth, has been coerced into joining the Covin. Lith'rian is sulking in his sky tree, determined to throw away his life in futile defiance, and Raspnex we believe to be holed up in a Zarkian jail."

Kadie said, "Jail, Papa?" in scandalized tones.

"A shielded jail. It is probably the safest place he could be. Every sorcerer seems to agree that open hostilities will break out on Longday, the day after tomorrow. That happens to be when the thanes of Nordland gather in moot to proclaim war against the Impire."

Kadie bit her lip. "And that's where Gath went?"

"He went to Nordland," Inos said soothingly. "It is extremely unlikely he will manage to attend the moot."

"And all the longships will be loaded with warriors when they head south," Rap added. "They certainly won't carry tourists. So Gath will remain in Nordland. He may actually have found himself a very safe stall."

Kadie looked from one face to another, obviously wondering if she should believe this. Her concern for her twin was a good sign, though. Yes, she was better since that record-breaking weep with her mother.

"All sorcerers in the world know of the impending struggle," Rap said, continuing his review, and wondering if the right word was *struggle* or just *rout*. "How many will elect to join in remains to be seen. If the first clash goes badly, I expect most of them will remain in hiding—no one joins lost causes. If we can put up a good show initially, we may enlist more support."

Who was *we*? Who was left? He suspected Zinixo was picking off the opposition like flies on a window. Olybino had gone. Grunth had gone. There had been no groundswell of support for them. Now he was out of it, also, unless the Keeper relented.

Thaïle had been studying her hands, hunched in her chair like a woman four times her age. She looked up now with a frown.

"You don't have any idea of numbers?"

"None. I don't know how strong the Covin is. Hundreds, I expect, and it includes at least two of warden rank. Zinixo raided the Nogids and snatched more than half the anthropophagi. He must have collected a majority of the dwarves in his twenty years of plotting. Probably all goblin sorcerers were votaries of Bright Water, so he would have inherited them, apart from the two Raspnex found at Kribur. But Azak's private little covin of djinns is still at liberty, as far as I could tell.

Shandie unearthed—I use the word advisedly—a sizable contingent of gnomes, who indicated that they might support him under the right circumstances."

It sounded even worse put into words than it did when he thought about it in private.

He sighed. "I admit that it looks bad, Archon. Thaïle, I mean. The anthropophagi and trolls who went to Dragon Reach must have been betrayed by Grunth, or most of them. The rest of the trolls would much prefer to stay in their jungle. Imps . . . I have no idea, although imps probably outnumber other races in sorcerers, so there must be many still at large."

"But less than half?" Thaïle said coldly.

"Very likely. The elves won't fight, except to defend their sky trees. The pixies won't fight, either."

She raised her eyebrows. "Do you still say we should?"

Put like that, the question had a horribly obvious answer.

"That leaves jotnar and merfolk," Rap said, avoiding it. "The merfolk I know nothing about. Jotnar? I doubt that Nordland has many sorcerers. Jotnar despise sorcery."

Silence.

A pair of butterflies danced across the shadowed circle and waltzed away into the sunshine again. Rap thought of pixies. The Keeper was right. You should not try to turn butterflies into hornets.

"You have omitted one factor from your appraisal, Rap," Thaïle said quietly.

He looked at her in surprise. She seemed so young and so much an innocent country maid that it was easy to forget the wisdom her great power must have brought her.

"What's that?"

"That you have been removed from the battle."

"Me? I doubt that I would make any difference at all. I must be the weakest sorcerer in the world."

"But you are the acknowledged leader of the counterrevolution. So now it is leaderless. What of the imperor?"

"As far as we know, he is in jail with Raspnex."

Inos intervened. "Shandie cannot be the leader. First, he's a mundane. Second—Raspnex says—the other races will never rally behind an imp, and especially that one."

"And I'm a half-breed?" Rap said. "A mongrel? Is that what he implied?"

"Not at all."

"I never wanted to be leader."

"Exactly. He said that it was only because you had repeatedly refused a warlock's throne that everyone would be willing to accept you."

Now there was perverse logic! It sounded more like an elf's than a dwarf's. So what was the purpose of this discussion? Was Thaïle hinting that she might be able to help Rap escape from Thume if he still wanted to go and take charge of the war? And did he really want to? His review of the situation had emphasized just how horribly hopeless it was. Every race in Pandemia seemed to have lost more than half its sorcerers to the Covin, which meant that his cause was mathematically hopeless already. The few exceptions were hardly encouraging: djinns and merfolk totally unknown quantities, the jotnar probably of little account. That left gnomes. What hope of them ever even showing up?

Common sense said he should accept the safe haven he had found in Thume and let the world fend for itself.

"Thaïle . . ." He stopped. "Something wrong?"

The pixie was staring blankly into space. She muttered an apology and rose to her feet.

Kadie jumped off her chair. "What's the matter?"

"Nothing," Thaïle murmured. "Have business to attend to . . ."

She faded away like smoke. Kadie screamed in alarm.

3

The sorrel gelding was a big, strong fellow, although he had a lazy streak. Ylo had been delighted to get him and had paid a ridiculous price for him. The roan was gentler, a placid little mare with a good seat, chosen for Eshiala. Now he could see that he need not have been so fussy—that woman could ride a whirlwind!

Try as he might, he could not catch up. The mare was just no match for the sorrel, especially bearing Ylo's weight. The two horses smoked across the hayfield with Eshiala steadily drawing out in front. Faintly Ylo heard little Maya's howls over the thunder of hooves. The next hedge was coming up ahead, and Eshiala had obviously seen the gate in it. It wasn't a gate, though, just a gap blocked by a wicker hurdle. She put the sorrel straight at it and soared like a bird. Then she was gone.

Ylo's heart turned over. *Gods, woman!* Think of our child!

Think of badger holes.

Don't think of badger holes.

Then he was coming at the hurdle and gathering the mare for the jump. From the way her ears flattened, he guessed she'd had no training in jumping, but she took his orders and cleared it like a veteran. They came down in unripe grain and Eshiala was farther in the lead than ever.

Utter insanity! Didn't the woman know she was *pregnant!*?

He looked back, but saw only the hedge, which was already fast receding into the distance. Here he was on the crest of the divide. He could see nothing in any direction but corn below and blue sky above, plus more hedges. This time there was no gap ahead. Eshiala did not seem to have realized that. She was still kicking for more speed, humped over to hold her child tight, holding the reins with one hand.

When he'd first met her, she'd seemed just a delicate wild-flower wilting in the sultry hothouse of the court. He had soon discovered that she was a wild animal caught in a cruel and intricate trap, and had adjusted his plans accordingly. Before he could make his move, the collapse of the old order had thrown her into terrible danger, but it had also released her from her captivity. Since then she had shown no fear that he had been able to see. Even after he had rescued her from Yewdark, the flower had not been ready for the picking, nor the trophy for the wall. She had made him wait for his reward until she was ready to grant it. Then she had given herself without stint.

Were Shandie to return from the dead, he would not recognize this new Eshiala, this confident, courageous concupiscent woman. Her palace terrors had been forced upon her because her inappropriate marriage had compelled her to be something she was not. She had been required to feign affection for a man she had not loved, a man incapable of loving her as anything except a mythical ideal. No one could be brave in the face of the unknown or the inexplicable, and Eshiala would rather face armored legions than a gaggle of corseted dowagers. Against danger she could understand, she was valiant as any battle-hardened warrior.

And she was riding the pants off him! He would never have expected the gelding to put out for her like this. Still, in her condition this was rank insanity. He would catch up with her at the hedge and tell her so.

She was riding straight at the hedge.

By the Powers, woman! Stop! It's too high. You don't know

*what's on the other side, or how wide it is. The horse will balk
and throw the pair of you straight into the thorns.* Make that
all three of them! The wind blew cold on his sweat. He wanted
to scream at her and the distance was too great, and he might
distract her anyway. The hedge was a windbreak, full of trees,
and Eshiala had chosen a gap between trees but the thorns and
shrubbery were higher there, taller than a man. The horse
would refuse . . .

The horse didn't. It showed momentarily in the gap against
the sky and then Ylo was riding alone through the corn. And
he couldn't tell if his love was alive or dead on the far side.

Well, if she could do it, he could. He patted the roan's neck.
"Did I mention that I am an extremely skilled horseman?" He
got no reply. He risked one last glance around and saw no pursuit yet. The hedge loomed over him.

He thought of Star, his first pony, and how Big Brother
Yshan had set up a knee-high hurdle and dared him to try his
first jump. He had done it and lived and had never truly feared
a jump since—until this one. A blind jump with an untried
horse too small for his weight. Even jail seemed good, suddenly.

He took the poor roan over it by brute force, and aged about
ten years. They went through the top in a blizzard of thorny
branches. She stumbled on landing and recovered, then he felt
the sickening jerk of a limp in her right foreleg. *Bloody blas-
phemy!*

Well-cropped pasture sloped down into another valley.
Eshiala was halfway across, angling to the left with cattle
stampeding out of her path. She was aiming for a gate in the
north boundary.

Beyond this field lay more fields, no cover in sight, very
few buildings. Water glinted in the valley bottom, but beyond
the river—forest! Suddenly there was hope. The silvery chain
of the stream divided the valley into vastly different halves.
This side was all cultivated and pastured. The far slope seemed
like uninhabited wilderness, stretching for leagues. If the fugitives could cross the river, they could hide from anything but
dogs. They might starve to death, but someone must live in
that forest. Charcoal burners or game wardens—such men
could be bribed with much less gold than still jangled at Ylo's
saddle.

Eshiala was almost at the gap, another hurdle. *Remember
you are jumping him downhill, love!* There was no field be-

yond it, just a narrow lane and another hedge. She could jump, but did she have room to land? Why did she not just wait for him to come and move the hurdle? He closed his eyes. When he opened them, the gelding was gone and must be presumed safely over and heading to the right, downhill. Oh, bravely, bravely done! That sorrel was a steeplechaser born. They would have a clear run down the lane to the river. *Just don't drop Maya now, darling!*

The roan was slowing, limping harder. All Ylo's training in horsemanship screamed at him to let her stop before he killed her. His father's ghost pounded on him. Yshan and Yyan, long-dead brothers, howled in his ears. He kicked and kicked, urging the mare onward toward that exit.

Again he took a quick glance back, and there were three horsemen in the pasture with him. A fourth came over the hedge even as he looked, then down and down, crumpling and rolling in disaster on the grass. One less—but that didn't matter. Three would be enough. He had a sword, but he couldn't fight three.

Gate coming up. The roan was too lame to jump. He wasn't going to make the river on a lame horse.

4

"For gods' sake, Kadie!" Inos said, hugging her frantic daughter. "Thaïle's only gone away for a few minutes. Stop making such a scene!"

She transfixed her husband with a penetrating green stare.

Rap said, "Huh?" and "Oh, yes. Well, I was thinking of going for a swim. Anyone else fancy a swim? No? Be back shortly, then."

He strode off across the glade.

Women!

Kadie's problem must be even worse than he had realized if she became hysterical every time her heroine left her for a moment. She was still only a child and he was her father, so he eavesdropped, knowing that Inos would expect him to, or at least would have no objection. As he pushed through the scrub and poplar saplings, his eyes and ears were back at the cabin—in a manner of speaking.

"Now come and sit here with me," Inos was saying sternly. "Your father doesn't know the difference between a chair and a double bed. I've always wondered if he was color blind and now I'm sure of it. There. Well, we might as well lie back."

They stretched out side by side on the cushions. Kadie had not stopped whimpering and weeping on her mother's shoulder.

"Mph!" Inos said crossly. "Perhaps a good slap was what you needed. What sort of princessy behavior is this?"

Rap came to the edge of the bank and slithered down in a shower of pebbles. The tide was out, exposing a wide expanse of white sand punctuated with slimy rocks. Wind stirred his hair. He began to trudge seaward and returned his mind to the conversation.

"Family is family," Inos was saying, "and friends are friends. Good friends are more precious than fine jewels, and greatly to be treasured. But you never *own* your friends. They're not pets. They have their lives to lead, too."

Reaching damper sand, he paused to strip and put his clothes in a heap. Cool salty wind caressed his hide. The entire bay was empty as far as he could see. Perhaps in the real-world Thume it was inhabited, but not in this one, the College Thume. He padded forward again, enjoying the wetness under his feet.

Inos had not yet managed to start Kadie talking, apparently.

"You were very, very lucky that she found you, and she has been very kind to you. I understand why you feel as you do. But tell me this: What does Thaïle get out of your friendship? What do you provide her in return for all the help and care she has given you?"

Kadie just sniveled.

"I said you can't treat a friend as a pet, Kadie. You can't behave like a pet, either. If you pester Thaïle too much, she may not want to be quite as friendly. You must be considerate in return for her kindness."

Rap was wading into the sea, eyeing the big breakers ahead. He'd learned to body-surf back at Durthing, years ago, and it would be fun to try that again. Perhaps not today, though.

Kadie now: ". . . doesn't mind. She's told me so lots of times." *Sniff!* "Says I'm good company for her 'cause she—" *Sniff!* "—doesn't have any friends here, either. They killed her baby!" *Weep.*

Undertow sucked at his knees and a glistening green wall rose up menacingly in front of him.

"Do you know why sorcerers never marry other sorcerers?" Inos asked.

The breaker hung in the sky, light shining through it. He dived into the base of it and was snatched underneath, through cool green silence.

Inos still: "I don't suppose she could. Words of power don't let themselves be talked about. But I can tell you. I'm probably the only person in the world who can tell you!"

Rap's head broke surface and he struck out seaward, hearing the crash of falling surf behind him.

". . . don't know any words now. I'm the only ex-sorcerer in the world, and so I'm the only person who knows these things and can also talk about them. So listen. Four words make you a sorcerer. In most cases a fifth word will destroy you. Almost nobody has enough control over magic to stand the power of five words. It's an overload, too many bales on the camel. Anyone who can survive, though, is a demigod. Like the Keeper. Like your father was once. Demigods are enormously strong, far beyond ordinary sorcerers, but they live in constant pain, fighting the power trying to destroy them."

"Destroy them how?" Kadie whimpered.

"Well, I saw a sorceress learn a fifth word and she burst into flames like tinder."

The next swell lifted Rap heavenward in cool bliss, not far from a bobbing white bird, a feathered boat with a cynical gold eye.

"Yes, it was horrible," Inos said. "She burned away completely. And that's why sorcerers mustn't fall in love with other sorcerers. They daren't! Men and women making love are not always, er, well, not always quite in command of what they do or say. It would be too easy to share a word of power at such a time."

"Thought they were hard to say!" Kadie objected, watching her mother with red-rimmed green eyes.

Rap sank downward into the trough, relishing the effort and unfamiliar exercise.

"In this case it's different," Inos was saying. "Because there's love involved. It's a special case. Maybe sometimes sorcerers do fall in love and deliberately do share five words, but then something completely different happens."

Inos was doing remarkably well! Rap took a deep breath and submerged.

"Your father and I had this problem, you see. Two people plus five words plus love . . ."

"What's the matter?" Kadie demanded.

Rap chuckled to himself, fighting himself down into deeper, darker green. He'd been expecting this. From the expression on Inos' face, she was experiencing a sudden attack of nausea.

"There's more than just the words keep that secret, dear. The Gods don't . . . Ouch!"

In the depths of the sea, Thaïle appeared to him.

"Rap? Your Majesty?" she said. She was perfectly audible, and apparently completely dry down there.

"What—" Taken aback by this apparition, Rap released a cloud of bubbles and began to choke.

"We need your help, Rap. Come, please."

Suddenly he was standing in a forest—stark naked, soaking wet, convulsively coughing up seawater.

5

Ylo checked the lathered roan and slid from the saddle. He landed her a grateful pat or two on her wet neck, for the poor brute had given him all she could. He tied the reins to the hurdle. It was a nasty thing, woven from thorny branches and lashed to the hedge at both ends with strong-looking rope. He had no time to take his dagger to it, and no need. He squeezed through under one end of the barrier, scratching himself mightily in the process. He took off down the road.

As soon as he was hidden by the hedge he doubled back to the edge of the gap and waited, his heart a pounding hammer in his chest.

He glanced behind him. Eshiala was nowhere to be seen. Then she came into sight out of a dip. She was well down the lane and still going, although the gelding was obviously tiring. She twisted around to look for him and he froze, resisting an urge to wave—if she saw him dismounted she might be stupid enough to come back for him.

Hooves drummed on the turf and the roan whinnied. He stooped to find a rock, a heavy rock, the sort of rock that might knock a rider off his horse. He had left the mare blocking the gap—would the horseman dismount to move the barrier? The hooves slowed. Then the hurdle creaked as the frightened roan tried to back out of the way. The hooves drummed harder and ceased abruptly. Ylo hurled the rock. As soon as it left his hand he knew it was aimed too low. Man and horse came through the air and the missile struck the horse just below its eye.

It was enough to throw the beast off its landing. It came down on knees, neck, shoulder, rump high in the air, mount and rider one huge mass of flesh toppling together. The mailed man clanged on the road and the horse rolled on him.

That left two. In a momentary silence Ylo heard more hooves coming.

The man he had felled was obviously no longer a threat. If the Gods were feeling kind, then his horse might just be well enough to ride. It struggled to right itself, hampered by its rider's foot caught in a stirrup, then collapsed again. Dog food! The Gods were not benevolent. Ylo felt much worse about the horse than the man.

He looked for Eshiala. She had reached the bottom of the hill, was heading for another gate. One more field to cross and she would be at the water. He wanted to cheer. *Don't stop now, my darling! Go! Go! Go!*

The sound of hooves grew louder. The roan mare whinnied and backed away, ripping off half the hurdle and leaving a barrier scarcely knee-high.

Ylo drew his sword.

Rap stood in the shadow of a forest, mostly beeches and chestnut. Beside him were Archon Thaïle and several other people. Nudity in other people was nothing to sorcerers, who could see through stone walls. Nudity in oneself was something else. Even before he had stopped throwing up saltwater, he created a pair of trousers on himself. They turned out the same surprising shade of purple as the chairs back at his Place, but that didn't matter. Beechnuts prickled his feet, but shoes could wait, also.

Thaïle he recognized, and Raim, and the other two were archons, whose names escaped him. They were standing at the top of a low cliff, sheltered by bushes. Below the cliff, trees sloped gently to a river. Beyond the river lay fields and farmland that could only be the Impire, probably Qoble.

He stopped coughing. "You called?" he gasped.

"Can you see what is happening?" Thaïle demanded. Everyone was studying something on the far bank. Tension crackled in the ambience and his levity had been misplaced.

"No." His farsight range was sadly restricted now.

He was granted power in a surge that shocked him. It brought vision that would make a hawk blink, and then he saw everything. A woman was riding a chestnut horse, clutching a child in front of her and going down a lane at breakneck speed, heading for the river. Farther away, half a dozen horsemen came in pursuit, spread out all the way to the skyline at the height of land. They all wore the chain mail of legionaries and at least three sported the white crests of centurions. One man had come a cropper trying to jump a hedge and was sitting on the grass clutching his right ankle. His horse grazed peacefully nearby, seemingly unharmed.

There was another horse and another man, a civilian. He had dismounted at a gate and left his horse behind in the field. He was waiting in obvious ambush for the first of the pursuers. What chance did he think he had against horsemen?

"Fugitives?" Rap said. "You must get them through here all the time, surely?"

"A woman with child!" Thaïle said. "She has a child with her and she is herself with child. There is a prophecy!"

He wanted to shrug. He wanted to say: *But I helped you three nights ago, and what good did it do me?*

Instead he said, "What do you want me to do? Again I point out that you must get fugitives dropping in all the time. Why four archons for this lot? Why me?"

"You do not see?" Raim said. "Look in the ambience."

Powers preserve us! Faint, like smoke, two great eyes hung in the sky. They were insubstantial, and yet stony, a ghost of a cliff face, a hint made up of cloud and shadow against the blue. Of course it was illusion. It was only Rap's own mind trying to make sense of the inconceivable, but the image was enough to chill him to the marrow. It was the same symbolism his brain had used when the Almighty had come searching the ambience for him in Ilrane. He was sensing the Covin. The Covin, too, was watching the drama unfolding in the valley.

Why?

The audience grew larger as more archons materialized at his side.

"Well, it seems you do have a problem," Rap said. "Not an hour ago Thaïle was telling me that only sorcery could injure Thume. Those folk down there are all mundane, aren't they?"

"Seemingly," Thaïle said. "But why are they of interest to the Almighty?"

"You expect me to know?" Rap exclaimed. "Just like that?" Had the pixies any idea of how big the outside world was or how many people lived in it?

The first pursuer jumped his horse over the gate by the watcher and went down in a gruesome tangle. Certainly that man was—or had been—no sorcerer.

It was the Azak problem all over again. If the Keeper used power to repel the invaders, then the Covin would notice. If the fugitives were allowed to cross the river they would vanish behind the inattention spell, and the Covin might wonder.

Who could these runaways be that they should merit such a pursuit and such an observer? Rap focused his superhuman vision on the woman. His shock alerted the other sorcerers.

"Who is it?" Thaïle cried.

He could not believe it himself, but he said it. "It's Impress Eshiala. The child is her daughter, the princess imperial."

How in the world had Eshiala managed to come to Thume? Shandie had left her in a safe house close to Hub. Why would she have come here?

"And the man?" one of the archons demanded.

The man? The civilian by the gate? He had his sword out. He was making no attempt to rescue the injured legionary, whose horse was obviously now crippled and who might be dead himself. Had the civilian contrived that fall? If so, he was fighting a very dirty battle.

Gods have mercy—it was Ylo! Signifer Ylo. His face was scratched bloody and streaked with dust and sweat also, but there was no mistaking it. Good looks like that were rare enough to be unforgettable.

Oh, of course.

"The man is Shandie's signifer." Thumian lacked such a word and Rap spoke the impish term. "That's an assistant . . . He's a lecher, a woman chaser. When I met him, he was after the impress. Apparently he got her."

Ylo had been with Shandie when the goblins caught him. Rap had not thought to ask Inos what had happened to him. There had been many, far more important things to discuss than Shandie's signifer.

"Then it is the woman the Almighty hunts?" Raim asked.

"It must be. Or the child. Ylo's a pretty lad and he has some good qualities, but there's nothing much to him." Rap pulled his wits together. "Look, call my wife here."

"Why should we need her?" a quiet voice in the background asked.

Without turning his head, he glanced behind him. The Keeper was standing back under the trees, a dark shape leaning on a staff, a shadow in the shadows.

"I am only trying to be helpful, Holiness," he said. "I am a friend of Thume's, remember?"

"Bring her," the Keeper said.

But the second legionary was nearing the gate, and apparently that civilian was about to tackle an armored, mounted opponent. *Nothing much to him?* That could not be the same Ylo Rap had met. Or else he'd gone crazy.

The impress cleared the gate into the water meadow and her horse stumbled and went down under her. The child rolled free.

"Good!" the Keeper said.

The opponent approaching would wield a legionary's short sword. Ylo wore no chain mail and his rapier was a gentleman's weapon. He must use his advantage in reach immediately, before his blade could be knocked aside or perhaps even cut through. He was on the man's right, and much would depend on whether the man had already drawn his sword. This battle was turning into a very dirty fight, but the Imperial Army had never cared much for rules except the one that said *The good guys must win and we are always the good guys.*

The knell of hooves slowed. The rider must have seen his predecessor go down and might be expecting an ambush. Or perhaps he was merely watching his footing. The fragment of hurdle remaining was no great barrier, but it could trip a weary horse.

He put his mount over it in proper jump style, which meant he was crouched low in the saddle. Possibly his attention had wandered to the casualty sprawled in the dirt, or possibly he expected a conventional attack from the left. Ylo leaped forward and lunged upward. The point of his rapier screeched on chain mail and went through the gap in the armpit. That was not a stroke to kill a man instantly, but it could do a lot of damage and it certainly served Ylo's purpose. The rider keeled over with a bubbling scream. The horse shied from the sudden attack and bucked. Ylo's sword came free. The downed horse tried again to rise and again collapsed on its motionless rider.

The second horse reared, tipping the legionary off completely. The wounded man flailed and screamed as he fell into the hedge. Ylo grabbed the cheek strap. There was a wild skirmish with clattering hooves and loud cursing. Then Ylo more or less had control of his new mount. Holding its reins, he grabbed up the rapier he had dropped. The horse backed away from him, whinnying with terror and rolling white-rimmed eyes. Fortunately it backed itself into the hedge; he was able to move in close and mount from the wrong side.

In the saddle he was master.

The wounded man had fainted, or was stunned. He was probably fated to drown in his own blood anyway.

Fury roared in Ylo's head. He felt wild exultation. Two down! He was invincible, irresistible!

The third rider was coming, galloping across the pasture, crouched over his horse's neck. Another two had come over the skyline. Eshiala . . .

Eshiala was staggering across the meadow on foot, carrying Maya, heading for the river. Oh, Gods! She had fallen? She could not be seriously hurt if she was walking. Could she? She had a long way to go.

For a moment Ylo dithered.

Then he turned to face the pursuit. There was no hope of faking any more accidents, but he must hold the gate to give Eshiala time to reach the forest. The good guys always win!

Beyond the hedge the third opponent reined in and straightened up in his saddle. Ylo saluted with his rapier.

"You crazy popinjay!" Hardgraa roared, drawing his sword with a blood-chilling scrape. "Think you can stop me, do you?"

There were ten watchers in the forest now, for all the archons had arrived.

"That is the one!" the Keeper said. "That soldier is the one the Covin watches."

How she could tell that, Rap had no idea and no chance to ask. With a squeal from Inos and a shriek from Kadie, his womenfolk appeared at his side, still huddled together as if lifted straight out of their chairs. They staggered. He clutched Inos' shoulders to steady her.

"Shandie!" he said. "When he was captured—did he say anything about Ylo, his signifer?"

Inos glanced over the audience and the geography and raised

her eyebrows. "We have another emergency? No, not then he didn't."

"Later?"

"Kadie!"

Ignoring her mother's exclamation, Kadie rushed to Thaïle's side. The pixie gave her a distracted smile and put an arm around her.

Inos said, "Later he said he thought that his companion had escaped."

"Nothing more?" Rap asked. "Not that he had given Ylo any special instructions, for instance?"

Inos frowned in annoyance at being thus interrogated when she did not know what was going on. "He hinted that he didn't trust Ylo not to go chasing after his wife. That was all."

Rap groaned. There was no other explanation, then. "Ylo did. Did go after her. They're here."

"Here?"

"Over there. Across the river. The impress is heading for the water—see? And Ylo's up that road there, facing off with . . . God of Mercy!"

With Centurion Hardgraa.

"Gladiator scum!" Ylo bellowed. "Come and get me! You think an Yllipo is scared of you, you dreg?"

Last of the Yllipos! Bred of mighty warriors! His heart soared. He was exultant with bloodlust. He was fighting for his woman and his unborn child. Chain mail or no chain mail, that stinking legionary was never going to get past Ylo.

Hardgraa turned to stare back up the hill. His two minions were still coming, but one horse was obviously lame. Ylo fought down the temptation to charge while his opponent was apparently distracted.

"I don't fall into those traps, cretin!"

Crazy with terror and the stench of blood, his horse skittered and danced, and he held it in place without a thought. He had the advantage and was going to keep it. That poxy-eyed no-good centurion had to come by him, and there was half a barrier still. Hardgraa was good with a sword and knew every dirty trick ever invented, but he wasn't in Ylo's class with a horse.

Still staring behind him, Hardgraa slammed his spurs into flanks already bloody—typical sneaky tactics! His horse hurtled through the gap as if to clear Ylo's mount out of its way by brute force alone.

Ylo rose in the stirrups, leaning forward, lunging at the centurion's eyes, trying to use his greater reach. Hardgraa parried contemptuously with his heavier blade. The two mounts collided with screams, swords clanged again, rapier against gladius. Ylo tried to back off, then realized his error. As the better horseman, wielding the longer sword, he would normally try to keep his distance. Conversely he had expected the centurion to keep the fight close. But Hardgraa wanted only to get by, so Ylo must seek to block him. For a moment the match was a melee, with knees and heels and hooves doing far more than arms. Dust swirled in choking clouds.

Then Ylo ducked below a stroke that would have removed his head, and Hardgraa's horse bucked, throwing him forward. The point of Ylo's rapier scraped over his helmet. Damn, that had been close! Fast as a viper, the legionary recovered and swung his gladius upward. Ylo felt the wind of its passing on his face as he swayed aside. Before he could even draw back his elbow for another lunge, Hardgraa spurred forward and struck again. Ylo parried a blow that would have taken off his sword arm, but a rapier was not meant to be used that way. It bent like an earthworm. Hardgraa's sword screeched along it and sliced deep into Ylo's thigh. The impact on the bone was stunning—pain and fear and nausea. As the horses danced apart, he threw both arms around his mount's neck and his rapier clattered to the dirt. Blasts of pain shot through him like thunderbolts. A hot tide of blood poured down his leg. He held his breath, waiting for the quietus.

"I'll finish you off later!" Hardgraa bellowed, spinning his horse around. He dug in his spurs and was off at a gallop down the road.

"He got him!" Rap cried.

"Who got him?" Inos shouted, squeezing his arm. "Ylo? The one on the gray is Ylo? Who's the other?"

"Hardgraa."

The archons were muttering. The ambience flickered in aurora of emotion. In the sky the illusion of eyes persisted, cold, stone eyes watching the tiny drama below. The impress was still staggering on foot across the meadow, burdened by her load and obviously close to collapse. And Hardgraa was racing down the hill.

"I think the emergency is over," the Keeper said in a small, satisfied whisper.

"Who is Hardgraa?" Inos demanded.

Rap kept his gaze on the chase. "One of Shandie's men. He was Eshiala's guardian. Looks like he followed them all the way here."

"You mean she ran off with this Ylo man?"

"She probably thinks that Shandie is dead," Rap said. "Of course she does! All of them do! They think that child is reigning impress! That's why Hardgraa's here!"

"Rap!" Inos shouted. "What do you mean?"

"He's after the child." Rap stared at those monstrous eyes in the sky. Hardgraa was probably in the power of the Covin. Mundanes could be votarized just as sorcerers could. That must be what the Keeper had detected. Knowingly or not, Hardgraa had brought the Covin with him.

It looked as if he was certain to win.

Except that Ylo was coming in pursuit.

He lashed the gray with the flat of his dagger. The world was fading in and out of gray mist. Every hoofbeat sent waves of agony up from his thigh, and he knew he must be spilling a trail of blood along the road. He had very little time before he blacked out. The world was disappearing from the edges of his vision and drums beat in his ears. All he could see was the hateful back of Hardgraa ahead of him. All he had to do was catch up. All he had to fight with was a dagger, against an armored legionary.

Yllipo! Yllipo! Last of the Yllipos. Father, Yyan, Yshan help me! Let me live just that long.

Hardgraa must have thought the hooves were one of his cronies coming to help. At the last minute he turned his head and an expression of comical shock showed even under his helmet. By then it was too late—his foe was to his left and he could not bring his short sword to bear.

The centurion spurred again, started to pull out ahead.

Using his hand to move his useless leg, Ylo pulled his right foot from the stirrup. He raked his horse with the point of the dagger. It spasmed forward. With a final, killing effort, clutching the mane, he let himself slide over, wounded leg drooping, and he struck at the only target he could be sure of, Hardgraa's mount. Even as his grip failed and he began to fall, he felt the dagger bite into the hamstring.

He thought, *Eshiala!* and that was all.

Hardgraa's horse went down. Ylo's fell on top of it. The centurion rolled free, stunned. Ylo was somewhere in the middle.

The impress plodded grimly toward the river.

Nauseated, Rap and Inos put their arms around each other.

"Rap of Krasnegar!" the Keeper cried from the shadows. "You must go down and make her turn back. I shall cloak you again in the spell of inattention."

"Me?" Rap shouted. "Never! Let her in, you heartless old bitch! If you do not pity her, then have mercy on her child!"

The archons reeled back in unison like a ballet corps. Inos said, "Sh!" nervously.

"It is the woman with child of your prophecy!" he said, just as loudly. He had no idea what the prophecy said, but obviously it mattered. "I think the Gods have rolled your dice, Keeper!"

She wailed. "No! We must stop her!"

Rap pushed Inos aside. His temper blazed out of control, jotunn fury. "You think that would save you? Two days ago an army turned back in the east. Today a fugitive is turned back in the west? Do you call Zinixo an idiot? You think he will not wonder now? Thume is exposed, Keeper! The trumpets are sounding!"

A yell of triumph from the Keeper and archons made Rap spin around. The impress had fallen. The child was sitting up, howling, but the woman lay still, not far from the riverbank. The two horsemen were racing down the hill, almost to where two prone men and two struggling horses marked the scene of the second battle. Rap's heart sank without trace.

"We are saved indeed, faun!" the Keeper cried.

The first horseman jumped from his mount and knelt beside Hardgraa. Rap saw the centurion speak, though he could not make out the words. The second horseman was almost there, his mount limping. The first straightened, beckoned to him, and vaulted back into his saddle. Hardgraa had told them to catch the woman before they tended to him.

"It's all over!" Inos said.

Rap nodded grimly. Nothing he could do, and Ylo's gallant battle had been in vain. Ylo was almost certainly dead.

Failure.

No! The Keeper howled like a dog—two more players had

come on stage. Two girls were splashing across the river, going to help. White blouses, long skirts . . .

Rap had felt nothing in the ambience, but he had known that Thaïle was a mighty sorceress. She had moved Kadie and herself down to the edge of the barrier without a flicker that he had detected. She had even evaded the Keeper.

One of the archons cried, "Stop them, Holiness! They will be seen!"

They had already been seen. The ghostly eyes in the clouds narrowed at the sight of these mysterious newcomers. How long would the Covin be content to watch and do nothing?

Inos threw her arms around Rap. "That's Kadie, isn't it?"

He nodded and hugged her. "Nothing I can do," he muttered miserably. Nothing anyone could do without making things worse, and nothing would draw the Covin's fires more certainly than Rap himself appearing. But he felt like the worst sort of coward. Sweat trickled cold down his face.

Side by side, Thaïle and Kadie leaped up the Qoble bank and ran to the fugitives. Kadie lifted the little princess, Thaïle raised the impress. The two horsemen had stopped at the gate and seemed engrossed in struggling with the fastening. *Thaïle, you are using sorcery in the sight of the Covin!*

"Holiness!" the same archon protested. "You must stop her!"

"Me?" the Keeper screamed. "I can do nothing now. It is not my fault! I told you! Why do you think she goes to rescue a child? Did I not warn you that the Gods might yet be wroth for what you did? This is your doing, you fools! Childslayers! See what you have made of the Chosen One!"

Archons tumbled to their knees before her fury. Kadie and the babe were halfway back across the stream. Leaning heavily on Thaïle, the impress was close behind. The horsemen were heading back up the hill toward Hardgraa.

Overhead, the watching eyes turned their gaze on Thume itself. The Almighty's frown darkened the sky like an imminent thunderstorm—puzzled, searching. Rap's scalp prickled and his arm tightened around Inos. He knew those eyes of old. Obviously they could not see him, though. If Zinixo had detected Rap he would have attacked at once, so the spell was holding.

Then the cloudy vision faded away. Either the dwarf had realized that he was being observed, or he had gone off to think over these peculiar events. Certainly he had seen enough to arouse his suspicions. It had never taken much to do that.

The fugitives had emerged from the water, safe on the Thume side. Safe for now, at least. The two horsemen were loading Hardgraa onto a mount as if he were hurt but conscious. They had cut the injured horses' throats. Ylo lay like a corpse in the lane, ignored.

Rap turned. The archons still groveled before the Keeper. His fury boiled up again. "Keeper, you have failed! Now the Covin knows that there is power and mystery in Thume!"

The hooded figure seemed to shrink away from him. "No!"

"Yes!" he roared. "You can hide no longer! Join the battle now, before it is too late!"

She raised her head and howled. "It is already too late! Your cause is hopeless! I have failed my people! Keef forgive me!" Her wail soared higher and higher, a thin shrill note of despair that cut like a knife.

Rap clapped his hands over his ears. The archons were doing the same. Power flooded the ambience, brighter and brighter, unbearably bright. The Keeper's bones shone through her flesh like the sun in mist. He turned his back on her and shut off his farsight. He did not want to watch.

"Rap!" Inos cried. "The Keeper! It's like Rasha, isn't it? She's burning! What happened?"

"It's the Gods' justice," Rap said. The Keeper had given up the struggle. Seven years of unrelenting pain, leading inevitably to this—he should feel sorry for her, but he could find no pity. "Good riddance!"

Behind him, the Keeper's death cry faded away.

He stared miserably at the carnage beyond the river.

Slumped in the saddle, Hardgraa was being led away toward the nearest farm, past the bodies of the two men Ylo had slain.

Ylo's body lay abandoned in the dirt between the slaughtered horses. Two ravens floated down from the sky.

A necessary end:

> The valiant never taste of death but once.
> Of all the wonders that I yet have heard,
> It seems to me most strange that men should fear;
> Seeing that death, a necessary end,
> Will come when it will come.

> Shakespeare, *Julius Caesar, II, ii*

❦ ELEVEN ❧

Rolling drums

1

Maya had gone to sleep, and that was good. There was shade under the willow, where Eshiala sat clutching her daughter, and that was good, too. The little river chattered on its pebbles under a silver glare of sunshine. Birds were chirping. But someone was missing. Something was wrong, and she couldn't remember exactly . . .

She'd hurt her leg, hadn't she? Perhaps not, for it seemed to be all right now. Riding a horse. Jumping. Everything was very muddled. Someone missing? Girls. There had been two young women, or girls. No, someone else.

Twigs crackled. She jumped and turned to look.

"Let me see the child," the man said, sitting down on the moss at her side. He was big and shaggy-chested, wearing only hideous purple trousers, but his ugly face seemed concerned and oddly familiar.

"It's all right," Eshiala said. "She's having a nap."

"More than that," he said. "And you're in bad shock yourself. You remember me? I'm Rap."

"She's asleep," Eshiala explained. "Poor thing, she was very frightened earlier. But she's asleep now. She'll be alarmed if she wakes up with a stranger holding her."

"I won't let her be frightened. I can calm her like I've calmed you." The man took Maya gently in his arms and frowned at her. "Trouble is, I can't do more than one thing at a time anymore. Didn't see where that scatty daughter of mine went, did you?"

Eshiala's boots were full of water. Her skirt was soaked, and badly torn. Daughter? The man had a daughter, too?

She wondered if she should mention the two girls, but perhaps she had dreamed those. She might be dreaming now. Everything was so muddled. There was something she ought to be doing, if she could just remember what it was.

"You're right, she is asleep," the big man said. "Must be Thaïle's doing. Nothing serious, just bruises. I'll fix them and then wake her up."

Memory . . . worry. "If she's all right with you, then I'd best go back right away. I have a friend to help. He must have been delayed." She started to rise.

"Sit down!" the man said. "That's better. You're not really conscious, you know! You're running around in a daze. You took a bad fall. I don't know how you managed to walk all that way. I don't know how you walked at all."

Daze? It was true that things were rather muddled in her mind. Riding down a road and looking back for Ylo. Where was Ylo? Why wasn't Ylo here? Sunlight glaringly bright on the water, moss warm, skirt all wet and tattered.

"Thaïle would have fixed you up, I'm sure," the man said, still frowning down at Maya, holding her as if she weighed nothing. "But she was called away." He turned and glanced at the trees behind. "And that halfwit daughter of mine is floundering around in the briars. Excuse me . . . *Kadie! Come back here!*"

Maya slept on, undisturbed by that ear-splitting bellow.

Where was Ylo? Why was he taking so long?

"My wife'll be here shortly. You do remember me, don't you? Rap from Krasnegar?"

Eshiala's court training came to her rescue. "Of course I remember you. It has been a long time, hasn't it? Have you been keeping well?" Where? He did look vaguely familiar. Count Rap? Senator Rap? An innkeeper, perhaps.

Maya opened her eyes. "Mommy, I'm hungry." Then she looked up doubtfully at the big, bare-chested man holding her on his lap.

He grinned a faun's wide grin at her. "Don't suppose you remember me, Princess. I was on the ship. Do you remember the ship? My, but you've grown! I'm Rap." He smiled again.

She returned his smile trustingly. "I'm hungry!"

"What would you like to eat?"

"Chocolate cake."

He sat her down on the moss at his side and gave her a plate of chocolate cake—several slices—and a glass of milk.

"That should keep you happy," he said. Then he turned big gray eyes on Eshiala.

Winds began to move the mists in her head. Things cleared. Ylo! Armed men on horses! She tried to rise and the man laid a large, powerful hand on her shoulder.

She yielded unwillingly. "I must go back and look for someone. He should have been here by—"

"Just wait a minute, your Majesty. I haven't quite finished. I wish Thaïle had been able to do this. You've been through quite an ordeal."

Terror and horrors lurked behind the mist. She did not want to see. "We must hide!" she said, scanning the far bank over the silver glare of water. *Panic!* "Hide my daughter. The soldiers—"

"They've gone away," he said. "Now do you remember me? Rap, from Krasnegar."

"The king! Sorcerer?" The ferry on Cenmere . . . *"How did you get here?"*

"That's a very long story." His big faun mouth was smiling, his eyes were not. "And you've had quite a journey yourself, your Majesty."

"You're mistaking me for someone else," she said automatically. Ylo! Where was Ylo? Gods, how was she going to manage in the forest without Ylo?

"You are Impress Eshiala. I'm a friend, remember?"

She nodded. Oh, yes, she remembered. He was a friend of Shandie's. Another one who might try to steal Maya away and take her to the palace, just like Hardgraa and Ionfeu. She clenched her fists.

"You are quite safe here." He shook his head. "No one is going to take the child from you. The soldiers won't come. You'll be looked after."

She shivered and stared longingly at the meadow across the river, willing Ylo to appear, riding over the grass. There had been two girls . . .

"Your horse fell after you cleared the last gate," the man said. "I don't suppose you even remember the jump. But you made it to safety. You're all right. Your child will be all right."

Startled, she looked at him. Which child did he mean? She wasn't showing her condition yet, but he was a sorcerer.

Ylo! There was still no sign of Ylo.

"Where is my husband?" she demanded.

The big man winced. He glanced behind him, at the trees. "My wife will be along in a moment. *Kadie! This way! Over here!*"

"They caught Ylo? Is that what you're hinting? No!"

He shook his head. "He stopped them from catching you. He felled three armored men single-handed. He defended the woman he . . . He defended his impress, I mean. To the death."

No! "You can't possibly know that!" she said angrily. "You were here, he was over there." No, she would not believe it! "You're making that up." It was all lies!

Again he shook his head. "I'm sorry."

"I won't believe it. He's my husband!"

King Rap gritted his teeth. "When were you married? How long ago?"

"Some weeks ago," she said evasively. She had started the baby before that.

"Your Majesty, Ylo did not lie to you, but he was mistaken if he said that the goblins killed the imperor. Shandie was rescued. As far as I know he's still alive, and well. I admit I have no recent news of him, but if your wedding was more than nine or ten days ago . . . well, you weren't married. It wasn't valid. And it probably couldn't have been valid at any time, unless something has happened to Shandie very recently."

She shook her head, dumb with horror. Shandie alive? What had she done? Betrayed her husband, her imperor? That would be treason! Oh, Ylo! What would Ylo say?

"Ah!" the big man said, springing up. "At last! This is my wife, Queen Inosolan of Krasnegar. And my daughter Kadie."

Eshiala clambered to her feet as two women emerged from the undergrowth from opposite directions. The first was tall and striking, not quite a jotunn. Her eyes were a startling green, her hair the color of summer honey, but she lacked the fierce angularity of jotnar. Ignoring her husband's attempt at formalities, she swept Eshiala into a comforting embrace and hugged her.

"Oh, Kadie!" Rap said. "For Gods' sake stop moping!"

"Thaïle disappeared again!"

Oh! So the girls had not been part of the nightmare. This was the one who had carried Maya across the stream. She seemed on the verge of tears. Her skirt was torn, her face scratched, and her long black hair had twigs in it.

"What if she did?" King Rap said crossly. "She's not your pet dog. The Keeper's dead. Thaïle had to go away with the other archons. She has duties. She can't spend every minute of her life with you, even if she wants to."

"More cake?" Uomaya said, holding up the plate. She was the only one still seated, and her face was chocolate from ear to ear.

"Maya! That is not polite!" Eshiala said despairingly.

"But it's good sense," the king said. "True impish practicality. How about some sherbet instead?"

"Rap!" Queen Inosolan said in a voice of menace. "Where do we go from here? Do we spend the rest of the day digging bait in this jungle, or can we go somewhere civilized? And by the way, you look like a serf."

He shrugged and began buttoning up a shirt that he had not been wearing an instant before. "I don't know what happens now. We're in the real Thume, you see. I can't move us back to the College—I nearly broke my neck coming down that hill."

"And I had to do it without sorcery!" the queen said icily. "You might have left me a good pair of boots."

He groaned and ran his fingers through his hair. "The only way back to the College will be one of their Gates, and I have no idea how to find one."

"Sherbet is nice, thank you," Maya remarked wistfully.

"What color sherbet?"

"I can't leave yet," Eshiala said, casting a yearning glance at the far bank.

Inosolan put an arm around her again. "I am truly sorry about Ylo. He died very nobly."

"You saw, too?"

"No. But if Rap says it happened, then it happened."

Ylo! Ylo! Ylo! She would not believe it. Lies! "I must go back. I should not have left him. I should have gone back as soon as I realized he was lagging."

"You did exactly right," Inosolan said. "You did exactly what he would have told you to do if he could, what he wanted."

"Chocolate sherbet, please," Maya said, "or strongberry."

The king said, "Ah! Archon Neem, her Imperial Majesty the Impress Eshiala."

The newcomer must have just stepped out from behind a tree, or somewhere. He had an odd face, with slanted yellow eyes and extraordinary pointed ears. His clothes were green, and more like city wear than peasant garments. Was his name all *Archonneem* or was some of that a title? He bore an air of authority. His expression was bleak. He nodded to her but did not bow.

Everyone began talking at once. He raised a hand for silence. "The Keeper told me to come and fetch you."

"The Keeper?" Inosolan and Rap and their daughter repeated the words in chorus.

"The new Keeper, of course."

The Kadie girl screamed. "Thaïle? Not Thaïle!" She had turned white. Queen Inosolan put an arm around her.

"Keeper of what, Archonneem?" Eshiala asked.

Rap answered for him. "Keeper of Thume."

"Thume, the Accursed Land?"

That was why she could not categorize the yellow-eyed man. East of Qoble, of course. He must be a pixie. "It's true, then?"

"It's true," Rap muttered.

"I like strongberry and I like chocolate, too."

"Thaïle is the new Keeper?" the girl cried.

Archonneem frowned. "That was her name before she became Keeper. Impress, her Holiness suggested you and your child might stay at the Baze Place. Goodman Baze is a former archon. He and Goodwife Prin are both elderly, but they have room for you, and will make you welcome. The location is pleasant."

"I think she should come back to the Rap Place first," Inosolan said firmly. "She and I need to have a long talk."

"The Keeper will be obeyed!"

"You've told her a fifth word?" Kadie wailed. "It will kill her! It will torture her!"

Eshiala's head was spinning. Pixies?

"Shut up, Kadie!" Rap said. "Archon, what news of the Covin?"

Neem fixed him with a forbidding stare. "Nothing here."

"Then where?"

Reluctantly the old man said, "The djinn army has halted but is not pitching camp. There is activity in Dragon Reach."

"He's raising the dragons?"

"Not yet, but perhaps soon."

"Chocolate sherbet, please," Maya said. "Or more cake."

"How long would it take dragons to fly to Thume?" Inosolan demanded, looking from the pixie to her husband and back again.

The two men exchanged glances.

"Two days maybe," the king said.

"They haven't risen yet."

"So they can be here by Midsummer?"

"Unlikely. But Longday may be only the beginning."

"And the caliph, also?"

Eshiala could not keep track of all this. Her mind would not stop shouting for Ylo, wanting to know what he would say about pixies, about Shandie being still alive. Where had the soldiers gone? And *dragons*? She must have gone crazy. She was in a home for the insane.

"Mommy?" Maya said. "Mommy! Mommy! Mommy! Where Ylo?"

2

"Three ravens," Gath said. "A head with an ax in it. A bloody hand. A woman with . . . Yuck! Two sea dragons and—"

Blood Wave II had arrived at Nintor and was sailing just off-shore, skirting the gray beach where the longships lay. Although they were drawn up on the shingle, clear of the water, they had their sails spread. Normally raiders' sails bore only the orca symbol of a thane, but for the Longday Moot they had been decorated with their owners' personal emblems, and Gath was reading them off before they came in sight. Drakkor had chosen to approach upwind, probably because that was tricky with a single square sail and let him show off his seamanship. Sounds of cheering followed his progress along the shore—he was the thane who had spoken for war at the last two moots, and now all of Nordland was behind him.

"Next three all show a white bear with red paws," Gath added. "I'll show up if I look farther."

"Try it," said Thewsome.

Gath stretched his prescience another few moments. "Two ships with a red shark. Three with raiders holding axes. Oh, *Gods!* A bloody phallus!"

"Yes, you're showing! Well done! You've got it now!"

Like all the rest of the crew, the two of them were leaning

on the gunwale and waving obscene gestures at the shorebound audience—the lanky boy and the enormous Thewsome. He was the largest man aboard, bigger even than Red. His arms and shoulders bulged like pillows, his fists were the size of horses' hooves, misshapen from innumerable fights. Not even another jotunn raider would ever pick a quarrel with Thewsome—which was why he looked that way.

"About five minutes is safe, then?" Gath said.

The giant nodded, and smiled. His eyes were a pale foggy gray, surprisingly gentle. He turned back to studying the passing shore, spray shining like diamonds on his flaxen hair and beard.

To Gath's great relief, the wind had held for the journey from Gark. The crew had not been required to row. After Afgirk and Kragthong's departure, Thane Drakkor had been remarkably merciful in administering punishment to the upstart atheling—a single punch that had laid him flat on the floor and left a purple bruise that still showed in the middle of his chest. When Gath had somehow wobbled to his feet and managed to raise his fists again, Drakkor had roared with laughter, thumped him on the shoulder, and told him to go board *Blood Wave*. Furthermore, that embarrassing rebuke had been delivered in the privacy of the thane's own quarters, with no bystanders present to mock. All in all, Gath had been let off amazingly lightly.

His relief had turned to alarm when the longship had sailed without the skald aboard. A few cable lengths from shore, his prescience had inexplicably returned. Even then, he had not guessed.

For an island so famed in legend, Nintor was a dismal sight. It was low and grassy, and so small that few charts would show it. Thewsome had explained that it had no water, so nobody lived there. He meant that no one would bother to fight over a place so worthless and thus it could safely be decreed sacred, but even he would not go so far as to put that cynical thought into words. It was a barren strip of dark green under the milk-blue arctic sky, backed by the ragged peaks of Hvark beyond it to the north. Longships flanked the shore like a row of teeth. Gath had not realized that there were so many jotnar raiders in the world. Fifty men to a keel; he had lost count at eighty-some, and still they kept coming into view.

"There!" Thewsome said, pointing an arm as thick as a flayed goat carcass. "See?"

A few upright stones showed on the skyline. There were no other rocks in sight, and those were too regular to be natural.

"The Place of Ravens?" Gath shivered. "Is that where the thanes meet?"

The giant chuckled. "That is where thanes *die*! The Moot is held at the Moot Stow, which is being a hollow on the south side."

"There won't be any Reckonings this year, though, will there?"

The fog-pale eyes turned to stare at him disbelievingly. "You think that all thanes are accepting Drakkor as leader without argument?"

Gath said, "Oh!" and nothing more. He tweaked his prescience again: another red fist, two crossed axes . . .

Thewsome muttered, "Careful!"

It had been several hours after *Blood Wave* set sail that Gath had realized Twist was aboard. He had not noticed the extra crewman—nobody had. The others knew him, of course, for he had sailed with them before. They had paid him no special heed. They seemed to have no realization that he only appeared once a year, on the Nintor jaunt, and was never seen around the thorp.

Gath had been sitting in the bow, being inconspicuous, when the great tattooed giant had settled down beside him and smiled at him with Twist's pearly eyes. Even then Gath would not have known him, had he not been allowed to.

"Is being traditional," he had explained. "I told you—not all of us are skalds. Some are women, some priests. So we are always coming in disguise. For Longday Moot, I am Thewsome. Is a good name, right?"

Gath had wondered how it felt for a despised cripple to be a whole man for a few days each year. Thewsome claimed that his excessive size was designed to avert challenges. To brawl would require him to use sorcery, which a jotunn regarded as cheating. But he could have diverted a challenge with sorcery just as easily, so his fearsome appearance probably had another explanation—it must feel good, too.

Having established his identity, Twist had set to work teaching Gath how to control his prescience. It was not conspicuous, but it could be detected, he had said, and there would certainly be Covin spies at the moot. Lessons from a sorcerer were like no others, involving adjustments to the pupil's brain, but now Gath was able to reduce his range all the way to zero if he wanted, as if he were turning off a spigot. He had even started to extend it, to two hours or more, and Twist-Thewsome said he might be able to raise it farther when he had more time to practice—but not to try that at Nintor.

Still the shore curved away ahead. Still the longships lay like basking sharks on the shingle just above the weeds that draped the high tide mark. Here and there groups of half-naked jotnar sprawled on the grass beyond, apparently asleep in the unending summer sunshine. Others were tending kit and weapons, or clustered around fistfights, hooting and jeering. Cooking fires smoked, but as *Blood Wave* went floating by them, the crews abandoned all other pastimes to run down to the water and cheer Thane Drakkor.

Drakkor himself held the steering oar and mostly ignored the applause. Once in a while he would raise a hand in salute to someone ashore, but he did not join in the vulgar gesturing. His babyish face was expressionless. As far as Gath was aware, he had not exchanged one word with his brother on the journey.

Gath glanced to his right to make sure his neighbor there was engrossed in other matters, then turned back to Thewsome. "There is a sorcerer for every ship?"

The skald spat over the side. "Oh, no. One for every thane, more like. But this year every thane is bringing all the ships he can muster. I have never seen so many."

War moot! Fire and slaughter. Gath tried to imagine all these men charging brandishing swords and axes, howling in bloodlust. He couldn't imagine it, but he could come closer than he wanted to. He had decided he was not as much a jotunn as he had thought. He wasn't even enough of a jotunn to want to be that much of a jotunn.

"And where is the Commonplace, where the secret moot is held?"

Thewsome pointed a finger as thick as a dagger hilt. "North. You can't see it from here."

The end of the line was near. It would come into sight in another few minutes. Then Drakkor could beach his ship. The cheering swelled as *Blood Wave* swept past some allies.

"Nobody's booing," Gath said. "Your brother seems to be the popular favorite."

"Do not be calling him my brother!" the giant growled. "Not here!"

"Sorry."

"And they will cheer his killer if he dies. But Drakkor is not the only one in danger, I am thinking."

The wind was chill and laden with salty spray. Clad only in breeches like everyone else, Gath was already having trouble persuading his teeth not to chatter, but the implications of those words made him feel much colder.

"You, you mean?" he asked hopefully.

Thewsome chuckled ominously, still studying the island. Boards and ropes creaked ... "Where is my world expert in sorcery? Are you not being aware of the problem?"

Gath had been thinking of little else but the problem for days now. The danger was much like the danger he and Mom and Warlock Raspnex and the imperor had faced in Dwanish, but there were differences. The trickery that Mom had dreamed up then would not work twice. He hoped Twist could think up an equally effective strategy, because *he* couldn't.

"You mean the Covin sorcerers are going around turning all the others into votaries like themselves? Ganging up on them? You may be enslaved as soon as you step ashore!"

And him, too.

Seeming deep in thought, the giant scratched a dragon tattoo half hidden by the hairy mat on his chest. "Is not happening that way, though! I am not hearing any sorcery at all—which is why I keep reminding you not to use your prescience. The island is quiet as a grave."

It might be quiet in sorcerous terms, but in Gath's world the cheering was waxing louder and a small army of men had started running along the shore. It was heading for the place where *Blood Wave* would beach, gathering mass like a snow-ball as it went.

Mention of graves made Gath feel even colder. Perhaps the damage was done, and every sorcerer already ashore had been bent to the will of the Almighty. Best not to worry about that possibility! "Is the Commonplace shielded?"

Now Thewsome turned to look at him with Twist's pale eyes. There was no hint of a smile in them, though. "It is."

"So ..." No, discard that idea ... "That's good, isn't it? If war breaks out in there, then the Covin itself can't interfere!"

"Shielding is only as strong as the sorcerer who made it," Thewsome remarked softly, "but likely you are being right."

"If the odds are on the Covin's side already, then the case is hopeless," Gath continued. To think he had hated schooling back in Krasnegar! Here the penalties for mistakes did not bear thinking about. "We'll lose. So we must just hope the odds are on our side, and we'll win the battle in the Commonplace."

"What battle?" Thewsome shrugged the obscene pictures on his shoulders and went back to watching the shore. Somehow he had implied disappointment, that Gath was overlooking something.

"But when we all come out again . . . ?"

The giant said nothing, merely scratching a few more tattoos. That was not the problem, then, or not the worst part of it.

"If all the sorcerers come in disguise," Gath suggested wildly, "then you can't tell which ones have loyalty spells on them! And we agreed that you probably can't rely on knowing them anyway?"

Thewsome nodded, waving a vulgar finger at some man ashore. What had he seen that Gath had not? The best way to get answers was to ask questions, Dad had always said.

"Then how do you tell the good guys from the bad guys? How do you tell the sheep from the wolves?"

"Ah! Well, my lad, one way is that sheep mill around in herds and wolves run in packs."

Was there a difference between a herd and a pack? Cold fingers closed around Gath's heart. Oh, God of Horrors!

"Twist! What happens at the Moot Stow if the thanes vote for war?"

Twist-Thewsome looked down at him with approval, baring yellow teeth in flaxen beard. "Then they choose a leader. If needs be, the candidates fight it out at the Place of Ravens. But once a leader is chosen, then all the other thanes do homage to him."

"Is it possible for a sorcerer to lie to another sorcerer?"

"Not usually."

Gath shivered. His teeth chattered briefly. Then he brought them under control. "Homage can be done to a deputy, can't it? An agent?"

The giant nodded.

"Was that why you let me come?"

"Whatever do you mean, Atheling? You came because you wanted to." Thewsome uttered a gruesome jotunn laugh. Then he gripped Gath's arm, and his fingers went all the way around. He squeezed painfully. "Will you do it? Are you man enough?"

This was Dad's war. Here was Gath's part in Dad's war. He

had chosen it himself, even if he hadn't known he was doing so. This was what his craziness at Urgaxox had brought him to! He had no one to blame but himself. He straightened up and forced out the words, his knuckles white on the gunwale.

"No, I'm not man enough, but yes, I'll do it, if it will help."

"It is the only way I can think of, Atheling."

"Then of course I'll do it."

"It is dangerous!"

"I said I'd do it!" Gath shouted angrily.

That was how to tell the sheep from the wolves—set a trap. With him as the bait.

3

Inos came along the Way in the evening sunshine. A whiff of sea tang and a muted rumble of surf told her she was approaching the Rap Place. As she emerged from the trees she was greatly relieved to see Rap himself stretched out on one of the ugly purple lounges. He sprang up to greet her and they hugged.

"Funny," she murmured into his neck. "I think I missed this more than anything—just being held."

He grunted. "Well, it's a start. Sit down and let me make you a drink."

She sank down wearily, wondering if she was too old for all this wild adventuring or just unaccustomed to the Thumian climate. "Something stunning."

"Elvish brandy?" He gave her a crystal beaker the size of a small bucket. She needed both hands to hold it.

"You were always generous," she muttered. "I said stun, not kill." It was cool and delicious and not elvish brandy.

Rap perched on the edge of the chair beside her and smiled happily.

"Kadie?" she said.

He glanced at the cottage. "Stretched out cold on our bed. I don't think she slept all night."

"Not much, anyway." Inos took another draft and eyed him over the rim. "I wish I understood why you can't heal her!"

He shrugged. "I can heal bodies. Souls belong to the Gods."

"You cured me!"

He turned his face away as if to study the trees. "Not really," he muttered.

"Rap!"

"Well . . . I did hurry your own healing along a little. You're a strong, mature woman. You knew that what Azak wanted was to hurt and humiliate you, so you fought back against that. To recover was to defeat him, right? I just helped. Kadie's problem is much worse, much deeper. What would you have me do—take away her memories? People are made of their memories, darling. Personalities are. I mean, I daren't meddle in that. I might turn her into a mushroom."

He ran his hands through his hair. "Besides, she's right to be worried about her friend, isn't she?"

Inos made a noncommittal noise. Friendship was one thing, obsession another. She laid the drink on the table beside her so she was free to squeeze Rap's arm. "I'm sure you're doing all you can, love."

"How's the impress?"

"Better. She's a strong woman." For a twenty-year-old who had been through several consecutive hells, the girl was a marvel.

Rap nodded, staring at nothing.

Inos said, "Prin and Baze are sweet."

"Yes."

"Rap? Is she pregnant?"

He nodded again.

Inos took another drink and thought yet again about Shandie. Having now met Eshiala, she could understand his infatuation. The impress' beauty was every bit as incredible as he had claimed, but he had never been a sensitive or understanding husband. How would he react to her now that she carried another man's child?

"I suppose that's a fairly small problem really, isn't it?" she said. "With the world at stake, what's one more little bastard? Even an Imperial bastard. Minor problem."

So was Kadie. Tomorrow was Longday. None of them mattered compared to that, not Eshiala or Kadie or Rap or Inos.

"How's your day been?"

Rap shrugged. "Frustrating. The Way won't always do what I want it to. I can't reach any of the archons' Places I know of. I can't find any trace of the Chapel, and I think Kadie tried for the Thaïle Place a hundred times. Mostly I've been following her around in circles, keeping an eye on her."

"Any news of the Covin?"

He sighed. "The djinn army's back where it was four days

ago. If it advances tomorrow, it'll enter Thume before mid-day."

"How's Azak?"

"Don't know."

"His sorcerers may have cured him?"

"If they weren't frightened of the Covin, they might. Or Zinixo may have done so. Or he may have died. I have no idea."

"We should have killed the bastard," Inos muttered, "when we had the chance. Him and his whole murdering horde." She saw Rap wince. Why? What did he know about Azak that he wasn't saying? "Dragons?"

He brightened. "That's interesting! Apparently they're restless, but not going anywhere. They rise, circle, then return to their nests."

"So why is that interesting?"

"Because either something is troubling them, or the dwarf suspects something."

"He always suspects something! Such as?"

"I think," Rap said, "that some of the anthropophagi must be still at large. Zinixo's frightened to raise the dragons in case he triggers a trap or something. Or else the worms themselves sense the trap—they're not entirely mundane, remember." He ran fingers through his hair again. "All right! I'm clutching at straws. It just seems indecisive, see?"

Zinixo was notoriously indecisive, but let the man dream. And how had he learned all this if he hadn't been able to reach the archons?

"What else did the new Keeper tell you?"

Rap shot her an admiring glance. "She was here. Not twenty minutes ago. Briefly."

"How is she?"

"Can't tell with demigods."

"Did Kadie know?"

"Kadie was asleep."

Mm. "Is Thaïle going to be more cooperative than her predecessor?"

"She will be, I think. If the Covin has noticed Thume, then she has no choice."

"So what else did she say?"

"Not a great deal."

"Darling, after all these years you think I don't know when you're being evasive?"

He chuckled. He swung his feet up, stretched out beside her on the pallet, and proceeded to kiss her at length and with great attention to detail. Inos began to appreciate that the Thumian climate might have certain advantages after all. It was several more minutes before he gave her a chance to speak.

"That was wonderful," she said breathlessly. "And I shall cooperate fully at the first suitable opportunity. But we were talking business. No!" She pushed his busy hands away from her buttons. "Rap, I mean it!"

"Later!"

"Now! What were you not telling me?"

"The new Keeper has appointed a replacement archon."

Inos studied his face for a moment, as it was all she could see—he was almost on top of her already. "I thought archons were exceptionally potent sorcerers?"

"She says she wants experience and counsel."

Idiot! "You accepted?"

"You think I had any choice?"

"Yes."

"I accepted."

She could tell nothing from his smile. So he was worried sick and using sorcery not to show it.

This was Midsummer Eve. There might be no more chances.

"I've never had an archon make love to me before," she said. "Can you make sure we won't be interrupted?"

Rap said, "Yes," huskily.

Inos reached for his buttons.

4

It was Midsummer Eve, and the Imperor was hosting a garden party. Anyone who was anyone was there. No one who was anyone was not. Someone who did not wish to be there was there. That one could see everyone, and he could also see some ones he was not supposed to see, sorcerers who were not one person but two. Skulking unobtrusively in the shadows between two fuchsias near a buffet table, Lord Umpily nibbled fervently on a heap of canapés and cursed his double vision.

Orchestras droned. Crowds strolled on the lawns below swaying rows of lanterns strung on cables; couples danced on a dance floor laid out in the Rose Garden. Bonfires hurled fountains of sparks into the summer night. There would be fireworks later. It was all very convivial.

Caviar, stuffed olives, peeled grapes, lark tongues on ginger crackers ... Umpily ate convulsively. He knew he should go more slowly, to make the spread last. At this rate he would soon empty the plate and have to go back for more, but somehow his fingers insisted on staying busy. His teeth could barely keep up with them.

A globular moon was rising behind the willows. The lanterns strung over the lawn burned brighter now, reflecting the jewels and finery of the multitude strolling below them.

He returned a nod and a smile as the Countess of Somewhere wandered by his place of concealment. He stepped back a pace.

One partridge wing, two frogs' legs, three turtle eyes ... he really ought to slow down!

He really ought to parade around and let himself be seen. Once he had done that, he could safely depart, and if anyone inquired he could claim to have been present.

For three weeks he had skittered amid the shadows of the court like an overweight cockroach. Somehow he had managed to avoid the fake imperor and impress, but it was impossible to stay away from sorcerers. The Opal Palace was stiff with sorcerers, as if the Almighty had moved the entire Covin in with him. To mundane eyes they were always unexceptional—footmen, female domestics, miscellaneous flunkies—but to Umpily's occult double vision their true selves showed, weedy youths or ancient crones or anything in between. Almost every race was represented: imps, elves, fauns ... and dwarves. Possibly one of the many dwarves he had seen had been Zinixo himself, but not likely so, for none had resembled last year's vision in the preflecting pool.

Lobster, smoked oysters, blue cheese, pistachio and curry—he continued to cram the succulent morsels into his mouth, chewing and swallowing convulsively, hardly aware of the flavors. When he had emptied the plate, he promised himself, he would saunter off across the lawn and mingle with a few hundred guests, greet a few dozen by name. And then scarper.

Oh, no!

Oh, *yes*! The imperor and impress! The royal party had just emerged from the throng, heading in his direction—Shandie and Eshiala, escorted by a fawning mob of senior courtiers.

The impress was recounting some witty tale and the sycophants were hanging breathless on her words. At her side,
Shandie was listening with a tolerant smile, nodding graciously to the bowing, curtseying onlookers as he strolled by.
She wore a stunning white crinoline, glittering with pearls,
and a diamond tiara that could almost rank as a crown. He
was in uniform, bronze flashing under the lanterns. They were
a fairy-tale couple.

They were total illusion. Prince Emthoro and Duchess
Ashia stepped in their footsteps and occupied their same
space. He looked drunk, eyes blurred and rolling, unshav-
en, bedraggled. She was a frump, her hair tangled and unkempt. She seemed to be laughing hysterically, but making no
sound.

And behind them?

Who or what was that vague misty darkness at their heels?

Umpily could guess. His enchantment was not powerful
enough to penetrate the Almighty's invisibility but was seemingly catching hints of it. The Almighty would certainly detect his awareness, his terror. In moments he would be
unmasked as the spy he was! *Terror!*

Still clutching his plate of canapés, Lord Umpily spun
around and crashed away through the shrubbery.

He did not run very far before a biting pain in his chest
brought him to a halt. He thought he was having a heart attack.
It was either that or severe heartburn, and he had always had
an excellent digestion. Just an attack of nerves, hopefully. He
sat down on an ornamental urn at the side of the road and
drooped in misery, waiting to see if he would die.

In the distance, the orchestras played on. Faint echoes of jollity drifted through the summer night. The moon crept up the
sky and the air cooled.

He could not stand any more of this cat-and-mouse existence! To have evaded the Covin's notice for three whole
weeks was a miracle; he could not expect the Gods to favor
him that way forever. He must flee to some safe refuge as soon
as possible. Trouble was, he had been trying to think of such
a sanctuary for three weeks and so far he had come up with an
utter blank.

Eventually the urn's unsuitability as a seat impressed itself
upon his awareness. He realized, too, that he was for some reason racked by a terrible thirst. Also there were people wander-

ing around in his vicinity. Lovers, perhaps. Inquisitive visitors. Guards, maybe. Possibly even sorcerers, although the Covin would not need to send out scouts in the flesh if it wanted to know what was going on. That was an unnerving thought in itself. By sitting here alone, he was behaving suspiciously.

With a private moan, he heaved himself to his feet, discarded the empty plate he had been clutching all this time, and began to walk. A sedate, purposeful stroll would attract no especial attention. He was a bona fide resident of the palace; he could walk where he wished. A gentleman could always claim to be going to the gentlemen's room.

He brooded as he wandered, not noticing where he was headed. Some considerable time later, he realized that his feet ached and he had arrived at Emine's Rotunda, its great dome gleaming in the moonlight. He had never quenched that thirst, which now thrust itself back into his attention. His throat was a fiery desert.

He glanced around dubiously. There were few buildings close to the Rotunda, and most of those were unfamiliar to him. They were all dark, too. But the door of the Rotunda itself was open, and a faint glow showed through it. Most probably there were workmen toiling there, installing the new seating for the coronation, or something. He knew the building well, including its many cloakrooms and antechambers.

He plodded up the steps and went in. The light came from a discarded lantern just inside the door, standing on a stack of timber beside some sacks of what seemed to be plaster. He could hear no sawing or hammering anywhere. The workmen had most likely slipped away to steal a look at the imperor's garden party. Taking the lantern, Umpily went in search of water. He found some in the first room he tried and enjoyed a long, refreshing drink.

Then, moved by a vague curiosity to see how the alterations were progressing, he wandered farther into the great warren. Craftsmen's supplies were piled everywhere: stone slabs, rolls of fabric, lumber, ladders, mysterious barrels. When he reached an entrance to the main auditorium, the Rotunda itself, he was much annoyed to discover it locked against him. He backtracked, detoured along more cluttered corridors until he had reached the next quadrant, and there he tried again. This time the great door swung open at his touch. His lamp flickered twice and died.

He cursed under his breath. Finding his way out again in the dark would be hazardous. The Rotunda itself was bright enough, with moonlight pouring down through the panes of the great dome, and since he was here he might as well look—he advanced along the canyon between the banks of seats. He squinted uncertainly. He seemed to be seeing the Opal Throne on its dais in the center, straight ahead. He should not be able to. The four warden thrones that had once stood at the end of the entrance passages had all been destroyed the night the usurper came, but the Covin had replaced them, hadn't it? Yes, of course it had! He had seen the replacements at the fake Shandie's spurious enthronement ceremony, for there had been thrones for the imposter wardens to occupy. They had been there when he watched the imposter address the Senate, too. Or at least Umpily could not recall them being absent, nor anyone commenting that they had been missing. They must have been there! They might have been taken away to make more space for the coronation.

He emerged from the canyon where the seating reached floor level. The great amphitheater was awash with silver light and quiet as a tomb, banked seating soaring up from the arena's perimeter to the base of the dome. The Opal Throne smoldered in uncertain greens and blues in the exact center. From its dais, the four points of the mosaic star ran out to the lower platforms where the thrones of Four had stood for three thousand years: red, white, gold, blue.

They were there now, and they weren't there.

Ah! It was that Evilish enchantment of Olybino's again. The replacement thrones were sorcerous, apparently, and Umpily could simultaneously see them and not see them. That was all! He felt oddly relieved to have solved the mystery. Mysteries upset him. He poked a finger gingerly at East's throne. He felt the clammy touch of gold. He stroked it. Yes, only his eyes could detect the illusion; his other senses were deceived. That was why he had not been able to hear Ashia's hysterics.

The new seating for the spectators was coming along very well. Both eastern quadrants were complete, resplendent in the new green. Northwest was still in its shabby old purple plumage, while southwest was a confused mess, halfway between caterpillar and butterfly perhaps.

He stared thoughtfully across at the Opal Throne. It was facing east now—someone gave it a quarter turn each day, but he had no idea who. Probably there was some hereditary office involved. Just for a moment he was tempted to go and sit on it. Just for a moment. See what it felt like to be imperor.

He didn't. It would seem like sacrilege.

A year ago he had been granted a vision of Zinixo sitting there, in the center of the world, but that prophecy had never been fulfilled. It had been a warning only, not intended to be taken literally.

Oh, how he wished he had taken it a great deal more seriously at the time! They had all been at fault there. Acopulo had been advised to seek out Doctor Sagorn and had done nothing much about it. Of course Ylo had claimed to have found the woman he had been shown—lusty young Ylo was not the sort of lad to ignore a hint like that, and ten to one he had bedded her on his first attempt—but had Shandie ever located the boy of his vision? Umpily had no idea, and would likely go to his grave without ever knowing the answer. He wondered sadly how his former friends were doing now, and where they all were.

His occult view of the Opal Throne had not been from this level. Around to the right a little, and six or seven rows up . . . Moved by sheer whimsy, Umpily turned to the nearest stairs and climbed. Yes, about this height—along about here, maybe?

He sat down and studied the angle. Close enough. He yawned. One empty throne, no dwarf. And that was just as well! Zinixo was occupied elsewhere, playing puppeteer at the garden party, so here was as safe as anywhere, for the moment. These new seats were a big improvement. Gods, he was tired! His eyelids drooped.

5

Shivering and covered with goosebumps, Gath strode over the coarse grass of Nintor, all alone. Behind him trailed his shadow, stretched and gaunt, as if reluctant to follow him into danger. He was barefoot, clad only in leather breeches too large for him, bunched at his waist by a thong. The cold wind ruffled his hair. If Mom saw that hair now she would tell him to get it cut—it was a terrible bush, and yet it was short compared to any other man's on the island. Real jotunn hair didn't stand on end like his. She would scold him for his dirty feet, too, and for not dressing more warmly. He decided he wouldn't mind a bit of mothering at the moment. That was a very unmanly thought, but his was the only chin on Nintor without whiskers and Nintor was a long, long way from home.

The sky was a sickly blue, and cloudless. Straight ahead stood the peaks of Hvark, with Frayealk the most conspicuous. Frayealk lay due north of Nintor, Twist had told him, and the sun cleared the summit one day in the year. It was very close now, moving eastward of course. When it stood directly over the mountain, that would mark midnight and the start of Longday.

The jotnar were already gathered at the Moot Stow—thanes down on the floor of the hollow, their followers assembled on the slopes, all unarmed. They had been singing ancient hymns, waiting on the sun. One by one the sorcerers had slunk away unnoticed. Gath could see a few of them ahead of him still, pale figures moving north over the tundra. Thewsome had told him to follow when the sun was one handsbreadth from the peak.

He had an astonishing faith in Gath's courage.

Those last few sorcerers were still in sight ahead, all walking alone, heading for the Commonplace, whatever that was. They all seemed to be able-bodied young men, just a random selection from the thousands of jotunn raiders now infesting the island. Doubtless many were not what they seemed. Some would be women, Twist had said.

Which were the wolves and which the sheep?

The sun was almost over Frayealk.

The effort of not using prescience was starting to give Gath a headache.

The standing stones of the Place of Ravens were just off to his right. If somehow the Gods ever did take him back to Krasnegar, then he would be able to brag to his jotunn friends about seeing the holy of holies. They would want all the details, though. How could he ever admit that he had been so close and not seen it properly? It would not take him far off his path. He risked a peek at the next few minutes and knew that there was nobody up there. The sorcerer stragglers were still in plain view. He changed direction slightly.

A few minutes later he stepped between two of the towering monoliths. There was nothing to see, only a circle of weathered boulders, larger than he had expected, maybe. And grass. Any cemetery was as exciting. There were no ravens in sight, just a few seagulls sitting on the stones at the far side, preening themselves. Was the grass a little greener within the circle, perhaps—fertilized by the blood of thanes? No, that was just the long shadows of the rocks.

He shrugged, shivering in the wind. Midnight sun. Should he cut across the edge of the circle? Peek . . .

No!

He would cut his feet if he tried that. The long grass was full of bones, old and brittle, weathered white. He saw a skull and then two more. There was a hazard he had never thought of! The combatants fought naked, or almost naked, and certainly barefoot. How many fatal duels had been decided by a careless misstep—tripping over a pelvis or planting a foot on a sharp vertebra? The skalds' sagas would never stoop to mentioning that hero so-and-so had lost his head because he had stubbed a toe.

Cutting across the Place of Ravens would be unwise, perhaps even sacrilege. Gath went back out the way he had come in, and hurried around the outside.

Frayealk came in sight again. The sun was over the mountain. It was almost past the mountain. Longday had begun.

The wind faltered for a moment and he thought he heard a distant roar. Then it had gone. Had that been the sound of surf, or was the moot in open bedlam already? The vote for war would take no time at all, Thewsome had predicted. Choosing a leader would be another matter.

In sudden alarm, Gath quickened his pace, eyes scanning the green slopes ahead, squinting against the low sun. Where were his guides? He had no idea what the Commonplace looked like—Thewsome had just said he couldn't miss it. If he did miss it, he was going to seem like a complete idiot. Worse! He would look like a coward! There was nobody else in sight. He was completely alone.

He began to run.

Then he forced himself to drop back to a fast walk again. Panic would not help, and he certainly did not want to arrive panting and sweating. Peek again—Yes! He was going to find it!

And there it was. Couldn't have missed it, even without prescience. He'd mistaken it for a hillock, but it was too regular to be natural, a flattish dome with grass growing over it. In a few minutes he was going to notice that the turf had been trampled by many feet, converging into a path. Recently, too. The entrance was a low cave mouth in the south side. The

Commonplace looked very much like some ancient, forgotten tomb.

The future inside it was a blank, meaning it was shielded, so there was no mistake, this must be the Commonplace. The first danger, Twist-Thewsome had said, was that he might not be allowed in, for he was not a sorcerer.

Horribly conscious of his pounding heart, Gath raised his chin and strode toward the doorway. Dad would approve, wouldn't he? He could hear nothing except the wind in the grass. He could see nothing within except darkness.

He stumbled down a gritty slope and stopped when the passage widened into a chamber. Not even a sound of breathing broke the age-old silence. A quick peek of prescience told him there were people there, though. They were probably all looking at him. He was against the light of the door, and sorcerers could see in the dark anyway. He could see nothing of them. He waited. The air was icy cold and earthy-smelling, the ceiling oppressively low.

Dazzled from staring into the sun, his eyes took a moment to adapt. Then he began to make out a spectral shape glimmering before him, a glowing outline of a head ... *Argh!*

Sorcery? No, trickery! It was only a man, lit from behind by a single beam of sunlight. His hair and beard and bare shoulders burned with golden fire and the rest was darkness. He must be even bigger than Thewsome.

"Who comes?" he demanded.

Gath jumped and clenched his fists. There was no echo. Why not even the sound of breathing from the onlookers?

"Who comes?" demanded that voice again, louder, more threatening. It was a deep, very male voice.

Never in his life, Gath thought, had he ever been really scared before. Not like this.

"Gath." Twist must have told them he was coming.

"Who?"

God of Courage! Why had Twist not given him more instructions? Gath took a deep breath. Might as well be hung for a horse as a pony, Dad always said.

"I am Atheling Gathmor of Krasnegar, son of Thane ... son of *Rap Thaneslayer*." Was that stupid or smart? He swallowed with difficulty and added, "I come in peace."

"You'd surely scare the piss out of me if you didn't!"

Sniggers ran off into the darkness.

That had been another voice, a youth's voice, or a woman's.

Gath's eyes were adjusting to the gloom. The circular chamber was about ten paces across. He could see the shapes of people—vaguely, just indications of pale jotunn chests, silver hair. They were sitting all around the walls, on a bench, perhaps, tightly packed together. Some were smaller and darker than others, more covered—women?

"Gods' bullocks!" roared the very large man—a very angry one, too—standing in the center. "Stripling, you blunder in where you are not invited. State your business or pay the penalty!"

Where in the Name of the Good was Twist? He had not warned Gath of any of this. Perhaps he had not known what to expect, because of the shielding. He had certainly not suggested having a speech ready.

Wiser not to. Would have scared him away completely.

The sheep and the wolves. The herd and the pack. The pack was united, loyal to Zinixo and the Covin. The free sorcerers had no leader, Twist had said. Being jotnar, they would take hours to choose one, if they could ever agree, and by then it might be too late.

That was why Gath was here. He was to be a rallying point, a symbol. Bait.

Faces were becoming visible—unfriendly faces. Yes, some women. Some very old men. One or two hale warriors. Several cripples, but still Gath's frantic searching had not located Twist. Not a smile in the place.

"Come here!" demanded the man in the middle of the chamber. He was standing on a low slab, of course. Even without that, he was big, his flaxen head almost touching the stones of the ceiling. His glare was visible now. Gath had often seen its like in Krasnegar, and blood had always flowed right after.

A few firm strides put him directly in front of the speaker, and his eyes were lower than the giant's furry chest. The sunlight was shining in through a shaft in the roof, and now it stabbed over the man's shoulders into Gath's eyes.

"Say what you expect of me, son of Rap Thaneslayer!"

Gath breathed a silent prayer. This was going to be suicide! He looked up defiantly. "I want you to do homage."

"To you?" roared the jotunn.

"To my da— I will accept your homage to, er, for my father, who is leader of the battle against the Alm . . . the dwarf . . ." Gath swallowed again and wiped sweat out of his eyes. Why was he so wet outside and dry inside? He desperately wanted to peek at the future, but his prescience would be detected and might seem like cowardice.

The jotunn raised a fist the size of a small anvil, right in front of Gath's nose. "Tell me why I should kneel to you, boy!"

Speech!

Gath put his hands on his hips and shouted up at him. "Would you sooner kneel to a dwarf? You know the war that hangs over us! Some of you here are votaries of the usurper and are planning to enslave all the rest of you. Your only hope of remaining free people is to join the army my dad leads. Him and the imperor and the wardens against the dwarf." Gods, this was coming out all muddled! He should never have mentioned the imperor! "The Protocol doesn't protect the jotn . . . us . . . anymore. If the thanes go to war this time, they'll be fighting against sorcery. My dad has promised a new protocol, which will stop votarism. You can trust him. I want you to help. He's fighting for freedom. Your freedom, too."

Gods, that had sounded really awful! He'd fouled it all up! Why hadn't Twist warned him he would have to make a speech?

"That's it?" the big man snarled, his breath reeking of fish and sour beer.

"That's it!" Gath said, and braced himself to be knocked senseless.

"Sounds like a smart move." The big man stepped back, off the plinth. "Get up there."

Bewildered, fighting not to use his prescience, Gath stepped up on the flat rock. The sunbeam dazzled him. He felt shamefully shaky and his eyes were still not level with the sorcerer's, but then the big man dropped to his knees and raised his great hands, palms together as if in prayer.

"I am Drugfarg son of Karjiarg and I am your father's man," he said loudly.

For a heart-stopping moment Gath stared down at those huge hands, while his mind whirled in search of the correct response. He found it in a faint memory of one of the fairy-tale plays that Kadie wrote and made all her friends perform at Winterfest. The words he would have to invent, but he recalled the gesture. Kadie knew all that sort of stuff.

He clasped Drugfarg's hands between his own. His were colder.

"In the name of my father, Rap Thaneslayer, I accept your homage, Drugfarg son of Karjiarg."

The giant waited.

There was more? Oh, yes. Gath bent to grip the sorcerer's meaty elbow and raise him. Of course he could no more have truly lifted Drugfarg than he could have drunk the Winter Ocean, but that was the correct gesture. Drugfarg rose smoothly to his feet and stepped back without a smile or a word. He turned his back and walked away. Another man rose and came forward to take his place. Older and smaller, he also knelt before Gath and raised his hands.

"I am Gustiag son of Prakran and I am your father's man."

Gath bent to clasp the hands. His mind turned cartwheels. He was accepting the homage of sorcerers! There must be sixty or seventy of them in this chamber.

"In the name of my father . . ."

Sixty or seventy sorcerers! Not all of them would be willing to do homage to him, of course. Members of the Covin would not. They *could* not, for they were already bound to Zinixo—and they could not just pretend, Twist said, because in something like that they could not deceive the others. So when the sheep had all lined up behind Rap's deputy, leaving the wolves . . .

Gath stole a peek at the future and saw—

He was about to die!

The world exploded, in pain and fire and thunder.

6

It was laughter that wakened Lord Umpily. For a moment he was bewildered, not understanding where he was or what he was doing—low moonlight shining straight in his eyes, coldness, cramp from sleeping in a chair, and what chair anyway? Rows of seating? He must have dozed off in the middle of some theatrical . . .

Reality struck him like a brick. He flashed straight from confusion to gibbering paralysis.

The Rotunda was filling up. People were climbing the aisles, filing along the rows, taking seats. In the ghostly blue light he could make out imps, dwarves, fauns, elves, trolls . . . Even as he was drawing breath to scream, more arrivals flowed in along the entrance canyons. Others flickered into existence on the floor below him and then headed for the stairs. He did not need occult vision to know that these were sorcerers, and in fact none of them was wearing any sort of glamour. They needed no disguise at a gathering of the Covin itself.

God of Terror!

He choked back the scream and looked wildly around for some means of escape. To his left, the way he had come in was already blocked by a trio of female dwarves settling into position, elderly, squat, and ugly. Fortunately they were all deep in conversation, mumbling in guttural whispers. He turned to look the other way just as a youngish faun entered the far end of the row and headed toward him. Two imps and an elf followed.

Blocked!

The intruder cowered down in his seat. The Covin was assembling. There must be several hundreds present already, and more arriving all the time. Pouring in now. He heard the hum of innumerable conversations, heard undertones of excitement, as if something major was about to happen.

What about an execution to start the proceedings? How could he possibly hope to remain undetected amid so many sorcerers? Any second now someone would notice the solitary mundane spy and raise the alarm.

Raise the alarm? No, they would just swat him where he sat.

The juvenile faun sat down a couple of places away. From the smell of him, he had just come from the stables. Ignoring the fat old imp, the boy turned at once to study the crowd.

So did Umpily. Everyone else was, so he would. Trolls? One or two of the giants seemed to be completely unclothed. The dark savages must be anthropophagi. Innumerable imps. Could those two pale ones be mermen? Not a jotunn in sight, though. Odd. Nor a gnome, either, although gnomes were never conspicuous. Mostly imps.

Wiping his streaming forehead with a very shaky hand, Umpily tried to estimate numbers and got nowhere. Certainly many hundreds. He could not remember the capacity of the Rotunda, and most of one quadrant was out of commission, still in the process of renovation. He had never guessed there could be so many sorcerers in the world.

Then he saw a woman he recognized, an enormous, silver-haired troll. She marched in from the south corridor with two or three other trolls at her back, beef on the hoof. He had seen her once before, at the real Shandie's enthronement—*Witch Grunth!* She had not been a Zinixo supporter then, but she must be one now. Hastily his eyes raked the hall, searching for signs of Raspnex or Lith'rian.

The assembly was apparently complete. A few latecomers came running in and teleported themselves up to seats to avoid the lines on the stairs. But the stairs cleared quickly. Movement along the rows died away as the last arrivals found places. The entire company was seated then, falling silent in a hush of eager expectation. Waiting for . . .

Oh, Gods!

The throne! Umpily's terror-filled gaze turned to the center and the glowing, somber mass of the Opal Throne. The *prophecy*! The true horror of his situation dawned. The preflecting pool had warned him of his greatest danger, that which he must most seek to avoid. The forgotten scream bubbled up again and was suppressed again. He had walked right into that very peril!

Even as he watched, the prophecy was fulfilled. A dwarf materialized on the Opal Throne.

Cheers! The congregation leaped to its feet with a roar to acclaim its leader. Applause thundered. Six or seven rows back from the front, Lord Umpily rose to clap and cheer with the best of them. To do anything else was unthinkable and would give him away instantly. *Harder! More enthusiasm!*

The tiny figure of the Almighty sat motionless on the great throne of Pandemia, a nondescript dwarf whose boots dangled above the floor. *Louder!* No expression showed through the metal-gray beard as he accepted this standing ovation from his massed followers. The Covin cheered and clapped, clapped and cheered. *Jubilation!* And so did Lord Umpily. Waves of adulation echoed through the vast Rotunda. Zinixo just sat, stony gaze sliding suspiciously over the multitude.

Soon Umpily's hands were raw, his arms aching, his throat sore. Still he clapped, still he cheered. *More! More!* Still the ovation continued. Who would dare be the first to stop? And who, in this congregation of devoted vassals, would want to?

7

"You're all right, Atheling! You're all right!"

There were many faces looking down, but that had been Twist's familiar voice. Gath lay on the cold dirt, surrounded by people kneeling and more standing behind them. The chamber was still dark and cold. He felt very peculiar.

"What happened?" he mumbled. Something important . . .

"There was being a bit of a fight, but we won. You died."

"I *what*?"

"Here—up with you."

Many hands lifted Gath to his feet, and the other people all stood up around him. Smiling? Why smiling? There was a strange smell of burned meat in the air.

"I killed you," said a new voice. "I am truly sorry."

Gath spun around, staggered, and was steadied.

The speaker was a young jotunn little older or taller than himself. He had a scant reddish beard and a fuzz of red hair in the middle of his chest. From the look of his shoulders, he did not row longships for a living, and he bore no tattoos. The most notable thing about him, though, was that his eyes were closed, as if he were blind. Yet his mouth smiled right at Gath.

"I am Jaurg. I killed you. Will you accept my apology?" People laughed. Jaurg thrust out a hand.

Gath took it. "I don't feel dead."

Jaurg's palm was horny, but not as horny as a sailor's. He played fair, too, not trying to crush.

"You are all right now," Jaurg said. "I am glad."

"Don't do it again, though!" Gath said, and was rewarded with chuckles. He glanced around and recognized misshapen little Twist leaning on a crutch at his side and the enormous Drugfarg beyond. The other faces were unfamiliar. Most of them seemed to be smiling.

What was going on here? He ran fingers through his hair, and it had a curious sticky feeling. Burned hair? What was that smell? Everyone in the chamber was gathered around him, and he found the attention unpleasant.

"Your plan worked, Atheling," Twist said. "The traitors—I mean votaries—saw the trap and were reacting with violence. Luckily there were few casualties." He grinned his distorted teeth.

My plan? Gath thought. *Your plan, you mean!* "Except me?"

"You were being one of them, yes."

"I didn't know sorcerers could bring the dead back to life."

"Normally we cannot, but your heart stopped for only a few seconds. There was much power available. You are a fortunate person, I am thinking."

"It's my friends!" Gath muttered, but his head had stopped spinning now, and he could work out the details—Twist's strategy succeeding, the Covin spies seeing how they were going to be isolated, attempting a preemptive attack, being overpowered and released from their votary spells. All good guys now.

"I was a votary of the Covin's," the blind Jaurg said. "Now I am not. I will gladly do homage to you, Atheling Gathmor, if you will accept me as your man."

"That isn't necessary now, is it?" Gath was seized by a frantic desire to leave this underground pit of horrors, this close press of sorcerers around him. He wanted sunshine and fresh air, not dark mystery and a stink of overdone steak.

"I think it is! And if I may, I will do it to you, not to your father. I owe you this."

"It doesn't matter—"

"Up on the Speaker Stone, Atheling!" Twist said brusquely.

Apparently it did matter, then. The crowd parted. Gath stepped forward to mount the center slab again and the blind Jaurg knelt before him to do homage. The others backed away and resumed their places on the bench around the walls.

Of course it mattered—there might still be Covin votaries present who had not revealed themselves. Every man must prove his innocence by paying homage to King Rap's deputy, and every woman, also.

"I am Jaurg the bastard and I am your man."

Two cindery heaps lay by the doorway. That was where the smell was coming from.

"In the name of my father, Rap Thanesl—"

"*Your* man, I said, Atheling Gath!"

It couldn't matter, but it felt good, a sort of Kadie make-believe. "Then I accept your homage, Jaurg the bastard."

I died today! Gath thought, as he raised his new vassal, the man who had confessed to killing him. His heart had stopped. Had he also been charred to a crisp like those two at the door? Was that why his hair felt funny? His breeches seemed like a better fit than before, so perhaps they were not the same breeches. Roast Gath—his gut turned a somersault.

One by one, the sorcerers were coming forward to kneel to him. Most took their cue from Jaurg and did homage to Gath himself. They didn't mean that, surely—it was all just a formality anyway, wasn't it, just make-believe? He accepted in his own name or Dad's, as they wanted.

Eventually the procession ended. He stood alone on the slab in the center and everyone else was sitting on the shelf around the walls. They had all passed the test. Now what? He could guess now what, but again it was something from one of Kadie's stories that told him what to say. He glanced around. Which?

"I yield to Drugfarg son of Karjiarg," he said. Since Drugfarg had held the floor when he intruded, that was fair.

He quit the Speaker Stone and the audience broke into applause, some even cheering. Unable to believe this was all happening, Gath hurried over to Twist, who grinned triumphantly at him and made a space on the shelf. Gath squeezed in between him and Jaurg. The huge Drugfarg rose and came forward to resume his place in the center.

"In respect to our liege lord," Drugfarg boomed, "I move that this debate shall continue in words."

A chorus of groans returned from the outskirts, but no one argued.

"Brothers and sisters," Drugfarg proclaimed, "we have now all established our loyalty . . ."

He was winding up for a speech. Gath glanced at Twist and whispered, "How many were there?"

"At least a dozen."

"There were fifteen of us," Jaurg said softly, not looking around. "You have made thirteen lifelong friends today, Atheling."

Gath stole a squeamish glance at the two odious corpses.

"They took their own lives," Jaurg murmured.

Twist said, "Sh!"

The jotnar Gath knew preferred actions to words, but Drugfarg evidently fancied himself as an orator. He was in full torrent already, denouncing the Almighty and demanding that the sorcerers of Nordland, here assembled, now prove their valor, be true to their pledges of allegiance, and rally to the banner of Rap Thaneslayer.

Fine! Gath thought. *Where to find that banner, though?*

It would be a historical battle, the sorcerer proclaimed. Skalds would sing of it for centuries.

Not if Zinixo wins, they won't.

The audience sat in stony silence around the cold, dim crypt.

Easy for them! They can magic themselves warm.

Et cetera, et cetera . . . At long last the big man reached his inspiring peroration. "I have spoken!" he concluded unnecessarily, and stepped down from the Speaker Stone. A few of the listeners clapped politely. Half a dozen of them rose to their feet.

Drugfarg looked them over and pointed. "I yield to Osgain,

daughter of Gwartusk." One of the women hobbled to the center to take the podium. She was very old and bent.

She was also very long-winded. Certainly the jotnar must support Thane Rap, she agreed, for he was of jotunn blood himself and his cause was the more just of the two. Nevertheless, as she understood the issues, the revolutionaries were not proposing to restore the Protocol of Emine, which had for three thousand years protected Nordland from the abuses of sorcery . . .

A protection that the thanes had shamefully abused, in Gath's opinion, although he could not imagine himself saying so in this company. The stone bench was cold and most horribly uncomfortable. This moot was going to go on all day, and the Gods alone knew what might be happening outside.

How long? He opened the spigot on his prescience. Ten minutes, twenty . . .

Twist rammed an elbow in his ribs. Oops! To use foresight when people were making speeches would be bad manners, like glancing at a clock.

At long last Osgain announced that she had spoken. The next speaker observed briefly that the Covin was certainly waiting for the company to emerge from the Commonplace, and the danger was extreme. They were trapped! Should not the meeting be considering means rather than ends?

That seemed like good sense to Gath.

But the speaker after that went back to discussing principles. He started to hint that a scout should be dispatched to open negotiations with the Covin. A few angry murmurs broke the silence. Suddenly men began jumping to their feet. They said nothing, but apparently the move implied dissent. When about a dozen had risen, the speaker took the hint and yielded the floor to another.

And he, in turn, to another.

An hour or more crept by like a dying snail.

Perhaps, suggested one oldster, the jotnar should offer to remain neutral. More angry growls . . .

This was becoming ridiculous! They had all sworn allegiance to Dad or to Gath himself, and now they were threatening to renege. What sort of jotnar were they?

Sensible, probably. They seemed to have very little grasp of correct debating procedure, for they wandered from topic to topic, but perhaps as sorcerers they knew a hopeless cause when they saw one. How *were* they going to escape from this cellar under the eyes of the Almighty?

How would they ever find Dad, who might be anywhere at all? What was happening outside, in the real world? What was going on at the Moot Stow?

8

Rap gazed up drowsily at the rafters, working out what had wakened him. Shafts of moonlight angled down from window to bed, reflecting enough light to show the ceiling. It was around midnight, the start of Longday.

Nothing stirred in the mundane world. In the other room, Kadie fretted through a nightmare on her cot. Inos slept deeply at his side, one arm across his chest. He summoned memories of their lovemaking and cherished them—first outdoors, then again in bed. Not since the first nights of their marriage had they so utterly abandoned themselves to raw passion, like wild, crazy youngsters. A sense of impending doom had contributed to that, but of course a little sorcery did help compensate for advancing years . . .

He had been summoned.

Keeping Inos asleep, he slid magically from her embrace and from the bed. When he released the spell, she stirred and rolled over on her back. The moon cast silver light over her face, her breasts, the tracery of her hair on the pillow. He stared in rapture for a moment. Then with a sigh he turned to his duty.

He clad himself, making the sort of sensible artisan work clothes he wore at home in Krasnegar. He could change them for cooler pixie garb when the day grew hot. He added a cowled cloak of dark flimsy cotton, archon uniform. He said, *"Ready!"* and was snatched away.

The Chapel was huge and dark, but not silent, susurrous with the beat of rain on the jungle outside. The archons were assembled, kneeling around Keef's grave. He saw them by farsight—three women, four men. In the ambience they reacted with consternation; obviously they had not been informed that Thaïle had chosen a demon as her replacement.

To hurry in such sanctity was unthinkable. He walked forward slowly, boots tapping on the ancient stone. He was disinclined to kneel to Keef, but even less inclined to antagonize his new associates. He knelt, completing the circle.

Young Raim shot him a smile of welcome in the ambience. Several of the others radiated strong disapproval.

The Keeper materialized outside the group and the archons bowed their heads. Rap joined them willingly in that token of respect, paying homage to her pain, the agony he so well remembered.

She was garbed as she had been when she came to the Rap Place the previous evening, in a white robe, cowled like her predecessor's. It was impervious to farsight and he could detect no hint of her feelings or expression. She was a glimmering wraith in the darkness, barely visible.

Her voice was flat. "The djinn army is preparing to strike camp. I seek your counsel. Should I trigger the trap or let them advance into our land?"

More shock from the archons told Rap that the previous Keeper had not asked for advice like this. But then she had managed to avoid making this decision and had surely never been required to make a worse one.

"Archon Raim?"

The youngster's distress showed as a writhing glow in the ambience. After a moment he spoke aloud. "I think not, Holiness," he said hesitantly. "That would be a crime beyond remorse. We have already offended the Gods enough. To slaughter sixty thousand . . ." His voice faded off into the sound of the storm.

"Archon Quaith?" The Keeper was taking them in order of age.

Quaith wrung her hands and then whispered, "No."

"Reason?"

"It will reveal our existence to the Covin!"

But the Covin already knew, Rap thought. Or if it didn't know, it suspected, and Zinixo could never live with suspicion. As had been prophesied, a woman with child had brought evil to the Accursed Land.

Rap should probably have been next after Quaith, but Thaïle passed him over. All seven pixies spoke, and all seven said no. They mostly gave the same reasons as the first two, but Toom said that war now seemed likely and to initiate brutality on such a scale would antagonize potential allies—a logic that Rap thought showed the best sense yet. It was wrong, though.

Neem was the oldest and last. His reedy voice quavered.

"No, Holiness. Surely we can mask our land in power so that the horde passes through without conflict? This has been done before."

Not when Zinixo was running things, Rap thought.

Thaïle had given no reaction yet. And finally—

"Archon Rap?"

Rap's mouth was dry, and he felt sick. "Yes. If the duty were mine, I would spring the trap."

Eight cowled heads remained bent over the ice-coated grave. Seven shocked faces stared horror at him in the ambience.

"Reason?"

"Two reasons. First, you cannot now avoid war with the Covin. In war you must seek to win. Backed by magic, that djinn army alone will ravage your land utterly, so you must destroy it while you have the chance. Second, the Covin has won every skirmish so far—the wardens, the imperor, the goblins, the legions, dragons, Warlock Olybino . . . It has met with no resistance. Unless we can chalk up a victory soon, our cause dies stillborn. To smite the djinns will send a signal to all those we must enlist, the sorcerers still uncommitted. It will show that the Covin can be beaten."

The dread words died away into the steady beat of the rain on the forest canopy.

"Will it not cause revulsion, though?" Thaïle said. "As Raim suggested, will they not recoil from joining an ally who launches such mass slaughter?"

"The djinns are not innocent peasants," Rap said grimly. He hated his own logic, but he was sure he was right. "They are professional soldiers bent on aggression. And Zinixo began the atrocities. You saw the field of Bandor. Have you forgotten the legions?"

Thaïle sighed. "No. It shall be done."

She was gone.

One by one the archons rose to their feet until they were all standing.

"Well?" Rap said harshly. "I seem to have convinced the Keeper. Have I changed any of your minds?"

Neem vanished without a word. Then Toom.

In a moment only Raim was left.

The youngster grinned. He strode around the grave and pumped Rap's hand in a firm clasp. "You changed mine! In fact, I think I'd have voted the other way if I hadn't been first. They all sounded so, well, timorous!"

His sincerity was appealing, yet very juvenile.

"I do not feel happy with my reasoning," Rap confessed, "but the alternative would be worse."

The pixie nodded. "The others will come around. They will support the Keeper." He chuckled. "Being outvoted by a demon has upset them."

"It takes a demon to fight demons," Rap said sadly. He had given Thaïle a horrible beginning to her reign. He should be feeling soiled by his own words, yet he had a strange hunch that the advice had been irrelevant, the whole scene staged for some other purpose altogether.

"Come!" Raim said. "Let us go and watch!" He was excited.

Rap hesitated. To refuse to witness the results of his own counsel seemed the worst sort of hypocrisy, but to do so would be ghoulish. He shook his head.

Raim scowled at him and disappeared. Rap stared for a while at Keef's grave, and then turned and headed for the door.

He came back to the Rap Place in clear moonlight. Kadie still tossed in nightmares. He sent her a deeper slumber. Inos slept on in the other room just as he had left her.

He wanted to go in and join her, to lie there in her arms. He could waken her and tell her what he had done; she would hold him while he wept, and comfort him.

He could never do that to Inos. He sat down on the steps and cradled his head in his arms.

9

Who never sleeps?

In the silence of the night, Thaïle stood for a long while by the river. The site of the Leéb Place was a pond now. Nothing moved in the deep dark of the flooded crater except a silvery gleam of fish, although once in a while a breath of warm wind moved ripples of moonlight over its surface. Ugly charred tree trunks in the background marked the edge of the forest and the limits of her destruction.

Here she had loved. Here she had been happy. Here she had brought forth a child, not half a year ago. Here she had fought the Keeper.

Now she was Keeper. Now she knew, with wisdom greater than human, that her predecessor had been blameless in that iniquity. Not the Keeper but the archons had slain her child and her love.

It had been foretold that Thaïle of the Gaib Place would save the College and Thaïle of the Leéb Place would destroy it. Lain had expunged the revelations from the records, but the words were still preserved in the archons' memories, easily visible to a demigod. By their own misdeeds, the archons themselves had brought the prophecy to pass. It had been the bereaved Thaïle of the Leéb Place who had rescued the woman with child.

She had goaded them a little this night. What fools they seemed now! They were not even worthy of vengeance. Sinning out of stupidity, in folly they had unchained the hounds of fate and been driven by them to calamity. The end of that chase had seen Thaïle herself bring in the woman with child, as the auguries had warned. Her pity had been folly, also, of course—yesterday she had been as addle-witted as the rest of the archons—but had the archons left her to dwell in peace here with Leéb, then Thume might have eluded the Almighty's notice for ever.

She would weep, were the pain not so great.

How little time the Gods had granted her for happiness! Yet even less time had passed since that final morning when Leéb had departed to fetch the old woman. If They sent him back to her now, he would not know her. She was no longer a peasant child content with a peasant's love, a peasant's life. Leéb had died and the Thaïle he had loved so staunchly had died, also. She was not that same Thaïle now. She was the Keeper.

With a Keeper's responsibilities. With a Keeper's pain.

Lain had been Keeper for seven years. Many of their predecessors had endured longer, but in the end they all failed. In the end they all broke under the strain. They all died as Lain had died, consumed by unbearable power.

Thaïle had never doubted that she must spring the trap on the djinn army, so why had she summoned the archons to give her counsel she had no intention of heeding? For spite? To demonstrate how far above them she was now? Petty, Thaïle, petty! But if that had been her purpose, then why had she involved the faun?

Perhaps she had hoped for reassurance that her destruction of the djinns could be justified by necessity and was not motivated by resentment and pain. Only the faun had given her that comfort.

A good man, the faun. He would be a bastion of strength for her in the struggle to come. He was the only one she could call on for wisdom about the Outside. He knew the world as no pixie did, or ever could, not even her, and few saw reality as clearly as he did. He had said that the djinns must be destroyed although he had hated himself as he did so.

She looked for him then and found him moping on his own doorstep, grieving for the death of his foes. A dark cloud of impending loss hung over him and she turned away quickly. To pry into the future this night was to risk madness and despair—she would not, must not.

Almost a thousand years ago, Keef had foreseen this day. For almost a thousand years, Thume had waited for it. Now it had come and the cause seemed hopeless. Thaïle gazed again at the dark, still pond.

Farewell, child I never saw! Farewell, Leéb, my only love!

The moon was near to setting. Dawn stirred in the east like a wakening ogre, lightening the sky, staining the ranges with blood. Thaïle flew north and came to rest on a frosty peak above the long lake. Here she stood on the extreme limit of her realm.

In the shadowy valley downstream, the djinn army was forming up, blighted to her eyes by a shimmer of the Covin's sorcery. The order of march left no doubt that it planned to advance into Thume. As King Rap had said, this was her only chance to avert the threat. Only here, striking from behind the occult barrier, could she hope to take the Covin by surprise.

She reached out to the trigger. Centuries ago, one of her predecessors had seen the deadly potential of this gorge and made it ready. It needed so little power to start the process that she had done it almost before she realized. A mountain began to move. Slowly at first, barely perceptible, then gathering speed and force, half a landscape fell away and plunged down.

A white cloud rushed out over the still surface, impossibly fast. The lake fled from the intruding rock, rising into a dark hill of water, which swelled into the far reaches of its basin and bulged upward until it leaped over the threshold where the little stream had carved its notch. No warning tremor of sorcery alerted the army, only a great wind coming ahead of the disaster, lifting men and tents and animals like leaves. Behind it came the giant wave, white now, surging irresistibly down the canyon, bringing trees and rocks and death, rending sixty thousand souls, hurling a momentary occult agony searing across the world.

Thaïle whimpered and curled herself small upon her vantage crag, blotting out the horror. *Leéb, Leéb, what would you think of me now?*

When she looked again, there was nothing. The valley was a barren cleft in the hills, scoured to bedrock all the way to the sea. Landslides still tumbled from the walls. Waves were spreading far out on the ocean, staining it orange and masking it with spray. The caliph and his army had ceased to exist.

Far away in Hub, black flames of rage spouted up as the Covin realized how it had been outwitted. Thunder shook the ambience. Power slammed against the walls of Thume like a mighty boot, like a child's tantrum. The barrier trembled, and held.

First the woman had been snatched away from the soldiers, now this. Now there could be no doubts. The Almighty's eyes glared fury and hatred at this unexpected defiance from an unknown opponent. For a moment Thaïle braced herself to resist all-out frontal assault on Thume. Then the danger passed—for the time being. The Covin settled back to consider its enemy, as a dog might study a cat on a fencepost.

Fire in the northwest proclaimed the sun. Longday came racing across the world.

10

Tiptoeing and carrying his boots, Rap was heading back to bed at last. Dawn was brightening the sky outside the windows. He was cold and damp with dew. Too late, he realized that Kadie was awake.

"Papa?"

"Morning, beloved," he whispered. "Try to go back to sleep."

"Where have you been?"

"Sitting outside. Thinking."

"Thinking of what?" Kadie demanded crossly.

Thinking of tens of thousands of men screaming as they died.

"About the war. I think it's going to start today."

"Have you talked with Thaïle?"

Rap sighed and went to perch on a chair alongside her cot.

Kadie pulled the sheet up under her chin and stared distrustfully at him.

"Yes, I was with the Keeper for a little while."

"Is she all right?"

"She's fine. Just very busy."

"But she hurts? The words hurt her?"

He sighed. "Kadie, Kadie! Thaïle has an enormous ability to
control sorcery! An incredible, historic ability. That's what
matters. She can live with five words when other sorcerers
would be destroyed by them. Some Keepers have survived to
be very old, so Archon Toom told me. Don't worry about
Thaïle. She'll outlive all of us, I promise you."

"I want to see her!"

Rap stood up. "I told you, she's very busy. She's queen of
Thume, remember, and she has many things to worry about. I
expect she'll send for you when she has time. Now you try
to—"

"Rap!" the Keeper said, her image flickering into view in
the ambience. *"The dragons are rising! Come, please!"*

Seeing him start to fade, Kadie opened her mouth, but he
was gone.

He staggered and dropped his boots. To his astonishment, he
was standing in one of the little cabanas of the Meeting Place.
There was no sign of the Keeper, or anyone else, either. Why
had she brought him here?

The glade was heavy with shadow under a pale-blue sky, the
grass dewy. Even the flowers seemed still asleep, but birds
were waking in the forest. He sat down on a bench and
reached for a boot.

Then he was whirled into the ambience beside Thaïle. All of
Pandemia opened before him. He saw the northern lands glowing under their unending daylight, Zark already baking in
morning heat, the steaming jungles of Guwush. The towering
sky trees of Ilrane were catching the first rays of the dawn. Beyond them darkness . . . and power, the alien taint of dragon.

He was overwhelmed. Suddenly he was a demigod again, as
he had been in his youth, but he had never been this great.
How could mortal mind stand so much? Thaïle was sharing
her omniscience with him, and he even thought he could feel
hints of her torment, the torturing burn of too much power.
Krasnegar—the town was still there! And Hub, roiling under
the evil anger of the Covin. Azak . . . gone!

And Dragon Reach—power flaming. Conflict!

"What's happening?" he demanded.

"I hoped you could tell me." She was projecting fear and indecision, no longer hiding behind her impenetrable Keeper persona. Despite her might, she was still only a girl, little older than Kadie. *"I have not seen its like before."*

"Nor I!" Rap thought. *"Try this."* He conjured a vision of Tik Tok—tattoos and sharpened teeth and a bone in his nose.

Thaïle registered shock and then unexpectedly sniggered. She reached out to that confusion of forces. *"Ah! Yes. I see traces of him."*

Before Rap could tell her that was a good sign, all of Dragon Reach erupted with destruction. Waves of power rolled outward across Pandemia, lighting a myriad of momentary sparks like stars as individual sorcerers reacted to the shock. Hub blazed in black flame.

"The dragons!" Thaïle cried. *"The dragons are gone!"*

And so they were. Utterly.

Rap crowed in triumph. *"It worked! Tik Tok and Thrugg! And the others! They did it! They must have set a trap . . ."*

Wonderful! Marvelous! First the djinn army and now the dragons! The Covin had taken two staggering blows. He yelled out his excitement like a boy, and the Keeper smiled.

Zinixo screamed in fury and hurled devastation upon Dragon Reach. Mountains reeled. Power flashed and roared. The world shuddered.

"Save them, Keeper!" Rap cried. *"We need them!"*

"You call them!" She thrust strength into him like coursing fire in his veins. *"Bring them!"*

Rap called.

"Thrugg! Tik Tok! Sin Sin! Murg!" One by one he declaimed the names of the band who had been his companions on *Dreadnought*. He knew that some had fallen to the Covin—Grunth in particular—but many must have survived to organize that incredible annihilation of the dragons.

"Rap?" A faint image of Tik Tok's nightmare shape flickered into view. He was distant and clearly in distress. *"You are indeed a site for psoriasis!"*

"Come, friend! All of you! Come now!" Rap reached out in the metaphor plane of the ambience, feeling his hands grasped by many hands. He heaved; power surged across the world and a horde of sorcerers exploded into the cabana. Its flimsy wicker walls bulged and burst, spilling trolls and anthropoph-

agi out into shrubbery. Roars of sorcery filled the glade. Water birds exploded off the lake in terror. Thaïle gasped at the sight of these savage figures.

"Twenty-four?" Rap yelled. "No, twenty-six! Welcome to Thume! Well done, all of you!" He saw burns and wounds vanishing as the sorcerers healed themselves. Giant trolls lurched to their feet, growling. Jingling bones, a laughing Tik Tok hurled himself at Rap and enveloped him in a rib-cracking embrace.

The ambience rumbled and Rap was back with Thaïle again. Waves of black fire boiled above the Qoble Mountains, shaking the occult ramparts to their foundations. Thaïle hurled power into them and the attack faltered. Then it ceased, as abruptly as it had begun.

But it had been close! Clearly the Covin had traced that rescue to its source. It knew its enemy now. How long could Zinixo tolerate a rival?

"Gods!" Rap said. *"We can't take much of that, can we? Summon your sorcerers, Keeper! All of them! We must organize defenses."*

Thaïle nodded. Raim materialized, recumbent upon the grass outside the cabana. He had no clothes on and neither did the lovely Sial clasped in his arms. They looked up in shock and outrage. Sial screamed. Thaïle snapped out a command and the two figures vanished again.

"I'll bet he remembers that one!" Rap said under his breath. "Thrugg, you big monster!" But events were racing ahead too fast for friendly greetings.

"Rap!" the Keeper shouted. "Proclaim your war! You said you had friends? Bring them!"

Again Rap felt the surge of her power elevate him. Again he saw Pandemia spread out before him. He stood above it like a giant, a shining cloud in the shape of a man. He had been given no time to prepare his proclamation, and he bellowed the first words that came into his head.

"Sorcerers! I am Rap, king of Krasnegar. Today we destroy the Covin! Today we begin the new protocol! Today freedom dawns! Come and enlist in the cause of right!"

Bolts of lightning buzzed up at him from Hub and were deflected by the age-old defenses of the Accursed Land—how long until Zinixo analyzed this alien sorcery and took its measure?

"Come now and join the cause!"

For a moment the ambience was still, shadowy nothing, silent as a crypt. The world seemed to hold its breath. Then a familiar figure shimmered into view—a slim youth with golden skin and eyes of many-colored gem. He, too, bestrode the world with power, smiling an infinitely cynical smile.

"King Rap demonstrates a remarkable potency and heralds a spectacular cause. I am Lith'rian, warlock of the south. I place my powers and all the sorcerers of Ilrane at his disposal."

God of Wonders!

"Come, and welcome!" Rap grabbed. A blizzard of shooting stars flashed in the ambience and the Meeting Place was filled with elves. A hundred? Well, several dozen, anyway. Too choked with relief and excitement to say a word, he bowed low to the warlock.

Lith'rian sighed. "Your Doctor Sagorn is a remarkable advocate, your Majesty. He bludgeoned me into submission with sheer loquacity."

"I had sooner believe that Jalon inspired you with jotunn battle songs, your Omnipotence!"

"Actually it was what you did to the djinns that persuaded us. Exquisite barbarity!" Lith'rian chuckled. "And obviously you were correct about Thume." Then he discovered Thaïle and his big eyes widened in shock. He glanced apprehensively at Rap.

"Her Holiness, the Keeper," Rap said.

"Your humble servant, ma'am!" The elf sank gracefully to one knee and bowed his head. Whatever his faults, Lith'rian always had style.

"And I am Raspnex," another voice boomed, jolting Rap's attention back to the ambience, *"warlock of the north. I also join King Rap and my dearly loved brother of the south in their campaign."* The familiar ugly face twisted with what a dwarf regarded as a grin, showing teeth like quartz pebbles in a beard of iron turnings.

Raspnex! He was closer, just over the mountains, and with him were two other dwarves—and Jarga, by the Powers!—and a *goblin* and a shadowy figure who might be another goblin, and . . . and . . . And then Thaïle yanked them all to the Meeting Place. That last one had been a mundane.

"Shandie!"

The imperor was thinner than he had been, gaunt and glittering of eye, clad in a nondescript and none-too-clean

Zarkian robe. He beamed at Rap quickly, and then glanced around the glade with understandable astonishment. Pixies were materializing all over, answering Raim's summons. Half of them were still in a state of undress, emitting shrill squeals of alarm as they registered the presence of so many demons. The archons were calling out occult reassurance, but Rap blanked that from his mind.

"Keeper! This mundane is the imperor! Let him also speak."

No sooner thought than done—Shandie staggered in confusion as the occult world opened before him.

"Summon your imps!" Rap prompted in his ear. There must still be impish sorcerers at large. "Proclaim the new protocol!"

Shandie was an old hand at making rousing speeches. As he announced himself the true imperor, a small voice spoke from the east.

"King? We had certain assurances from your mate concerning Imperor's good intentions."

Rap stared in delight at the tiny man. *"Ishist, you old rascal! I gladly confirm the imperor's good faith."*

"This is strange, Rap!" Thaïle whispered. *"The Covin is letting them come! Why does it not seek to block this assembly?"*

"We come, then, King!" the old gnome said, clutching Rap's occult hand. A horde of male and female gnomes pattered down into the Meeting Place, scores of them.

Horde of gnomes? A mob of gnomes? A *dump* of gnomes, perhaps? No matter! Their help was welcome. Rap spared a brief glance Hubward. The Covin was indeed holding its fire, as the Keeper said. Why? Had Zinixo panicked at this sudden revolution? Again no matter! The freedom fighters would be more effective if they were all gathered together. If nothing else, that would make control easier and desertion almost impossible.

Now voices clamored everywhere in the ambience, demanding admission. Rap recognized old Vog and Wurnk in the far-off Mosweeps, with a large herd of trolls. He brought them. Thaïle had set the archons to work, also, pulling in scattered bands from all over Pandemia—djinns, imps, dwarves, even a dozen female goblins from the taiga. The sorcerers of the world were rallying to the cause, and the Meeting Place was filling up.

"Rap!" Shandie said. "How can you be sure all these recruits are what they seem? There must be Covin agents among them!"

Rap thumped the imperor on the shoulder. "No. They're being vetted. They can't come in unless they're brought. Deception is impossible, just about."

"Just about?"

"Impossible. By the way, your wife and daughter are here in Thume."

Shandie's face went rigid with shock.

"King Rap," the Keeper said, "there is something going on in the north. That is what is holding the Covin's attention."

Shandie was clutching Rap's shoulders and shouting questions. The Meeting Place was a tumult as the various races organized themselves in groups, every group eyeing all the others with wary suspicion. The ambience flashed and rumbled as the archons brought in more, and more.

Rap tried to see what was concerning Thaïle, but it was too far off for him, and there was too much going on in between.

"Probably the Nordland Moot," he said. *"Perhaps they have some sorcerers there. Not too many, I expect."*

Thaïle eyed him darkly. *"What's wrong?"*

"It doesn't matter."

Gath was somewhere in Nordland.

The God had warned Rap that he must lose a child in this war. Kadie was safe, here in Thume.

Still, Gath would never have managed to penetrate the thanes' moot and he wasn't a sorcerer, so whatever the Covin was up to could not concern Gath. If that Nordland diversion was keeping the Covin distracted, then it was a Godsend and must not be interrupted. Meanwhile Shandie—

"What? Yes, they're quite safe. Ylo brought them."

"Ylo?"

Rap needed no sorcery to recognize the apprehension. "Ylo's dead. I'm sorry. Two days ago. He died defending your wife and child from the Covin. No, I can't explain at the moment. And no, you can't go to her. Now shut *up*! I'm busy. Inos is here, too, by the way. And Kadie."

Shandie said, "Congratulations!" in tones to be expected of an imperor who had just been told to shut up.

The Meeting Place was becoming crowded, but the races were sorting themselves out in groups. Mostly pixies, of course, a couple of hundred pixies. Thirty or forty elves stood by themselves in aloof disapproval. Imps were rarer, perhaps twenty. With his incongruous black kibr swishing around his ankles, Shandie went stalking over to deliver an oration to them. Thirty djinns at least, and those chattering near-naked little folk were fauns. The dwarves had assembled as far from the elves as they could get, but Raspnex had them under control. The trolls had wandered into the trees, sampling as they went.

The fifty or so gnomes had vanished under flower bushes, out of the sunlight. Unfortunately they were upwind.

And merfolk! Sitting in a cluster by the edge of the lake—at least two dozen blue-haired merfolk! Rap had missed their arrival. As sorcerers they could use power to restrain their racial curse, but it was still an eerie sensation to see a group of merfolk in the crowd. In the army. His army!

He wanted to throw back his head and scream his triumph to the skies. He might yet lose the battle, but at least there was going to be a battle. Zinixo would not win by default.

In the Outside world the ambience was growing quieter as the last few stragglers clamored for recognition, eager to be admitted before the Covin retaliated. The archons were still busy, but inducting them in ones and twos now. Whatever was going on in Nordland was still happening and keeping the Covin distracted. Long may it last!

"Your Holiness," Rap said formally, "I think we are about done recruiting. I suggest you make a speech, welcoming our allies to your land."

Thaïle looked at him sadly. Then she pulled up her hood and became again the inscrutable Keeper, a white-clad enigma. "It would be more fitting if you made that speech, Archon Rap. You are the general and they are your warriors."

Rap's heart chilled. "You are not hopeful? You foresee defeat?"

"I cannot, will not, try to read the outcome."

"How many are we?"

Thaïle glanced around. "More than four hundred, but not many more. Make your speech, General."

Hastily gathering his thoughts, Rap took a last quick glance at the ambience Outside.

11

Gath squirmed. He was stiff and cold on the gritty stone bench. Above all, he was bored to distraction by the unending speeches. Nothing had been decided or seemed likely to be decided for hours yet. What was happening on this fateful day while he sat here in this shielded madhouse?

The sunlight had already abandoned two windows and was starting to creep in through a third. The shafts were positioned to shed light on the Speaker Stone, and he had decided that this was a very clever device that probably only worked on Longday itself. On other days the sun would not be in the right position. So what?

He had also realized the true purpose of the meeting. These men and women were the loneliest people in the world. All sorcerers were forced to be solitary, but power was especially despised in Nordland, and their duties forced them to live their lives far apart. Once a year the Nintor Moot gave them the chance to meet and be themselves and know others of their own kind. That was why they were all being so atrociously long-winded, and why they wanted to be. He might have to stay here all day!

Longday was living up to its name.

"Go ahead!" whispered a tiny voice in his ear. It came from Jaurg, although he had not moved or spoken aloud.

Gath pondered. Dare he try to address the group? He risked a tiny peek of prescience—and apparently he would be heard. He was their liege, wasn't he?

What did he have to lose? He'd died once already today.

He stood up in the middle of a long digression on the merits of Dad's new protocol.

The speaker was Gustiag, the older man who had been the second to do homage. He frowned at this insolent interruption.

"May I say one thing?" Gath asked quietly, marveling at his own courage.

"I yield to Atheling Gathmor!" Obviously reluctant, Gustiag stepped down but did not return to his seat.

Well!

Gath stalked forward and took the vacant stone.

"I appreciate your courtesy in holding this debate in words for my sake," he said loudly, "but I'm sure you could get finished faster if you used occult means."

Silence—very cold silence.

"Is this your father's command to us?" Gustiag inquired.

Gath wilted before the sarcasm. "No . . . merely a sugges-tion of my own . . . I do think the situation is urgent."

Still no reaction from the onlookers.

He mumbled, "Thank you, er, I have spoken," and stepped down.

Gustiag took his place. "As I was saying . . ."

Gath slunk back to his seat. Twist smiled mockingly at him. Jaurg was holding hands with Fraftha, a girl of about Gath's age. As he squeezed into his previous place, Gath realized that this was the kiddies' corner. The four of them were the young-sters of the group, expected to maintain a respectful silence while their elders debated, and he was the youngest of all. He had been wrong to stand up.

Gustiag ended and recognized an elderly woman as his suc-cessor. Her speech was the shortest yet, and about the shortest possible: "I yield to Jaurg the bastard."

Eyes still firmly closed, Gath's neighbor rose and strode for-ward to mount the stone. Blindness would be small handicap to a sorcerer and bastardy could be no great shame in Nordland, for at least a dozen of those present had been unable to name their fathers when they did homage.

"Brothers and sisters, I speak for those who were enslaved and now are free." He spoke softly and simply, spurning the dramatic tricks that many speakers had attempted. "For that re-lease, we are eternally grateful to the rest of you, although we were happy in our servitude. We expected an attempt to un-mask us and feared it, but did not think it would succeed.

"It would not have done, I am sure, without the valor of one man. Some of you may feel that your pledge of homage to him was mere formality, a way of demonstrating your independ-ence. I assure you that we who were enthralled do not think of it that way. We honor Atheling Gathmor for his father's sake of course, but we honor him also in his own right. How many mundanes would have defied a gathering of sorcerers as he did today? He is not pure jotunn, I agree, but does any man or woman here claim to be his superior in courage?"

The whole chamber broke into applause. Oh, horrors! Shame! Gath curled up and hid his face on his knees. They all knew how frightened he had been when he came in, so this was just cruel, hateful mockery! Perhaps they were getting back at him for having had to kneel at his feet. He thought bit-

ter thoughts about the despicable Jaurg, who had seemed quite
a solid sort of guy until then.

The clapping died away into open laughter, and then stilled.
Jaurg chuckled. "He does not believe us! Let us prove our
sincerity. On your honor, brothers and sisters, let any here who
feels demeaned by having knelt to this man today now stand
and ask to be released from his homage."

Warily Gath lifted his head a little and peered around the
chamber. No one was standing. What sort of game were they
playing with him now?

Jaurg sighed loudly. "He is still modest—that must come
from the nonjotunn part of him! But I must get down to business. As you can guess, our mission and purpose was to enlist
all the rest of you to the cause that we so wholeheartedly then
supported. When we set out for Nintor there were five of us
loyal to the Almighty. Our ships encountered others at sea, and
some stopped to make wassail at ports on the way. When we
came ashore, we were twelve."

He paused a moment, to let his audience reflect on that.

"We enlisted three more on Nintor itself, but then the arrivals overwhelmed us. We were outnumbered and dared try no
further recruitment lest we reveal ourselves. We waited for this
meeting, planning to take possession of the building in advance
and entrap each of you in turn as he or she entered. You all
know how Twist son of Kalkor thwarted us . . . Are you aware
of that, Atheling Gath?"

"No," Gath said.

Because of his closed eyes, Jaurg's smile seemed to imply
that he was dreaming happy dreams. "He suggested that this
year we assemble outside and enter by lot. Thus were we
balked! To him also we are now grateful.

"Our alternative plan, of course, was to leave first, and overpower you singly as you emerged. We failed in the first attempt and shall not now try again, but the Usurper was most
certainly watching who entered. Oh, yes, he can see this far!
Right at the start, he warned us that we might fail. He said he
would give us three hours. That time, I believe, is almost up.
I have spoken."

Jaurg stepped down from the stone and waited for others to
rise. No one did. Several voices shouted: "Speak on!" "Then
what?" "Tell us more!"

Drugfarg's weighty bellow drowned them all out. "You
mean he's going to overpower us as we leave?"

The blind man stepped back up on the podium. "No. He will simply destroy the Commonplace and us with it."

Half the sorcerers leaped to their feet, and then more followed, but no one said anything at all. Puzzled, Gath glanced at Twist. The cripple was showing his tangled teeth in a grimace and concentrating blank-eyed on something. So, apparently Jaurg had succeeded where Gath had failed and the debate was now being conducted at an occult level. Gath himself could no longer hear it, that was all.

Jaurg shrugged and walked back to his seat between Gath and Fraftha. He put an arm around the girl.

"That livened things up a little," he remarked cheerfully.

"You were serious?"

"Quite serious."

How could he be so calm? Gath wanted to scream. He had visions of that low ceiling collapsing, burying him under the hill. His skin felt like cold maggots were eating it already.

"But why would Zinixo kill you all? There must be sixty sorcerers—"

"Sixty-four here."

"Doesn't he want you, to serve him? He *collects* sorcerers, doesn't he?"

Jaurg yawned. "Not any more, apparently. He probably feels he has so many now that he may as well just exterminate the rest. Hub's a long way off. At this range . . . hard to explain. Take my word for it, it's easier to stamp than grab."

Gath said, "Oh!" and tried to look unworried.

He wasn't that good a liar. He opened his mental spigot and grabbed all the future he could foresee. He said, "Awrk!"

In about three minutes the roof was going to blow right off the Commonplace.

In sudden urgency, Jaurg straightened, releasing Fraftha. He grabbed Gath's wrist in an astonishingly powerful grip. "Hold tight, Atheling! We meld. I'll try to take you in with me."

Gath clutched Jaurg's wrist also—he was in a mood to clutch at anything. He felt Twist grip his other arm in a similar double hold, and then they were all on their feet.

"In where?"

"Into the ambience." The blind youth smiled again. "I'm not sure it's possible for a mundane, but we'll try."

"Otherwise," Twist added, "you will be finding things even more confusing."

"More confusing than what?"

"Than anything."

Gath saw double.

Within the dim chamber, the sorcerers stood around the walls, many holding hands. Superimposed on that was an image that seemed to make no sense at all. It was bright and yet without light. It had no points of reference at all, no place, no being—no underground chamber, no world or sky. This must be how a sorcerer saw things. Within that shadowless nothingness the sixty-odd jotnar were clustered tightly around him, many smiling at him, *and none of them seemed to have any clothes on!* He found Drugfarg the armorer and old Gustiag the healer—and how did he know their professions? And the women. Gods! No clothes. Some were as solid as boulders, others almost transparent. Then he located Twist the skald and Blind Jaurg the cobbler, and between them a faint image of a lanky young man with unruly blond hair and a stern, worried expression. That one seemed oddly familiar.

By the Powers! He knew that one! He really had grown lately, hadn't he? No beard yet, but ... well, getting there. Hey, not bad! He would rather have breeches on, though.

"Now!" Atheling Twist said. He had been chosen leader, because he was as strong as any, also brother to the thane who was certainly going to be war leader of the Nordland Host and how did Gath know all these things? A mighty fist punched upward and the roof of the Commonplace dissolved in a spray of flying dirt and boulders.

Was that real?

There were many things to see then.

The Moot Stow. Drakkor had been raised on a platform of shields held by a dozen husky jotnar. He was haranguing the mob, promising blood and loot and rape, and the warriors were cheering their lungs out for him, thanes and churls ...

The Commonplace from the outside, apparently undamaged.

All of Nintor, as if seen by a bird soaring at cloud height.

Sixty-odd sorcerers racing over the grass, heading for the longships drawn up on the beach—not running, for crippled Twist was moving as fast as any, but traveling faster than a hunting hawk.

A roiling dark evil ... Eyes. Huge, hateful dwarvish eyes filling the sky and staring contempt right at him.

A voice, booming: "The faun's son! So there you are! Got you at last!"

There was no doubt who that was.

"Go puke yourself, you squat-eyed gray horror!" Gath roared, and registered laughter and approval all around him. "My dad squashed you once and he's going to squash you again!"

Fury boiled in the sky. "Die, stripling!"

A fiery foot descended.

The meld of sorcerers slid sideways, evading that giant stamp. The ground erupted in flame where it struck.

That was not real. That was only an image, perhaps invoked by something Jaurg had said earlier. The reality behind it was something else but just as dangerous.

At the Moot Stow the crowd stilled and turned to see where the noise had come from . . .

Voices all around him, the melded mind of the sorcerers: "To the ships—is the boy with us?—where can we go?"

Another fiery stamp. Another explosion of dirt and rock, high in the air. And another dodge. Another blast from the Covin, another fast evasion. Pillars of smoke rose above Nintor.

The horde at the Moot Stow dissolving in panic—

The beach. A ship. Any ship. When in danger take to the sea.

Thane Afgirk's *Raven Feast* . . .

"It will do—all aboard—lift her now—"

Sorcerers poured aboard. The longship leaped from her berth a moment before blasts of fire smote the shingle where she had lain. Her former neighbors exploded in red flame and a blizzard of pebbles. She hit the sea with a shower of spray and was a league away before the Covin's next bolt struck in steam and boiling eradication. Southward. No time to set sail. No time to run out the oars. Leap. Impact. Leap again. Like a giant marlin, *Raven Feast* vaulted over the face of the ocean while the Covin's strokes exploded the green sea behind her in white breakers and clouds of mist.

Nothing was real except perhaps the longship itself and the fierce grips on Gath's wrists. The voices of the meld roared in his ears.

"We can't keep this up forever—he's sure to catch us eventually. Where can we go—where is King Rap?"

The Covin's volleys were closing in, pillars of steam bursting all around.

"Atheling!" Twist bellowed in Gath's ear. "Where is your father?"

"I don't know!"

"Find him for us! We need sanctuary! Call him! He will recognize you!"

Call him?

Gath saw the shiny sea and the sky and the distant peaks of Nordland. He saw the evil of the Covin and its blasts of power. He saw sixty-four sorcerers and a mundane boy.

They were appealing to *him*?

Call Dad?

The last news of Dad had been months ago, when he had been somewhere down near the Mosweeps, about as far from Nordland as it was possible to be. These maniacs expected Gath to *call* to him?

A near miss showered *Raven Feast* with icy seawater, half swamping her. The shock and cold almost jerked Gath out of the meld. He was sprawled on the gratings with Twist hanging on one arm and Jaurg on the other, tearing him apart. Overhead the bare mast whirled against blue sky.

"Try, Atheling!" Twist howled. *"Or we are being undone!"*

"Give him power, everyone!" Jaurg shouted. *"Give him all you can!"*

"Save us, Atheling! Call on your father!"

The world swelled.

The world was round.

Nordland shrank to a cluster of barren islands, swathed in pack ice to the north. Land swam into view to the south—that would be Guwush, and the shimmer of silver beyond that the Morning Sea and the green to the west must be the Impire, shadows of night still rushing away to the southwest. The sun was white and hot at his side.

There was the Winter Ocean, and if he tried he could probably see all the way to Krasnegar, but he mustn't waste time looking there. Dad wouldn't be in Krasnegar. People—more than the land itself he could see the teeming millions of people. Imps, gnomes, many races. Mountains to the south, sparkling with snow and ice but very tiny, and the sky trees of Ilrane that Kadie had talked of, little crystal pinecones against the deep blue of the Summer Seas. That black fire roaring in the middle of the world was the evil of the Covin and ignore those hateful eyes and think where Dad might be . . .

"*Dad!*" he howled.

No response.

"*Dad, it's me, Gath!*"

Contact?

"*Dad!*"

A tiny whisper, very far away . . .

"*Gath?*"

Dad's voice!

"*Dad? King Rap? It's Gath! I've got some sorcerers for you!*"

"*Gath? Is that you? Where are you?*"

"*Dad, I'm here! In Nordland!*"

Near miss—the sea exploded. *Raven Feast* rolled below a vast green wave. Icy surf sucked at the crew, sweeping oars and baggage overboard. Gath had water in his eyes, up his nose. For a moment the longship seemed ready to turn turtle. Slowly she fought to straighten herself. The meld shimmered and began to break up. Gath felt power draining away. The craft was swamped. One more blast would do it.

"*Dad! Save us!*"

"*Got you!*" The whisper swelled into command: "*Gath! Here! Come now!*"

Rolling drums:
> Thy voice is heard thro' rolling drums,
>   That beat to battle where he stands;
> Thy face across his fancy comes,
>   And gives the battle to his hands.
>   Tennyson, *The Princess, vi*

❦ TWELVE ❧

God at war

1

On being wakened by a howl of alarm from Kadie, Inos had realized that Rap was not in bed at her side, where he belonged. When she had calmed her daughter, she learned that he had gone, returned, and then disappeared again by sorcery. On this ominous day, she was disinclined to go back to sleep after that news.

Breakfast presented a problem, as there was no food in the cabin and no resident sorcerer to produce any. Mother and daughter set out for the Commons. They found nobody there, which was definitely odd. Had the entire College been abandoned? Something vital must be happening, somewhere.

"We'll try the Meeting Place!" Inos said firmly, and they set off through the woods again.

In a few minutes Kadie exclaimed, "That sounds like the sea!"

The Meeting Place was nowhere near the sea. There was certainly something noisy ahead, though. "Or a large crowd?"

Kadie jumped and uttered another howl, the second of the day. The poor girl's nerves were in terrible shape, Inos thought, and then stifled a scream of her own. A monstrous mushroom-colored giant was grinning at her from the bushes. It was browsing on a banana tree and it had no clothes on. It . . . she

357

. . . mumbled something incomprehensible through a mouthful of juicy leaf.

"Er, good morning to you, too," Inos said politely, and walked quickly past, towing Kadie by the hand. "Only a troll," she whispered airily, as if trolls had always been commonplace in her life. Trolls in Thume? Behold the millennium! She sniffed. "And there are gnomes around somewhere. Come on! This is becoming exciting!"

"Exciting? I don't want anything else exciting!"

"History being made? Would you rather call it 'romantic,' then?"

Kadie smiled wistfully. "I think I would rather be at home in Krasnegar and never have another adventure as long as I live."

"Now you are making sense!" Inos said, but it was not the sort of sense a fourteen-year-old should make. She was sickened by the change in her daughter. The old Kadie would never have made such a remark.

Hand in hand, they emerged into the Meeting Place. It was full of people, all the way from the encircling woods down to the little lake in the center—pixies, of course, but also clumps of bright-clad folk, clumps of drab-clad folk, and groups showing much bare skin.

"See?" Inos said with a calm that belied her thumping heart. "I expect they're all sorcerers. Your father has been collecting allies. Elves over there? And imps, of course . . ."

"Inos!" Shandie came running through the crowd in a resplendent doublet of imperial purple, bedecked with several jeweled orders and strewn with chivalrous sashes. He swept her into a hug. "And Princess Kadolan!"

Kadie curtseyed low. The imperor pulled her up and hugged her, too. He put an arm around both mother and daughter, laughing and trying to speak at the same time. His excitement was much at odds with his very formal dress. "Rap told me you were here, and my wife, too, I understand, and of course old Raspnex—"

"Things are going well, obviously?" Inos said. Those brown bushy-haired people must be the anthropophagi Rap had mentioned. They seemed to be wearing nothing but paint and bones.

"Things are going marvelously!" Shandie said. "I was worried about you, but Raspnex swore you'd be safe enough with the caliph." His eyes were asking questions his mouth wasn't.

Inos would not inform Shandie of her experiences with Azak, even were Kadie not present. Raspnex ought to lose his warlocking license. "I assume that Rap is busy at the moment?"

"Very! This is a historic occasion! There are sorcerers here from all over the world, all gathered to combat the Covin."

"Fauns? And goblins!" There were more pixies than anyone else, of course. They must be terrified by this invasion.

Then Inos located the center of the action, halfway around the clearing, with Rap himself towering over a group of assorted races, probably the leaders of the various factions. Certainly that was Warlock Lith'rian at his side, looking no older than he had twenty years ago. The male troll was even taller than Rap and twice the width, and there was a brown man with a bone through his nose. Another anthropophagus? That small, white-cowled figure was probably the Keeper, but fortunately Kadie had not noticed her yet.

"I don't see any jotnar," Inos remarked. "Except Jarga." She returned a smile and a wave from the big sailor, who was conspicuous within a group of two or three dozen dwarves.

"No, she's the only jotunn," Shandie said.

"Mama!" Kadie cried. "Down by the lake—those are merfolk!"

"Where? Good Gods! Shandie, are those . . . Kadie, how do you know about merfolk?"

"Don't worry about them," the imperor said confidently. "They're sorcerers, so there'll be no trouble."

"I've never seen merfolk before!"

Shandie scowled. "Remember Ythbane? He was part merman."

Inos decided that merfolk were odd-looking fish, with their pale skins and blue hair. She did not think she could ever find any merman attractive, whatever the legends said. She was still staring at them, and hence at the little lake, when a Nordland longship materialized upon it with a crack of thunder. Waves leaped shoreward, crashed into the banks, drenched the closer bystanders with silver sheets of water—merfolk and djinns, mostly. Others, all the way from the elves to the dwarves, were sprayed. Cries of alarm echoed through the glade, and half the pixies winked out of existence.

"Recent information," the imperor said, "hints that the Nordland contingent may have just reported for duty."

Kadie screamed for the third time that morning, but this

time she was indicating joy. The sinister craft was packed with oversize fair-haired, fair-skinned people, men and women both, but there was no doubt which one mattered to her. A lanky young man had leaped up on the gunwale and was balancing there, windmilling his arms as the longship rolled. He wore leather breeches like all the other men aboard, but he was the only member of the crew whose hair did not lie flat and he was grotesquely lank. He yelled, "Dad! Dad! I brought you some sorcerers!" and took a flying leap to shore.

He slipped on the muddy bank and disappeared amid the rushes with another violent splash.

Kadie squealed piercingly. "Gath! That's Gath!" She vanished into the crowd like an arrow from a bow.

As a sodden Gath emerged and scrambled out, Rap came plowing through sorcerers and archons and warlocks. The two of them crashed into an embrace.

"Inos?" Shandie said reprovingly. "You're weeping!"

True! The Meeting Place had disappeared in crystal mist and the pain in her throat was unbearable. She turned to the imperor and hugged him, burying her face in his velvet collar. "Rap safe, Kadie safe, and now Gath safe! Just a week ago I thought I'd never see any of them again!" She could hardly force the words out—sentimental idiot! This was becoming a habit. She stepped back, wiping away tears. Then she saw that Rap was holding his son at arm's length with one arm, studying him, and his other hand was surreptitiously wiping his eyes, also. It was catching.

Shandie regarded her with fond amusement. "Well, from now on, you can brag about that boy of yours. He seems to have succeeded where you and I dared not even try! Congratulations!"

"Thank you." Gath was taller than his father!

"If he ever wants a job, just send him to me."

"I plan to leave him mine." How strange! Inos recalled that not so very long ago, she and Rap had seriously doubted Gath's talents and prospects for future kingship. Not assertive enough, they had thought. So now the kid had taken off on his own to the Nintor Moot—and that exploit alone would guarantee him the lifelong worship of all the jotnar in her kingdom—and come wandering back from the market with a few dozen sorcerers in tow . . .

"He must have been incredibly lucky!" she said.

"In my experience, luck is more output than input," Shandie said dryly. "I understand my wife and daughter are safe, also?"

How much had Rap told him? "Yes, they're well," Inos said, intently watching her son and husband's reunion, Kadie's frantic progress around the lake, the jotnar disembarking, the panicky pixies' efforts to distance themselves from those ultimate terrors, the white-haired demons.

"But not Ylo?"

"No," she said, "not Ylo." She glanced cautiously at Shandie.

His expression was bleak. The glint in his eye was a challenge to their friendship. "I must stay here. Can you bring my wife to me?" It was as close as he could ever come to pleading.

Kadie had reached her twin. Gath lifted her bodily into the air and whirled her around, the two of them screaming with excitement. Rap was grinning like a maniac. The jotnar crowded in around them, hiding the family reunion from view.

Things were under control there. Inos was not needed there. She would congratulate her son in due course. The imperor needed her more.

"Yes, I can fetch Eshiala here, Shandie," she said. "But first let's find somewhere to sit and talk. I have some things to tell you."

2

"This is the leader of the Nordland sorcerers," Gath said proudly, "Atheling Twist, son of Kalkor."

Rap could not tear his eyes away from this astonishing young man who had replaced the boy he remembered. So tall already! Then the name penetrated . . . His heart missed a beat. He swung around to look at the little youth on his crutch. "Son of *Kalkor*?" And a sorcerer? Jotnar were addicted to blood feuds.

Twist leered up at him with a grotesque mouthful of crooked teeth. "Also brother of Drakkor, the war leader, a sturdy man with an ax—but we come in peace, Thaneslayer." The cripple's very pale eyes twinkled as he registered Rap's apprehension.

"I am delighted to hear it, and you are all most welcome. The Keeper . . ." Rap glanced around. Where was Thaïle? And why had the jotnar chosen this unfortunate runt to lead them?

"We are having already done homage to you as leader of the righteous, Thane."

"You have?"

"I accepted their oaths on your behalf, Father," Gath said, obviously enduring agony from his efforts to appear humble. "But some of them preferred to swear to me personally. Of course my vassals and I are at your command! Did I do wrong?"

"I don't recall delegating such powers to you, but under the circumstances I shall waive the usual death penalty for exceeding authority. How many of you, Sorcerer?"

"Sixty-four, Thane. Is this all of your army, though?"

Many of the pixies had departed but were now returning.

"Most of it," Rap said. He had just realized that several of the jotnar contingent were women, and very few of them seemed to be sailors.

"How many?"

"With you, we must have almost five hundred."

"Ah!" Twist sighed. "Jaurg?"

A blind youth at the back said, "Leader?"

"How many in the Covin?"

"Something over two thousand."

Rap staggered. "*What?* You're joking! How do you know this?"

"Because I was one of them. Several of us were enthralled. Athelings Gath and Twist contrived our release, but I know there were at least twenty-two hundred sorcerers in the Covin, and that was some weeks ago."

Rap's mouth was suddenly drier than the heart of Zark. He could not comprehend such numbers. Where had all those sorcerers come from? No wonder Zinixo had been displaying confidence! "We also have a demigod on our side."

With his eyes still closed, Jaurg smiled at him over blond heads. "Then it should be a good fight."

Gath was registering worry in the background. "We can win?"

Jaurg turned to the voice and smiled again. "No, Atheling my liege, we cannot win. But it should be a good fight."

Odds of four to one? It would be a fight, but not a very good one.

"We must coordinate our strategies," Rap said, suddenly aware that even jotnar might be easier to handle than a mixture of touchy warlocks, archons, a demigod, sophisticated elves, and deadly cannibals—

A scream of agony rent the morning, stilling the babble of conversation. Everyone stopped talking to stare. Over in the pixie sector, old Archon Neem had fallen writhing to the grass. Spectators were backing away hastily. In the ambience, he was enveloped in black flame. A moment later and a few paces away from him, Archon Puik erupted in black flame, also.

Each archon was attuned to the section of border he guarded.

The Keeper's cry told the company what they had all already guessed. *"Rally!"* Thaïle shouted. *"Meld! The attack has begun!"*

3

Thaïle had not dared use foresight on the events of this fateful day, but she had guessed all along that the cause was hopeless. Had there been any chance of victory at all, her predecessor would not have capitulated so easily, for Lain had been no weakling; only certainty of failure could have driven her to despair. The testimony of the cobbler Jaurg had thus been merely confirmation. Overhearing it, Thaïle had peered into the very depths of his soul, suspecting a deeply buried treachery. She had discovered only a peaceable young man, honest and sincerely obedient to the Gods and the Good. A very unusual jotunn, in fact.

Mundane logic alone said that disaster was inevitable. Even were the two sides evenly matched in strength, the issue could not be in doubt, for the Covin's thousands were united under the will of the Almighty. The diverse assembly in the Meeting Place had no discipline, no unanimity, no single vision. These ragtag revolutionaries had no practice in acting together. They even lacked an overall leader. Thaïle herself, for all her superhuman power, was a naive country lass, inexperienced in command. Rap was a midget sorcerer and too much a decent human being to be a successful general—he had a statesman's vision, but he lacked the arrogance needed to impose his own will on everyone else. The two warlocks were so wary of each other's distrust that neither dared exert himself lest he provoke a rupture.

At Thaïle's command the company tried to meld and produced only a welter of confusion. Each of the twelve races making up the Thumian army rallied to its own leader first. Then imp clashed with jotunn, gnome with djinn, merman with anthropophagus, elf with dwarf. The fauns tried to argue. Trolls froze in horror and pixies shattered like glass.

In essence the Covin was hurling raw power at the barrier over the Qoble Mountains, where Neem's sector joined with Puik's. The contest held no more subtlety than two mountain rams battering heads together beside a herd of ewes. Normally the physical world would have paid no heed, but in this case the energies released were so great that the earth shook and avalanches tumbled from the crags. Soon streams were boiling and forests smoked.

The real battle was staged in the ambience. There, too, there was only insistence against resistance. Thaïle could observe the truth but mere sorcerers interpreted the ambience in metaphor. Different observers saw it in different ways, and she was overwhelmed by all the conflicting reactions around her. Many saw fire—white, red, and black. The jotunn mostly visualized a rampaging horde of warriors. Dwarves saw mighty hammers and merfolk giant waves. Struggling against this massive confusion, the Keeper fought to sustain the ancient walls and rally her supporters at the same time.

Every one of the five hundred seemed to be calling on her—advising, beseeching, arguing, lamenting, while Neem and Puik thrashed in terminal agony. The Meeting Place roiled with fear and anger. Reduce the perimeter, launch a counterstroke at Hub, divide the army into columns . . . Five hundred sorcerers clamored with five hundred plans and suggestions.

One tiny voice trilled on a different note. One small thread of emotion was different from all the others. Puzzled, Thaïle managed to spare a transitory fragment of attention for that one, and saw Kadie's frightened mundane green eyes staring at her.

"You all right, Thaïle?"

Sympathy? That's what it was! Someone cared for Thaïle herself.

"Yes, I'm fine!" she said aloud. She smiled gratefully and turned her attention back to the Qoble front.

Too late. The thousand-year sorcery collapsed, Puik and Neem dissolved utterly, and the Covin's wrath raged untrammeled into Thume.

And there, for a moment, it was balked. The stony eyes of the Almighty glared around, seeking an enemy. He found no army drawn up in battle, no fortresses to overthrow or cities to besiege. He saw only sleepy rustic countryside and a scattered population of herders, fishermen, and peasant farmers. Typically, he reacted with wanton spite.

Pixies began to die. Bolts of power struck them down as they reaped and tilled. Men at their labors, women tending children, the children themselves at play—a wave of death surged forward over the Accursed Land. Cottages exploded in flame, livestock fell lifeless. Watermills and beehives burned. Nothing in the War of the Five Warlocks or the innumerable wars before it had ever been more cold-blooded than this systematic annihilation.

The Meeting Place stiffened into paralysis. Horror froze the defenders as the destruction spread.

King Rap was the first to recover. *"Keeper!"* he bellowed. *"They have found the Gates! Abandon the College quickly!"*

Abandon? . . . Then Thaïle saw what the faun had seen. The Covin had just discovered that there were two Thumes. The mass slaughter was being inflicted on the real land, the home of the pixie folk. Above that, glimmering everywhere in a silver web of sorcery, lay the network of the Way, spreading out from the Chapel, linking Meeting Place with Library, Commons, Gates, Market, and all the facilities of the College. Innumerable threads led off to the humble Places where the sorcerers lived with their mundane partners.

It was all horribly vulnerable. As soon as the Almighty realized where his enemies were hiding, he could detach the web from the real world. He need exert a mere fraction of his power to do that, and in an instant he would hold Pandemia unopposed, for the College would be gone forever, and everyone in it also.

Thaïle blazed out a command: *"To the Chapel! Archons, round up the mundanes and bring them, also. Now!"*

Thunder rumbled over the sunlit Meeting Place. The sorcerers vanished, leaving an empty space of much-trampled grass and clumps of bedraggled shrubs. Half the cabanas were in need of repair and an incongruous Nordland longship listed to starboard in the lake. Only the six surviving archons remained—plus the imperor, Queen Inosolan, Kadie, and Gath.

"Hey!" Gath said. "Where did everybody go?"

4

Rap had always known that the battle would be brief, for that was the way of sorcery, but he had not expected such instant catastrophe. For a moment the transition took his breath away.

Then he pulled his wits together. The five pixies were still in a state of shock. He slammed power at them with all the feeble strength he could summon.

"You!" he barked at Toom. "That way. You—take the west . . . Summon all the mundanes!" He distributed the four cardinal points and turned to the fifth pixie, Raim. "Adjust the Way!"

They nodded, and rallied.

Then he looked to the four mundanes. Gath and Kadie were already standing at his side, white-faced and bewildered. Inos and the imperor came running up.

"Where is everybody?" Shandie demanded.

"At the Chapel," Rap said. "We must join them or—"

Temptation opened before him like a chasm. The war was as good as lost. The ancient barrier had offered a slim chance, but now it had fallen he could see no hope at all. Two thousand sorcerers! Odds of four or five to one—Zinixo was going to win in a pushover.

So . . .

So even if the Almighty did not detach the College from the real world, Rap himself and the archons might be able to do so. The alternative Thume would continue to exist. Assuming every sorcerer in the College had children and a wife or husband, it would be inhabited by a couple of thousand people. That was a viable population, and some of the sorcerers might manage to scramble back aboard before the severance was complete.

"There are two Thumes," he mumbled, struggling with honor and conscience. "The Almighty may be able to cut us off from the real world. If he does that, then he can never recapture us."

He stared in dismay at the wife he loved, his son and daughter. What would be their fate if Zinixo caught them? And what would be his own? Thume was a pleasant land. The four of them might dwell there in peace for the rest of their days. Kadie and Gath could survive to adulthood and find partners among the younger pixies. He and Inos would grow old in contentment, dangling grandchildren on their knees. It would be exile, but a safe exile.

It was the fate he had chosen for the fairies. When he had been a demigod and had banished their race forever from the real world, he had not doubted that he was doing them a favor. Why, now, should he not choose the same solution for himself and his loved ones? The alternative was defeat and probably the most horrible deaths a mad sorcerer could devise.

Shandie and the kids stared at him in bewilderment.

But Inos understood, and her green eyes flashed disapproval. "Desert the cause?" she said.

"The cause is lost!"

"Duty?"

Duty. Once before she had given him that answer in similar circumstances. Long ago, the two of them had faced a decision even more tempting than this one. Rap had known five words of power then. Five words alone destroyed, but five words plus love made a God. Together they could have taken on immortality, eternal bliss, and infinite authority. Together they had chosen duty instead.

Gath and Kadie, then? Leave them? But they were not children any longer. What right had Rap to make this decision for them?

None. But he had no time to explain it all. The archons were calling out to the mundanes, their voices echoing along the web of power to the farthest ends of Thume. Men and women and children were answering the occult summons, hurrying to the Way. Raim had changed the settings, so the Way now led only to the Chapel and whatever was happening there. There was no time to explain and reflect, so Rap would have to decide, and Inos' expression told him what his decision should be.

"We must go to the Chapel," he said. "Come on!"

He grabbed Kadie's hand and started to run over the grass to the white path. He sensed the others following.

Fool! he thought. *Fool!*

The Way sloped steeply through the forest now, and it was packed with refugees. Men bore toddlers on their shoulders, women and youngsters carried babies, and children milled around them all. Even the adults reacted with terror at the sight of demons, so Rap used sorcery to mask himself and his companions and clear a path ahead. The five of them ran, five people hand in hand, pelting down the slope Raim had just created.

The trees became larger, thicker, darker. The air took on the muggy scents of jungle. Shandie and Gath kept gasping out questions. Inos and Kadie were trying to explain—the Chapel was the center, the site of power, the heart of Thume.

And also Keef's tomb, Rap thought, but the Chapel existed on both planes. Once there, they would be back in the real world.

Even before the ancient ruin emerged from the forest, he could feel the crackle of sorcery and hear its echoes. The battle had reached the Chapel already. A mob of mundanes milled in dark confusion before the entrance. Still towing Kadie—who in turn towed Gath, Inos, and Shandie—he plunged into the undergrowth.

"Back door!" he shouted over his shoulder. Swamp sucked at his legs, branches tore at his eyes. He fought his way through the tangled vegetation, around the corner of the crumbling ruin, and along to the little side portal. He arrived panting, covered in mud to his thighs. The handle resisted his efforts to turn it, so he exerted power again, ripping the door bodily from its hinges and hurling it away.

Gath murmured an appreciative "Wow!" in the background. Rap dived through, and his chain of followers followed.

Battle raged in the great chamber like a thunderstorm.

To the left, the torrent of mundanes had poured in through the two entrances and then congealed, barring any more from following. The vestry must be packed solid behind them, while those who had entered stared in bewildered terror at the contest in progress.

To the right, the few hundreds of the righteous were being driven steadily back on Keef's grave in the far corner. Thaïle was in the front rank, with the leaders around her—Lith'rian, Raspnex, Thrugg, Twist, little Ishist, and some others. Fire and thunder clamored over them. Behind them the lesser sorcerers struggled to maintain their meld against the searing pain of manifest power.

And in the center stood the Almighty.

Of course it was only an illusion—Zinixo would never risk his own hide in a battle. But the human mind sought explanations and that vortex of raw power demanded form. Thus Rap saw the usurper himself, shining in black fire and three times the height of the tallest jotunn. Wielding the melded force of his minions, the giant dwarf hurled havoc upon the retreating defenders. The Chapel trembled in the blasts of power.

Disaster! Rap gazed in despair upon the unequal struggle and knew that he had arrived in time to see the conclusion, no more. The outcome was inevitable. Nothing could resist the Almighty.

Nothing Rap could do would make the slightest difference. For a moment he considered flight, but he knew he could never force his way back up the Way now. He released Kadie and took Inos in his arms.

"It's all over!" he shouted through the echoing thunders. "We have failed!"

Shandie shouted, "No! Do something!"

Inos kissed her husband's cheek and hugged him.

Gath said, "Oh, shit!" in a manly baritone.

Then his prescience warned him. He yelled, and grabbed hold of Kadie.

The resistance collapsed. All of the assorted freedom fighters tumbled helpless to the floor: imps, gnomes, jotnar . . . Only Thaïle remained, a tiny defiant figure wrapped in the angry blasts of the Covin's power. For a heart-rending moment the demigod alone defied the overweening sorcery.

Then Thaïle also yielded. She cried out and was wreathed in fire. Brighter and brighter she blazed, echoes of her despair tearing at the onlookers. Despair and surrender—it was the inevitable fate of Keepers.

"Let me go!" Kadie screamed, struggling wildly in her brother's clumsy embrace.

Rap's heart was being torn apart. A God's prophecy rang mercilessly in his ears: *You must lose a child!* This was what had been foretold. The fate of Pandemia swung in the balance now, and this was why the God had spoken. This was where duty led.

"Let her go!" he barked.

"But, Dad!" Gath protested, trying to avoid Kadie's kicks. She was squirming and clawing like a wildcat. Thaïle's howl was a knife in the eardrums, her flames blazing ever brighter.

"Let her go, I said!"

"But, Dad—"

"I know! *Let her go!*" Rap grabbed the pair of them. For a

moment all three of them wrestled together, until Rap hauled Kadie free from her brother's grasp.

And released her.

She ran. Gath tried to follow. Rap hung on to him, and then it was Gath who was the wildcat, fighting, kicking, screaming warnings. Inos, also, dived forward, and Rap somehow won a hand free from his other struggle to grab her arm. Again there was a three-way tussle.

Kadie raced across the empty floor, skirted the towering triumph of the Almighty, and hurled herself upon the blazing demigod. Inos screamed and turned her back. Rap still struggled with a son frantic to go to the rescue of his twin. Gath was taller, but all bone and sinew, and he could not break free of his father's muscle. There could be no rescue.

For a moment princess and pixie clung to each other in incandescent embrace. White inferno roared in the Chapel. Clothes, hair, flesh dissolved in brightness greater than the sun.

Sobbing, Gath slumped limply to the floor.

There was nothing left. They had gone. The vision faded, except for green after-images. Darkness flooded back into the Chapel, stillness and sorrow.

"You knew!" the boy howled, staring up at his father in disbelief.

Rap turned away, unable to meet the awful accusation in his son's face.

He had known ever since Gath came safely back to him that Kadie was the one he must lose, and he had been fairly sure how it must happen.

"Yes, he knew!" Inos said, and her glare was worse. "I hope he thinks it is worth it."

Kadie, Kadie!

The sorcerers were scrambling to their feet and bowing to the obscenity that rejoiced in the center, the exultant mirage of the Almighty. They were all votaries now. The ice on Keef's grave had melted.

The battle was over. Zinixo had won.

His monstrous image turned to look at the mundanes. Especially at Rap.

5

Dawn had long since reached Hub. Lord Umpily had not the faintest idea how long he had been crouching in his seat in the

Rotunda. His limbs were cramped, his clothing clammy with sweat. He could guess that the decisive struggle of the war was being fought and that he was trapped in the middle of the enemy's army. He suspected he was liable to be destroyed with it if his own friends won; he would certainly be executed as a spy if he were detected, but the worst part of his torment was that *he had no idea how the battle was going*! Ignorance was driving him crazy.

Ever since the Almighty had stopped the standing ovation with a single gesture, the Rotunda had been eerily silent. Everyone but Umpily had remained locked in a trance. Once in a while an involuntary sigh or murmur would rustle through the great hall, but that was all. He felt like a blind man watching a gladiatorial contest with his head in a bag. At first most of the Covin had looked south, then northeast. Then their faces had swung around to the southeast, but every eye had stared blankly at things he could not see.

To begin with, he had stared where the others were staring, but eventually his neck grew agonizingly stiff and he just crouched down low, as if somehow that position might hide him from so many sorcerers. Once in a while one of the congregation would cry out, and sometimes one of the older ones would crumple as if overcome by too much effort; most of them revived in due course and joined in the struggle again. He had wondered often whether he might try to slip out unnoticed, but he had never found the courage to try.

Besides, in his humble fashion he was one of the players, so he may as well stay and see the ending. He might be saved if Shandie won. Otherwise he would die forgotten, but that was any soldier's duty.

In the center, the Almighty sat motionless, glaring southeastward. Apart from that one change of direction, he had not moved for an hour. The vast bulk of the Opal Throne could make even an imperor seem small; Zinixo looked like a child in it.

Suddenly he came alive. He jumped down and raised his arms overhead, waving his fists in triumph. The audience recovered at the same instant—it surged to its feet and roared.

They were back into standing ovation again.

That one probably did not last more than fifteen minutes. Of course Umpily knew then who had won and who had lost, but he banged his bruised hands together and screamed with the worst of them. Why? he wondered. Why bother to hide any longer? Why not just cock a snoot at the little horror and die with honor?

Again the Almighty gestured for silence. Again it came instantly. His votaries resumed their seats, grinning and panting with excitement.

Three seats away, the young faun turned to Umpily, smirking and raising an eyebrow. Asking a question?

"Oh, yes! Marvelous!" Umpily said, forcing his mouth into a rictus of smile.

The rustic frowned, puzzled. Then threateningly. His gray eyes widened in astonishment. Power had nothing to do with age or employment—quite likely the kid was capable of analyzing the fat imp's enchantment and seeing that it was not a loyalty spell, that the man inside it was not a sorcerer . . .

Then everyone's attention flicked back to the center. Zinixo had risen, and now he spoke for the first time all night.

"Bring them in! Welcome your new associates!" His voice was the deepest Umpily had ever heard.

The floor of the Rotunda shimmered and was suddenly crowded. Towering blond jotnar, hulking trolls, dozens of tiny gnomes, elegant elves. In sorcerous wars the losers were not necessarily destroyed. Sometimes they joined the ranks of the victors, and this must be Shandie's army.

He had done very well, Umpily decided. There were hundreds of them. But in the end the odds had been impossible— Zinixo had gathered four or five times as many. So now the rebels were kneeling to him. Probably every sorcerer in all Pandemia was here, loyal to the Almighty. The war was over. Never in the history of the world had anything like this happened before.

Who in the Name of Evil were those pointy-eared people?

Umpily shot a nervous sideways glance at the young faun, but he was entranced by the spectacle unfolding on the floor and had apparently forgotten the mysterious mundane. How long until he remembered? The three dwarvish women were muttering excitedly together.

A rustle of movement . . . The defeated sorcerers had risen to their feet. They bowed once to the throne and were dismissed. They vanished from the floor. The seats between Umpily and the faun groaned in protest as two enormous half-naked jotnar appeared on them; a pair of silken-garbed elves flickered in on his left. All over the Rotunda, places that had been empty were now filled.

And down on the floor their departure had revealed—

Warlock Raspnex and an elf, who must surely be Warlock Lith'rian. Those two were kneeling. A group of others stood nearby—Shandie! Impress Eshiala and the child. And King Rap, with a blond woman who must be his wife—Umpily could recall seeing her at court many years ago, back in Ythbane's time. And a gangly jotunn youth in sailor breeches. Was that the boy Shandie had seen in the pool? Umpily did not know and probably never would.

A slight disturbance amid the seats at the far side and Witch Grunth appeared on the floor alongside the other two wardens. She knelt, also.

Ex-wardens.

Zinixo had resumed his seat and was leering joyfully at this ragtag collection of captives. An eager hush settled over the Rotunda.

"We are merciful toward those who were misguided." The usurper rubbed his massive hands. "But We draw the line at wardens. You three We shall deal with at Our leisure! We wish to be entertained. You will devise the program yourselves. You will propose for Our consideration the longest, most painful deaths you can imagine!"

Lith'rian bent over in obeisance. "We shall be honored," he announced in an elf's sweet tones, "to provide Your Godhood with any amusement we can."

Raspnex and Grunth proclaimed their agreement together.

Umpily shivered. They meant it! As votaries they would co-operate fully in their own executions if ordered to do so.

"Stand aside now!" Zinixo commanded with a wave. "Let us see what other fish we have caught in our net."

The wardens scrambled to their feet and moved away. They chose a location beyond the Gold Throne, where Umpily could not see them very well. But that did not matter, because the dwarf had turned his smirk on the mundanes.

"Welcome back to Hub, Emshandar!"

"May the Gods rot your guts!"

Zinixo was too triumphant to be displeased. He probably welcomed Shandie's show of resistance. "And your wife's beauty was not exaggerated! I shall enjoy making her acquaintance."

Shandie opened his mouth again and was apparently struck dumb.

"Your understudies have begun to find their tasks onerous," the dwarf continued teasingly. "But we can dispense with understudies from now on, can't we? *Come and pay homage, Emshandar!*"

Umpily could not suppress a whimper when the rightful imperor hurried forward and mounted the two steps to his own throne. As Shandie knelt to the usurper occupying it, Umpily closed his eyes.

Utter disaster!

"And dear Rap!" the hateful, sepulchral voice said.

Umpily opened his eyes. Shandie had finished his public apologies and protestations of future obedience. He had returned to the floor and was gazing up at the Almighty with starry adoration.

Zinixo had lost interest in the imperor. His manner implied that he had left the best till last.

"Will you plead with Us, King Rap? Plead for mercy? Plead for a quick death, relatively speaking?"

"It would be a waste of breath!" The faun did not seem to speak loudly, but his voice filled the hall. He was not dressed like a king. His garments were commonplace workman's garb, bedraggled and muddy; his hair was a tangle. He had his feet apart and his arms folded; he held his chin high. He looked like a king.

His wife, in a white blouse and a green skirt, was a queen born. Her haughty gaze dismissed that upstart on the throne as unworthy of serious consideration. Consciously or not, the youth at her other side had adopted the same defiant, folded-arm stance as his father.

Again Zinixo rubbed his hands. "Will you plead then for your wife or the people of Krasnegar?"

"Never."

Umpily shivered. How long could a prisoner defy a captor as ruthless as Zinixo? What price would the king be willing to pay for his pride?

"Indeed? Then let Us see how your son moves you. Come here, brat."

The jotunn boy began to walk forward. He shot a look of horror back at his father, but he did not stop walking until he stood before the Opal Throne. There he spread his feet, folded his arms again, and raised his head to stare up at the dwarf.

The Almighty leaned forward. "We are going to kill you. Slowly."

There was a moment's pause. Then the boy said, "With the throne. Go ahead, toad." And he spat on the steps.

The Rotunda buzzed with anger.

Umpily was speechless. He was speechless mostly because his mouth was as dry as a mummy and his tongue had shriveled to ashes. There was an excellent reason why spitting was a sign of contempt—only a very brave man could spit in the face of danger.

"You have foresight!" the dwarf exclaimed.

"A little," the kid admitted. "Prescience." The husky adolescent voice was almost as steady as his father's had been.

"And what do you foresee?"

"About five minutes left now. After that—I don't know."

Zinixo chortled. "Well, you will find out! This morning you predicted that your father would squash Us like a bug. Now you are going to plead with him to beg Us for your life."

"Never!" But the word lacked the conviction his father had given it.

The boy's legs collapsed under him. He sprawled to the floor and rolled over on his back. After a moment, he turned his head to look to his parents. The king and queen of Krasnegar each had an arm around the other and were watching the drama in silence.

The Opal Throne floated off its dais, carrying the Almighty. When it was directly over the young jotunn, it stopped. A dozen trolls could not have lifted that great monolith, but it hung rock steady in midair, less than an arm's length above its spread-eagled victim.

It began to settle downward. Slowly, very slowly. Inexorably. Gradually the boy disappeared from Umpily's view.

A minute.

Umpily could hear himself whimpering. He knew his tears would surely betray him, but he was past caring.

Two minutes.

The throne must be almost on the boy's chest—it was hard to believe that there was still room for a living body in that gap. Only one hand and a wrist showed now. The boy himself had said five minutes. He had overestimated.

"Well, dear Rap?" The dwarf's soft question seemed as loud

as trumpets in that dread silence. "You still have your powers, such as they are. Will you stop his heart to spare him an agonizing death?"

The king of Krasnegar said nothing.

"You had better start pleading soon!" The dwarf seemed annoyed, as if his enjoyment was less than he had hoped.

"I shall never ask favor of you!"

"Inosolan, then? Will you not try to persuade your son to plead with his father to plead with Us?"

The queen said nothing, but she glanced sideways at her husband as if puzzled by his silence.

"Oh, well!" Zinixo growled. "Juice time."

The throne sagged down another inch. A faint gasp came from under it . . .

"*Stop!*" a shrill voice screamed. All eyes swung around in astonishment. "Monsters! Do you not see that you serve the Evil?"

To his unspeakable horror, Umpily realized that he was on his feet, waving his arms, and that was himself he could hear yelling hysterically. "To crush an innocent boy? You are all guilty! Atrocity! Throw off his foul compulsion! He is evil, evil, evil . . ."

Something lifted him bodily, sucked him through the air, and dropped him stunningly on the floor in front of the throne. He sprawled helplessly, winded, dazed. Zinixo peered down at him in furious disbelief.

"Who . . . ? Well, well, well! It is the blubber man himself! Who removed your loyalty spell, worm?"

Umpily raised his face from the stone. His nose hurt like the torments of the cursed and was probably bleeding. Under the throne, the boy was trying to twist his head around to see what was happening.

"Well?" the dwarf thundered.

"Olybino," Umpily mumbled. Oh, his nose! And his knees! And what crazy impulse of honor had ever moved him to try to be a hero? He struggled to rise and only managed to get his elbows under him.

"Olybino!" Zinixo screeched. "You have been spying on Us all these last three weeks? Foul slug! We shall devise an especially lingering . . . Or were you volunteering to take the brat's place? You have left it too late! There is no room for one of your size!"

He smiled, showing his pebbly dwarvish teeth all around the

Rotunda. His massed minions roared with obedient laughter at their leader's wit.

A quiet whisper came from under the throne: "Thanks for trying, sir."

Umpily gulped. "Couldn't let you steal all the heroism, lad. You're doing great!" Funny—he felt better. He really did. Clean again. He glanced around and saw Shandie staring at him with a very perplexed expression. He knew what it was like to be under a votary spell . . .

The laughter had faded away.

"We shall leave the mundane snoop for later," the dwarf announced. "It would be a shame to waste so much tallow—turn him into a candle for the coronation, perhaps? But now . . . King Rap? Your last chance to save the brat!"

Umpily looked in horror at the faun. Everyone looked to the faun.

In silence, he sank to his knees. His wife joined him as calmly as if they were in a chapel service.

From under the deadly throne a muffled voice shouted, "Dad, no! Mom! Don't!"

"We do not plead with the madman, Gath," the king said. He raised clasped hands. "I direct my prayers to the Gods! Unworthy as I am, and acknowledging my past sins against Them, I call on Them now. God of Rescues, save us, I beg You!"

Zinixo seemed disconcerted. He frowned. "There is no God of Rescues!"

"There is now!" said a new voice.

The sun dimmed. Three thousand voices screamed in pain, six thousand hands covered eyes to shut out the wondrous glare.

A real God stood within the Rotunda.

God at War:

> There saw she direst strife; the supreme God
> At war with all the frailty of grief,
> Of rage, of fear, anxiety, revenge,
> Remorse, spleen, hope, but most of all despair.
>
> Keats, *Hyperion II, 1 92*

❡ THIRTEEN ❡

The game again

1

Zinixo had shriveled into a knot in the depths of the Opal
Throne, leaving nothing of himself visible except boots and
shins and forearms. The king and queen of Krasnegar were already on their knees; the little princess imperial buried her face
in her mother's skirt. Everyone else tried to kneel to the God.

The seating had been built for imps. Even they had trouble
finding room for kneeling. So did djinns and merfolk. Jotnar
and trolls just made room, and sounds of splintering timber exploded through the Rotunda. Then there was only the child
weeping and Zinixo's shrill screaming.

"Let there be silence!" the God said, and there was silence.
The voice of a God was not especially loud, yet it rolled like
thunder.

Sounding muffled, Gath said, "*KADIE?* Is that you, Kadie?"

"No longer," the God said. *"Come out from under that
throne, silly!"*

Gath squirmed and wriggled until he got his arms free and
could gain leverage on the base of the throne. Then he hauled
himself out, began to rise ... He choked, averting his face
away from the incandescent glory. He settled on his knees beside Lord Umpily and bowed his head in reverence.

Slowly, all over the Rotunda, hands were rising to cover
eyes as people peered over seats and bent shoulders. The God

was a figure of roiling white flame, too bright to look upon, although They cast no shadow.

The Opal Throne crashed to the paving with a bang that shook the Rotunda and could be felt through the bones. Zinixo bounced. Ears rang.

"Rap?" the God said, and Their voice, although still tuneful and feminine, was subtly different. *"Why do you weep?"*

"For the loss of . . ." His voice broke. "Loss of my daughter!"

"But she is not lost. Rather do We weep for you, who are mortal and transient! This glory We know should by rights have been yours. Do you understand now?"

"I understand. Forgive my lack of faith, God."

"You see now why you had to be warned?"

"I do. There would not have been time, else."

"Gods are made of love, but there is more than one kind of love! And Inosolan? Do you also accept?"

There was a long pause, then the queen said, "The Gods' will be done."

There was another pause before the God continued, still in the second voice. *"It will suffice. We are the God of Rescues, for in our mortal form We prayed for rescue and We did rescue, each to each. It is traditional for a new God to announce Their presence by a public miracle, so that Their name may be added to the lists. All now present bear witness! We hereby decree, as token of Our Godhead, that this chamber and this place shall be for all time proof against the use of sorcery."*

"Great!" Gath said. He was closest of all—it seemed amazing that the white radiance did not scorch him. "What happens with the merfolk?"

"That, too, of course!" the God said snappily, in Their first voice. *"We'd thought of that, stupid."*

"Sorry," Gath muttered.

"Now, Sorcerers, We shall see what good you can find in the evil of this day."

With those dread words, the God vanished.

The first to recover was the dwarf.

Zinixo leaped from the throne and sprinted toward the eastern exit. Dwarves were not built for sprinting, and several male jotnar were sitting next to the passageway he had chosen. They sprang over the edge and plunged into the canyon as he passed beneath them. Whether any of them actually landed on him is unknown, but he was caught before he reached the door. He screamed once.

The jotnar returned to the auditorium, carrying him. They paraded around the arena, waving to the hysterically jubilant crowd. There were four of them—that much is certain, because two circled clockwise and two counterclockwise. Later reports that the usurper had been ripped into five pieces may therefore have been slightly exaggerated.

2

The loyalty spell had snapped in a pang of heartbreaking loss. Shandie felt as if he had just awakened from a nightmare, or discovered that his best friend was a traitor. He needed time to adjust, and if he felt that way, having been enthralled for only a few minutes, what of those who had been Zinixo votaries for years? They might not recover for months. At last he had a chance to speak with his wife and child . . . He turned to Eshiala as the jotnar went raining down on the dwarf. Zinixo screamed.

The killers' lightning-fast reaction told Shandie that he had no time for family or personal feelings. The next few minutes would be a pivot point in history. No one had expected this! With the old order in ruins, a new order must be proclaimed or chaos would prevail. *Something* would replace what Zinixo had torn down. The new millennium began now, for better or for worse. It was up to Shandie to seize control of the gathering.

He ran across to the Opal Throne—passing Lord Umpily, who was just now struggling to his feet—and sprang up onto the seat the dwarf had so recently vacated. He was standing there with his arms raised in triumph as the blood-spattered giants returned and marched around, waving their gruesome trophies. He let the first hubbub fade a little, then bellowed at the top of his lungs:

"Praise to the Gods for this deliverance!"

A ragged "Amen!" rolled through the Rotunda.

The audience had given him its attention, but only for a moment. Perhaps he had an advantage in that he had never been a sorcerer. If sorcery was banned from the chamber, then most of the audience must be feeling blind and deaf, but he could sense their mood changing by the second as they began to comprehend all the implications of the God's miracle.

The thrones of the Four had disappeared. No matter . . .

"Wardens, take your places!"

The three shot him odd glances. Then Lith'rian, Raspnex, and Grunth stalked to the platforms where those thrones had been. A mutter of disagreement rumbled and grew like an approaching earthquake. Men were rising to their feet.

"Emine's Protocol is ended!" Shandie cried at the top of his voice. "The new protocol begins!"

That was a little better. That was more what the audience wanted. It raised a halfhearted cheer. But other voices were rising, also. Imminent riot crackled in the air like lightning.

"I made certain promises!" Shandie yelled. "I now confirm them! Sorcerer Ishist?"

Gnomes? What did the emperor want with gnomes? The muttering dwindled as speakers paused to listen. Some of those who had risen sat down again.

"I am here, Imperor!"

The thin voice was barely audible. Half the crowd said *Sssh!* to the other half.

"I stand by my promise to Oshpoo. I shall pull my legions from Guwush! Will you save time and further bloodshed? When the orders are cut, will you convey them to the troops by sorcery?"

"Gladly we will!"

The hubbub died to an astonished muttering as the spectators realized that history was taking shape in front of their eyes.

"Witch Grunth?"

The huge woman stood on the western dais, hunched and grizzled, eyeing the young imperor with open skepticism. "Yes, Mundane Brother of the Center?"

"I shall take immediate steps to end the impressment of trolls in Pithmot! You have our word."

She bared her great fangs. "My son is more concerned with that than I am. Convince him of your good faith—if you can."

Sweat trickled into Shandie's eyes. If he could not even hold the wardens on his side, then explosion was inevitable. "I hereby appoint him proconsul with plenipotentiary powers. Will that satisfy you?"

A troll? Astonishment rippled across the hall. Some of the imps cried out in disgust, but that rallied the other races. A gruff bass voice began a cheer and it was taken up. That was better, but there was still no real enthusiasm. Shandie caught his breath. At eighteen he had begun his military career in earnest when he faced down the Creslee Mutiny. This was worse than that, because he had a wife and child here with him. He had learned a few things since those days, though.

"Friends, we are one warden short. Let us give tribute to Warlock Olybino, who died to proclaim the new protocol! A minute's silence for a hero and a martyr!"

It was a sleazy trick, but it worked. They had all seen Olybino die. Most of them had helped kill him.

Of course only Shandie himself could end the silence. He allotted the dead hero about forty seconds, then spoke again. "The warlock decreed that in future new wardens should be elected, and I heartily agree. Let us make that a keystone of the new protocol that we must now forge! Let his own replacement be the first elected warden! Whom do you wish to be the new warlock of the east?"

The reaction was even faster than he had expected. The audience roared a name.

Rap and Inos and their son had been locked in a three-way embrace, mourning their own loss and paying no heed to millennia turning. Now the king broke loose and swung around, his face black.

"No!" Rap said.

Shandie chuckled silently. Some chance!

He raised his arms and his voice again. "He declines! Tell me once more: Whom do you wish to be the fourth warden?"

This time the roar was instantaneous and seemed likely to lift the dome off the Rotunda.

"You seem to be the unanimous choice, your Majesty!" Shandie said.

The faun scowled horribly and looked to his wife and son. They grinned at him.

"No!" Rap said.

Only two or three people in all history had ever refused a warden's throne, and this made five times for him. He had invented the protocol, led the revolt, been the only sorcerer in the world not votarized by Zinixo, and he had no mundane loyalties except to his own obscure little kingdom, not even a loyalty of race. His prayer had brought the God. He was the inevitable choice.

Shandie looked around cheerfully. "We must convince a faun, brothers and sisters! Tell me that name again."

Louder still: *RAP!*

Rap glared at Shandie and shook his head.

With anyone else, Shandie might have brought up the daughter's sacrifice, but not with this man.

"King Rap! Remember the millennium! Will you have the history books mourn for what might have been? 'If only Rap had accepted the warlock's throne,' they will say, 'then the bad times might have been averted.' "

Rap scowled.

His wife gave him a gentle push.

With a grimace, he stalked across to the vacant platform where the Gold Throne had once stood. He stopped before it, paused for a moment, head down, as if in thought. The Rotunda was breathless. Then he turned.

"I have conditions! Four conditions."

"Name them!"

"First, there shall be no more votarism."

"Agreed!" Shandie said, and looked to the audience. "Agreed?" He did not ask the wardens. At the moment they did not matter.

"Agreed!" roared the assembled sorcerers.

"And no more shielding! Sorcery shall be done openly, and never to do harm!"

"Agreed!"

Again Rap pulled a face, as if he had been hoping for an excuse to withdraw. "Third . . . You heard the God decree this building immune to sorcery. This is Longday. Let us hold a Sorcerers' Moot here on Longday every year—to elect wardens, to judge their performance, and to approve their actions."

This time the roar was louder yet, and tailed away slowly. Shandie glanced around. Raspnex was leering. Grunth looked impressed. Lith'rian was white with fury.

Rap seemed to sigh. "And finally, I think we need a Council of Sorcery to advise the wardens. Twelve, one delegate elected from each race. Their first task will be to draw up the text of the new protocol."

The cheering began slowly for that one, then surged higher and higher as the audience saw the implications. Shandie had never heard an inkling of this proposal before, but it was brilliant. It would shackle the wardens hand and foot and neck, as the Emine's Protocol never had. Rap could not possibly have made that up on the spur of the moment. He must have foreseen this whole little drama, but when had he had time to do that?

Three thousand sorcerers were on their feet now, a rhythmic shout of *Rap! Rap! Rap!* beating the air like a drum.

The new warlock stepped up on the platform and bowed to the assembly.

3

This could go on all day! Inos looked around the crowded rotunda. Everyone seemed ready to stay put until winter. The fat imp, whoever he was, was sitting all alone on the floor, clutching a handkerchief to his bleeding nose. He seemed to have forgotten it, though, being totally engrossed in the proceedings. Shandie was making another speech, something to do with elections for the proposed Council of Sorcery. Glittering in his orders and decorations up there on the throne, he was displaying a remarkable skill in politics, but he had been trained for that all his life. What of his family? Ignored if not forgotten, Eshiala knelt on the floor, trying to comfort a hungry, terrified, and desperate child.

Inos herself had not had anything to eat yet, either, and felt faint because of it.

And what of Krasnegar? Against his will, Rap had been sucked into a geopolitical swamp. He would do a fine job, but he would not wriggle free of it in short order, so Inos would have to attend to their kingdom by herself. Gath? Gath was staring entranced at his father the warlock, but Rap would have no more spare time for fathering than he would for ruling Krasnegar, and the thought of a fourteen-year-old heir apparent loose in the jungles of the Imperial court was enough to give her a migraine. Once the mothers of Hub learned about him, he wouldn't last a week.

Inos opened her mouth—

And then closed it. Gath was still only a boy, but he had fought with sorcerers, sailed with raiders, and proved himself a hero in public—and that was just this morning. What else he might have achieved in the last couple of months did not bear thinking about. If she tried to order her son around now like the child he was, she would create a major conflict. Tact was needed.

"Gath?" she whispered.

He jumped and looked down at his mother with his father's gray eyes. "Mom?"

"I need your help!"

"Oh?" He swelled. "Yes, Mom?" His smile revealed the
tooth that Brak had broken for him, the day they left
Krasnegar. She wondered if young Brak had been rotting in the
royal dungeon ever since.

"Krasnegar!"

He blinked as if he had never heard the name before. "What
about it?"

"I must go back there! You have sorcerer friends, don't
you?"

"Yes!" He beamed. "Several, actually."

"I knew I could depend on you! Come on, then."

She walked over to Eshiala. Even such beauty as the impress' was barely proof against such a day. She looked up with
pathetic relief as she saw help approach.

Inos smiled comfortingly. "This will go on for hours!" she
said. "Why don't you come and have lunch with me?"

As they left the auditorium, Inos looked back and saw both
Rap and Shandie staring after them. She waved a cheerful farewell and kept on going, along a corridor half full of stacked
lumber.

"I'm not sure I know the way!" Eshiala said.

"Master Jaurg can find it. Can't you?" Inos said.

The blind youth smiled sadly. He had a hand on Gath's
shoulder. "Not easily, your Majesty. Once we are outside the
Rotunda, then I shall be a sorcerer again."

"Of course—foolish of me. Well, let's just try. I wonder
where all the workmen are?"

"Longday is a holiday," the impress pointed out. "But what
if there are guards on the outer doors?"

"You're the impress!" Inos said cheerfully. "Order them to
report to Guwush immediately. Gath, can you carry Uomaya?"

Gath obviously realized now how he had been trapped. He
scowled, but he lifted the little girl. Maya was almost beyond
protest.

"Just don't tell me to comb my hair!" he muttered crossly.

"I was thinking of it," Inos said.

It was early morning in Krasnegar. The sky was a washy
blue, the sun lower than expected and the air cool, as the royal
party materialized in the forecourt of the castle. A few wandering pedestrians gaped in rank amazement. The man-at-arms at
the gate dropped his pike with a clang.

"Well, it's still here, anyway!" Inos said. Dear, dowdy, down-at-the-heels little town! How small and shabby it looked!

Registering relief, Gath deposited a squirming Maya on the cobbles. "Everything seems all right." He grinned. "We're going to eat soon! Not you, though, Mom." His prescience was working again.

Inos shivered as the climate bit through her thin Thumian skirt and blouse. "Why not me?"

"Because the council's in session!"

She felt a rush of relief that made her tremble. If the council was still meeting, then the kingdom had not dissolved in civil war. And it had not been flattened by the usurper. "Who's in charge?"

"Er—That's queen's work." Gath's face had assumed an odd expression. "Jaurg and I will be disposing of a roast kid." He glanced at the impress. "With your help, too, ma'am, of course."

"Excellent beer you have here, Atheling," Sorcerer Jaurg remarked with a smile—either to show that Gath was not the only one with prescience, or just to give his mother something else to worry about. Gath was a beer drinker now?

Eshiala was staring up in astonishment at the spiky towers of Inisso's castle, black against the pale northern sky. Maya had uttered a whoop and gone racing off after the white pigeons. Bystanders were dropping to their knees to honor their long-lost queen. Ignoring his fallen pike, the guard rushed in through the gate to spread the news.

"Come on, then!" Inos said, starting for the gate. She waved graciously at the kneeling citizens, and they began to cheer. Pigeons clattered noisily upward to escape the princess imperial.

They were halfway across the bailey when a small impish woman in a fancy gown and bonnet came scurrying out the main door to meet them.

Inos felt a jolt of surprise. Who was this? If the council was indeed in session—and while Gath might evade questions, he was never wrong when he did issue a prediction—then officials like Lin would be unavailable. But why had the guards summoned this unknown matron? The woman curtseyed. "You are welcome, welcome, your Majesty! Welcome back!" Whoever she was, her manner hinted that she was returning the keys.

"Thank you. It is good to be back."

The small woman glanced at the others and her eyes widened. "And Prince Gathmor! You have grown, your Highness, if I may say so!" She bobbed a smaller curtsey to him, glanced over Eshiala and Maya inquisitively and then said, "And his Majesty is also well?"

Inos drew a deep breath, but fortunately Gath's supernormal reactions diverted her explosion.

"Oh, Dad will be along later. He's busy saving the world, still. Mom, this is Mistress Sparro."

"I don't believe we have met?" Inos inquired sweetly.

"I never had the honor of being presented, ma'am. The chairman and I were married after you left."

"The chairman?"

Gath was purple with suppressed secrets. "The chairman of the council, of course, Mom. Who do you think has been holding the kingdom together while you've been away?"

That was precisely what Inos did not know. Gath was only aware of such things because he was going to find them out shortly. He was not going to tell her anything.

"Indeed, and my husband has done a wonderful job, if I may say so!" Mistress Sparro declared. Modesty was apparently not one of her greater afflictions.

Inos would prefer to judge the state of the kingdom for herself. "Eva and Holi?"

"They're fine!" Gath said enthusiastically. "Boy, has Holi grown!"

That was all right, then. The children could be greeted when she had time to greet them properly. "Mistress Sparro, please see to our guests." Inos pulled a name out of the sky. "Lady Aquiala and her daughter, and Master Jaurg . . ."

Mistress Sparro was curling her lip at the young jotunn. His breeches might be adequate dress in Nordland, but Krasnegarians regarded short sleeves as daring and bare chests as obscene.

"Master Jaurg is our new court sorcerer," Inos added spitefully. With Mistress Sparro's squeal of alarm ringing in her ears, the queen swept into her castle.

She stormed along corridors and raced up stairs—always stairs, in Krasnegar. People leaped out of her way with cries of astonishment and joy. She threw open the door of the council chamber and marched in.

There were only a dozen or so gathered along the big table.

At this time of year, most of the citizens had duties elsewhere. Familiar faces turned with frowns to the intruder and broke into smiles of delight. Chairs scraped back. Elderly men and women heaved themselves to their feet, and for a moment nobody said a word. They were, perhaps, too overcome with surprise. Inos was completely out of breath.

And speechless. The man at the head of the table was old Captain Efflio—retired sailor, and a recent arrival in Krasnegar. She had forgotten all about Efflio, the most junior member of the council. But of course when Kadie had dragged her away from a meeting of the council, she had put the captain in charge. He had been the only one present not worked up over some trivial argument, and she had expected to be gone for only a few minutes. So *Efflio* had continued to run the kingdom all this time?

She smiled then, at the others, the lifetime friends and loyal subjects. Ancient old Foronod, Kratharkran the smith huger than ever, Mistress Oglebone, ancient Bishop Havermore, Lin with his monstrous walrus mustache . . . She was home, and it was all right. Home was safe!

"Good morning!" she said.

"Welcome back, your Majesty!" Efflio bowed, spoiling the effect with a loud wheeze. The spell was broken and all the rest of the council echoed him, bowing and curtseying.

"It is wonderful to be home! And I gather you ladies and gentlemen have kept the plants watered while I was away? You are looking very well, Factor . . ."

By the time she had moved around the table, greeting all of them—even allowing Lin to give her a hug—Efflio had moved away from the president's chair. He wore a nervous smile and his wheezing was more noticeable.

Inos had recovered her breath. "And you, Captain! I gather you have managed to keep the dogs and cats from coming to blows?" Muddled metaphor! Oh, well, they must all know what she meant.

"My honor, ma'am!"

"I am most grateful," Inos said. And lucky! Probably only this wily old outsider could have kept peace between imp and jotunn for so long. She sat down, and the others resumed their seats. Clutching a bundle of papers, Efflio moved to a vacant chair.

"Can you bring me up to date quickly?" Inos said. She saw dismay on the impish faces, especially Lin's. "Or perhaps I should start by bringing you up to date! It is a very long story, though. I am well, as you can see. I have been traveling in far lands, involved in very important matters."

She considered telling them that she had begun her day in Thume, at the other end of the world, and then decided to take it more slowly. "My husband is well, also. He has assumed some duties that may require a good deal of his time. He has just been appointed—" she drew a deep breath "—warden of the east."

Jaws dropped.

Eyebrows rose. King Rap had always denied being a sorcerer.

"Prince Gath has returned with me, and he is well. You probably won't recognize him! And I gather Eva and Holi are well, also?"

The pain under her heart throbbed. She fell silent, waiting for the inevitable question—Princess Kadie? What could she tell them? Probably nothing at all, because the Gods kept Their origins secret.

"It's wonderful to know you are all safe!" the bishop proclaimed. "We should have the bell rung! And a special service of thanksgiving, of course! How soon do you suppose his Majesty will be able . . ."

They were not going to ask!

Well, that was a problem to consider at leisure, or perhaps a solution to a problem. She waited for a momentary pause in the ecclesiastical diatribe—

"Now, how fares Krasnegar?" She turned to Efflio.

He shook his head sadly. "In dire straits, ma'am! Or it will be soon. No ships have come this year—none at all, none even from Nordland!"

"Well, that's hardly surprising!" Inos said. Then she registered their blank stares. They did not know! This was sleepy little Krasnegar at the rim of the world, and it had never heard the news.

"There has been a major war! The goblins invaded the Impire. Most of Julgistro has been devastated. That's why they sent no ships! And the jotnar have, ah, other plans this year."

"And why no goblins came?" old Foronod exclaimed in his creaky voice.

"Of course! The goblins have been virtually wiped out."

She watched them wrestle with the horrible tidings. True disaster was hard to comprehend in Krasnegar, where a lost fishing boat could plunge the kingdom into mourning. Except for Efflio and the bishop, none of them had ever been more than ten leagues from home in their lives.

Efflio's wheezing was growing even louder. He was leaning back in his chair, struggling. Inos looked at him in alarm.

"I shall be . . . all right, ma'am. Just the shock." He chuckled with difficulty. "Relief, I mean! The Impire is safe?"

"It is now, but it has suffered a cruel blow."

"And we?" Lin said loudly from farther down the table. "Without the supplies from the south, Inos, we face serious shortages for the winter—salt and grain especially. Medicines, too. We were talking about it when you came in."

"Oh, that's all right!" She laughed, and saw their amazement. She was going to enjoy this . . .

The door creaked open, and a young man walked in with his eyes closed. He wore a floor-length black gown emblazoned with stars and occult symbols in gold and silver, and his conical hat almost reached the ceiling. His former wispy red beard had become a magnificent torrent of ginger hair reaching to his waist. He inclined his head respectfully to Inos and calmly headed for a vacant chair. The counselors gaped.

Gath's friend the sorcerer was very little older than Gath himself. Which of them had dreamed up that grotesque outfit?

"You may have need of me, ma'am," he remarked confidently.

"Indeed, I believe we do have need of you," Inos said, making the best of things. "Ladies and gentlemen, this is Master Jaurg, who has agreed to join us here for a while. As I told you, my husband will have other demands on his time in the near future. I have therefore appointed Master Jaurg court sorcerer in his absence."

A sorcerer? In *Krasnegar*? As Inos spoke the counsellors' names, the youth turned a grave blind face on each in turn and they shrank back in their chairs, almost gibbering. Obviously Jaurg was enjoying himself, and she could not honestly deny that she was, too.

"Now, Master Jaurg, we seem to have need for certain supplies. Salt, for example."

"Quite easy, ma'am. Just tell me where you want it put."

"And medicines?"

Jaurg opened his mouth and then paused. He turned a disapproving frown on Captain Efflio, whose labored breathing now sounded like a bag of newborn kittens on their way to the harbor. Sailors were notoriously superstitious.

"Is that noise necessary, Captain?"

Unable to speak, Efflio just shook his head.

"The captain is afflicted with asthma, Sorcerer," Inos said.

"Oh?" The jotunn's silver brows drooped lower. "Do you mind if I cure him, then?"

Sudden silence.

"Now, ma'am," the sorcerer said. "Medicines, you said. What do you need medicines for?"

4

The Queen's parlor at Krasnegar was a shabby, homely room. It had a lived-in air composed of peat scent mingled with hints of candles and polish and leather and dogs. The pictures and paneling had faded, the rug was worn almost threadbare in front of the sagging, overstuffed chairs. Accumulated clutter of generations lurked in corners, on bookshelves, all over the mantel shelf of an enormous stone fireplace—ornaments, well-thumbed volumes, stuffed birds, golden candlesticks, silver inkwells, carved crystal decanters.

Eshiala had never seen any chamber quite like it. Her parents would have dismissed it as hopelessly dowdy and old-fashioned, and it would certainly be spurned by servants within the palace in Hub. Yet somehow it fitted her mood like a favorite old slipper.

She felt more relaxed than she could remember being in months. Twelve months, probably—ever since Shandie had returned from Qoble and resumed their marriage. She had eaten a large meal. Maya had been whisked away by servants and Princess Eva. The usurper was dead, most horribly dead.

Ylo was dead, too, and Shandie was alive . . .

A small pile of peat smoldered in the great hearth, although the warmth was not needed. In fact, one of the windows was open, and a murmur of surf drifted up from the sea far below, but now Inos was pulling the drapes, leaving only a slit of light from each of the windows.

"What time is it anyway?"

Inos chuckled and settled into the opposing chair. "Middle of the afternoon, I think." She wriggled herself comfortable, pounding a stubborn cushion. "But Krasnegar time is not the same as Hubban time, or Thumian time, so I'm thoroughly confused."

"Will the sun set at all?"

"Not on Longday. It's never easy to tell the time in summer here. People forget to sleep for days, and then suddenly drop in their tracks. It can be quite funny to see."

"I should be going back."

Her hostess shook her head. "Shandie knows where you are. You'd be one more problem he doesn't need right now. Can't have two impresses around the palace! He knows where you are and he knows you're safe. I'm sure he's glad not to have to worry about you for the time being."

That was wonderful rationalization. What else was there to say?

The green eyes were as sharp as rapiers. "He still loves you, you know. He may not be very good at showing it, but I'm sure he still loves you. Shandie is a very clever man and he will want you back."

Eshiala nodded miserably. She was afraid of that. She did not love Shandie. She had never loved him. Ylo had taught her what love felt like, and it had been quite, quite different. Her heart had died with Ylo.

"An impress of Pandemia bearing another man's child?" she said. "That's treason! Shandie can have me put to death for that."

Inos laughed. "Not very likely!" She sounded quite sure, but she probably knew the imperor now much better than Eshiala ever had. "Never mind what he wants! What do *you* want?"

"I don't know. I honestly don't know." She had given the future no thought, except to acknowledge that it would be a desert, a barren solitude stretching as far as mind could reach, with no Ylo in it. With Ylo, anywhere would be a paradise. Without him, nowhere could be.

She would much prefer never to see the court again. A nunnery would suit her perfectly, or Krasnegar, even—any quiet haven where no one knew her or ever wanted to put her on display. But Maya was heir presumptive and belonged to the realm. Maya would be returned to the palace. Eshiala had lost the man she loved and now must lose her child, too.

Inosolan had lost a child today, also. A few hours ago she had watched her daughter burned away until not even ash remained. Not dead, but lost forever. If Inos could bear her bereavement so well, then Eshiala should try to be as strong. But few women could ever match Inos. She was determined and gentle, motherly and queenly, understanding and assertive, all at the same time.

"I am sorry about Kadie!" Eshiala blurted.

Inos shrugged wistfully. "The Gods warned us that we must lose a child. We had two years' warning, two years to adjust to the idea. And in a sense she is not really lost." She stared at the quietly hissing fire. "When I am as old as the castle, Kadie will still be as she is now. When Krasnegar crumbles to dust, she will be here to see. That takes a little getting used to, that idea! But it is a comfort."

"What will you tell the people?"

"Nothing. The Gods do not allow that secret to be spoken of. It seems that others will not even miss her. That helps, and yet it doesn't help, if you can—"

There was a tap on the door.

Inos stretched herself comfortably into her chair and covered a yawn. "That will be Shandie, I expect."

Eshiala quailed. "How can you tell?"

"Because I said I was not to be disturbed except by Rap or a visitor from the Impire. I didn't know what name he'd use. If you don't want to see him, then say so. He's not imperor here."

"He will have a sorcerer with him!"

Inos smiled grimly, not moving from her chair. "The castle gates are closed. I've never ordered that before! But the castle is shielded from sorcery, so he can't enter unless you want him to. Say the word and he will be sent away."

That thought conjured strange visions: the Impire besieging the castle at Krasnegar, the Imperial Navy in the harbor, an imperor bringing an army to rescue his daughter . . .

"Of course I must see him."

Inos smiled approvingly and rose. "May as well get it over with! I'll send him in here, then. You will not be disturbed." She came over and laid a comforting hand on Eshiala's shoulder. "Be honest, all right? Only absolute truth will serve now, for both of you. And for Maya, too."

Eshiala nodded, and was alone.

Ten minutes, she thought. Five minutes to send word to the gate and five more for Shandie to arrive. Perhaps a few more for Inos to lecture him. She stood at a window and stared out at the blue of the Winter Ocean, white scars of breakers over the reefs, white birds. She rehearsed her Speech, the Speech she had been preparing for three days, the Speech that would never come out the same way twice and reached no sort of ending but just went on and on.

She must, of course, submit to whatever he wanted. He was the imperor and would decide: to put her in a nunnery, send her into exile, chop off her head . . . or take her to bed. *Gods!* She shivered. Not that! Not so soon, please Gods! Lying on her back in the dark, with Shandie pulling up her nightdress and her trying not to remember Ylo's touch, Ylo's banter, Ylo's body . . .

She was standing by the fireplace when Shandie opened the door, came in briskly, and turned to close it. She sank to her knees on the hearth mat and bowed her head so she need not look at him as he strode across to her.

His silver-buckled shoes came into view, and then his pearl-gray hose as he knelt down, also, about an arm's length in front of her. What? Why? Was this some sort of trick? Disconcerted, she forgot the Speech completely. She froze. Only her heart was still alive, clamoring like an alarm bell.

"I came as soon as I could," he said. "I just couldn't get away any sooner! You do understand that?"

She nodded, not looking up. No matter how tightly she clenched her hands, they would not stop shaking.

"I am deeply, deeply sorry about Ylo," Shandie said. "I mourn him greatly. He was the most valuable aide I had or could ever hope for, but I shall miss him even more as a friend. I know your loss is far greater than mine, though. I offer my deepest sympathy."

She looked up then, shocked beyond measure, but the coal-black eyes were solemn. If this was some cruel mockery, then it was well hidden.

Shandie had always been thin. He was thinner. He was weatherbeaten and needed his second shave of the day. His plain gray doublet was nothing like the finery he had sported in the Rotunda. His eyes were burning brighter than ever. She could not meet them.

He seemed puzzled by her reaction. "Did you think . . . I honor his memory! If Ylo were here, I would make him a prince of the realm! He died defending my child and the woman I love—how can I not honor him? Had he lived, how could I not reward him? Nothing would be too good for him."

The lump in her throat was choking her. Why must he speak of Ylo?

"And he saved me, too, Eshiala. Did he tell you of that?"

She shook her head, staring at the hearth.

"No, he wouldn't. Ylo never saw himself as a hero, although he was, many times. He never took himself seriously. And he saved you at Yewdark. Oh, that unspeakable Ionfeu! If I ever set eyes on that man again, I shall have him racked!" Shandie growled furiously. "Hardgraa, too. Idiots! Blundering, witless *idiots*!"

"They meant well," she whispered.

"So did I, and I left you in the care of a pair of bungling cretins! Will you ever forgive me?"

"My lord! It is I who must ask forgiveness."

"No, it isn't!" Shandie snapped. He was blushing like a boy. "Eshiala, I was not faithful to you!"

But—

"I let Ylo talk me into . . . No, I will not blame him! I am responsible for my own sins. Waitresses, bar girls! It was disgraceful, and I am abjectly, thoroughly ashamed! I never did that before, you know, and I swear I never will again. Please, please, will you forgive me?"

She felt her face flame. "You mock me, my lord!"

"No! Never!"

"But Ylo and I—"

"That was nothing! You thought I was dead, didn't you?"

"Well, yes . . ."

"I did not have any such excuse!"

"Ylo said the gobl—"

"He wasn't lying. He saw me go down and the goblins take me. That's what he told you, isn't it? Well, then, Ylo did not lie to you. You believed yourself a widow. I knew I was committing adultery."

This was all, crazily, backward! A married woman carrying another man's child and her husband was asking forgiveness? She blinked tears away. "But I knew how Ylo was with women and I let him . . ."

"Ylo?" Shandie was trying to smile, although the red flames still burned on his cheeks. "Ylo was the most incredible womanizer the Impire has ever known. Of course I should have guessed what was going to happen when he said he had seen the most beautiful woman in the world in the magic pool— who else could it have been? But I didn't. You had no one else to turn to. You made the only possible decision. He didn't bargain, did he?"

"No. Never. It—"

"I was sure he wouldn't have. That was not his way. He would never have stooped to blackmail. He enjoyed the sport too much. But then he *married* you, right? And he gave his *life* for you! That's different. That's not the game he played with the others. Ylo loved you. He must have loved you. And you must have loved him? Must still love him, love his memory?"

She nodded, utterly bewildered.

Shandie sighed. "Who can blame you? Not me! I left my wife in the care of a blockhead and went off whoring across Julgistro! I need forgiveness far more than you do. If Ylo had ... This is easy to say now, Eshiala, but I swear I mean it. If Ylo had survived and the two of you wanted to live together, then I would agree to it. Divorce or something ... I don't know how it could have been done, and it doesn't matter now, because he isn't. But I swear I would not have stood between you."

"But why? Why?"

"Because I owed him my life. Because he was my friend and I admired him. Above all because I want you to be happy."

Nothing was coming out the way she had expected. Shandie was not behaving like a wronged husband at all. He was certainly not behaving like Shandie, cold and inscrutable. She had been prepared for that. Even bluster and threats would have been easier to deal with than this.

"I carry Ylo's *child*!"

He nodded. "So Inos told me. And Rap told her. And Rap says it's a girl, so it—she, I mean—she won't come between Maya and the throne. And if we—" He stopped and swallowed. "If I later have a son, then he will take precedence, so it will matter even less. Bring forth Ylo's daughter, darling, and we shall raise her as our own." He smiled sadly, as if hurt by her astonishment. "Did you think I would abandon a child of Ylo's? Or of yours? Never! Nobody will know. As far as the world is concerned, you and I have been living together as man and wife all these months, so she will be another princess, Maya's sister."

He held out his hands. She took them. Her fingers were icy and his were hot. He stood up, raising her. She braced herself, thinking he would kiss her, but he led her across to one of the two matching, overstuffed chairs, then turned and went to sit on the other. He stretched out his legs, crossed his ankles, and studied her.

"I have much unhappy news," he muttered.

"My lord?" She saw him wince. "I mean, what news?"

"Well, first, your sister is far from well. Emthoro's in even worse condition. They have both had an Evilish, terrible time. I got a couple of sorcerers to help, and they did help them a bit, but they're both in need of a lot of care." He glanced around the friendly, cozy parlor. "I wonder if Queen Inos would take Ashia in? A quiet little refuge like this may be exactly what she requires."

Ashia? In a backwater hickdom like Krasnegar? *Boggle!*

Shandie scratched his cheek and studied his boots. "You want to stay here for a while? You and Maya?"

"I haven't thought about it." She had expected to be told what to do, as always. Was this Shandie's own idea, or Inosolan's?

"It might be a good idea, you know! Eshiala, I had no inkling—The Impire's in chaos! Not just Julgistro and Pithmot—all of it! The army's wandering all over the place, there's famine and riot and . . ." He shook his head. ". . . and chaos! Why open revolution hasn't broken out already, I have no idea. Thank the Gods we now have sorcery to help us. At least I hope we do! Rap's working on the wardens and this new council of his right now." He thumped a fist on the arm of the chair and a cloud of dust rose. "*Gods!* I hope he can pull it off!"

"King Rap? Pull what off?"

Shandie looked up again, and she saw a worry there she had never seen before. "Don't you understand? If votarism reappears, then all the sorcerers will vanish again. And if that happens, then everything's going to fall apart! We need them desperately! Zinixo may not have been the prophesied disaster at all. He's gone, but the millennium will still happen. And it's all my fault!"

"Yours? But that's not fair!"

He shrugged. "Who ever said anything about fair? As far as the people are concerned, I've been imperor for half a year and just about destroyed the Impire! They're burning me in effigy."

"Shandie, that's terrible! Awful! Can't you explain?"

"No."

"Why not?" she demanded.

"Who would believe me? It would seem like the most absurd excuse ever invented. 'That wasn't me, it was my cousin, and he couldn't help what he did, either'? The Senate would chain me up in the violent wing. No, it's going to take years to put things back together." He sighed, and she saw how tired he was.

"The Senate?" he muttered. "Oh, the Senate! And the consuls!" He cursed bitterly. She had never heard him use such language. Perhaps he was only thinking aloud, but she had never heard him do so before. He had never, ever, mentioned anything to do with politics in her hearing. "Those consuls have got to go! Oh, by the way—I postponed the coronation. The treasury can't stand anything like that just now. Even the rich . . ."

He scratched his chin and looked at her quizzically. "Something Ylo said once . . . He told me you don't enjoy formal balls and parties?"

"*Enjoy* them? I detest them! You mean you didn't know that?" How could he possibly not know the terror she felt? Some nights she had been almost ill beforehand.

"No, I had no idea! I never guessed . . . You fooled me!" He grinned sheepishly. "I hate them, too, you see—rather fight a battle any day! I suppose I was always in such a cold sweat . . ."

"You?"

They stared at each other, and very slowly they both began to smile.

"Yes, me!" Shandie said. "All that dressing up, standing around . . . But we shan't have to worry about sumptuous parties for quite a while! Even the richest families have been battered to the ground."

Truly, as the priests said, there was some good in every evil. Without that awful burden, the palace would not hurt so badly.

"Which reminds me," Shandie said. "Count Ipherio? You sat next to him at Ishipole's one night . . . Would he make a consul, do you think?"

"You are asking *me*?"

He blinked. "Well, you had to listen to him for three hours. Did he make any sense?"

"No. He was drunk before we sat down and got drunker as the meal went on."

"Trash him then," Shandie said offhandedly.

Had he been testing her judgment or had she really just

ruined a man's political career? Did the king and queen of Krasnegar sit around on the long winter nights, tossing affairs of state back and forth across the great hearth like this? And Shandie was still talking—

"You know there are packs of starving people running like wild dogs in Julgistro? Reports of *feral children*! Gods, what a mess! I must do something about the children, but what? If I order the army to round them up, they'll use dogs or nets or something and throw them in cages . . ." He paused. "I'll have to put someone on it right away, but who can I trust to deal with *children*?"

Perhaps he wasn't really asking her, but she answered.

"A woman."

He pouted. "Good idea, but I'm no judge of women! Name one!"

"Lady Eigaze."

He grabbed. "Is she competent?"

"Extremely. She and Ylo ran circles around her husband and the centurion to get me away, but I think she did most of it."

Shandie's smile was almost a smirk. "Excellent! Wonderful! Well, that's one thing settled. That leaves two million, nine hundred thousand et ceteras! Ylo would surely be useful now!" he added wistfully. He moved as if about to pull himself out of the chair.

"If I can help—"

He sank back. He studied the fireplace and chewed a knuckle, which was a very exuberant gesture for him. "Help? Of course you could help! I can think of a hundred things you could do. Make a list of the competent and incompetent people you know, for instance. Organize a relief fund for the homeless, nurse your sister back to health . . . but . . . if you wouldn't mind . . . Umpily's already picking up rumors of coups being plotted, you see, and at the moment sorcery's completely out of control, which is something our predecessors never had to worry about . . ."

She had never heard him so hesitant. "What are you getting at?"

"If you wouldn't mind . . . I honestly think you could help best—just for the next few weeks, at least—by staying right where you are, darling! I know you're safe, then, and Maya's safe. I can announce that you're paying a state visit. And you're pregnant, of course. Great excuse."

"I won't mind." Marvelous! Stay in Krasengar? Peace to

heal after all those months of flight! This must be Inosolan's doing.

He smiled, looking relieved. "Good. I am very grateful! But I shall come and visit you every day. Or at least I shall come and visit Maya, because I want to get to know my daughter before I march her down the aisle to marry some chinless aristocratic miracle. If you choose not to see me, then I shall just visit with Maya."

She stared.

"What's wrong?" he asked, his eyes twinkling.

"Nothing. I mean, of course there's lots of things wrong, but . . . Nothing."

Shandie chuckled, looking pleased. "Not quite the old Shandie? I have changed, Eshiala! I really have! Ylo started it. He lectured me about taking life too seriously. Maybe the bar girls helped, too. I certainly learned a lot of surprising things about, well, you know."

The bar girls were starting to irk.

"About what, my lord?"

He colored again. "All right, I'll say it! The first woman I took to bed called me a clumsy, impatient, inconsiderate oaf!"

After a long silence, Eshiala said, "Gracious! Did she really?"

Now the imperor's face burned as red as any schoolgirl's. "I don't suppose Ylo was, was he?" he said through his teeth.

"Ylo was a revelation."

Shandie nodded grimly. "Very well. I deserved that. I learned! I learned quite quickly, I think, although I'll never come up to Ylo's standards. I kept thinking of you. I don't mean . . . What I mean is, then the goblins caught me. For two days I was sure I was going to die very horribly. Believe me, please, but one of my greatest regrets was that I had never made love to you as you deserved! Maybe one day . . . And then I met Inos."

"No!" Eshiala exclaimed.

"No," he admitted. "I was tempted to try a time or two, though. Amazing woman, that! But Inos taught me some things, in a less intimate way. Ylo taught me how men could be friends. Inos taught me how a man and a woman could be friends."

His dark eyes gazed solemnly at her as if that were an earth-shaking revelation. Maybe it had been, for Shandie. He had

had a very strange childhood. And why was he telling her all this? Inos had warned her that he was a very clever man.

Shandie rose, gesturing to stop Eshiala when she would have risen. He walked over to the bell rope and tugged it. Then he came to her and sank down on one knee.

"Inos said to ring if I needed food. I haven't eaten all day. You won't mind watching me guzzle? And I have a request to make."

"Request?" She tried to pull her wits together. They refused to come. "You have only to command, Sire."

He shook his head impatiently. "Request. Petition. Plea. I know you are in mourning for the man you loved. I respect that. I mourn him, also, dearly."

Those could not be tears in his eyes, could they? *Shandie's* eyes?

"But, after the baby . . . In a year or so? When you have had time. No hurry! No hurry at all! I know it sounds callous to say this, but time does heal, Eshiala! When it does—I want your permission to pay court to my friend's widow."

"I don't understand!" she cried. Nothing had happened as she had expected.

"It's quite simple. I don't deserve you. I never wooed and won you. The contest was never fair. Do you suppose your mother learned who I was by accident? Oh no!—I cheated! Now I want to play by the rules and win on my own merits, as a man, not as prince or imperor. You married Ylo for love and I respect that. Ylo won you! Ylo died saving you from the Covin. You need time to adjust, I know. Lots of time! But you are a young woman yet. I ask only that I may be your first suitor, when you are ready to consider suitors. That is all I ask of you. And if I cannot win your hand honestly, then I do not deserve you. May I hope for that? And until then, may we be friends?"

It was the most generous offer he could have made, and far beyond her dreams. It was too good to be sincere.

"You mean that for the first time in my life I would actually be free to make a decision for myself?"

He winced, then nodded.

She felt Ylo's presence. She felt him at her side.

She felt as she had when she rode the horse at the hedges in Qoble, fleeing the soldiers, knowing that she was risking her life and the life of her daughter. She had survived that—she could survive this.

What would Ylo say now? Ylo would ask what was in it for him.

Her mouth was almost too dry for speech. "And what if you do not win me, my lord? Do we go back to rape? Do I get to choose between that and giving up my children? Do I also have a chance to win something?"

Shandie stood up. He went back to the big chair opposite and sat down, stretching out his legs. He smiled lazily, confidently. She noticed that his fists were clenched, though.

"Inos warned me that the kitten was growing tiger stripes. Name the stakes, ma'am."

"Divorce."

The darkness of his eyes burned brighter. "On what grounds?"

"Failure to give the imperor a son. There are precedents."

"There are," Shandie admitted grimly. His knuckles showed white now. "And the children?"

"I remain at court as their governess. They will be in my charge, completely, whether or not you remarry. Or I remarry."

He bared his teeth. "By the Gods, you drive a hard bargain, my lady!"

"So your wooing will be all pretense? However I choose, I lose?"

"By the Gods!" he muttered again. "Anything else?"

She could hear Ylo's laughter.

"That's if I refuse you. I may have conditions for accepting you, you understand—a limit of one formal function a month, perhaps . . . And I shall require at least two years to decide."

"That's all?"

"That's all for now."

He sighed. "I accept the stakes. I can refuse you nothing."

Their eyes met. He smiled. Could he actually be *pleased* by her new assertiveness? "I mean it! I will swear any oath you ask. I will pay any price and risk anything to win your love— when you are ready to love again." Suddenly the smile became a mischievous grin. "I did warn you that Ylo had given me lessons, didn't I?"

It was so much what Ylo might have said that it brought tears to her eyes, but she laughed in spite of them.

"And me, too!" she said, and then fumbled hastily for a handkerchief.

Moments later, a footman delivered a loaded tray. Thereafter Shandie sat and ate like a starved man, and talked.

Mostly he spoke of Ylo.

5

Meanwhile, in a corridor of the castle . . .

Krasnegar had not changed at all. Not a thing. World capital of dull. The same soup bubbled in the same pots, the same seagulls stood on the battlements, the same dogs erupted all over a long-lost friend. The only difference was that Kadie was not around to share it. Kadie was never going to be around again. When Gath mentioned her to their friends, they became confused and upset and changed the subject.

Friends? The imps seemed devious, curious, and garrulous to him; domestic jotnar were a wishy-washy imitation of the wild variety he had come to know. All this peace and serenity was going to take a lot of getting used to, an Evilish lot! Gath had not faced death even once in the last hour. What he needed was exercise and entertainment to stop him moping about Kadie.

This was the most promising future he could find.

"Gath!" exclaimed the burly redhead.

"Oh, hello, Brak!" Gath said airily, rising from the bench he had been waiting on. Yes, he was a handsbreadth taller than Brak! He had known, but it was good to see. Wonderful! Best thing yet!

Behind Brak stood Arkie and Koarth. They had grown, too, but Brak was in front and clearly still the leader.

"Where have you *been?*"

"Oh, all sorts of places," Gath said modestly. "Helping my dad the warlock, mostly."

"The *what?*"

"Warlock." Gath flexed his arms hopefully. There was a fifty-fifty future of Brak calling him a liar now, and Gath slaughtering him. Arkie and Koarth exchanged interested glances.

But Brak peered up at the returned traveler for a long, cautious moment and apparently disliked what he saw.

"That's great news for Krasnegar," he muttered.

"This is Longday. I was at the Nintor Moot this morning. Very interesting."

"This morning?"

"You heard what I said."

This time the pause was longer. Arkie coughed. Koarth hummed and tapped a boot on the flagstones.

Brak wiped his forehead. "We'd like to hear about that, Gath," he said faintly.

Gath sighed. Hopeless! "That's a fantastic ear you've got, lad. I wonder you can hold your head straight. Did I do that, or has someone else been giving you lessons?"

"That was you." Brak pulled a grin, although it displayed hints of desperation. "We both put up quite a show that day, didn't we, Gath? The guys talked of it for weeks. I know I knocked you out in the end, but you did a lot more damage to me than I did to you . . . we could kinda call that one a draw, couldn't we?"

Gath's mouth felt full of tooth, because an hour or two ago Jaurg had replaced the piece Brak had broken off. Maybe Brak wasn't too bad really, especially compared with Vork or some of the men of their age in Gark. It was sort of good to see him again. Gath returned the grin. "I suppose we could."

Brak released a long breath of relief. Arkie and Koarth welcomed Gath back. Gath said it was good to see them all.

"Er, which throne did your, er, the king, get?" Koarth asked.

"The gold."

"Why not north?"

"Wasn't available. Of course, as East, he runs the Imperial Army. Keeps him busy, you know. And he's rewriting Emine's Protocol. With the help of some pixies. Funny people, pixies."

Three sets of blue eyes blinked, but no one questioned.

Gath yawned. "I'm heading down to the Beached Whale for a beer or two. Wanna come along and hear about the Nintor Moot?" And there would be action there later . . .

"They won't let us into the Beached Whale!" Brak said.

Puke! No, they wouldn't! This was Krasnegar. Mom made all the rules here. Gath frowned and reached for prescience. Oh, of course! "Then let's go and find my friend Jaurg. He'll get us in."

The game again:
 And many a broken heart is here and many a broken head;
   But tomorrow,
 By the living God, we'll try the game again!
                                        Masefield, *Tomorrow*

❦ POSTSCRIPT ❧

MINUTES
of a joint meeting of
THE WARDENS
and
THE COUNCIL OF SORCERY
held at Hub,
Longday, 2999

The meeting was called to order at noon. The Warden of the Day, having taken the Chair *pro tempore* and having called for nominations for Chairman and no other nominations having been received, the said WARLOCK KING RAP was elected CHAIRMAN by acclamation. The Chairman requested that the meeting elect WARLOCK LITH'RIAN as SECRETARY and this was unanimously approved.

THE CHAIRMAN REMARKED THAT with the mundane population of many areas presently enduring severe hardship of famine, disease, and civil disorder, the advantages of employing sorcery as a force for good had never been more obvious or necessary;

THAT divine intervention having released all votaries of the late Sorcerer Zinixo, the unique opportunity to craft a new order of occult affairs must not be wasted;

AND THAT until the new protocol had been drafted and rat-

405

ified, he hoped the Wardens and the new Council of Sorcery
would work together in harmony to resolve all problems before they could become troublesome.

THE SECRETARY then distributed a draft agenda. On MO-
TION by Witch Grunth, the Agenda was unanimously
adopted.

Item 1: The matter of Thume.

MOVED by Delegate Raim, SECONDED by Delegate Countess Ymmi:

BE IT RESOLVED that the sorcerers of Thume, having agreed
that they will not appoint a replacement Keeper, are hereby
authorized, for an interim period of one year, to expel intruders, provided they employ no unnecessary force; and

BE IT FURTHER RESOLVED that the Protocol Committee
shall consider Thume's distinctive vulnerability and devise
legal protection for it on a permanent basis.

IN FAVOR: *Wardens* Grunth, Lith'rian, and Raspnex, *Delegates* Fial'rian, Ishist, Moon Baiter, Raim, Shup-Uth, Tho-
ik-Esh, Proconsul Thrugg, Tik Tok, Twist, Countess Ymmi,
and Wirax.

OPPOSED: *Delegate* Furkar.

MOTION CARRIED

Item 2: The matter of Nordland.

MOVED by Delegate Countess Ymmi, SECONDED by Delegate Ishist:

BE IT RESOLVED that the Warden of the East is hereby authorized and instructed to deputize a force of not more than
twelve sorcerers to constrain the Nordland fleet within its
own territorial waters by means of such weather as he may
deem appropriate for the duration of the present fighting
season; the Warden of the North having waived his prerogative in this instance, without prejudice.

IN FAVOR: *Wardens* Grunth and Lith'rian, *Delegates* Fial'rian,
Ishist, Moon Baiter, Raim, Tho-ik-Esh, Proconsul Thrugg,
Tik Tok, Countess Ymmi, and Wirax.

OPPOSED: *Delegates* Furkar and Shup-Uth.
ABSTAINED: *Warden* Raspnex, *Delegate* Twist.

MOTION CARRIED

Item 3: The matter of the Impire.

MOVED by Delegate Countess Ymmi, SECONDED by Warlock Lith'rian:
BE IT RESOLVED that in areas of civil unrest, use of sorcery
to assist the military in restoring law and order is permissible, provided always that the minimum necessary force is
used; and
BE IT FURTHER RESOLVED that this edict shall be proclaimed at the conclusion of this meeting.
IN FAVOR: *Wardens* Grunth, Lith'rian, and Raspnex, *Delegates* Fial'rian, Ishist, Moon Baiter, Raim, Tho-ik-Esh,
Proconsul Thrugg, Tik Tok, Countess Ymmi, and Wirax.
OPPOSED: *Delegates* Furkar, Shup-Uth, and Twist.

MOTION CARRIED

Item 4: The matter of Dwanish.

MOVED by Warden Raspnex, SECONDED by Delegate
Countess Ymmi:
BE IT RESOLVED that the Warden of the North is hereby au-
thorized and instructed to negotiate immediate withdrawal of
Dwanishian forces within national borders, or to impose
such withdrawal by force.
IN FAVOR: *Wardens* Grunth and Raspnex, *Delegates* Ishist,
Moon Baiter, Raim, Tho-ik-Esh, Proconsul Thrugg, Tik Tok,
Twist, and Countess Ymmi.
OPPOSED: *Warden* Lith'rian, *Delegates* Fial'rian, Furkar, and
Shup-Uth.
ABSTAINED: *Delegate* Wirax.

MOTION CARRIED

Item 5: The matter of Zark.

MOVED by Delegate Furkar, SECONDED by Delegate Shup-Uth:

BE IT RESOLVED that civil order having broken down throughout Zark, use of sorcery to establish Prince Krandaraz of Arakkaran as caliph is permissible.

IN FAVOR: *Delegates* Furkar and Shup-Uth.

OPPOSED: *Wardens* Grunth, Lith'rian, and Raspnex, *Delegates* Fial'rian, Countess Ymmi, Ishist, Moon Baiter, Raim, Tho-ik-Esh, Proconsul Thrugg, Tik Tok, Twist, and Wirax.

MOTION DEFEATED

MOVED by Delegate Raim, SECONDED by Delegate Countess Ymmi:

BE IT RESOLVED that the Warden of the East is authorized and directed to deliver the emerald sash of Arakkaran, presently held as a trophy of war in Thume, to Prince Krandaraz ak'Azak in recognition that he has the best claim to succeed his father as sultan of that city, and to secure release of the said prince from captivity in Dreag; and

BE IT FURTHER RESOLVED that the said Warden of the East is charged to be especially vigilant in prohibiting any further political use of sorcery whatsoever within Zark.

IN FAVOR: *Wardens* Grunth, Lith'rian, and Raspnex, *Delegates* Fial'rian, Countess Ymmi, Ishist, Moon Baiter, Raim, Tho-ik-Esh, Proconsul Thrugg, Tik Tok, Twist, and Wirax.

OPPOSED: *Delegates* Furkar and Shup-Uth.

MOTION CARRIED

Item 6: The matter of Dragon Reach.

Delegate Shup-Uth having moved that the territory hitherto known as Dragon Reach be renamed North Sysanasso and the motion having failed for lack of a seconder, the said Delegate asked that her views be recorded in the minutes.

Delegate Countess Ymmi having moved that the territory hitherto known as Dragon Reach be recognized as an extension of the Impire and the motion having failed for lack of a seconder, the said Delegate asked that her views be recorded in the minutes.

MOVED by Delegate Countess Ymmi, SECONDED by Delegate Twist:

BE IT RESOLVED that ownership of the land of Dragon Reach is a matter of mundane politics and therefore lies outside the responsibility of this meeting.

IN FAVOR: *Wardens* Grunth and Raspnex, *Delegates* Moon Baiter, Raim, Countess Ymmi, Twist, and Wirax.

OPPOSED: *Warden* Lith'rian, *Delegates* Fial'rian, Furkar, Ishist, Shup-Uth, Tho-ik-Esh, Proconsul Thrugg, and Tik Tok.

                              MOTION DEFEATED

At this point the SECRETARY, Warlock Lith'rian, advised the meeting that he had previously taken steps to remove the indigenous fauna of the area from the grasp of both sides in the recent dispute, that the said fauna should be returning shortly, and that anyone who thought he could take over Dragon Reach unopposed was going to receive a very nasty surprise indeed.

This item was TABLED without further discussion.

Item 7: Delegation of committees to draft the New Protocol.

After extensive discussion, this item was TABLED until the next meeting.

Item 8: Allocation of responsibilities between Wardens and the Council of Sorcery.

After extensive discussion, this item was TABLED until the next meeting.

Item 9: Definition of votarism and permissible loyalties.

After extensive discussion, this item was TABLED until the next meeting.

At midnight, the Chairman declared the Meeting ADJOURNED.

⫷ EPILOGUE ⫸

The return of the legendary Faun Sorcerer was greeted in Hub with intense excitement. The gossips soon whispered that he had worked an even greater miracle on Emshandar V than he had on his grandfather, for it was only now that the new imperor began to justify the hopes he had raised before his accession. He took command of the realm with an unprecedented series of edicts and decrees that won the admiration of even his most stubborn opponents in the Senate. Famine and civil war were averted. By the time winter approached, the new millennium was being hailed as a time of hope and renewal. The healing had begun.

Lacking the caliph, Zark collapsed back into a melee of independent sultanates. The Impire recognized Guwushian independence, the Dwanishian army was demobilized, severe storms in the Spring Sea kept the jotnar away.

The epochal document known as the New Protocol was eventually drafted and accepted. All of the Four signed it, even Warlock Lith'rian, who detested it, and all twelve Delegates to the Council of Sorcery.* A whole new system of occult law was established, designating occult power itself as a weapon, and its abuse a crime. Skeptics mocked, but all the sorcerers of

---

*The means by which Warlock Rap obtained the signature of the faun delegate, Mistress Shup-Uth, were never officially revealed, but in private the warlock admitted that he had merely threatened to wring her neck.

Pandemia were determined never to be votarized again, and their leaders could draw on Thume's thousand years of experience in regulating sorcery. In practice the new system worked better than almost anyone had dared to hope.

One morning the following spring, in the middle of a private working breakfast with the Head of the Bureau of Internal Statistics—more commonly known as the secret police—the imperor unveiled an inspiration that had come to him in the bathtub.

"An exclusive new order of chivalry!" he said. "To be called The Companions of the *White Impress*. Its emblem will be an Imperial Crown in opal, outlined in diamonds. Membership will be restricted to that handful of men and women who escaped with us from Hub to the ferryboat on the night of our accession."

"Brilliant!" Lord Umpily murmured, brandishing a carving knife like a saber. "Some more roast swan, your Majesty?"

"No more for me, thank you. You go ahead. My wife and daughter will be included, of course, plus Warlock Raspnex, Sorceress Jarga, and King Rap. And yourself, needless to say."

Lord Umpily beamed around a mouthful of swan. He was very happy in his new duties, as they required him to find out everything about everyone. "Do try the truffles in raspberry and olive oil sauce, Sire. An elvish recipe. Countess Eigaze certainly deserves membership, but what of her husband?"

Shandie pouted. "I think not. He disgraced himself at Yewdark!"

"Ah! Another cup of chocolate? Some lobster preserve? Centurion Hardgraa, whom you banished for life to the Mosweeps?"

"Certainly not!"

"Mm." The fat man chewed busily for a moment. "Queen Inos and Prince Gath, then? They were certainly your companions during much of the adventures that followed, but never on *White Impress*."

Shandie crumbled a fragment of roll to nothing. "I should include them, of course." He frowned uneasily.

Umpily gestured vaguely with a loaded fork. "Then what about the daughter? Is it blasphemous to offer a mundane honor to a God? Would it be sacrilegious not to?"

Shandie bit his lip.

"And Sir Acopulo, Sire?"

Conversation stopped completely while they thought about Sir Acopulo. A letter purporting to be from him had turned up at Winterfest, explaining that he had entered the cloister and would henceforth dedicate his life to certain unspecified labors of love. The news had not been entirely unexpected, for he had always been a devout man, if not quite the sanctimonious prude that Ylo had called him.

"You still believe that letter was genuine?"

"The handwriting was his, if a trifle shaky. Won't you try this Guwushian blue cheese?"

"Uh! No, please! I had rather you moved it farther away. Have you had any success in locating a monastery called the Refuge of Constant Service?"

"None whatsoever," Umpily admitted regretfully. "And what of that other handful of men, the former sequential set? Of the five, two were present on *White Impress*, as I understand. Senator Sagorn?"

Shandie growled a military expression under his breath. He had let Warlock Rap talk him into appointing the renowned sage to the Senate. Alas, with advancing age, his word of power diluted, and lacking the advantages given him by the ancient spell, he was not the man he had once been. He had rapidly established a reputation as the most boring and long-winded speaker in an assembly notorious for loquacity.

"And Master Thinal," Umpily murmured. "I am told he is showing great promise in his new position?"

"He is." Shandie did not elaborate. He tried to keep the Bureau of Internal Statistics from meddling in affairs of other government departments—rarely with much success. "The other three never set foot on the ferryboat."

"They are not available anyway, Sire. The jotunn warrior was executed by the elves. Minstrel Jalon has remained in Ilrane, painting and collecting songs. Although his talents are much reduced from what they were, he is reported to be content." Umpily had incredible sources of information.

"The other one, the lover? Andor? Was that his name?"

"Indeed. He frequently claims to be a baronet. He returned to Hub briefly, but has since departed."

Shandie raised an eyebrow. Umpily smirked.

"His somewhat clumsy advances offended a certain young lady. He departed the city in haste a few weeks ago, hotly pursued by her four brothers, all of whom are celebrated duelists. I could probably track him down for you, if that is your wish."

The imperor sighed. "I have always depended on you for frank and honest advice, old friend."

The fat man dabbed at his mouth with a serviette, possibly to conceal a blush. "Then to be honest, Sire, I feel the venture may be ill-advised. What of Signifer Ylo? Why reopen wounds that still ache? Furthermore . . . this is in strictest confidence, of course . . . I have reason to believe that neither Warlock Raspnex nor Sorcerer Jarga will be available for very much longer."

"Why not?" Shandie demanded sharply.

"Just rumor," Umpily said smugly. "I do recommend these savory eels in ginger."

Recognizing that there were some secrets even the imperor could not be trusted with, Shandie changed the subject, and the Order of the Companions of the *White Impress* was never heard of again.

Umpily's prediction was fulfilled, though. A few weeks later, a new warlock of the north was elected to fill a sudden vacancy. Sorceress Jarga disappeared at about the same time. Shortly thereafter, a God of Lost Causes was added to the lists.

Prince Gathmor, having visited the Nintor Moot in the summer and been dubbed duke of Kinvale on his fifteenth birthday by the imperor, discovered he was the young lion of Krasnegar, worshipped by imp and jotunn alike. He also discovered the problem of girls and the advantages of prescience in solving it. It was at about that time that his mother began pulling out gray hairs; she prayed frequently to the God of Rescues.

Eshiala was delivered of a fine baby daughter, proclaimed throughout the Impire as Princess Ylla.

The imperor wooed his wife tirelessly, but it was many months after the coronation and Ylla's birth that she accepted him again as her husband. Thereafter they lived a long and happy life together, and were later blessed with a third daughter.

Prince Emthoro eventually recovered from his ordeal as surrogate imperor, and Duchess Ashia from hers as surrogate impress. The tribulation they had shared had forged a bond between them. The aged duke of Hileen having died, Ashia thereupon married the prince. She later bore him several handsome children, surprising nobody more than he.

* * *

On the very night of Princess Ylla's birth, ancient Mistress Ukka died at Yewdark. By then spring was returning. Trees were budding around the abandoned mansion, crocuses flowered unseen, and the shoots of daffodils sprouted already amid the weeds.

Ukka died as she had lived much of her life—alone and yet convinced that she was not alone. In her last hours she chattered busily to the invisible Voices that only she could hear; she laughed as if their messages were amusing. A spark from her final candle, perhaps, or spontaneous combustion amid the heaps of litter in the cellars . . . something fired the great house soon after she died, and it burned to the ground. The Voices were heard no more—if indeed they had ever been heard.

Some years later, the emperor had a more modern edifice constructed on the site and donated it to his wife as a summer home. They spent many happy days at Yewdark with her children, and Princess Ylla resided there often after her marriage.

Rap served two years as warlock and then resigned his throne. Over all protests, he returned to his beloved Krasnegar. By that time the little kingdom had acquired several magic portals and lost its isolation forever. He became an elder statesman, consulted by secular and occult authorities from all over Pandemia. Many a deadlock in the Council of Sorcery was broken when King Rap's opinion was made known.

The years passed. Prosperity returned to Pandemia. More than anyone else, Thinal deserved credit for restoring Imperial finances. He was acknowledged to be the most brilliant Minister of Inland Revenue the Impire had ever known. He served three times as consul and died a senator.*

Lord Umpily refused all public honors. At his death he left an extensive library of memoirs. The imperor promptly ordered them destroyed, and supervised that destruction in person.

Emshandar V himself outlived all of them except his daughters, dying in 3063, full of years and widely mourned. He had ruled with compassion and imagination, delivering peace and justice and prosperity. The impire he bequeathed to his successors was a far different realm from the one he had inherited, for his reign coincided with the transformation that sociologists

*And immensely wealthy.

later termed the Sorcerous Revolution, when the powers released by the new protocol so dramatically improved the quality of life in Pandemia. The old man never applied his own name to the basic document, but by then everyone else knew it as Emshandar's Protocol and history gave him the credit for it, calling him Emshandar the Great.

He was succeeded by his daughter Uomaya, who was herself elderly and also childless. When she died after a very brief reign, the throne passed on to her nephew the duke of Rivermead, oldest son of the late Princess Ylla.

Had Lord Umpily's memoirs survived, then someone might have realized that this was a change of dynasty. Agraine's line was ended and a grandson of Signifer Ylo sat upon the Opal Throne. Mortals' memories are short, though, and to mortals Emshandar IV was by then only a name in the history texts, the last of the "old" imperors, his achievements irrelevant and even his crimes forgotten. The Gods remembered better, and in the fullness of time They had rendered justice for the Yllipo massacre.

But perhaps not even the Gods recalled how the Statue had prophesied this, one blustery summer day back in the previous millennium.

Coming soon to bookstores everywhere.
Published in hardcover by Del Rey Books.

THE CURSED
by Dave Duncan

In the beginning were the gods, dispensing
unto mankind in equal measure their light and
their darkness, their sorrow and their joy, their
blessing and their curse . . .

Read on for a sneak preview
of THE CURSED . . .

SHOOL is Time, the Slow One, stealer of youth, guardian of what has been and what is to be, maker of ends and beginnings

IVIEL is Health, Star of Evening, bringer of wounds and sickness, Star of Morning, the healer, the comforter

MUOL is Passion, the Red One, bringer of love and hatred, maker and destroyer

AWAIL is Change, the Inconstant One, the Fickle One, Ruler of the Night

OGOAL is Chance, the Swift One, the joker, spinner of fortune

JAUL is Thought, who is Reason, the Bright One, dispenser of truth and falsehood, maker and breaker of law and justice

POUL is Destiny, the Great One, giver of life and death, the Mover, Queen of Days

1

In Tolamin, it began with a runaway wagon. Two
horses came careering down the narrow street in panic,
trying to escape from the terrible racketing monster pursuing them. Its load of pottery ewers clattered and
rolled; every few seconds another would bounce right
out to explode on the stones and splatter contents everywhere. Bystanders leaped for the safety of doorways or
pressed back against walls. There was no sign of the
driver.

A child stood directly in the wagon's path, thumb in
mouth, an infant clad only in a wisp of cloth, staring
blankly at the doom hurtling down upon him.

The boy's mother rushed out to snatch him away to
safety, but her foot slipped and the two of them sprawled
headlong together, directly under the plunging hooves.
Horses and wagon flashed over them and continued their
headlong progress to certain destruction at the river. The
woman scrambled to her feet, clutching her child. Apparently neither had suffered as much as a bruise.

"There!" Jasbur screeched. "You see that?"

"Lucky," Ordur muttered.

"Lucky? You call that lucky? I say it's impossible. I say somebody is influencing!"

Ordur scratched his head and thought about it. He wasn't thinking too clearly these days. "Suppose it could be."

"Suppose? Hah! You're even stupider than you look, you know that?"

"You, too!"

"You look like a moron, but you're not that smart. You don't have the brains of a lettuce."

"You, too!"

That was the best Ordur could manage in repartee these days. He knew he was slow. It wasn't fair of Jasbur to call him ugly, though. Maybe he was ugly, but this time Jasbur was just as bad—short and bent, almost a hunchback. His face was a grayish, swarthy shade, as if it had not been washed for years, and gruesomely wrinkled. The whites of his eyes were yellow; he slavered all the time. Although the fringe of hair around his head was silver, its roots were dark. There were patches of shadowy dark stubble on his cheeks and more on his bald pate. His teeth were nastily prominent, his clothes tattered and filthy.

The wagon had reached the dock. The horses veered to right and left; trappings broke miraculously to free them. The wagon sailed on by itself, passing narrowly between two moored barges and vanishing into the water. Jasbur crowed witlessly at this further evidence of fatalist *influence* upsetting the normal probabilities of the world.

But talk of lettuce had reminded Ordur that his belly ached. He peered up the long street, then down it. There were a lot of people standing around, mostly staring after the wagon. An excited group had gathered around the woman and her child, babbling about their miraculous escape.

"I'm hungry. Haven't eaten all day!"

422

Jasbur shrieked in derision. "All day? It's barely dawn! You mean you didn't eat all day yesterday!"

"And I'm still hungry."

"Whose fault is that? You're supposed to be a beggar, but you look so bad you give children hysterics. Women set their dogs on us because of your ugly face."

"You, too."

"Half the people in this town don't eat. It was your idea to come to Tolamin, and it was a stupid idea."

Ordur didn't think it had been his idea, but he wasn't going to argue with Jasbur today. Maybe tomorrow would be better. "You eaten today?"

"No, nor yesterday neither!"

"Don't like this town," Ordur announced. "It smells."

"Curd brain! It's all the burned buildings. It was sacked, you numskull."

As if to emphasize the point, a ruined shell of a house farther up the hill collapsed out into the street in a cascade of bricks and charred timbers. Dust flew up in black clouds. People screamed.

"There!" Jasbur cackled. "Months it's been standing, and it falls down now. I tell you, there's somebody *influencing*!"

"Who?"

"How should I know?"

Lightning flashed, and thunder cracked almost overhead. Ordur jumped. "Oughta get out of here!"

"Naw. Thunder at this time of day? How often d'you see that?"

"Don't *see* thunder, Jasbur. See lightning. Hear thunder."

"Bah! There's an Ogoalscath around here somewhere. Let's find him." Jasbur hobbled off down the hill on bandy legs.

Ordur strode after him. "Why? How'd you know he's this way?"

"I don't, but he will be, you'll see."

Surely wise people would go away from an Ogoalscath, not toward him? But if Jasbur said to go

423

this way, then Ordur would have to. Jasbur wasn't being very nice to him just now, but he did seem to be the smart one. He said he was, so it must be true.

Lightning flashed again, thunder rumbled, rain began to fall in grape-sized drops.

2

In Tharn Valley, it began with a bad tooth. Bulion Tharn was no stranger to having teeth pulled. Any man who lived long enough to outlast his teeth had been blessed by the fates—that was how he liked to look on the matter. He had been fortunate in having Glothion around. Glothion was the blacksmith, the largest of his sons, with limbs like an oak. Old teeth tended to shatter when gripped with pliers, but Glothion could pull them with his bare fingers. It felt as if he were about to snap the jawbone, and the way he steadied his victim's head under his arm would surely crush some unfortunate's skull one day, but nine times out of ten he could yank a tooth cleanly out.

This time had been one of the other times. Bulion should have stood the pain a week or two longer, perhaps, to let the rotting molar rot some more. He hadn't. He'd been in too much of a hurry, and Glothion had pulled the crown off.

That meant real bloodshed. Wosion had insisted they wait three days, until the fates were propitious, and by then Bulion had been almost out of his mind with the pain. It had taken Glothion and Brankion and Zanion to hold their father down while Wosion himself tried to cut out the roots with a dagger.

He hadn't found all of them, obviously. Now, two days later, Bulion's face was swollen like a pumpkin and nigh hot enough to set his beard on fire. He was running a fever. The pain was a constant throb of lightning all through his head.

He was very likely going to die of this.

There were surgeons in Daling. The odds that he

could survive the two-day ride there were slim. The odds that any leech or sawbones could help him now were even slimmer.

It seemed the fates were ready to close the book on Bulion Tharn.

3

In Daling, it began when Tibal Frainith came to Phoenix Street.

Gwin was helping Tob the stableboy replace the wheat sheaf over the door. She was needed only when a cart came along and threatened to sweep ladder and Tob and wheat sheaf all away together, but her presence discouraged passing urchins from attempting the same feat. Meanwhile, she could clean off the road with a broom—not just because it made the entrance more appealing, but because it meant less dirt to be tracked inside. She could have sent a servant to do all that, but then it would have taken twice as long. She welcomed an excuse just to go outside. It seemed she did not leave the hostel for weeks at a time nowadays.

Meanwhile, the staff indoors were probably sitting around eating and talking when they should be working. Morning was busy time. The last guests had just left. There was a stable to be shoveled out, water to carry, beds to make, bread to bake, bedding to air, and all the interminable cleaning. The Flamingo Room needed fumigating again, having still not recovered from the sailors who had infested it with bedbugs the previous week.

Morning sunlight brightened the narrow streets of Daling like a baby's smile. Stonework shone in the color of beech wood. The cobbles were polished little islands, each one set off by dark mire in the crevices between them, giving the roadway a texture of coarse cloth, a cobble carpet, dipping here and there into noxious puddles, although even they reflected the sun. Exterior windows were rare, but a few bronze grilles gleamed joyously; and all the doors were limed to a brilliant white.

Phoenix Street was occupied by pedestrians and horsemen and much idle gossip. Every few minutes, and ox cart would come clattering and rattling along, usually being chased by small children trying to cadge a ride, being shouted away by the carter. Strolling hawkers called their wares, stopping to talk with the women at the doorways.

The old wheat sheaf hit the cobbles, disintegrating into a cloud of dust and a mess of rotted straw where Gwin had just swept. She clucked annoyance and hastened to pass up the replacement bundle to Tob. He took it without a word. Not even his own mother could call him swift. The only good thing about Tob was that he was too stupid to be dishonest.

She laid into the straw with her broom, spreading it out for hooves and wheels to crumble. She tried not to remember that self-same sheaf being hung—thirty-six weeks ago, a day as hot as this one promised to be. She had been helper then, too, but it had not been a half-wit stable boy up the ladder. It had been Carp himself. Now Carp was rotting in an unmarked grave somewhere near Tolamin. Karn and Naln had followed their father. She was the only one left now—widow, bereaved mother, innkeeper, Gwin Nien Solith.

"Gwin!"

She spun around, blinking into the sun.

The speaker was tall, lean, clean-shaven. He bore a bulky packsack on his shoulders. His smock and breeches had never been dyed and now were a nondescript gray. They were ordinary Kuolian garb, yet of an unfamiliar cut, as if they had traveled far from the loom that birthed them. He had steady gray eyes, brown tangled hair, worn shorter than was normal for men in Daling. Bone and sinew lay close under his skin. Yes, tall. He was smiling at her as if the two of them were old friends, close friends. She had never seen him before in her life.

"I don't . . ."

He started. "Sorry! I am Tibal Ambor Frainith." He bowed.

"Most honored, Tibal *Saj*. I am Gwin Nien Solith."

"Yes. I mean I am honored, Gwin *Saj*." He was blushing.

Blushing?

Pause.

The expectant look remained in his eyes. She could not recall being thrown off balance like this for years. She did not forget faces. He was at least as old as she was, so why were his cheeks flaming red like that?

A stranger in town would seek out a hostelry. Carp Solith had won a good reputation for the Phoenix Street Hostel; his widow had sustained it so far. Most of her business came from repeats, established customers—merchants, farmers, ship captains—but first-timers were not rare.

So why was she gazing tongue-tied at this man? Why was he staring down at her with that blush on his cheeks and that wistful, disbelieving expression in his gray eyes? There was something strange about his gaze that she could not place.

"The Phoenix Street Hostel," he said in his unfamiliar accent. "Everyone will . . . Everyone told me that it's the best hostelry in the city, Gwin *Saj*." He spoke too softly, stood a little too close.

A lead pair of oxen emerged from Sailors' Alley, with another following.

"They spoke no less than the truth, Tibal *Saj*."

"I need a room, Gwin." He still seemed mildly amused that she had not recognized him. He was a little too quick dropping the honorific.

"Rooms are my business, Tibal *Saj*." Why else display a wheat sheaf above the door?

Tob was still up the ladder, tying the sheaf to the bracket. The ox cart was advancing along the road. Tibal backed into its path, holding up a hand to stop it, all without ever taking his eyes off Gwin.

"You came by way of Tolamin?" she said. He must have done, to be arriving in the city so early in the day.

He hesitated and then nodded. The wagoner howled curses at him.

"How is it?" she asked.

Tibal blinked and frowned. "Much the same," he said vaguely.

Whatever did that mean? The Wesnarians had sacked it in the fall.

The teamster hauled on the traces and brought his rig to a clattering halt with the lead pair's steaming muzzles not an ell from the lanky stranger—who still ignored it all, still stared at Gwin.

Tob came slithering down the ladder, leering with pride at having completed an unfamiliar task. "All done, Gwin *Saj*."

"Take the ladder down, Tob."

"Oh. Yes." The lout moved the ladder. Tibal stepped out of the way, so the team could proceed.

"You almost got yourself jellied there," she said.

"What?" he glanced at the cart and its furious driver as if he had been unaware of their existence until she spoke. He shrugged. "No."

There was something definitely odd about Tibal Frainith, but he raised no sense of alarm in her. Almost the reverse—he seemed to be signaling friendship. Not asking for it, just assuming it. Curiously reassuring, somehow . . . clothes neither rich nor poor . . . carried his own pack. Not a rich man, therefore. Soft spoken. Not a soldier. Not a merchant. A wandering scholar, perhaps? At least he wasn't proposing marriage yet. Lately she spent half her days fighting off suitors who wanted to marry a hostel, and she was going to lose the battle.

She opened the door, setting the bell jangling. "I'll show you the rooms we have available." They were all available, but she would not admit to that.

He stepped past her. As she was about to follow him inside, a voice said, *It has begun.*

Startled, she jumped and looked around. There was no

one there. Tob was just disappearing into the alley with the ladder, heading around to the back. The wagon had gone. The voice had not come from Tibal Frainith.

So who had spoken? Her nerves must be snapping if she were starting to hear voices. With a shiver of fear, she followed her guest inside, shutting the door harder than necessary.

And so it begins . . .

Dave Duncan

THE CURSED

Coming soon from Del Rey Books!